1 MONTH OF
FREE
READING

at
www.ForgottenBooks.com

By purchasing this book you are
eligible for one month membership to
ForgottenBooks.com, giving you
unlimited access to our entire
collection of over 700,000 titles via
our web site and mobile apps.

To claim your free month visit:
www.forgottenbooks.com/free792675

ISBN 978-0-483-62748-2
PIBN 10792675

This book is a reproduction of an important historical work. Forgotten Books uses state-of-the-art technology to digitally reconstruct the work, preserving the original format whilst repairing imperfections present in the aged copy. In rare cases, an imperfection in the original, such as a blemish or missing page, may be replicated in our edition. We do, however, repair the vast majority of imperfections successfully; any imperfections that remain are intentionally left to preserve the state of such historical works.

Microreproductions / Institut canadien de microreproductions historiques

1995

Technical and Bibliographic Notes / Notes techniques et bi

The Institute has attempted to obtain the best original
copy available for filming. Features of this copy which
may be bibliographically unique, which may alter any
of the images in the reproduction, or which may
significantly change the usual method of filming, are
checked below.

L'Institut a m
lui a été possib
exemplaire qui
bibliographiqu
reproduite, ou
dans la méthod
ci-dessous.

☑ Coloured covers/
Couverture de couleur

☐ Coloured
Pages de

☐ Covers damaged/
Couverture endommagée

☐ Pages
Pages

☐ Covers restored and/or laminated/
Couverture restaurée et/ou pelliculée

☐ Pages
Pages

☐ Cover title missing/
Le titre de couverture manque

☑ Pages
Pages

☐ Coloured maps/
Cartes géographiques en couleur

☐ Pages
Pages

☑ Coloured ink (i.e. other than blue or black)/
Encre de couleur (i.e. autre que bleue ou noire)

☑ Show
Transpen

☑ Coloured plates and/or illustrations/
Planches et/ou illustrations en couleur

☐ Quality
Qualité i

☐ Bound with other material/
Relié avec d'autres documents

☐ Continuou
Pagination

☐ Tight binding may cause shadows or distortion
along interior margin/
La reliure serrée peut causer de l'ombre ou de la
distorsion le long de la marge intérieure

☐ Includes in
Compren

Title on

ks

L'exemplaire filmé fut reproduit grâce à la
générosité de:

Bibliothèque nationale du Canada

Les images suivantes ont été reproduites avec le
plus grand soin, compte tenu de la condition et
de la netteté de l'exemplaire filmé, et en
conformité avec les conditions du contrat de
filmage.

Les exemplaires originaux dont la couverture en
papier est imprimée sont filmés en commençant
par le premier plat et en terminant soit par la
dernière page qui comporte une empreinte
d'impression ou d'illustration, soit par le second
plat, selon le cas. Tous les autres exemplaires
originaux sont filmés en commençant par la
première page qui comporte une empreinte
d'impression ou d'illustration et en terminant par
la dernière page qui comporte une telle
empreinte.

Un des symboles suivants apparaîtra sur la
dernière image de chaque microfiche, selon le
cas: le symbole ⟶ signifie "A SUIVRE", le
symbole ▽ signifie "FIN".

Les cartes, planches, tableaux, etc., peuvent être
filmés à des taux de réduction différents.
Lorsque le document est trop grand pour être
reproduit en un seul cliché, il est filmé à partir
de l'angle supérieur gauche, de gauche à droite,
et de haut en bas, en prenant le nombre
d'images nécessaire. Les diagrammes suivants
illustrent la méthode.

3

1

2

MICROCOPY RESOLUTION TEST CHART

(ANSI and ISO TEST CHART No. 2)

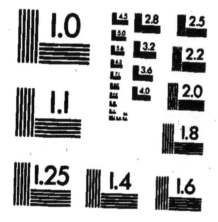

 APPLIED IMAGE Inc

1653 East Main Street
Rochester, New York   14609   USA
(716) 482 - 0300 - Phone
(716) 288 - 5989 - Fax

Gladys Berry

THE PRINCE OF GRAUSTARK

Her eyes were starry bright, her red lips were parted

(Page 381)

THE
PRINCE OF GRAUSTARK

BY
GEORGE BARR McCUTCHEON
Author of "Graustark," "Beverly of Graustark," etc.

With Illustrations by
A. I. KELLER

TORONTO
WILLIAM BRIGGS
1914

CONTENTS

ILLUSTRATIONS

THE PRINCE OF GRAUSTARK

—

CHAPTER I

"MY DEAR," said Mr. Blithers, with decision, "you can't tell me."

"I know I can't," said his wife, quite as positively. She knew when she could tell him a thing and when she couldn't.

It was quite impossible to impart information to Mr. Blithers when he had the tips of two resolute fingers embedded in his ears. That happened to be his customary and rather unfair method of conquering her when an argument was going against him, not for want of logic on his part, but because it was easier to express himself with his ears closed than with them open. By this means he effectually shut out the voice of opposition and had the discussion all to himself. Of course, it would have been more convincing if he had been permitted to hear the sound of his own eloquence; still, it was effective.

She was sure to go on talking for two or three minutes and then subside in despair. A woman will not talk to a stone wall. Nor will she wantonly allow an argument to die while there remains the slightest chance of its survival. Given the same situation, a man would get up and leave his wife sitting there with her fingers in her ears; and, as he bolted from the room in high dudgeon, he would be mean enough to call at-

1

tention to her pig-headedness. In most cases, a woman is content to listen to a silly argument rather than to leave the room just because her husband elects to be childish about a perfectly simple elucidation of the truth.

Mrs. Blithers had lived with Mr. Blithers, more or less, for twenty-five years and she knew him like a book. He was a forceful person who would have his own way, even though he had to put his fingers in his ears to get it. At one period of their joint connubial agreement, when he had succeeded in accumulating a pitiful hoard amounting to but little more than ten millions of dollars, she concluded to live abroad for the purpose of educating their daughter, allowing him in the meantime to increase his fortune to something like fifty millions without having to worry about household affairs. But she had sojourned with him long enough, at odd times, to realise that, so long as he lived, he would never run away from an argument — unless, by some dreadful hook or crook, he should be so unfortunate as to be deprived of the use of both hands. She found room to gloat, of course, in the fact that he was obliged to stop up his ears in order to shut out the incontrovertible.

Moreover, when he called her "my dear" instead of the customary Lou, it was a sign of supreme obstinacy on his part and could not, by any stretch of the imagination, be regarded as an indication of placid affection. He always said "my dear" at the top of his voice and with a great deal of irascibility.

Mr. William W. Blithers was a self-made man who had begun his career by shouting lustily at a team of mules in a railway construction camp. Other drivers had tried to improve on his vocabulary but even the mules were able to appreciate the futility of such an ambition, and later on, when he came to own two or three railroads, to say nothing of a few mines and a steam yacht, his ability to drive men was even more noteworthy than his power over the jackasses had been. But driving mules and men was one thing, driving a wife another. What incentive has a man, said he, when after he gets through bullying a creature that very creature turns in and caresses him? No self-respecting mule ever did such a thing as that, and no man would think of it except with horror. There is absolutely no defence against a creature who will rub your head with loving, gentle fingers after she has worked you up to the point where you could kill her with pleasure — or at least so said Mr. Blithers with rueful frequency.

Mr. and Mrs. Blithers had been discussing royalty. Up to the previous week they had restricted themselves to the nobility, but as an event of unexampled importance had transpired in the interim, they now felt that it would be the rankest stupidity to consider any one short of a Prince Royal in picking out a suitable husband — or, more properly speaking, consort — for their only daughter. Maud Applegate Blithers, aged twenty.

Mrs. Blithers long ago had convinced her husband

that no ordinary human being of the male persuasion was worthy of their daughter's hand, and had set her heart on having nothing meaner than a Duke on the family roll,—(Blithers alluded to it for a while as the pay-roll)—, with the choice lying between England and Italy. At first, Blithers, being an honest soul, insisted that a good American gentleman was all that anybody could ask for in the way of a son-in-law, and that when it came to a grandchild it would be perfectly proper to christen him Duke —- lots of people did !— and that was about all that a title amounted to any-way. She met this with the retort that Maud might marry a man named Jones, and how would Duke Jones sound? He weakly suggested that they could christen him Marmaduke and — but she reminded him of his oft-repeated boast that there was nothing in the world too good for Maud and instituted a pictorial campaign against his prejudices by painting in the most allur-ing colours the picture of a ducal palace in which the name of Jones would never be uttered except when employed in directing the fifth footman or the third stable-boy — or perhaps a scullery maid — to do this, that or the other thing at the behest of her Grace, the daughter of William W. Blithers. This eventually worked on his imagination to such an extent that he forgot his natural pride and admitted that perhaps she was right.

But now, just as they were on the point of accept-ing, in lieu of a Duke, an exceptionally promising Count, the aforesaid event conspired to completely

upset all of their plans — or notions, so to speak. It
was nothing less than the arrival in America of an eligible Prince of the royal blood, a ruling Prince at that.
As a matter of fact he had not only arrived in America but upon the vast estate adjoining their own in the
Catskills.

Fortunately nothing definite had been arranged
with the Count. Mrs. Blithers now advised waiting
a while before giving a definite answer to his somewhat
eager proposal, especially as he was reputed to have
sufficient means of his own to defend the chateau
against any immediate peril of profligacy. She coun-
selled Mr. Blithers to notify him that he deemed it
wise to take the matter under advisement for a couple
of weeks at least, but not to commit himself to anything positively negative.

Mr. Blithers said that he had never heard anything
so beautifully adroit as " positively negative," and
directed his secretary to submit to him. without delay
the draft of a tactful letter to the anxious nobleman.
They were agreed that a Prince was more to be desired
than a Count and, as long as they were actually about
it, they might as well aim high. Somewhat hazily Mr.
Blithers had inquired if it wouldn't be worth while to
consider a King, but his wife set him straight in short
order.

Peculiarly promising to their hopes was the indis-
putable fact that the Prince's mother had married an
American, thereby establishing a precedent behind
which no constitutional obstacle could thrive, and had

lived very happily with the gentleman in spite of the critics. Moreover, she had met him while sojourning on American soil, and that was certainly an excellent augury for the success of the present enterprise. What could be more fitting than that the son should follow in the footsteps óf an illustrious mother? ˙ If an American gentleman was worthy of a princess, why not the other way about? Certainly Maud Blithers was as full of attributes as any man in America.

It appears that the Prince, after leisurely crossing the continent on his way around the world, had come to the Truxton Kings for a long-promised and much-desired visit, the duration of which depended to some extent on his own inclinations, and not a little on the outcome of the war-talk that affected two great European nations — Russia and Austria. Ever since the historic war between the Balkan allies and the Turks, in 1912 and 1913, there had been mutterings, and now the situation had come to be admittedly precarious. Mr. Blithers was in a position to know that the little principality over which the young man reigned was bound to be drawn into the cataclysm, not as a belligerent or an ally, but in the matter of a loan that inconveniently expired within the year and which would hardly be renewed by Russia with the prospect of vast expenditures of war threatening her treasury. The loan undoubtedly would be called and Graustark was not in a position to pay out of her own slender resources, two years of famine having fallen upon the people at a time when prosperity was most to be desired.

He was in touch with the great financial movements in all the world's capitals, and he knew that retrenchment was the watchword. It would be no easy matter for the little principality to negotiate a loan at this particular time, nor was there even a slender chance that Russia would be benevolently disposed toward her debtors, no matter how small their obligations. They who owed would be called upon to pay, they who petitioned would be turned away with scant courtesy. It was the private opinion of Mr. Blithers that the young Prince and the trusted agents who accompanied him on his journey, were in the United States solely for the purpose of arranging a loan through sources that could only be reached by personal appeal. But, naturally, Mr. Blithers couldn't breathe this to a soul. Under the circumstances he couldn't even breathe it to his wife who, he firmly believed, was soulless.

But all this is beside the question. The young Prince of Graustark was enjoying American hospitality, and no matter what he owed to Russia, America owed to him its most punctillious consideration. If Mr. Blithers was to have anything to say about the matter, it would be for the ear of the Prince alone and not for the busybodies.

The main point is that the Prince was now rustieating within what you might call a stone's throw of the capacious and lordly country residence of Mr. Blithers; moreover, he was an uncommonly attractive chap, with a laugh that was so charged with heartiness that it didn't seem possible that he could have a drop of royal blood in his vigorous young body. And the perfectly ridiculous part of the whole situation was that Mr. and Mrs. King lived in a modest, vine-covered little house that could have been lost in the servants' quarters at Blitherwood. Especially aggravating, too, was the attitude of the Kings. They were really. nobodies, so to speak, and yet they blithely called their royal guest "Bobby" and allowed him to fetch and carry for their women-folk quite as if he were an ordinary whipper-snapper up from the city to spend the week-end.

The remark with which Mr. Blithers introduces this chapter was in response to an oft-repeated declaration made by his wife in the shade of the red, white and blue awning of the terrace overlooking, from its despotic heights, the modest red roof of the King villa in the valley below. Mrs. Blithers merely had stated — but over and over again — that money couldn't buy everything in the world, referring directly to social eminence and indirectly to their secret ambition to capture a Prince of the royal blood for their daughter Maud. She had prefaced this opinion, however, with the exceedingly irritating insinuation that Mr. Blithers was not in his right mind when he proposed inviting the Prince to spend a few weeks at Blitherwood, provided the young man could cut short his visit in the home of Mr. and Mrs. King, who, he had asseverated, were not in a position to entertain royalty as royalty was in the habit of being entertained.

Long experience had taught Mr. Blithers to read the lip and eye language with some degree of certainty, so by watching his wife's indignant face closely he was able to tell when she was succumbing to reason. He was a burly, domineering person who reasoned for every one within range of his voice, and it was only when his wife became coldly sarcastic that he closed his ears and boomed his opinions into her very teeth, so to say, joyfully overwhelming her with facts which it were futile for her to attempt to deny. He was aware, quite as much so as if he had heard the words, that she was now saying:

"Well, there is absolutely no use arguing with you, Will. Have it your way if it pleases you."

Eying her with some uneasiness, he cautiously inserted his thumbs in the armholes of his brocaded waistcoat, and proclaimed:

"As I said before, Lou, there isn't a foreign nobleman, from the Emperor down, who is above grabbing a few million dollars. They're all hard up, and what do they gain by marrying ladies of noble birth if said ladies are the daughters of noblemen who are as hard up as all the rest of 'em? Besides, hasn't Maud been presented at Court? Didn't you see to that? How about that pearl necklace I gave her when she was presented? Wasn't it the talk of the season? There wasn't a Duke in England who didn't figure the cost of that necklace to within a guinea or two. No girl ever had better advertising than —"

" We were speaking of Prince Robin," remarked his wife, with a slight shudder. Mrs. Blithers came of better stock than her husband. His gaucheries frequently set her teeth on edge. She was born in Providence and sometimes mentioned the occurrence when particularly desirous of squelching him, not unkindly perhaps but by way of making him realise that their daughter had good blood in her veins. Mr. Blithers had heard, in a round-about way, that he first saw the light of day in Jersey City, although after he became famous Newark claimed him. He did not bother about the matter.

" Well, he's like all the rest of them," said he, after a moment of indecision. Something told him that he really ought to refrain from talking about the cost of things, even in the bosom of his family. He had heard that only vulgarians speak of their possessions. " Now, there's no reason in the world why we shouldn't consider his offer. He —"

" Offer? " she cried, aghast. " He has made no offer, Will. He doesn't even know that Maud is in existence. How can you say such a thing? "

" I was merely looking ahead, that's all. My motto is ' Look Ahead.' You know it as well as I do. Where would I be to-day if I hadn't looked ahead and seen what was going to happen before the other fellow had his eyes open? Will you tell me that? Where, I say? What's more, where would I be now if I hadn't looked ahead and seen what a marriage with the daughter of Judge Morton would mean to me in the long run?" He felt that he had uttered a very pretty and convincing compliment. "I never made a bad bargain in my life, Lon,' and it wasn't guess-work when I married you. You, my dear old girl, you were the solid foundation on which I —"

"I know," she said wearily; "you've said it a thousand times: 'The foundation on which I built my temple of posterity '— yes, I know, Will. But I am still unalterably opposed to making ourselves ridiculous in the eyes of Mr. and Mrs. King."

"Ridiculous? I don't understand you."

"Well, you will after you think it over," she said quietly, and he scowled in positive perplexity.

"Don't you think he'd be a good match for Maud?" he asked, after many minutes. He felt that he had thought it over.

"Are you thinking of kidnapping him, Will?" she demanded.

"Certainly not! But all you've got to do is to say that he's the man for Maud and I'll — I'll do the rest. That's the kind of a man I am, Lou. You say you don't want Count What's-His-Name,— that is, you don't want him as much as you did,— and you do say that it would be the grandest thing in the world if Maud could be the Princess of Grosstick —"

"Graustark, Will."

"That's what I said. Well, if you want her to be the Princess of THAT, I'll see that she is, providing this fellow is a gentleman and worthy of her. The only Prince I ever knew was a damned rascal, and I'm going to be careful about this one. You remember that measly —"

" There is no question about Prince Robin," said she sharply.

" I suppose the only question is, how much will he want?"

" You mean — settlement? "

" Sure."

" Have you no romance in your soul, William Blithers? "

" I never believed in fairy stories," said he grimly. " And what's more, I don't take any stock in cheap novels in which American heroes go about marrying into royal families and all that sort of rot. It isn't done, Lou. If you want to marry into a royal family you've got to put up the coin."

" Prince Robin's mother, the poor Princess Yetive, married an American for love, let me remind you."

" Umph! Where is this Groostock anyway? "

" ' Somewhere east of the setting sun,' " she quoted. " You *must* learn how to pronounce it."

" I never was good at foreign languages. By the way, where is Maud this afternoon? "

" Motoring."

He waited for additional information. It was not vouchsafed, so he demanded somewhat fearfully:

" Who with? "

" Young Scoville."

He scowled. " He's a loafer, Lou. No good in the world. I don't like the way you let —"

"He is of a very good family, my dear. I —"

"Is he — er — in love with her?'"

"Certainly."

"Good Lord!"

"And why not? Isn't every one she meets in love with her?"

"I — I suppose so," he admitted sheepishly. His face brightened. "And there's no reason why this Prince shouldn't fall heels over head, is there? Well, there you are! That will make a difference in the settlement, believe me — a difference of a couple of millions at least, if —"

She arose abruptly. "You are positively disgusting, Will. Can't you think of anything but —"

"Say, ain't that Maudie coming up the drive now? Sure it is! By gracious, did you ever see anything to beat her? She's got 'em all beat a mile when it comes to looks and style and — Oh, by the way," lowering his voice to a hoarse, confidential whisper, "— I wouldn't say anything to her about the marriage just yet if I were you. I want to look him over first."

CHAPTER II

PRINCE ROBIN of Graustark was as good-looking a
chap as one would see in a week's journey. Little
would one suspect him of being the descendant of a
long and distinguished line of princes, save for the unmistakeable though indefinable something in his eye
that exacted rather than invited the homage of his
fellow man. His laugh was a free and merry one, his
spirits as effervescent as wine, his manner blithe and
boyish; yet beneath all this fair and guileless exposition of carelessness lay the sober integrity of caste.
It looked out through the steady, unswerving eyes,
even when they twinkled with mirth; it met the gaze
of the world with a serene imperiousness that gave way
before no mortal influence; it told without boastful-
ness a story of centuries. For he was the son of a
princess royal, and the blood of ten score rulers of
men had come down to him as a heritage of strength.

His mother, the beautiful, gracious and lamented
Yetive, set all royal circles by the ears when she married the American, Lorry, back in the nineties. A
special act of the ministry had legalised this union
and the son of the American was not deprived of his
right to succeed to the throne which his forebears had
occupied for centuries. From his mother he had in-
herited the right of kings, from his father the spirit of

14

freedom; from his mother the power of majesty, from his fath^er the power to see beyond that majesty. When little more than a babe in arms he was orphaned and the affairs of state fell upon the shoulders of three loyal and devoted men who served as regents until he became of age.

Wisely they served both him and the people through the years that intervened between the death of the Princess and her consort and the day when he reached his majority. That day was a glorious one in Graustark. The people worshipped the little Prince when he was in knickerbockers and played with toys; they saw him grow to manhood with hearts that were full of hope and contentment; they made him their real ruler with the same joyous spirit that had attended him in the days when he sat in the great throne and "made believe" that he was one of the mighty, despite the fact that his little legs barely reached to the edge of the gold and silver seat,— and slept soundly through all the befuddling sessions of the cabinet. He was seven when the great revolt headed by Count Marlanx came so near to overthrowing the government, and he behaved like the Prince that he was. It was during those perilous times that he came to know the gallant Truxton King in whose home he was now a happy guest. But before Truxton King he knew the lovely girl who became the wife of that devoted adventurer, and who, to him, was always to be "Aunt Loraine."

As a very small boy he had paid two visits to the homeland of his father, but after the death of his par-

ents his valuable little person was guarded so jealously
by his subjects that not once had he set foot beyond
the borders of Graustark, except on two widely separated occasions of great pomp and ceremony at the
courts of Vienna and St. Petersburgh, and a secret
journey to London when he was seventeen. (It appears that he was determined to see a great football
match.)   On each of these occasions he was attended
by watchful members of the cabinet and certain military units in the now far from insignificant standing
army.   As a matter of fact, he witnessed the football
match from the ordinary stands, surrounded by thou-
sands of unsuspecting Britons, but carefully wedged in
between two generals of his own army and flanked by
a minister of police, a minister of the treasury and a
minister of war, all of whom were excessively bored by
the contest and more or less appalled by his unregal
enthusiasm.   He had insisted on going to the match
incog, to enjoy it for all it was worth to the real spectators — those who sit or stand where the compression
is not unlike that applied to a box of sardines.

The regency expired when he was twenty years
of age, and he became ruler in fact, of himself as well
as of the half-million subjects who had waited patiently for the great day that was to see him crowned
and glorified.   Not one was there in that goodly half
million who stood out against him on that triumphant
day; not one who possessed a sullen or resentful heart.
He was their Prince, and they loved him well.   After
that wonderful coronation day he would never forget

that he was a Prince or that the hearts of a half million were to throb with love for him so long as he was man as well as Prince.

Mr. Blithers was very close to the truth when he said (to himself, if you remember) that the financial situation in the far-off principality was not all that could be desired. It is true that Graustark was in Russia's debt to the extent of some twenty million gavvos,— about thirty millions of dollars, in other words,— and that the day of reckoning was very near at hand. The loan was for a period of twelve years, and had been arranged contrary to the advice of John Tullis, an American financier who long had been interested in the welfare of the principality through friendship for the lamented Prince Consort, Lorry. He had been farsighted enough to realise that Russia would prove a hard creditor, even though she may have been sincere in her protestations of friendship for the modest borrower.

A stubborn element in the cabinet overcame his opposition, however, and the debt was contracted, taxation increased by popular vote and a period of governmental thriftiness inaugurated. Railroads, highways, bridges and aqueducts were built, owned and controlled by the state, and the city of Edelweiss rebuilt after the devastation created during the revolt of Count Marlanx and his minions. There seemed to be some prospect of vindication for the ministry and Tullis, who lived in Edelweiss, was fair-minded enough to admit that their action appeared to have been for the best. The people had prospered and taxes were paid in full and without complaint. The reserve fund grew steadily and surely and there was every prospect that when the huge debt came due it would be paid in cash. But on the very crest of their prosperity came adversity. For two years the crops failed and a pestilence swept through the herds. The flood of gavvos that had been pouring into the treasury dwindled into a pitiful rivulet; the little that came in was applied, of necessity, to administration purposes and the maintenance of the army, and there was not so much as a penny left over for the so-called sinking fund.

A year of grace remained. The minister of finance had long since recovered from the delusion that it would be easy to borrow from England or France to pay the Russians, there being small prospect of a renewal by the Czar even for a short period at a higher rate of interest. The great nations of Europe made it plain to the little principality that they would not put a finger in Russia's pie at this stage of the game. Russia was ready to go to war with her great neighbour, Austria. Diplomacy — caution, if you will,— made it imperative that other nations should sit tight and look to their own knitting, so to say. Not one could afford to be charged with befriending, even in a round-about way, either of the angry grumblers.

It was only too well known in diplomatic circles that Russia coveted the railroads of Graustark, as a means of throwing troops into a remote and almost impregnable portion of Austria. If the debt were paid promptly, it would be impossible, according to international law, for the great White Bear to take over these roads and at least a portion of the western border of the principality. Obviously, Austria would be benefitted by the prompt lifting of the debt, but her own relations with Russia were so strained that an offer to come to the rescue of Graustark would be taken at once as an open affront and vigorously resented. Her hands were tied.

The northern and western parts of Graustark were rich with productive mines. The government had built railroads throughout these sections so that the yield of coal and copper might be given an outlet to the world at large. In making the loan, Russia had demanded these prosperous sections as security for the vast sum advanced, and Graustark in an evil hour had submitted, little suspecting the trick that Dame Nature was to play in the end.

Private banking institutions in Europe refused to make loans under the rather exasperating circumstances, preferring to take no chances. Money was not cheap in these bitter days, neither in Europe nor America. Caution was the watchword. A vast European war was not improbable, despite the sincere efforts on the part of the various nations to keep out of the controversy.

Nor was Mr. Blithers far from right in his shrewd surmise that Prince Robin and his agents were not without hope in coming to America at this particular time. Graustark had laid by barely half the amount

required to lift the debt to Russia. It was not beyond
the bounds of reason to expect her Prince to secure
the remaining fifteen millions through private sources
in New York City.

Six weeks prior to his arrival in New York, the
young Prince landed in San Francisco. He had come
by way of the Orient, accompanied by the Chief of
Staff of the Graustark Army, Count Quinnox,—
hereditary watch-dog to the royal family!—and a
young lieutenant of the guard, Boske Dank. Two
men were they who would have given a thousand lives
in the service of their Prince. No less loyal was the
body-servant who looked after the personal wants of
the eager young traveller, an Englishman of the name
of Hobbs. A very poor valet was he, but an cxcep-
tionally capable person when it came to the checking
of luggage and the divining of railway time-tables.
He had been an agent for Cook's. It was quite impossible to miss a train that Hobbs suspected of being
the right one.

Prince Robin came unheralded and traversed the
breadth of the continent without attracting more than
the attention that is bestowed upon good-looking
young men. Like his mother, nearly a quarter of a
century before, he travelled incognito. But where she
had used the somewhat emphatic name of Guggen-
slocker, he was known to the hotel registers as "Mr.
R. Schmidt and servant."

There was romance in the eager young soul of
Prince Robin. He revelled in the love story of his

parents. The beautiful Princess Yetive first saw Grenfell Lorry in an express train going eastward from Denver. Their wonderful romance was born, so to speak, in a Pullman compartment car, and it thrived so splendidly that it almost upset a dynasty, for never — in all of nine centuries — had a ruler of Graustark stooped to marriage with a commoner.

And so when the far-sighted ministry and House of Nobles in Graustark set about to select a wife for their young ruler, they made overtures to the Prince of Dawsbergen whose domain adjoined Graustark on the south. The Crown Princess of Dawsbergen, then but fifteen, was the unanimous choice of the amiable match-makers in secret conclave. This was when Robin was seventeen and just over being fatuously in love with his middle-aged instructress in French.

The Prince of Dawsbergen despatched an embassy of noblemen to assure his neighbour that the match would be highly acceptable to him and that in proper season the betrothal might be announced. But alack! both courts overlooked the fact that there was independent American blood in the two young people. Neither the Prince of Graustark nor the Crown Princess of Dawsbergen,— whose mother was a Miss Beverly Calhoun of Virginia,— was disposed to listen to the voice of expediency; in fact, at a safe distance of three or four hundred miles, the youngsters figuratively turned up their noses at each other and frankly confessed that they hated each other and wouldn't be bullied into getting married, no matter what *anybody* said, or something of the sort.

"S'pose I'm going to say I'll marry a girl I've never seen?" demanded seventeen-year-old Robin, full of wrath. "Not I, my lords. I'm going to look about a bit, if you don't mind. The world is full of girls. I'll marry the one I happen to want or I'll not marry at all."

"But, highness," they protested, "you must listen to reason. There must be a successor to the throne of Graustark. You would not have the name die with you. The young Princess is —"

"Is fifteen you say," he interrupted loftily. "Come around in ten years and we'll talk it over again. But I'm not going to pledge myself to marry a child in short frocks, name or no name. Is she pretty?"

The lords did not know. They had not seen the young lady.

"If she is pretty you'd be sure to know it, my lords, so we'll assume she isn't. I saw her when she was three years old, and she certainly was a fright when she cried, and, my lords, she cried all the time. No, I'll not marry her. Be good enough to say to the Prince of Dawsbergen that I'm very much obliged to him, but it's quite out of the question."

And the fifteen-year-old Crown Princess, four hundred miles away, coolly informed her doting parents that she was tired of being a Princess anyway and very much preferred marrying some one who lived in a cottage. In fine, she stamped her little foot and said she'd jump into the river before she'd marry the Prince of Graustark.

"But he's a very handsome, adorable boy," began her mother.

"And half-American just as you are, my child," put in her father encouragingly. "Nothing could be more suitable than —"

"I don't intend to marry anybody until I'm thirty at least, so that ends it, daddy,— I mean, your poor old highness."

"Naturally we do not expect you to be married before you are out of short frocks, my dear," said Prince Dantan stiffly. "But a betrothal is quite another thing. It is customary to arrange these marriages years before —"

"Is Prince Robin in love with me?"

"I — ahem! — that's a very silly question. He hasn't seen you since you were a baby. But he *will* be in love with you, never fear."

"He may be in love with some one else, for all we know, so where do I come in?"

"Come in?" gasped her father.

"She's part American, dear," explained the mother, with her prettiest smile.

"Besides," said the Crown Princess, with finality, "I'm not even going to be engaged to a man I've never seen. And if you insist, I'll run away as sure as anything."

And so the matter rested. Five years have passed

since the initial overtures were made by the two courts, and although several sly attempts were made to bring the young people to a proper understanding of their case, they aroused nothing more than scornful laughter on the part of the belligerents, as the venerable Baron Dangloss was wont to call them, not without pride in his sharp old voice.

"It all comes from mixing the blood," said the Prime Minister gloomily.

"Or improving it," said the Baron, and was frowned upon.

And no one saw the portentous shadow cast by the slim daughter of William W. Blithers, for the simple reason that neither Graustark nor Dawsbergen knew that it existed. They lived in serene ignorance of the fact that God, while he was about it, put Maud Applegate Blithers into the world on precisely the same day that the Crown Princess of Dawsbergen first saw the light of day.

On the twenty-second anniversary of his birth, Prince Robin fared forth in quest of love and romance, not without hope of adventure, for he was a valorous chap with the heritage of warriors in his veins. Said he to himself in dreamy contemplation of the long journey ahead of him: "I will traverse the great highways that my mother trod and I will look for the Golden Girl sitting by the wayside. She must be there, and though it is a wide world, I am young and my eyes are sharp. I will find her sitting at the road-side eager for me to come, not housed in a gloomy castle surrounded by the spooks of a hundred ancestors. They who live in castles wed to hate and they who wed at the roadside live to love. Fortune attend me! If love lies at the roadside waiting, do not let me pass it by. All the princesses are not inside the castles. Some sit outside the gates and laugh with glee, for love is their companion. So away I go, la, la! looking for the princess with the happy heart and the smiling lips! It is a wide world but my eyes are sharp. I shall find my princess."

But, alas, for his fine young dream, he found no Golden Girl at the roadside nor anything that suggested romance. There were happy hearts and smiling lips — and all for him, it would appear — but he passed them by, for his eyes were *sharp* and his wits awake. And so, at last, he came to Gotham, his heart as free as the air he breathed, confessing that his quest had been in vain. History failed to repeat itself. His mother's romance would stand alone and shine without a flicker to the end of time. There could be no counterpart.

"Well, I had the fun of looking," he philosophised (to himself, for no man knew of his secret project) and grinned with a sort of amused tolerance for the sentimental side of his nature. "I'm a silly ass to have even dreamed of finding her as I passed along, and if I had found her what the deuce could I have done about it anyway? This isn't the day for mediæval lady-snatching. I dare say I'm just as well off for not having found her. I still have the zest for hunting farther, and there's a lot in that." Then aloud: " Hobbs, are we on time? "

" We are, sir," said Hobbs, without even glancing at his watch. The train was passing 125th Street. " To the minute, sir. We will be in in ten minutes, if nothing happens. Mr. King will be at the station to meet you, sir. Any orders, sir? "

" Yes, pinch me, Hobbs."

" Pinch your Highness? " in amazement. " My word, sir, wot —"

" I just want to be sure that the dream is over, Hobbs. Never mind. You needn't pinch me. I'm awake," and to prove it he stretched his fine young body in the ecstasy of realisation.

That night he slept soundly in the Catskills.

CHAPTER III

I REPEAT: Prince Robin was as handsome a chap as you'll see in a week's journey. He was just under six feet, slender, erect and strong in the way that a fine blade is strong. His hair was dark and straight, his eyes blue-black, his cheek brown and ruddy with the health of a life well-ordered. Nose, mouth and chin were clean-cut and indicative of power, while his brow was broad and smooth, with a surface so serene that it might have belonged to a woman. At first glance you would have taken him for a healthy, eager American athlete, just out of college, but that afore-mentioned seriousness in his deep-set, thoughtful eyes would have caused you to think twice before pro-nouncing him a fledgling. He had enjoyed life, he had made the most of his play-days, but always there had hung over his young head the shadow of the cross that would have to be supported to the end of his reign, through thick and thin, through joy and sor-row, through peace and strife.

He saw the shadow when he was little more than a baby; it was like a figure striding beside him always; it never left him. He could not be like other boys, for he was a prince, and it was a serious business being a prince! A thousand times, as a lad, he had wished that he could have a few " weeks off " from being what

he was and be just a common, ordinary, harum scarum
boy, like the "kids" of Petrove, the head stableman.
He would even have put up with the thrashings they
got from their father, just for the sake of enjoying the
mischief that purchased the punishment.   But alas!
no one would ever dream of giving him the lovely
"tannings" that other boys got when they were
naughty.   Such joys were not for him; he was mildly
reproved and that was all.   But his valiant spirit
found release in many a glorious though secret enconn-
ter with boys both large and small, and not infre-
quently he sustained severe pummelings at the hands of
plebeians who never were quite sure that they wouldn't
be beheaded for obliging him in the matter of a
"scrap," but who fought like little wild-cats while they
were about it.   They were always fair fights, for he
fought as a boy and not as a prince.   He took his
lickings like a prince, however, and his victories like a
boy.   The one thing he wanted to do above all others
was to play foot-ball.   But they taught him fencing,
riding, shooting and tennis instead, for, said they,
foot-ball is only to be looked-at, not played,— fine
argument, said Robin!

Be that as it may, he was physically intact and
bodily perfect.   He had no broken nose, smashed ribs,
stiff shoulder joints or weak ankles, nor was he tooth-
less.   In all his ambitious young life he had never
achieved anything more enduring than a bloody nose,
a cracked lip or a purple eye, and he had been compelled to struggle pretty hard for even those blessings.

And to hi... the pity of it all was that he was as hard
as nails and as strong as a bullock — a sad waste, if
one were to believe him in his bitter Lamentations.

Toward the end of his first week at Red Roof, the
summer home of the Truxton Kings, he might have
been found on the broad lawn late one afternoon,
playing tennis with his hostess, the lovely and vivacious " Aunt Loraine." To him, Mrs. King would
always be " Aunt Loraine," even as he would never be
anything but Bobby to her.

She was several years under forty and as light and
active as a young girl. Her smooth cheek glowed
with the happiness and thrill of the sport, and he
was hard put to hold his own against her, even though
she insisted that he play his level best.

Truxton King, stalwart and lazy, lounged on the
turf, umpiring the game, attended by two pretty young
girls, a lieutenant in flannels and the ceremonious
Count Quinnox, iron grey and gaunt-faced battleman
with the sabre scars on his cheek and the bullet wound
in his side.

" Good work, Rainie," shouted the umpire as his
wife safely placed the ball far out of her opponent's
reach.

" Hi ! " shouted Robin, turning on him with a scowl.
" You're not supposed to cheer anybody, d' you understand? You're only an umpire."

" Outburst of excitement, Kid," apologised the umpire complacently. " Couldn't help it. Forty thirty.
Get busy."

"He called him 'kid,'" whispered one of the young girls to the other.

"Well I heard the Prince call Mr. King 'Truck' a little while ago," whispered the other.

"Isn't he good-looking?" sighed the first one.

They were sisters, very young, and lived in the cottage across the road with their widowed mother. Their existence was quite unknown to Mr. and Mrs. Blithers, although the amiable Maud was rather nice to them. She had once picked them up in her automobile when she encountered them walking to the station. After that she called them by their Christian names and generously asked them to call her Maud. It might appear from this that Maud suffered somewhat from loneliness in the great house on the hill. The Felton girls had known Robin a scant three-quarters of an hour and were deeply in love with him. Fannie was eighteen and Nellie but little more than sixteen. He was their first Prince.

"Whee-ee!" shrilled Mrs. King, going madly after a return that her opponent had lobbed over the net. She missed.

"Deuce," said her husband laconically. A servant was crossing the lawn with a tray of iced drinks. As he neared the recumbent group he paused irresolutely and allowed his gaze to shift toward the road below. Then he came on and as he drew alongside the interested umpire he leaned over and spoke in a low tone of voice.

"What?" demanded King, squinting.

"Just coming in the gate, sir," said the footman.

King shot a glance over his shoulder and then sat up in astonishment.

"Good Lord! Blithers! What the deuce can he be doing here? I say, Loraine! Hi!"

"Vantage in," cried his pretty wife, dashing a stray lock from her eyes.

Mr. King's astonishment was genuine. It might better have been pronounced bewilderment. Mr. Blithers was paying his first visit to Red Roof. Up to this minute it is doubtful if he ever had accorded it so much as a glance of interest in passing. He bowed to King occasionally at the station, but that was all.

But now his manner was exceedingly friendly as he advanced upon the group. One might have been pardoned for believing him to be a most intimate friend of the family and given to constantly dropping in at any and all hours of the day.

The game was promptly interrupted. It would not be far from wrong to say that Mrs. King's pretty mouth was open not entirely as an aid to breathing. She couldn't believe her eyes as she slowly abandoned her court and came forward to meet their advancing visitor.

"Take my racket, dear," she said to one of the Feltons. It happened to be Fannie and the poor child almost fainted with joy.

The Prince remained in the far court, idly twirling his racket.

"Afternoon, King," said Mr. Blithers, doffing his panama — to fan a heated brow. "Been watching the game from the road for a spell. Out for a stroll. Couldn't resist running in for a minute. You play a beautiful game, Mrs. King. How do you do! Pretty hot work though, isn't it?"

He was shaking hands with King and smiling genially upon the trim, panting figure of the Prince's adversary.

"Good afternoon, Mr. Blithers," said King, still staring. "You — you know my wife?"

Mr. Blithers ignored what might have been regarded as an introduction, and blandly announced that tennis wasn't a game for fat people, patting his somewhat aggressive extension in mock dolefulness as he spoke.

"You should see my daughter play," he went on, scarcely heeding Mrs. King's tactless remark that she affected the game because she had a horror of getting fat. "Corking, she is, and as quick as a cat. Got a medal at Lakewood last spring. I'll fix up a match soon, Mrs. King, between you and Maud. Ought to be worth going miles to see, eh, King?"

"Oh, I am afraid, Mr. Blithers, that I am not in your daughter's class," said Loraine King, much too innocently.

"We've got a pretty fair tennis court up at Blitherwood," said Mr. Blithers calmly. "I have a professional instructor up every week to play with Maud. She can trim most of the amateurs so —"

"May I offer you a drink of some kind, Mr. Blithers?" asked King, recovering his poise to some extent. "We are having lemonades, but perhaps you'd prefer something—" .

"Lemonade will do for me, thanks," said the visitor affably. "We ought to run in on each other a little more often than — thanks! By jove, it looks refreshing. Your health, Mrs. King. Too bad to drink a lady's health in lemonade but — the sentiment's the same."

He was looking over her shoulder at the bounding Prince in the far court as he spoke, and it seemed that he held his glass a trifle too high in proposing the toast.

"I beg your pardon, Mr. Blithers," mumbled King. "Permit me to introduce Count Quinnox and Lieutenant Dank." Both of the foreigners had arisen and were standing very erect and soldierly a few yards away. "You know Miss Felton, of course."

"Delighted to meet you, Count," said Mr. Blithers, advancing with outstretched hand. He shook the hand of the lieutenant with a shade less energy. "Enjoying the game?"

"Immensely," said the Count. "It is rarely played so well."

Mr. Blithers affected a most dégagé manner, squinting carelessly at the Prince.

"That young chap plays a nice game. Who is he?"

The two Graustarkians stiffened perceptibly, and

waited for King to make the revelation to his visitor.

"That's Prince Robin of —" he began but Mr. Blithers cut him short with a genial wave of the hand.

"Of course," he exclaimed, as if annoyed by his own stupidity. "I did hear that you were entertaining a Prince. Slipped my mind, however. Well, well, we're coming up in the world, eh? — having a real nabob among us." He hesitated for a moment. "But don't let me interrupt the game," he went on, as if expecting King to end the contest in order to present the Prince to him.

"Won't you sit down, Mr. Blithers?" said Mrs. King. "Or would you prefer a more comfortable chair on the porch? We —"

"No, thanks, I'll stay here if you don't mind," said he hastily, and dragged up the camp chair that Lieutenant Dank had been occupying.

"Fetch another chair, Lucas," said King to the servant. "And another glass of lemonade for Miss Felton."

"Felton?" queried Mr. Blithers, sitting down very carefully on the rather fragile chair, and hitching up his white flannel trousers at the knees to reveal a pair of purple socks, somewhat elementary in tone.

"We know your daughter, Mr. Blithers," said little Miss Nellie eagerly.

"I was just trying to remember —"

"We live across the road — over there in the little white house with the ivy —"

"— where I'd heard the name," proceeded Mr.

Blithers, still looking at the Prince. "By jove, I should think my daughter and the Prince would make a rattling good match. I mean," he added, with a boisterous laugh, "a good match at tennis. We'll have to get 'em together some day, eh, up at Blitherwood. How long is the Prince to be with you, Mrs. King?"

"It's rather uncertain, Mr. Blithers," said she, and no more.

Mr. Blithers fanned himself in patience for a moment or two. Then he looked at his watch.

"Getting along toward dinner-time up our way," he ventured. Everybody seemed rather intent on the game, which was extremely one-sided.

"Good work!" shouted King as Fannie Felton managed to return an easy service.

Lieutenant Dank applauded vigorously. "Splendid!" he cried out. "Capitally placed!"

"They speak remarkably good English, don't they?" said Mr. Blithers in an audible aside to Mrs. King. "Beats the deuce how quickly they pick it up."

She smiled. "Officers in the Graustark army are required to speak English, French and German, Mr. Blithers."

"It's a good idea," said he. "Maud speaks French and Italian like a native. She was educated in Paris and Rome, you know. Fact is, she's lived abroad a great deal."

"Is she at home now, Mr. Blithers?"

"Depends on what you'd call home, Mrs. King. We've got so many I don't know just which is the real one. If you mean Blitherwood, yes, she's there. Course, there's our town house in Madison Avenue, the place at Newport, one at Nice and one at Pasadena — California, you know — and a little shack in London. By the way, my wife says you live quite near our place in New York."

"We live in Madison Avenue, but it's a rather long street, Mr. Blithers. Just where is your house?" she inquired, rather spitefully.

He looked astonished. "You surely must know where the Blithers house is at —"

"Game!" shrieked Fannie Felton, tossing her racket in the air, a victor.

"They're through," said Mr. Blithers in a tone of relief. He shifted his legs and put his hands on his knees, suggesting a readiness to arise on an instant's notice.

"Shall we try another set?" called out the Prince.

"Make it doubles," put in Lieutenant Dank, and turned to Nellie. "Shall we take them on?".

And doubles it was, much to the disgust of Mr. Blithers. He sat through the nine games, manifesting an interest he was far from feeling, and then — as dusk fell across the valley — arose expectantly with the cry of "game and set." He had discoursed freely on the relative merits of various motor cars, stoutly maintaining that the one he drove was without question the best in the market (in fact, there wasn't an-

other "make" that he would have as a gift); the
clubs he belonged to in New York were the only ones
that were worth belonging to (he wouldn't be caught
dead in any of the others); his tailor was the only
tailor in the country who knew how to make a decent
looking suit of clothes (the rest of them were "the
limit"); the Pomeranian that he had given his daughter was the best dog of its breed in the world (he
was looking at Mrs. King's Pomeranian as he made the
remark); the tennis court at Blitherwood was pronounced by experts to be the finest they'd ever seen
— and so on and so on, until the long-drawn-out act
was ended.

To his utter amazement, at the conclusion of the
game, the four players made a dash for the house
without even so much as a glance in his direction. It
was the Prince who shouted something that sounded
like "now for a shower!" as he raced up the terrace,
followed by the other participants.

Mr. Blithers said something violent under his
breath, but resolutely retained his seat. It was King
who glanced slyly at his watch this time, and subsequently shot a questioning look at his wife. She was
frowning in considerable perplexity, and biting her
firm red lips. Count Quinnox coolly arose and excused
himself with the remark that he was off to dress for
dinner. He also looked at his watch, which certainly
was an act that one would hardly have expected of a
diplomat.

"Well, well," said Mr. Blithers profoundly. Then

he looked at his own watch — and settled back in his chair, a somewhat dogged compression about his jaws. He was not the man to be thwarted. "You certainly have a cosy little place here, King," he remarked after a moment or two.

"We like it," said King, twiddling his fingers behind his back. "Humble but homelike."

"Mrs. Blithers has been planning to come over for some time, Mrs. King. I told her she oughtn't to put it off — be neighbourly, don't you know. That's me. I'm for being neighbourly with my neighbours. But women, they — well, you know how it is, Mrs. King. Always something turning up to keep 'em from doing the things they want to do most. And Mrs. Blithers has so many sociable obli — I beg pardon?"

"I was just wondering if you would stay and have dinner with us, Mr. Blithers," said she, utterly helpless. She couldn't look her husband in the eye — and it was quite fortunate that she was unable to do so, for it would have resulted in a laughing duet that could never have been explained.

"Why," said Mr. Blithers, arising and looking at his watch again, "bless my soul, it is *past* dinner time, isn't it? I had no idea it was so late. 'Pon my soul, it's good of you, Mrs. King. You see, we have dinner at seven up at Blitherwood and — I declare it's half-past now. I don't see where the time has gone. Thanks, I *will* stay if you really mean to be kind to a poor old beggar. Don't do anything extra on my account, though, just your regular dinner, you know.

No frills, if you please." He looked himself over in some uncertainty. "Will this rag of mine do?"

"We shan't notice it, Mr. Blithers," said she, and he turned the remark over in his mind several times as he walked beside her toward the house. Somehow it didn't sound just right to him, but for the life of him he couldn't tell why. "We are quite simple folk, you see," she went on desperately, making note of the fact that her husband lagged behind like the coward he was. "Red Roof is as nothing compared to Blitherwood, with its army of servants and —"

Mr. Blithers magnanimously said "Pooh!" and, continuing, remarked that he wouldn't say exactly how many they employed but he was sure there were not more than forty, including the gardeners. "Besides," he added gallantly, "what is an army of servants compared to the army of Grasstock? You've got the real article, Mrs. King, so don't you worry. But, I say, if necessary, I can telephone up to the house and have a dress suit sent down. It won't take fifteen minutes, Lou — er — Mrs. Blithers always has 'em laid out for me, in case of an emergency, and —"

"Pray do not think of it," she cried. "The men change, of course, after they've been playing tennis, but we — we — well, you see, you haven't been playing," she concluded, quite breathlessly.

At that instant the sprightly Feltons dashed pell mell down the steps and across the lawn homeward, shrieking something unintelligible to Mrs. King as they passed.

"Rather skittish," observed Mr. Blithers, glaring after them disapprovingly.

"They are dears," said Mrs. King.

"The — er — Prince attracted by either one of 'em?" he queried.

"He barely knows them, Mr. Blithers."

"I see. Shouldn't think they'd appeal to him. Rather light, I should say — I mean up here," and he tapped his forehead so that she wouldn't think that he referred to pounds and ounces. "I don't believe Maud knows 'em, as the little one said. Maud is rather —"

"It is possible they have mistaken some one else for your daughter," said she very gently.

"Impossible," said he with force.

"They are coming back here to dinner," she said, and her eyes sparkled with mischief. "I shall put you between them, Mr. Blithers. You will find that they are very bright, attractive girls."

"We'll see," said he succinctly.

King caught them up at the top of the steps. He seemed to be slightly out of breath.

"Make yourself at home, Mr. Blithers. I must get into something besides these duds I'm wearing," he said. "Would you like to — er — wash up while we're —"

"No, thanks," interposed Mr. Blithers. "I'm as clean as a whistle. Don't mind me, please. Run along and dress, both of you. I'll sit out here and —

"You will excuse me if I leave you —"

"Don't mention it, old man," said the new guest, rather more curtly than he intended. "I'll take it easy."

"Shall I have the butler telephone to Blitherwood to say that you won't be home to dinner?"

"It would be better if he were to say that I *wasn't* home to dinner," said Mr. Blithers. "It's over by this time."

"Something to drink while you're —"

"No, thanks. I can wait," and he sat down.

"You don't mind my —"

"Not at all."

Mr. Blithers settled himself in the big porch chair and glowered at the shadowy hills on the opposite side of the valley. The little cottage of the Feltons came directly in his line of vision. He scowled more deeply than before. At the end of fifteen minutes he started up suddenly and, after a quick uneasy glance about him, started off across the lawn, walking more rapidly than was his wont.

He had remembered that his chauffeur was waiting

for him with the car just around a bend in the road —
and had been waiting for two hours or more.

"Go home," he said to the man. "Come back at
twelve. And don't use the cut-out going up that hill,
either."

Later on, he met the Prince. Very warmly he shook
the tall young man's hand,— he even gave it a prophetic second squeeze,— and said:

"I am happy to welcome you to the Catskills,
Prince."

"Thank you," said Prince Robin.

CHAPTER IV

" A most extraordinary person," said Count Quinnox
to King, after Mr. Blithers had taken his departure,
close upon the heels of the Feltons who were being
escorted home by the Prince and Dank. The venerable Graustarkian's heroic face was a study. He
had just concluded a confidential hour in a remote
corner of the library with the millionaire while the
younger people were engaged in a noisy though tem-
perate encounter with the roulette wheel at the opposite end of the room. " I've never met any one like
him, Mr. King." He mopped his brow, and still
looked a trifle dazed.

King laughed. "There isn't any one like him,
Count. He is the one and only Blithers."

" He is very rich? "

" Millions and millions," said Mrs. King.
" Didn't he tell you how many? "

" I am not quite sure. This daughter of his — is
she attractive? "

" Rather. Why? "

" He informed me that her dot would be twenty
millions if she married the right man. Moreover, she
is his only heir. 'Pon my soul, Mrs. King, he quite
took my breath away when he announced that he
knew all about our predicament in relation to the

Russian loan. It really sounded quite — you might say significant. Does — does he imagine that — good heaven, it's almost stupefying!"

King smoked in silence for many seconds. There was a pucker of annoyance on his wife's fair brow as she stared reflectively through the window at the distant lights of Blitherwood, far up the mountain side.

"Sounds ominous to me," said King drily. "Is Bobby for sale?"

The Count favoured him with a look of horror. "My dear Mr. King!" Then as comprehension came, he smiled. "I see. No, he isn't for sale. He is a Prince, not a pawn. Mr. Blithers may be willing to buy but —" he proudly shook his head.

"He was feeling you out, however," said King, ruminating. "Planting the seed, so to speak."

"There is a rumour that she is to marry Count Lannet," said his wife. "A horrid creature. There was talk in the newspapers last winter of an Italian duke. Poor girl! From what I hear of her, she is rather a good sort, sensible and more genuinely American in her tastes than might be expected after her bringing-up. And she is pretty."

"How about this young Scoville, Rainie?"

"He's a nice boy but — he'll never get her. She is marked up too high for him. He doesn't possess so much as the title to an acre of land."

"Extraordinary, the way you Americans go after our titles," said the Count good-naturedly.

"No more extraordinary than the way you Europeans go after our money," was her retort.

"I don't know which is the cheaper, titles or money in these days," said King. "I understand one can get a most acceptable duke for three or four millions, a nice marquis or count for half as much, and a Sir on tick." He eyed the Count speculatively. "Of course a prince of the royal blood comes pretty high."

"Pretty high," said the Count grimly. He seemed to be turning something over in his mind. "Your amazing Mr. Blithers further confided to me that he might be willing to take care of the Russian obligation for us if no one else turns up in time. As a matter of fact, without waiting for my reply, he said that he would have his lawyers look into the matter of security at once. I was somewhat dazed, but I think he said that it would be no trouble at all for him to provide the money himself and he would be glad to accommodate us if we had no other plan in mind. Amazing, amazing!"

"Of course, you told him it was not to be considered," said King sharply.

"I endeavoured to do so, but I fear he did not grasp what I was saying. Moreover, I tried to tell him that it was a matter I was not at liberty to discuss. He didn't hear that, either."

"He is not in the habit of hearing any one but himself, I fear," said King.

"I am afraid poor Robin is in jeopardy," said his wife, ruefully. "The Bogieman is after him."

"Does the incomprehensible creature imagine —"
began the Count loudly, and then found it necessary to
pull his collar away from his throat as if to save himself from immediate strangulation.

"Mr. Blithers is not blessed with an imagination,
Count," said she. "He doesn't imagine anything."

"If he should presume to insult our Prince by —"
grated the old soldier, very red in the face and
erect —"if he should presume to —" Words failed
him and an instant later he was laughing, but somewhat uncertainly, with his amused host and hostess.

Mr. Blithers reached home in high spirits. His
wife was asleep, but he awoke her without ceremony.

"I say, Lou, wake up. Got some news for you.
We'll have a prince in the family before you can say
Jack Robinson."

She sat up in bed, blinking with dismay. "In
heaven's name, Will, what have you been doing?
What *have* you been —"

"Cutting bait," said he jovially. "In a day or
two I'll throw the hook in, and you'll see what I land.
He's as good as caught right now, but we'll let him
nibble a while before we jerk. And say, he's a corker,
Lou. Finest young fellow I've seen in many a day.
He —"

"You don't mean to say that you — you actually
said anything to him about — about — Oh, my God,
Will, don't tell me that you were crazy enough to —"
cried the poor woman, almost in tears.

"Now cool down, cool down," he broke in soothingly. " I'm no fool, Lou. Trust me to do the fine work in a case like this. Sow the right kind of seeds and you'll get results every time. I merely dropped a few hints, that's all,— and in the right direction, believe me. Count Equinox will do the rest. I'll bet my head we'll have this prince running after Maud so —"

" What *did* you say? " she demanded. There was a fine moisture on her upper lip. He sat down on the edge of the bed and talked for half an hour without interruption. When he came to the end of his oration, she turned over with her face to the wall and fairly sobbed: " What will the Kings think of us? What will they think? "

" Who the dickens cares what the Kings think? " he roared, perfectly aghast at the way she took it. " Who are the Kings? Tell me that! who are they? "

" I — I can't bear to talk about it. Go to bed."

He wiped his brow helplessly. " You beat anything I've ever seen. What's the matter with you? Don't you want this prince for Maud? Well, then, what the deuce are you crying about? You said you wanted him, didn't you? Well, I'm going to get him. If I say I'll do a thing, you can bet your last dollar I'll do it. That's the kind of a man William W. Blithers is. You leave it to me. There's only one way to land these foreign noblemen, and I'm —"

She faced him once more, and angrily. " Listen to me," she said. " I've had a talk with Maud. She has gone to bed with a splitting headache and I'm

not surprised. Don't you suppose the poor child has
a particle of pride? She guessed at once just what
you had gone over there for and she cried her eyes
out. Now she declares she will never be able to look
the Prince in the face, and as for the Kings — Oh,
it's sickening. Why can't you leave these things to
me? You go about like a bull in a china shop. You
might at least have waited until the poor child had an
opportunity to see the man before rushing in with
your talk about money. She —"

"Confound it, Lou, don't blame me for everything.
We all three agreed at lunch that he was a better bargain than this measly count we've been considering.
Maud says she won't marry the count, anyhow, and
she *did* say that if this prince was all that he's cracked
up to be, she wouldn't mind being the Princess of
Groostock. You can't deny that, Lou. You heard
her say it. You —"

"She didn't say Groostock," said his wife shortly.
"And you forget that she said she wouldn't promise
anything until she'd met him and decided whether
she liked him."

"She'll like him all right," said he confidently.

"She will refuse to even meet him, if she hears of
your silly blunder to-night."

"Refuse to meet him?" gasped Mr. Blithers.

"I may be able to reason with her, Will, but — but
she's stubborn, as well you know. I'm afraid you've
spoiled everything."

His face brightened. Lowering his voice to a half-whisper, he said: "We needn't tell her what I said to that old chap, Lou. Just let her think I sat around like a gump and never said a word to anybody. We can —"

"But she'll pin you down, Will, and you know you can't lie with a straight face."

"Maybe — maybe I'd better run down to New York for a few days," he muttered unhappily. "You can square it better than I can."

"In other words, I can lie with a straight face," she said ironically.

"I never thought she'd balk like this," said he, ignoring the remark.

"I fancy you'd better go to New York," she said mercilessly.

"I've got business there anyhow," muttered he. "I — I think I'll go before she's up in the morning."

"You can save yourself a bad hour or two if you leave before breakfast," said she levelly.

"Get around her some way, Lou," he pleaded. "Tell her I'm sorry I had to leave so early, and — and that I love her better than anything on earth, and that I'll be back the end of the week. If — if she wants anything in New York, just have her wire me. You say she cried?"

"She did, and I don't blame her."

Mr. Blithers scowled. "Well — well, you see if you can do any better than I did. Arrange it somehow for them to meet. She'll — she'll like him and then — by George, she'll thank us both for the interest we take in her future. It wouldn't surprise me if she fell in love with him right off the reel. And you may be sure he'll fall in love with her. He can't help it. The knowledge that she'll have fifty millions some day won't have anything to do with his feeling for her, once he —"

" Don't mention the word millions again, Will Blithers."

" All right," said he, more humbly than he knew. " But listen to this, old girl; I'm going to get this prince for her if it's the last act of my life. I never failed in anything and I won't fail in this."

" Well, go to bed, dear, and don't worry. I may be able to undo the mischief. It — it isn't hopeless, of course."

" I'll trust you, Lou, to do your part. Count on me to do mine when the time comes. And I still insist that I have sowed the right sort of seed to-night. You'll see. Just wait."

Sure enough, Mr. Blithers was off for New York soon after daybreak the next morning, and with him went a mighty determination to justify himself before the week was over. His wily brain was working as it had never worked before.

Two days later, Count Quinnox received a message from New York bearing the distressing information that the two private banking institutions on which he had been depending for aid in the hour of trouble had decided that it would be impossible for them to make the loan under consideration. The financial agents who had been operating in behalf of the Graustark government confessed that they were unable to explain the sudden change of heart on the part of the bankers, inasmuch as the negotiations practically had been closed with them. The decision of the directors was utterly incomprehensible under the circumstances.

Vastly disturbed, Count Quinnox took the first train to New York, accompanied by Truxton King, who was confident that outside influences had been brought to bear upon the situation, influences inimical to Graustark. Both were of the opinion that Russia had something to do with it, although the negotiations had been conducted with all the secrecy permissible in such cases.

"We may be able to get to the banks through Blithers," said King.

"How could he possibly be of assistance to us?" the Count inquired.

"He happens to be a director in both concerns, besides being such a power in the financial world that his word is almost law when it comes to the big deals."

All the way down to the city Count Quinnox was thoughtful, even pre-occupied. They were nearing the Terminal when he leaned over and, laying his hand on King's knee, said, after a long interval of silence between them:

"I suppose you know that Graustark has not given up hope that Prince Robin may soon espouse the daughter of our neighbour, Dawsbergen."

King gave him a queer look. "By jove, that's

odd. I was thinking of that very thing when you spoke."

"The union would be of no profit to us in a pecuniary way, my friend," explained the Count. "Still it is most desirable for other reasons. Dawsbergen is not a rich country, nor are its people progressive. The reigning house, however, is an old one and rich in traditions. Money, my dear King, is not everything in this world. There are some things it cannot buy. It is singularly ineffective when opposed to an honest sentiment. Even though the young Princess were to come to Graustark without a farthing, she would still be hailed with the wildest acclaim. We are a race of blood worshippers, if I may put it in that way. She represents a force that has dominated our instincts for a great many centuries, and we are bound hand and foot, heart and soul, by the so-called fetters of imperialism. We are fierce men, but we bend the knee and we wear the yoke because the sword of destiny is in the hand that drives us. To-day we are ruled by a prince whose sire was not of the royal blood. I do not say that we deplore this infusion, but it behooves us to protect the original strain. We must conserve our royal blood. Our prince assumes an attitude of independence that we find difficult to overcome. He is prepared to defy an old precedent in support of a new one. In other words, he points out the unmistakably happy union of his own mother, the late Princess Yetive, and the American Lorry, and it is something we cannot go behind. He declares that his mother set an example that he may emulate without prejudice to his country if he is allowed a free hand in choosing his mate.

"But we people of Graustark cannot look with complaisance on the possible result of his search for a sharer of the throne. Traditions must be upheld — or we die. True, the Crown Princess of Dawsbergen has American blood in her veins but her sire is a prince royal. Her mother, as you know, was an American girl. She who sits on the throne with Robin must be a princess by birth or the grip on the sword of destiny is weakened and the dynasty falters. I know what is in your mind. You are wondering why our Prince should not wed one of your fabulously rich American girls —"

"My dear Count," said King warmly, "I am not thinking anything of the sort. Naturally I am opposed to your pre-arranged marriages and all that sort of thing, but still I appreciate what it means as a safe-guard to the crown you support. I sincerely hope that Robin may find his love-mate in the small circle you draw for him, but I fear it isn't likely. He is young, romantic, impressionable, and he abhors the thought of marriage without love. He refuses to even consider the princess you have picked out for him. Time may prove to him that his ideals are false and he may resign himself to the — I was about to say the inevitable."

"Inevitable is the word, Mr. King," said Count Quinnox grimly. "'Pon my word, sir, I don't know what our princes and princesses are coming to in these days. There seems to be a perfect epidemic of independence among them. They marry whom they please in spite of royal command, and the courts of Europe are being shorn of half their glory. It wouldn't surprise me to see an American woman on the throne of England one of these days. 'Gad, sir, you know what happened in Axphain two years ago. Her crown prince renounced the throne and married a French singer."

" And they say he is a very happy young beggar," said King drily.

" It is the prerogative of fools to be happy," said Count Quinnox.

" Not so with princes, eh? "

" It is a duty with princes, Mr. King."

They had not been in New York City an hour before they discovered that William W. Blithers was the man to whom they would have to appeal if they expected to gain a fresh hearing with the banks. The agents were in a dismal state of mind. The deal had been blocked no later than the afternoon of the day before and at a time when everything appeared to be going along most swimmingly. Blithers was the man to see; he and he alone could bring pressure to bear on the directorates that might result in a reconsideration of the surprising verdict. Something had happened during the day to alter the friendly attitude of the banks; they were now politely reluctant, as one of the agents expressed it, which really meant that opposition to the loan had appeared from some unexpected source, as a sort of eleventh hour obstacle. The heads of the two banks had as much as said that negotiations were at an end, that was the long and short of it; it really didn't matter what was back of their sudden change of front, the fact still remained that the transaction was as "dead as a door nail" unless it could be revived by the magnetic touch of a man like Blithers.

"What can have happened to cause them to change their minds so abruptly?" cried the perplexed Count. "Surely our prime minister and the cabinet have left nothing undone to convince them of Graustark's integrity and —"

"Pardon me, Count," interrupted one of the brokers, "shall I try to make an appointment for you with Mr. Blithers? I hear he is in town for a few days."

Count Quinnox looked to Truxton King for inspiration and that gentleman favoured him with a singularly dis-spiriting nod of the head. The old Graustarkian cleared his throat and rather stiffly announced that he would receive Mr. Blithers if he would call on him at the Ritz that afternoon.

"What!" exclaimed both agents, half-starting from their chairs in amazement.

The Count stared hard at them. "You may say to him that I will be in at four."

"He'll tell you to go to — ahem!" The speaker coughed just in time. "Blithers isn't in the habit of going out of his way to — to oblige anybody. He wouldn't do it for the Emperor of Germany."

"But," said the Count with a frosty smile, "I am not the Emperor of Germany."

"Better let me make an appointment for you to see him at his office. It's just around the corner." There was a pleading note in the speaker's voice.

"You might save your face, Calvert, by saying that the Count will be pleased to have him take tea with him at the Ritz," suggested King.

"Tea!" exclaimed Calvert scornfully. "Blithers doesn't drink the stuff."

"It's a figure of speech," said King patiently.

"All right, I'll telephone," said the other dubiously.

He came back a few minutes later with a triumphant look in his eye.

"Blithers says to tell Count Quinnox he'll see him to-morrow morning at half-past eight at his office. Sorry he's engaged this afternoon."

"But did you say I wanted him to have tea with us!" demanded the Count, an angry flush leaping to his cheek.

"I did. I'm merely repeating what he said in reply. Half-past eight, at his office, Count. Those were his words."

"It is the most brazen exhibition of insolence I've ever —" began the Count furiously, but checked himself with an effort. "I — I hope you did not say that I would come, sir!"

"Yes. It's the only way —"

"Well, be good enough to call him up again and say to him that I'll — I'll see him damned before I'll come to his office to-morrow at eight-thirty or at any other hour." And with that the Count got up and stalked out of the office, putting on his hat as he did so.

"Count," said King, as they descended in the elevator, "I've got an idea in my head that Blithers will be at the Ritz at four."

"Do you imagine, sir, that I will receive him?"

"Certainly. Are you not a diplomat?"

"I am a Minister of War," said the Count, and his scowl was an indication of absolute proficiency in the science.

"And what's more," went on King, reflectively, "it wouldn't in the least surprise me if Blithers is the man behind the directors in this sudden move of the banks."

"My dear King, he displayed the keenest interest and sympathy the other night at your house. He —"

"Of course I may be wrong," admitted King, but his brow was clouded.

Shortly after luncheon that day, Mrs. Blithers received a telegram from her husband. It merely stated that he was going up to have tea with the Count at four o'clock, and not to worry as "things were shaping themselves nicely."

CHAPTER V

LATE the same evening, Prince Robin, at Red Roof, received a long distance telephone communication from New York City. The Count was on the wire. He imparted the rather startling news that William W. Blithers had volunteered to take care of the loan out of his own private means! Quinnox was cabling the Prime Minister for advice and would remain in New York for further conference with the capitalist, who, it was to be assumed, would want time to satisfy himself as to the stability of Graustark's resources.

Robin was jubilant. The thought had not entered his mind that there could be anything sinister in this amazing proposition of the great financier.

If Count Quinnox himself suspected Mr. Blithers of an ulterior motive, the suspicion was rendered doubtful by the evidence of sincerity on the part of the capitalist who professed no sentiment in the matter but insisted on the most complete indemnification by the Graustark government. Even King was impressed by the absolute fairness of the proposition. Mr. Blithers demanded no more than the banks were asking for in the shape of indemnity; a first lien mortgage for 12 years on all properties owned and controlled by the government and the deposit of all bonds

held by the people with the understanding that the
interest would be paid to them regularly, less a small
per cent as commission. His protection would be complete,— for the people of Graustark owned fully four-
fifths of the bonds issued by the government for the
construction of public service institutions; these by
consent of Mr. Blithers were to be limited to three
utilities: railroads, telegraph and canals. These
properties, as Mr. Blithers was by way of knowing,
were absolutely sound and self-supporting. According to his investigators in London and Berlin, they
were as solid as Gibraltar and not in need of one-
tenth the protection required by the famous rock.

Robin inquired whether he was to come to New
York at once in relation to the matter, and was informed that it would not be necessary at present.
In fact, Mr. Blithers preferred to let the situation
remain in statu quo (as he expressed it to the Count),
until it was determined whether the people were willing to deposit their bonds, a condition which was
hardly worth while worrying about in view of the fact
that they had already signified their readiness to
present them for security in the original proposition
to the banks. Mr. Blithers, however, would give himself the pleasure of calling upon the Prince at Red
Roof later in the week, when the situation could be
discussed over a dish of tea or a cup of lemonade.
That is precisely the way Mr. Blithers put it.

The next afternoon Mrs. Blithers left cards at
Red Roof — or rather, the foot-man left them — and

on the day following the Kings and their guests received invitations to a ball at Blitherwood on the ensuing Friday, but four days off. While Mrs. King
and the two young men were discussing the invitation
the former was called to the telephone. Mrs. Blithers
herself was speaking.

"I hope you will pardon me for calling you up,
Mrs. King, but I wanted to be sure that you can come
on the seventeenth. We want so much to have the
Prince and his friends with us. Mr. Blithers has
taken a great fancy to Prince Robin and Count Quinnox, and he declares the whole affair will be a fiasco
if they are not to be here."

"It is good of you to ask us, Mrs. Blithers. The
Prince is planning to leave for Washington within
the next few days and I fear —"

"Oh, you must prevail upon him to remain over, my
dear Mrs. King. We are to have a lot of people up
from Newport and Tuxedo — you know the crowd —
it's the *real* crowd — and I'm sure he will enjoy meeting them. Mr. Blithers has arranged for a special
train to bring them up — a train de luxe, you may be
sure, both as to equipment and occupant. Zabo's
orchestra, too. A notion seized us last night to give
the ball, which accounts for the short notice. It's
the way we do everything — on a minute's notice.
I think they're jollier if one doesn't go through the
agony of a month's preparation, don't you? Nearly
every one has wired acceptance, so we're sure to have

a lot of nice people. Loads of girls,— you know
the ones I mean,— and Mr. Blithers is trying to arrange a sparring match between those two great prize-
fighters,— you know the ones, Mrs. King,— just
to give us poor women a chance to see what a real
man looks like in — I mean to say, what marvellous
specimens they are, don't you know. Now please tell
the Prince that he positively cannot afford to miss
a real sparring match. Every one is terribly excited over it, and naturally we are keeping it very
quiet. Won't it be a lark? My daughter thinks
it's terrible, but she is finicky. One of them is a negro,
isn't he? "

" I'm sure I don't know."

" You can imagine how splendid they must be when
I tell you that Mr. Blithers is afraid they won't come
up for less than fifteen thousand dollars. Isn't it
ridiculous? "

" Perfectly," said Mrs. King.

" Of course, we shall insist on the Prince receiving
with us. He is our *piece de resistance*. You —"

" I'm sure it will be awfully jolly, Mrs. Blithers.
What did you say? "

" I beg pardon? "

" I'm sorry. I was speaking to the Prince. He
just called up stairs to me."

" What does he say? "

" It was really nothing. He was asking about
Hobbs."

"Hobbs? Tell him, please, that if he has any friends he would like to have invited we shall be only too proud to —"

"Oh, thank you! I'll tell him."

"You must not let him go away before —"

"I shall try my best, Mrs. Blithers. It is awfully kind of you to ask us to —"

"You must all come up to dinner either to-morrow night or the night after. I shall be so glad if you will suggest anything that can help us to make the ball a success. You see, I know how terribly clever you are, Mrs. King."

"I am dreadfully stupid."

"Nonsense!"

"I'm sorry to say we're dining out to-morrow night and on Thursday we are having some people here for —"

"Can't you bring them all up to Blitherwood? We'd be delighted to have them, I'm sure."

"I'm afraid I couldn't manage it. They — well, you see, they are in mourning."

"Oh, I see. Well, perhaps Maud and I could run in and see you for a few minutes to-morrow or next day, just to talk things over a little — what's that, Maud? I beg your pardon, Mrs. King. Ahem! Well, I'll call you up to-morrow, if you don't mind being bothered about a silly old ball. Good-bye. Thank you so much."

Mrs. King confronted Robin in the lower hall a few seconds later and roundly berated him for shouting

up the steps that Hobbs ought to be invited to the
ball. Prince Robin rolled on a couch and roared with
delight. Lieutenant Dank, as became an officer of the
Royal Guard, stood at attention — in the bow window
with his back to the room, very red about the ears and
rigid to the bursting point.

"I suppose, however, we'll have to keep on the
good side of the Blithers syndicate," said Robin soberly, after his mirth and subsided before her wrath.
"Good Lord, Aunt Loraine, I simply cannot go up
there and stand in line like a freak in a side show
for all the ladies and girls to gape at. I'll get sick
the day of the party, that's what I'll do, and you can
tell 'em how desolated I am over my misfortune."

"They've got their eyes on you, Bobby," she said
flatly. "You can't escape so easily as all that. If
you're not very, very careful they'll have you married
to the charming Miss Maud before you can say Jack
Rabbit."

"Think that's their idea?"

"Unquestionably."

He stretched himself lazily. "Well, it may be that
she's the very one I'm looking for, Auntie. Who
knows?"

"You silly boy!"

"She may be the Golden Girl in every sense of the
term," said he lightly. "You say she's pretty?"

"My notion of beauty and yours may not agree
at all."

"That's not an answer."

"Well, I consider her to be a very good-looking girl."

"Blonde?"

"Mixed. Light brown hair and very dark eyes and lashes. A little taller than I, more graceful and a splendid horse-woman. I've seen her riding."

"Astride?"

"No. I've seen her in a ball gown, too. Most men think she's stunning."

"Well, let's have a game of billiards," said he, dismissing Maud in a way that would have caused the proud Mr. Blithers to reel with indignation.

A little later on, at the billiard table, Mrs. King remarked, apropos of nothing and quite out of a clear sky, so to speak:

"And she'll do anything her parents command her to do, that's the worst of it."

"What are you talking about? It's your shot."

"If they order her to marry a title, she'll do it. That's the way she's been brought up, I'm afraid."

"Meaning Maud?"

"Certainly. Who else? Poor thing, she hasn't a chance in the world, with that mother of hers."

"Shoot, please. Mark up six for me, Dank."

"Wait till you see her, Bobby."

"All right. I'll wait," said he cheerfully.

The next day Count Quinnox and King returned from the city, coming up in a private car with Mr. Blithers himself.

"I'll have Maud drive me over this afternoon," said Mr. Blithers, as they parted at the station.

But Maud did not drive him over that afternoon. The pride, joy and hope of the Blithers family flatly refused to be a party of any such arrangement, and set out for a horse-back ride in a direction that took her as far away from Red Roof as possible.

"What's come over the girl?" demanded Mr. Blithers, completely non-plused. "She's never acted like this before, Lou."

"Some silly notion about being made a laughing-stock, I gather," said his wife. "Heaven knows I've talked to her till I'm utterly worn out. She says she won't be bullied into even meeting the Prince, much less marrying him. I've never known her to be so pig-beaded. Usually I can make her see things in a sensible way. She would have married the duke, I'm sure, if — if you hadn't put a stop to it on account of his so-called habits. She —"

"Well, it's turned out for the best, hasn't it? Isn't a prince better than a duke?"

"You've said all that before, Will. I wanted her to run down with me this morning to talk the ball over with Mrs. King, and what do you think happened?"

"She wouldn't go?"

"Worse than that. She wouldn't let *me* go. Now, things are coming to a pretty pass when —"

"Never mind. I'll talk to her," said Mr. Blithers,

somewhat bleakly despite his confident front. "She loves her old dad. I can do *anything* with her."

"She's on a frightfully high horse lately," sighed Mrs. Blithers fretfully. "It — it can't be that young Scoville, can it?"

"If I thought it was, I'd — I'd —" There is no telling what Mr. Blithers would have done to young Scoville, at the moment, for he couldn't think of anything dire enough to inflict upon the suspected meddler.

"In any event, it's dreadfully upsetting to me, Will. She — she won't listen to anything. And here's something else: She declares she won't stay here for the ball on Friday night."

Mr. Blithers had her repeat it, and then almost missed the chair in sitting down, he was so precipitous about it.

"Won't stay for her own ball?" he bellowed.

"She says it isn't her ball," lamented his wife.

"If it isn't hers, in the name of God whose is it?"

"Ask her, not me," flared Mrs. Blithers. "And don't glare at me like that. I've had nothing but glares since you went away. I thought I was doing the very nicest thing in the world when I suggested the ball. It would bring them together —"

"The only two it will actually bring together, it seems, are those damned prize-fighters. They'll get together all right, but what good is it going to do us, if Maud's going to act like this? See here, Lou, I've

got things fixed so that the Prince of Groostuck can't
very well do anything but ask Maud to —"

"That's just it!" she exclaimed. "Maud sees
through the whole arrangement, Will. She said last
night that she wouldn't be at all surprised if you offered to assume Graustark's debt to Russia in order
to —"

"That's just what I've done, old girl," said he in
triumph. "I'll have 'em sewed up so tight by next
week that they can't move without asking me to loosen
the strings. And you can tell Maud once more for
me that I'll get this Prince for her if —"

"But she doesn't want him!"

"She doesn't know what she wants!" he roared.
"Where is she going?"

"You saw her start off on Katydid, so why —"

"I mean on the day of the ball."

"To New York."

"By gad, I'll — I'll see about *that*," he grated.
"I'll see that she doesn't leave the grounds if I have
to put guards at every gate. She's got to be reasonable. What does she think I'm putting sixteen millions into the Grasstork treasury for? She's got to
stay here for the ball. Why, it would be a crime for
her to — but what's the use talking about it? She'll
be here and she'll lead the grand march with the
Prince. I've got it all —"

"Well, you'll have to talk to her. I've done all
that I can do. She swears she won't marry a man
she's never seen."

"Ain't we trying to show him to her?" he snorted. "She won't have to marry him till she's seen him, and when she does see him she'll apologise to me for all the nasty things she's been saying about me." For a moment it looked as though Mr. Blithers would dissolve into tears, so suddenly was he afflicted by self-pity. "By the way, didn't she like the necklace I sent up to her from Tiffany's?"

"I suppose so. She said you were a dear old foozler."

"Foozler? What's that mean?" He wasn't quite sure, but somehow it sounded like a term of opprobrium.

"I haven't the faintest idea," she said shortly.

"Well, why didn't you ask her? You've had charge of her bringing up. If she uses a word that you don't know the meaning of, you ought to —"

"Are you actually going to lend all that money to Graustark?" she cut in.

He glared at her uncertainly for a moment and then nodded his head. The words wouldn't come.

"Are you not a trifle premature about it?" she demanded with deep significance in her manner.

This time he did not nod his head, nor did he shake it. He simply got up and walked out of the room. Half way across the terrace he stopped short and said it with a great fervour and instantly felt very much relieved. In fact, the sensation of relief was so pleasant that he repeated it two or three times and then had to explain to a near by gardener that he

didn't mean him at all. Then he went down to the
stables. All the grooms and stableboys came tumbling
into the stable yard in response to his thunderous
shout.

"Saddle Red Rover, and be quick about it," he commanded.

"Going out, sir?" asked the head groom, touching
his fore-lock.

"I am," said Mr. Blithers succinctly and with a
withering glare. Red Rover must have been surprised
by the unusual celerity with which he was saddled and
bridled. If there could be such a thing as a horse looking shocked, that beast certainly betrayed himself as
he was yanked away from his full manger and hustled
out to the mounting block.

"Which way did Miss Blithers go?" demanded
Mr. Blithers, in the saddle. Two grooms were clumsily trying to insert his toes into the stirrups, at the
same time pulling down his trousers legs, which had a
tendency to hitch up in what seemed to them a most
exasperating disregard for form. To their certain
knowledge, Mr. Blithers had never started out before
without boot and spur; therefore, the suddenness of
his present sortie sank into their intellects with overwhelming impressiveness.

"Down the Cutler road, sir, three quarters of an
hour ago. She refused to have a groom go along, sir."

"Get ap!" said Mr. Blithers, and almost ran down
a groom in his rush for the gate. For the information of the curious, it may be added that he did not

overtake his daughter until she had been at home for half an hour, but he was gracious enough to admit to himself that he had been a fool to pursue a stern chase rather than to intercept her on the back road home, which *any* fool might have known she would take.

His wife came upon him a few minutes later while he was feverishly engaged in getting into his white flannels.

"Tell Maud I'm going over to have tea with the Prince," he grunted, without looking up from the shoe lace he was tying in a hard knot. "I want her to go with me in fifteen minutes. Told 'em I would bring her over to play tennis. Tell her to put on tennis clothes. Hurry up, Lou. Where's my watch? What time is it? For God's sake, look at the watch, not at me! I'm not a clock! What?"

"Mrs. King called up half an hour ago to say that they were all motoring over to the Grandby Tavern for tea and wouldn't be back till half-past seven —"

He managed to look up at that. For a moment he was speechless. No one had ever treated him like this before.

"Well, I'll be — hanged! Positive engagement. But's it's all right," he concluded resolutely. "I can motor to Grandby Tavern, too, can't I? Tell Maud not to mind tennis clothes, but to hurry. Want to go along?"

"No, I don't," she said emphatically. "And Maud isn't going, either."

"She isn't, eh?"

"No, she isn't. Can't you leave this affair to me?"

"I'm pretty hot under the collar," he warned her, and it was easy to believe that he was.

"Don't rush in where angels fear to tread, Will dear," she pleaded. It was so unusual for her to adopt a pleading tone that he overlooked the implication. Besides he had just got through calling himself a fool, so perhaps she was more or less justified. Moreover, at that particular moment she undertook to assist him with his necktie. Her soft, cool fingers touched his double chin and seemed to caress it lovingly. He lifted his head very much as a dog does when he is being tickled on that velvety spot under the lower jaw.

"Stuff and nonsense," he murmured throatily.

"I thought you would see it that way," she said so calmly that he blinked a couple of times in sheer perplexity and then diminished his double chin perceptibly by a very helpful screwing up of his lower lip. He said nothing, preferring to let her think that the most important thing in the world just then was the proper adjustment of the wings of his necktie. "There!" she said, and patted him on the cheek, to show that the task had been successfully accomplished.

"Better come along for a little spin," he said, readjusting the tie with man-like ingenuousness. "Do you good, Lou."

"Very well," she said. "Can you wait a few minutes?"

"Long as you like," said he graciously. "Ask Maud if she wants to come, too."

"I am sure she will enjoy it," said his wife, and then Mr. Blithers descended to the verandah to think. Somehow he felt if he did a little more thinking perhaps matters wouldn't be so bad. Among other things, he thought it would be a good idea not to motor in the direction of Grandby Tavern. And he also thought it was not worth while resenting the fact that his wife and daughter took something over an hour to prepare for the little spin.

In the meantime, Prince Robin was racing over the mountain roads in a high-power car, attended by a merry company of conspirators whose sole object was to keep him out of the clutches of that far-reaching octopus, William W. Blithers.

CHAPTER VI

In order to get on with the narrative, I shall be as brief as possible in the matter of the Blitherwood ball. In the first place, mere words would prove to be not only feeble but actually out of place. Any attempt to define the sensation of awe by recourse to a dictionary would put one in the ridiculous position of seeking the unattainable. The word has its meaning, of course, but the sensation itself is quite another thing. As every one who attended the ball was filled with awe, which he tried to put forward as admiration, the attitude of the guest was no more limp than that of the chronicler. In the second place, I am not qualified by experience or imagination to describe a ball that stood its promoter not a penny short of one hundred thousand dollars. I believe I could go as high as a fifteen or even twenty thousand dollar affair with some sort of intelligence, but anything beyond those figures renders me void and useless.

Mr. Blithers not only ran a special train de luxe from New York City, but another from Washington and still another from Newport, for it appears that the Newporters at the last minute couldn't bear the idea of going to the Metropolis out of season. He actually had to take them around the city in such a

MICROCOPY RESOLUTION TEST CHART

(ANSI and ISO TEST CHART No. 2)

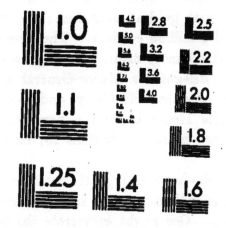

APPLIED IMAGE Inc

1653 East Main Street
Rochester, New York 14609 USA
(716) 482 - 0300 - Phone
(716) 288 - 5989 - Fax

way that they were not even obliged to submit to a glimpse of the remotest outskirts of the Bronx.

From Washington came an amazing company of foreign ladies and gentlemen, ranging from the most exalted Europeans to the lowliest of the yellow races. They came with gold all over them; they tinkled with the clash of a million cymbals. The President of the United States almost came. Having no spangles of his own, he delegated a Major-General and a Rear-Admiral to represent Old Glory, and no doubt sulked in the White House because a parsimonious nation refuses to buy braid and buttons for its chief executive.

Any one who has seen a gentleman in braid, buttons and spangles will understand how impossible it is to describe him. One might enumerate the buttons and the spangles and even locate them precisely upon his person, but no mortal intellect can expand sufficiently, to cope with an undertaking that would try even the powers of Him who created the contents of those well-stuffed uniforms.

A car load of orchids and gardenias came up, fairly depleting the florists' shops on Manhattan Island, and with them came a small army of skilled decorators. In order to deliver his guests at the doors of Blitherwood, so to speak, the incomprehensible Mr. Blithers had a temporary spur of track laid from the station two miles away, employing no fewer than a thousand men to do the work in forty-eight hours. (Work on a terminal extension in New York was delayed for a week or more in order that he might borrow the rails, ties and worktrains!)

Two hundred and fifty precious and skillfully selected guests ate two hundred and fifty gargantuan dinners and twice as many suppers; drank barrels of the rarest of wines; smoked countless two dollar Perfectos and stuffed their pockets with enough to last them for days to come; burnt up five thousand cigarettes and ate at least two dozen eggs for breakfast, and then flitted away with a thousand complaints in two hundred and fifty Pullman drawing-rooms. Nothing could have been more accurately pulled-off than the wonderful Blitherwood ball. (The sparring match on the lawn, under the glare of a stupendous cluster of lights, resulted in favour of Mr. Bullhead Brown, who successfully — if accidentally — landed with considerably energy on the left lower corner of Mr. Sledge-hammer Smith's diaphragm, completely dividing the purse with him in four scientifically satisfactory rounds, although they came to blows over it afterwards when Mr. Smith told Mr. Brown what he thought of him for hitting with such fervour just after they had eaten a hearty meal.)

A great many mothers inspected Prince Robin with interest and confessed to a really genuine enthusiasm: something they had not experienced since one of the German princes got close enough to Newport to see it quite clearly through his marine glasses from the bridge of a battleship. The ruler of Graustark — (four-fifths of the guests asked where in the world it was!)—was the lion of the day. Mr. Blithers was annoyed because he did not wear his crown, but was somewhat mollified by the information that he had neglected to bring it along with him in his travels. He was also considerably put out by the discovery that the Prince had left his white and gold uniform at home and had to appear in an ordinary dress-suit, which, to be sure, fitted him perfectly but did not achieve distinction. He did wear a black and silver ribbon across his shirt front, however, and a tiny gold button in the lapel of his coat; otherwise he might have been mistaken for a "regular guest," to borrow an expression from Mr. Blithers. The Prince's host manœuvred until nearly one o'clock in the morning before he succeeded in getting a close look at the little gold button, and then found that the inscription thereon was in some sort of hieroglyphics that afforded no enlightenment whatsoever.

Exercising a potentate's prerogative, Prince Robin left the scene of festivity somewhat earlier than was expected. As a matter of fact, he departed shortly after one. Moreover, being a prince, it did not occur to him to offer any excuse for leaving so early, but gracefully thanked his host and hostess and took himself off without the customary assertion that he had had a splendid time. Strange to say, he did not offer a single comment on the sumptuousness of the affair that had been given in his honor. Mr. Blithers couldn't get over that. He couldn't help thinking that the fellow had not been properly brought-up, or was it possible that he was not in the habit of going out in good society?

Except for one heart-rending incident, the Blitherwood ball was the most satisfying event in the lives of Mr. and Mrs. William W. Blithers. That incident, however, happened to be the hasty and well-managed flight of Maud Applegate Blithers at an hour indefinitely placed somewhere between four and seven o'clock on the morning of the great day.

Miss Blithers was not at the ball. She was in New York City serenely enjoying one of the big summer shows, accompanied by young Scoville and her one-time governess, a middle-aged gentlewoman who had seen even better days than those spent in the employ of William W. Blithers. The resolute young lady had done precisely what she said she would do, and for the first time in his life Mr. Blithers realised that his daughter was a creation and not a mere condition. He wilted like a famished water-lily and went about the place in a state of bewilderment so bleak that even his wife felt sorry for him and refrained from the " I told you so " that might have been expected under the circumstances.

Maud's telegram, which came at three o'clock in the afternoon, was meant to be reassuring but it failed of its purpose. It said: " Have a good time and don't lose any sleep over me. I shall sleep very soundly myself at the Ritz to-night and hope you will be doing the same when I return home to-morrow afternoon, for I know you will be dreadfully tired after all the excitement. Convey my congratulations to the guest of honor and believe me to be your devoted and obedient daughter."

The co-incidental absence of young Mr. Scoville from the ball was a cause of considerable uneasiness on the part of the agitated Mr. Blithers, who commented upon it quite expansively in the seclusion of his own bed-chamber after the last guest had sought repose. Some of the things that Mr. Blithers said about Mr. Scoville will never be forgotten by the four walls of that room, if, as commonly reported, they possess auricular attachments.

Any one who imagines that Mr. Blithers accepted Maud's defection as a final disposition of the cause he had set his heart upon is very much mistaken in his man. Far from receding so much as an inch from his position, he at once set about to strengthen it in such a way that Maud would have to come to the conclusion that it was useless to combat the inevitable, and ultimately would heap praises upon his devoted head for the great blessing he was determined to bestow upon her in spite of herself.

The last of the special coaches was barely moving on its jiggly way to the main line, carrying the tag end of the revellers, when he set forth in his car for a mid-day visit to Red Roof. Already the huge camp of Slavs and Italians was beginning to jerk up the borrowed rails and ties; the work trains were rumbling and snorting in the meadows above Blitherwood, tottering about on the uncertain road-bed. He gave a

few concise and imperative orders to obsequious super-
intendents and foremen, who subsequently repeated
them with even greater freedom to the perspiring foreigners, and left the scene of confusion without so
much as a glance behind. Wagons, carts, motor-
trucks and all manner of wheeled things were scuttling
about Blitherwood as he shot down the long, winding
avenue toward the lodge gates, but he paid no attention to them. They were removing the remnants of
a glory that had passed at five in the morning. He
was not interested in the well-plucked skeleton. It
was a nuisance getting rid of it, that was all, and he
wanted it to be completely out of sight when he returned from Red Roof. If a vestige of the ruins remained, some one would hear from him! That was
understood. And when Maud came home on the five-
fourteen she would not find him asleep — not by a long
shot!

Half-way to Red Roof, he espied a man walking
briskly along the road ahead of him. To be perfectly
accurate, he was walking in the middle of the road and
his back was toward the swift-moving, almost noiseless
Packard.

" Blow the horn for the dam' fool," said Mr. Blithers to the chauffeur. A moment later the pedestrian
leaped nimbly aside and the car shot past, the dying
wail of the siren dwindling away in the whirr of the
wheels. "Look where you're going!" shouted Mr.
Blithers from the tonneau, as if the walker had come
near to running him down instead of the other way

around. "Whoa! Stop 'er, Jackson!" he called to the driver. He had recognised the pedestrian.

The car came to a stop with grinding brakes, and at the same time the pedestrian halted a hundred yards away.

"Back up," commanded Mr. Blithers in some haste, for the Prince seemed to be on the point of deserting the highway for the wood that lined it. "Morning, Prince!" he shouted, waving his hat vigorously. "Want a lift?"

The car shot backward with almost the same speed that it had gone forward, and the Prince exercised prudence when he stepped quickly up the sloping bank at the roadside.

"Were you addressing me," he demanded curtly, as the car came to a stop.

"Yes, your highness. Get in. I'm going your way," said Mr. Blithers beamingly.

"I mean a moment ago, when you shouted 'Look where you are going,'" said Robin, an angry gleam in his eye.

Mr. Blithers looked positively dumbfounded. "Good Heavens, no!" he cried. "I was speaking to the chauffeur." (Jackson's back seemed to stiffen a little.) "I've told him a thousand times to be careful about running up on people like that. Now this is the last time I'll warn you, Jackson. The next time you go. Understand? Just because you happen to be driving for me doesn't signify that you can run over people who —"

"It's all right, Mr. Blithers," interrupted Robin, with his fine smile. "No harm done. I'll walk if you don't mind. Out for a bit of exercise, you know. Thank you just the same."

"Where are you bound for?" asked Mr. Blithers.

"I don't know. I ramble where my fancy leads me."

"I guess I'll get out and stroll along with you. God knows I need more exercise than I get. Is it agreeable?" He was on the ground by this time. Without waiting for an answer, he directed Jackson to run on to Red Roof and wait for him.

"I shall be charmed," said Robin, a twinkle in the tail of his eye. "An eight or ten mile jaunt will do you a world of good, I'm sure. Shall we explore this little road up the mountain and then drop down to Red Roof? I don't believe it can be more than five or six miles."

"Capital," said Mr. Blithers with enthusiasm. He happened to know that it was a "short cut" to Red Roof and less than a mile as the crow flies. True, there was something of an ascent ahead of them, but there was also a corresponding descent at the other end. Besides, he was confident he could keep up with the long-legged youngster by the paradoxical process of holding back. The Prince, having suggested the route, couldn't very well be arbitrary in traversing it. Mr. Blithers regarded the suggestion as an invitation.

They struck off into the narrow woodland road, not precisely side by side, but somewhat after the fashion

of a horseback rider and his groom, or, more strictly
speaking, as a Knight and his vassal. Robin started
off so briskly that Mr. Blithers fell behind a few paces
and had to exert himself considerably to keep from
losing more ground as they took the first steep rise.
The road was full of ruts and cross ruts and littered
with boulders that had ambled down the mountain-side
in the spring moving. To save his life, Mr. Blithers
couldn't keep to a straight course. He went from
rut to rut and from rock to rock with the fidelity of a
magnetised atom, seldom putting his foot where he
meant to put it, and never by any chance achieving a
steady stride. He would take one long, purposeful
step and then a couple of short "feelers," progressing
very much as a man tramps over a newly ploughed
field.

At the top of the rise, Robin considerately slack-
ened his pace and the chubby gentleman drew alongside, somewhat out of breath but as cheerful as a
cricket.

"Going too fast for you, Mr. Blithers?" inquired
Robin.

"Not at all," said Mr. Blithers. "By the way,
Prince," he went on, cunningly seizing the young
man's arm and thereby putting a check on his speed
for the time being at least, "I want to explain my
daughter's unfortunate absence last night. You must
have thought it very strange. Naturally it was una-
voidable. The poor girl is really quite heart-broken.
I beg pardon!" He stepped into a rut and came

perilously near to going over on his nose. "Beastly
road! Thanks. Good thing I took hold of you. Yes,
as I was saying, it was really a most unfortunate
thing; missed the train, don't you see. Went down
for the day — just like a girl, you know — and missed
the train."

"Ah, I see. She missed it twice."

"Eh? Oh! Ha ha! Very good! She might
just as well have missed it a dozen times as once, eh?
Well, she could have arranged for a special to bring
her up, but she's got a confounded streak of thriftiness in her. Couldn't think of spending the money.
Silly idea of — I beg your pardon, did I hurt you?
I'm pretty heavy, you know, no light weight when I
come down on a fellow's toe like that. What say to
sitting down on this log for a while? Give your foot
a chance to rest a bit. Deucedly awkward of me.
Ought to look out where I'm stepping, eh?"

"It really doesn't matter, Mr. Blithers," said
Robin hastily. "We'll keep right on if it's all the
same to you. I'm due at home in — in half an hour.
We lunch very punctually."

"I was particularly anxious for you and Maud to
meet under the conditions that obtained last night,"
went on Mr. Blithers, with a regretful look at the log
they were passing. "Nothing could have been more
— er — ripping."

"I hear from every one that your daughter is most
attractive," said Robin. "Sorry not to have met
her, Mr. Blithers."

"Oh, you'll meet her all right, Prince. She's coming home to-day. I believe Mrs. Blithers is expecting you to dinner to-night. She —"

"I'm sure there must be some mistake," began Robin, but was cut short.

"I was on my way to Red Roof to ask you and Count Quiddux to give us this evening in connection with that little affair we are arranging. It is most imperative that it should be to-night, as my attorney is coming up for the conference."

"I fear that Mrs. King has planned something —"

Mr. Blithers waved his hand deprecatingly. "I am sure Mrs. King will let you off when she knows how important it is. As a matter of fact, it has to be to-night or not at all."

There was a note in his voice that Robin did not like. It savoured of arrogance.

"I daresay Count Quinnox can attend to all the details, Mr. Blithers. I have the power of veto, of course, but I shall be guided by the counsel of my ministers. You need have no hesitancy in dealing with —"

"That's not the point, Prince. I am a business man,— as perhaps you know. I make it a point never to deal with any one except the head of a concern, if you'll pardon my way of putting it. It isn't right to speak of Growstock as a concern, but you'll understand, of course. Figure of speech."

"I can only assure you, sir, that Graustark is in a position to indemnify you against any possible chance of loss. You will be amply secured. I take it that you are not coming to our assistance through any desire to be philanthropic, but as a business proposition, pure and simple. At least, that is how we regard the matter. Am I not right?"

"Perfectly," said Mr. Blithers. "I haven't got sixteen millions to throw away. Still I don't see that that has anything to do with my request that you be present at the conference to-night. To be perfectly frank with you, I don't like working in the dark. You have the power of veto, as you say. Well, if I am to lend Groostork a good many millions of hard-earned dollars, I certainly don't relish the idea that you may take it into your head to upset the whole transaction merely because you have not had the matter presented to you by me instead of by your cabinet, competent as its members may be. First hand information on ar subject is my notion of simplicity."

"The integrity of the cabinet is not to be questioned, Mr. Blithers. Its members have never failed Graustark in any —"

"I beg your pardon, Prince," said Mr. Blithers firmly, "but I certainly suspect that they failed her when they contracted this debt to Russia. You will forgive me for saying it, but it was the most asinine bit of short-sightedness I've ever heard of. My office boys could have seen farther than your honourable ministers."

To his utter amazement, Robin turned a pair of beaming, excited eyes upon him.

"Do you really mean that, Mr. Blithers?" he cried eagerly.

"I certainly do!"

"By jove, I — I can't tell you how happy I am to hear you say it. You see it is exactly what John Tullis said from the first. He was bitterly opposed to the loan. He tried his best to convince the prime minister that it was inadvisable. I granted him the special privilege of addressing the full House of Nobles on the question, an honour that no alien had known up to that time. Of course I was a boy when all this happened, Mr. Blithers, or I might have put a stop to the — but I'll not go into that. The House of Nobles went against his judgment and voted in favour of accepting Russia's loan. Now they realise that dear old John Tullis was right. Somehow it gratifies me to hear you say that they were — ahem! — short-sighted."

"What you need in Groostock is a little more good American blood," announced Mr. Blithers, pointedly. "If you are going to cope with the world, you've got to tackle the job with brains and not with that idiotic thing called faith. There's no such thing in these days as charity among men, good will, and all that nonsense. Now, you've got a splendid start in the right direction, Prince. You've got American blood in your veins and that means a good deal. Take my advice and increase the proportion. In a couple of generations you'll have something to brag about. Take Tullis as your example. Beget sons that will think and act as he is capable of doing. Weed out the thin blood and give the crown of Grasstick something that is thick and red. It will be the making of your—"

"I suppose you are advising me to marry an American woman, Mr. Blithers," said Robin drily.

Mr. Blithers directed a calculating squint into the tree-tops. "I am simply looking ahead for my own protection, Prince," said he.

"In what respect?"

"Well I am putting a lot of money into the hands of your people. Isn't it natural that I should look ahead to some extent?"

"But my people are honest. They will pay."

"I understand all that, but at the same time I do not relish the idea of some day being obliged to squeeze blood from a turnip. Now is the time for you to think for the future. Your people are honest, I'll grant. But they also are poor. And why? Because no one has been able to act for them as your friend Tullis is capable of acting. The day will come when they will have to settle with me, and will it be any easier to pay William W. Blithers than it is to pay Russia? Not a bit of it. As you have said, I am not a philanthropist. I shall exact full and prompt payment. I prefer to collect from the prosperous, however, and not from the poor. It goes against the grain. That's why I want to see you rich and powerful — as well as honest."

"I grant you it is splendid philosophy," said Robin.

"But are you not forgetting that even the best of Americans are sometimes failures when it comes to laying up treasure?"

"As individuals, yes; but not as a class. You will not deny that we are the richest people in the world. On the other hand I do not pretend to say that we are a people of one strain of blood. We represent a mixture of many strains, but underneath them all runs the full stream that makes us what we are: Americans. You can't get away from that. Yes, I *do* advise you to marry an American girl."

"In other words, I am to make a business of it," said Robin, tolerantly.

"It isn't beyond the range of possibility that you should fall in love with an American girl, is it? You wouldn't call that making a business of it, would you?"

"You may rest assured, Mr. Blithers, that I shall marry to please myself and no one else," said Robin, regarding him with a coldness that for an instant affected the millionaire uncomfortably.

"Well," said Mr. Blithers, after a moment of hard thinking, "it may interest you to know that I married for love."

"It *does* interest me," said Robin. "I am glad that you did."

"I was a comparatively poor man when I married. The girl I married was well-off in her own right. She had brains as well. We worked together to lay the foundation for a — well, for the fortune we now pos-

sess.   A fortune, I may add, that is to go, every dollar of it, to my daughter.   It represents nearly five
hundred million dollars.   The greatest king in the
world to-day is poor in comparison to that vast estate.   My daughter will one day be the richest woman
in the world."

"Why are you taking the pains to enlighten me as
to your daughter's future, Mr. Blithers?"

"Because I regard you as a sensible young man,
Prince."

"Thank you.   And I suppose you regard your
daughter as a sensible young woman?"

"Certainly!" exploded Mr. Blithers.

"Well, it seems to me, she will be capable of taking
care of her fortune a great deal more successfully than
you imagine, Mr. Blithers.   She will doubtless marry
an excellent chap who has the capacity to increase
her fortune, rather than to let it stand at a figure
that some day may be surpassed by the possessions of
an ambitious king."

There was fine irony in the Prince's tone but no
trace of offensiveness.   Nevertheless, Mr. Blithers
turned a shade more purple than before, and not from
the violence of exercise.   He was having some difficulty in controlling his temper.   What manner of fool
was this fellow who could sneer at five hundred million
dollars?   He managed to choke back something that
rose to his lips and very politely remarked:

"I am sure you will like her, Prince.   If I do say it
myself, she is as handsome as they grow."

"So I have been told."

"You will see her to-night."

"Really, Mr. Blithers, I cannot —"

"I'll fix it with Mrs. King.   Don't you worry."

"May I be pardoned for observing that Mrs. King, greatly as I love her, is not invested with the power to govern my actions?" said Robin haughtily.

"And may I be pardoned for suggesting that it is your duty to your people to completely understand this loan of mine before you agree to accept it?" said Mr. Blithers, compressing his lips.

"Forgive me, Mr. Blithers, but it is not altogether improbable that Graustark may secure the money elsewhere."

"It is not only improbable but impossible," said Mr. Blithers flatly.

"Impossible?"

"Absolutely," said the millionaire so significantly that Robin would have been a dolt not to grasp the situation.   Nothing could have been clearer than the fact that Mr. Blithers believed it to be in his power to block any effort Graustark might make in other directions to secure the much-needed money.

"Will you come to the point, Mr. Blithers?" said the young Prince, stopping abruptly in the middle of the road and facing his companion.   "What are you trying to get at?"

Mr. Blithers was not long in getting to the point. In the first place, he was hot and tired and his shoes were hurting; in the second place, he felt that he knew precisely how to handle these money-seeking scions of nobility. He planted himself squarely in front of the Prince and jammed his hands deep into his coat pockets.

"The day my daughter is married to the man of my choice, I will hand over to that man exactly twenty million dollars," he said slowly, impressively.

"Yes, go on."

"The sole object I have in life is to see my girl happy and at the same time at the top of the heap. She is worthy of any man's love. She is as good as gold. She—"

"The point is this, then: You would like to have me for a son-in-law."

"Yes," said Mr. Blithers.

Robin grinned. He was amused in spite of himself. "You take it for granted that I can be bought?"

"I have not made any such statement."

"And how much will you hand over to the man of *her* choice when she marries him?" enquired the young man.

"You will be her choice," said the other, without the quiver of an eye-lash.

"How can you be sure of that? Has she no mind of her own?"

"It isn't incomprehensible that she should fall in love with you, is it?"

"It might be possible, of course, provided she is not already in love with some one else."

Mr. Blithers started. "Have you heard any one

say that — but, that's nonsense! She's not in love with any one, take it from me. And just to show you how fair I am to her — and to you — I'll stake my head you fall in love with each other before you've been together a week."

"But we're not going to be together for a week."

"I should have said before you've known each other a week. You will find —"

". Just a moment, please. We can cut all this very short, and go about our business. I've never seen your daughter, nor, to my knowledge, has she ever laid eyes on me. From what I've heard of her, she *has* a mind of her own. You will not be able to force her into a marriage that doesn't appeal to her, and you may be quite sure, Mr. Blithers, that you can't force me into one. I do not want you to feel that I have a single disparaging thought concerning Miss Blithers. It is possible that I could fall in love with her inside of a week, or even sooner. But I don't intend to, Mr. Blithers, any more than she intends to fall in love with me. You say that twenty millions will go to the man she marries, if he is your choice. Well, I don't give a hang, sir, if you make it fifty millions. The chap who gets it will not be me, so what's the odds? You —"

"Wait a minute, young man," said Mr. Blithers coolly. (He was never anything but cool when under fire.) "Why not wait until you have met my daughter before making a statement like that? After all, am I not the one who is taking chances? Well, I'm

"You will be her choice," said the other, without the quiver of an eye-lash

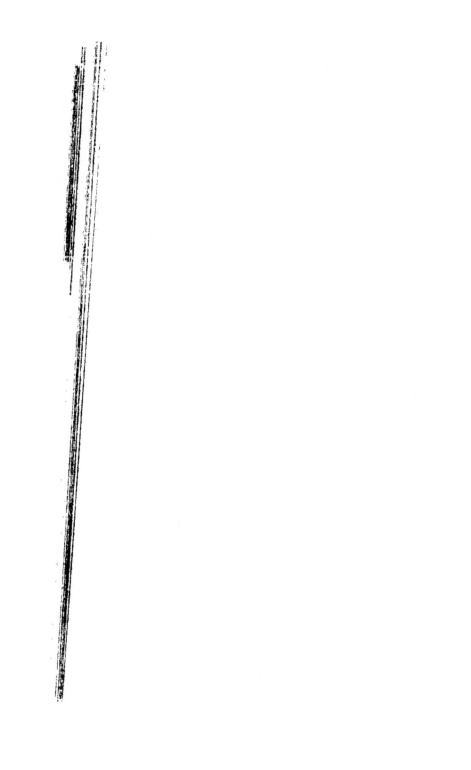

willing to risk my girl's happiness with you and that's
saying everything when you come right down to it.
She will make you happy in —"

"I am not for sale, Mr. Blithers," said Robin abruptly. "Good morning." He turned into the wood
and was sauntering away with his chin high in the air
when Mr. Blithers called out to him from behind.

"I shall expect you to-night, just the same."

Robin halted, amazed by the man's assurance. He
retraced his steps to the roadside.

"Will you pardon a slight feeling of curiosity on
my part, Mr. Blithers, if I ask whether your daughter
consents to the arrangement you propose. Does she
approve of the scheme?"

Mr. Blithers was honest. "No, she doesn't," he
said succinctly. "At least, not at present. I'll be
honest with you. She stayed away from the ball last
night simply because she did not want to meet you.
That's the kind of a girl *she* is."

"By jove, I take off my hat to her," cried Robin.
"She is a brick, after all. Take it from me, Mr.
Blithers, you - will not be able to hand over twenty
millions without her consent. I believe that I should
enjoy meeting her, now that I come to think of it. It
would be a pleasure to exchange confidences with a girl
of that sort."

Mr. Blithers betrayed agitation. "See here,
Prince, I don't want her to know that I've said anything to you about this matter," he said, unconsciously
lowering his voice as if fearing that Maud might be

somewhere within hearing distance. "This is between you and me. Don't breathe a word of it to her. 'Gad, she'd — she'd skin me alive!" At the very thought of it, he wiped his forehead with unusual vigour.

Robin laughed heartily. "Rest easy, Mr. Blithers. I shall not even think of your proposition again, much less speak of it."

"Come now, Prince; wait until you've seen her. I know you'll get on famously —"

"I should like her to know that I consider her a brick, Mr. Blithers. Is it too much to ask of you? Just tell her that I think she's a brick."

"Tell her yourself," growled Mr. Blithers, looking very black. "You will see her this evening," he added levelly.

"Shall I instruct your chauffeur to come for you up here or will you walk back to —"

"I'll walk to Red Roof," said Mr. Blithers doggedly. "I'm going to ask Mrs. King to let you off for to-night."

CHAPTER VII

MR. BLITHERS, triumphant, left Red Roof shortly
after luncheon; Mr. Blithers, dismayed, arrived at
Blitherwood a quarter of an hour later. He had had
his way with Robin, who, after all, was coming to
dinner that evening with Count Quinnox. The
Prince, after a few words in private with the Count,
changed his mind and accepted Mr. Blithers' invitation with a liveliness that was mistaken for eagerness
by that gentleman, who had made very short work of
subduing Mrs. King when she tried to tell him that
her own dinner-party would be ruined if the principal
guest defaulted. He was gloating over his victory
up to the instant he reached his own lodge gates.
There dismay sat patiently waiting for him in the
shape of a messenger from the local telegraph office
in the village below. He had seen Mr. Blithers approaching in the distance, and, with an astuteness
that argued well for his future success in life, calmly
sat down to wait instead of pedaling his decrepit bi-
cycle up the long slope to the villa.

He delivered a telegram and kindly vouchsafed the
information that it was from New York.

Mr. Blithers experienced a queer sinking of the
heart as he gazed at the envelope. Something warned

him that if he opened it in the presence of the messenger he would say something that a young boy ought
not to hear.

" It's from Maud," said the obliging boy, beaming
good-nature. It cost him a quarter, that bit of gentility, for Mr. Blithers at once said something that a
messenger boy ought to hear, and ordered Jackson to
go ahead.

It was from Maud and it said: " I shall stay in
town a few days longer. It is delightfully cool here.
Dear old Miranda is at the Ritz with me and we are
having a fine spree. Don't worry about money. I
find I have a staggering balance in the bank. The
cashier showed me where I had made a mistake in sub-
traction of an even ten thousand. I was amazed to
find what a big difference a little figure makes. Have
made no definite plans but will write Mother to-night.
Please give my love to the Prince. Have you seen
to-day's *Town Truth!* Or worse, has be seen it?
Your loving daughter, Maud."

The butler was sure it was apoplexy, but the chauffeur, out of a wide experience, announced, behind his
hand, that he would be all right the instant the words
ceased to stick in his throat. And he was right. Mr.
Blithers was all right. Not even the chauffeur had
seen him when he was more so.

A little later on, after he had cooled off to a quite
considerable extent, Mr. Blithers lighted a cigar and
sat down in the hall outside his wife's bed-chamber
door. She was having her beauty nap. Not even he

possessed the temerity to break in upon that. He sat
and listened for the first sound that would indicate the
appeasement of beauty, occasionally hitching his chair
a trifle nearer to the door in the agony of impatience.
By the time Jackson returned from the village with
word that a copy of *Town Truth* was not to be had
until the next day, he was so close to the door that
if any one had happened to stick a hat pin through
the keyhole at precisely the right instant it would have
punctured his left ear with appalling results.

"What are we going to do about it?" he demanded
three minutes after entering the chamber. His wife
was prostrate on the luxurious couch from which she
had failed to arise when he burst in upon her with the
telegram in his hand.

"Oh, the foolish child," she moaned. "If she only
knew how adorable he is she wouldn't be acting in this
perfectly absurd manner. Every girl who was here
last night is madly in love with him. Why must Maud
be so obstinate?"

Mr. Blithers was very careful not to mention his
roadside experience with the Prince, and you may be
sure that he said nothing about his proposition to the
young man. He merely declared, with a vast bitterness in his soul, that the Prince was coming to dinner,
but what the deuce was the use?

"She ought to be soundly — spoken to," said he,
breaking the sentence with a hasty gulp. "Now, Lou,
there's just one thing to do. I must go to New York
on the midnight train and get her. That woman was

all right as a tutor, but hanged if I like to see a daughter of mine traipsing around New York with a school teacher. She —"

"You forget that she has retired on a competence. She is not in active employment, Will. You forget that she is one of the Van Valkens."

"There you go, talking about good old families again. Why is it that so blamed many of your fine old blue stockings are hunting jobs —"

"Now don't be vulgar, Will," she cut in. "Maud is quite safe with Miranda, and you know it perfectly well, so don't talk like that. I think it would be a fearful mistake for you to go to New York. She would never forgive you and, what is more to the point, she wouldn't budge a step if you tried to bully her into coming home with you. You know it quite as well as I do."

He groaned. "Give me a chance to think, Lou. Just half a chance, that's all I ask. I'll work out some —"

"Wait until her letter comes. We'll see what she has to say. Perhaps she intends coming home to-morrow, who can tell? This may be a pose on her part. Give her free rein and she will not pull against the bit. It may surprise her into doing the sensible thing if we calmly ignore her altogether. I've been thinking it over, and I've come to the conclusion that we'll be doing the wisest thing in the world if we pay absolutely no attention to her."

"By George, I believe you've hit it, Lou! She'll

be looking for a letter or telegram from me and she'll not receive a word, eh? She'll be expecting us to beg her to come back and all the while we just sit tight and say not a word. We'll fool her, by thunder. By to-morrow afternoon she'll be so curious to know what's got into us that she'll come home on a run. You're right. It takes a thief to catch a thief,— which is another way of saying that it takes a woman to understand a woman. We'll sit tight and let Maud worry for a day or two. It will do her good."

Maud's continued absence was explained to Prince Robin that evening, not by the volcanic Mr. Blithers but by his practised and adroit better-half who had no compunction in ascribing it to the alarming condition of a very dear friend in New York,— one of the Van Valkens, you know.

"Maud is so tender-hearted, so loyal, so really sweet about her friends, that nothing in the world could have induced her to leave this dear friend, don't you know."

"I am extremely sorry not to have met your daughter," said Robin very politely.

"Oh, but she will be here in a day or two, Prince."

"Unfortunately, we are leaving to-morrow, Mrs. Blithers."

"To-morrow?" murmured Mrs. Blithers, aghast.

"I received a cablegram to-day advising me to return to Edelweiss at once. We are obliged to cut short a very charming visit with Mr. and Mrs. King and to give up the trip to Washington. Lieutenant

Dank left for New York this afternoon to exchange
our reservations for the first ship that we can —"

"What's this?" demanded Mr. Blithers, abruptly
withdrawing his attention from Count Quinnox who
was in the middle of a sentence when the interruption.
came.   They were on the point of going out to dinner.
"What's this?"

"The Prince says that he is leaving to-morrow —"

"Nonsense!" exploded Mr. Blithers, with no effort
toward geniality. "He doesn't mean it. Why,—
why, we haven't signed a single agreement —"

"Fortunately it isn't necessary for me to sign anything, Mr. Blithers," broke in Robin hastily. "The
papers are to be signed by the Minister of Finance,
and afterwards my signature is attached in approval.
Isn't that true, Count Quinnox?"

"I daresay Mr. Blithers understands the situation
perfectly," said the Count.

Mr. Blithers looked blank. He *did* understand the
situation, that was the worst of it. He knew that
although the cabinet had sanctioned the loan by cable,
completing the transaction so far as it could be completed at this time, it was still necessary for the Minister of Finance to sign the agreement under the royal
seal of Graustark.

"Of course I understand it," he said bluntly.
"Still I had it in mind to ask the Prince to put his
signature to a sort of preliminary document which
would at least assure me that he would sign the final

agreement when the time comes. That's only fair, isn't it?"

"Quite fair, Mr. Blithers. The Prince will sign such an article to-morrow or the next day at your office in the city. Pray have no uneasiness, sir. It shall be as you wish. By the way, I understood that your solicitor — your lawyer, I should say,— was to be here this evening. It had occurred to me that he might draw up the statement,— if Mrs. Blithers will forgive us in our haste —"

"He couldn't get here," said Mr. Blithers, and no more. He was thinking too intently of something more important. "What's turned up?"

"Turned up, Mr. Blithers?"

"Yes — in Groostock. What's taking you off in such a hurry?"

"The Prince has been away for nearly six months," said the Count, as if that explained everything.

"Was it necessary to cable for him to come home?" persisted the financier.

"Graustark and Dawsbergen are endeavouring to form an alliance, Mr. Blithers, and Prince Robin's presence at the capitol is very much to be desired in connection with the project."

"What kind of an alliance?"

The Count looked bored. "An alliance prescribed for the general improvement of the two races, I should say, Mr. Blithers." He smiled. "It would in no way impair the credit of Graustark, however. It is what you might really describe as a family secret, if you will pardon my flippancy."

The butler announced dinner.

"Wait for a couple of days, Prince, and I'll send you down to New York by special train," said Mr. Blithers.

"Thank you. It is splendid of you. I daresay everything will depend on Dank's success in —"

"Crawford," said Mr. Blithers to the butler, "ask Mr. Davis to look up the sailings for next week and let me know at once, will you?" Turning to the Prince, he went on: "We can wire down to-night and engage passage for next week. Davis is my secretary. I'll have him attend to everything. And now let's forget our troubles."

A great deal was said by her parents about Maud's unfortunate detention in the city. Both of them were decidedly upset by the sudden change in the Prince's plans. Once under pretext of whispering to Crawford about the wine, Mr. Blithers succeeded in transmitting a question to his wife. She shook her head in reply, and he sighed audibly. He had asked if she thought he'd better take the midnight train.

Mr. Davis found that there were a dozen ships sailing the next week, but nothing came of it, for the Prince resolutely declared he would be obliged to take the first available steamer.

"We shall go down to-morrow," he said, and even Mr. Blithers subsided. He looked to his wife in des-

peration.   She failed him for the first time in her life.
Her eyes were absolutely messageless.

"I'll go down with you," he said, and then gave his
wife a look of defiance.

The next morning brought Maud's letter to her
mother.   It said: "Dearest Mother: I enclose the
cutting from *Town Truth*.   You may see for yourself
what a sickening thing it is.   The whole world knows
by this time that the ball was a joke — a horrible joke.
Everybody knows that you are trying to hand me over
to Prince Robin neatly wrapped up in bank notes.
And everybody knows that he is laughing at us, and he
isn't alone in his mirth either.   What must the Truz-
ton Kings think of us?   I can't bear the thought of
meeting that pretty, clever woman face to face.   I
know I should die of mortification, for, of course, she
must believe that I am dying to marry anything on
earth that has a title and a pair of legs.   Somehow
I don't blame you and dad.   You really love me, I
know, and you want to give me the best that the world
affords.   But why, oh why, can't you let me choose
for myself?   I don't object to having a title, but I do
object to having a husband that I don't want and who
certainly could not, by any chance, want me.   You
think that I am in love with Channie Scoville.   Well,
I'm not.   I am very fond of him, that's all, and if it
came to a pinch I would marry him in preference to any
prince on the globe.   To-day I met a couple of girls
who were at the ball.   They told me that the Prince is

adorable. They are really quite mad about him, and one of them had the nerve to ask what it was going to cost dad to land him. *Town Truth* says he is to cost ten millions! Well, you may just tell dad that I'll help him to practice economy. He needn't pay a nickle for my husband — when I get him. The world is small. It may be that I shall come upon this same Prince Charming some place before it is too late, and fall in love with him all of a heap. Loads of silly girls do fall in love with fairy princes, and I'm just as silly as the rest of them. Ever since I was a little kiddie I've dreamed of marrying a real, lace-and-gold Prince, the kind Miranda used to read about in the story books. But I also dreamed that he loved me. There's the rub, you see. How could any prince love a girl who set out to buy him with a lot of silly millions? It's not to be expected. I know it is done in the best society, but I should want my prince to be happy instead of merely comfortable. I should want both of us to live happy ever afterwards.

"So, dearest mother, I am going abroad to forget. Miranda is going with me and we sail next Saturday on the *Jupiter* I think. We haven't got our suite, but Mr. Bliss says he is sure he can arrange it for me. If we can't get one on the *Jupiter*, we'll take some other boat that is just as inconspicuous. You see, I want to go on a ship that isn't likely to be packed with people I know, for it is my intention to travel incog, as they say in the books. No one shall stare at me and say: 'There is that Maud Blithers we were

reading about in *Town Truth* — and all the other
papers this week. Her father is going to buy a prince
for her.'

" I know dad will be perfectly furious, but I'm going
or die, one or the other. Now it won't do a bit of good
to try to stop me, dearest. The best thing for you
and dad to do is to come down at once and say good-
bye to me — but you are not to go to the steamer!
Never! Please, please come, for I love you both and
I do so want you to love me. Come to-morrow and
kiss your horrid, horrid, disappointing, loathsome
daughter — and forgive her, too."

Mr. Blithers was equal to the occasion. His vary-
ing emotions manifested themselves with peculiar vivid-
ness during the reading of the letter by his tearful
wife. At the outset he was frankly humble and contrite; he felt bitterly aggrieved over the unhappy
position in which they innocently had placed their
cherished idol. Then came the deep breath of relief
over the apparent casting away of young Scoville, followed by an angry snort when Maud repeated the remark of her girl friend. His dismay was pathetic
while Mrs. Blithers was fairly gasping out Maud's determination to go abroad, but before she reached the
concluding sentences of the extraordinary missive, he
was himself again. As a matter of fact, he was almost jubilant. He slapped his knee with resounding
force and uttered an ejaculation that caused his wife
to stare at him as if the very worst had happened: he
was a chuckling lunatic!

"Immense!" he exclaimed.   "Immense!"

"Oh, Will!" she sobbed.

"Nothing could be better!   Luck is with me, Lou.
It always is."

"In heaven's name, what are you saying, Will?"

"Great Scott, can't you see?   He goes abroad, she
goes abroad.   See?   Same ship.   See what I mean?
Nothing could be finer.   They —"

"But I do not want my child to go abroad," wailed
the unhappy mother.   "I cannot bear —"

"Stuff and nonsense!   Brace up!   Grasp the ro-
mance.   Both of 'em sailing under assumed names.
They see each other on deck.   Mutual attraction.
Love at first sight.   Both of 'em.   Money no object.
There you are.   Leave it to me."

"Maud is not the kind of girl to take up with a
stranger on board —"

"Don't glare at me like that!   Love finds the way,
it doesn't matter what kind of a girl she is.   But listen to me, Lou; we've got to be mighty careful that
Maud doesn't suspect that we're putting up a job on
her.   She'd balk at the gang-plank and that would
be the end of it.   She must not know that he is on
board.   Now, here's the idea," and he talked on in a
strangely subdued voice for fifteen minutes, his enthusiasm mounting to such heights that she was fairly
lifted to the seventh heaven he produced, and, for once
in her life, she actually submitted to his bumptious
argument without so much as a single protesting word.

The down train at two-seventeen had on board a

most distinguished group of passengers, according to
the Pullman conductor whose skilful conniving resulted
in the banishment of a few unimportant creatures who
had paid for chairs in the observation coach but who
had to get out, whether or no, when Mr. Blithers
loudly said it was a nuisance having everything on
the shady side of the car taken "on a hot day like
this." He surreptitiously informed the conductor
that there was a prince in his party, and that highly
impressed official at once informed ten other passengers
that they had no business in a private car and would
have to move up to the car ahead — and rather quickly
at that.

The Prince announced that Lieutenant Dank'had
secured comfortable cabins on a steamer sailing Saturday, but he did not feel at liberty to mention the name
of the boat owing to his determination to avoid newspaper men, who no doubt would move heaven and earth
for an interview, now that he had become a person of
so much importance in the social world. Indeed, his
indentity was to be more completely obscured than at
any time since he landed on American soil. He
thanked Mr. Blithers for his offer to command the
"royal suite" on the *Jupiter*, but declined, volunteering the somewhat curt remark that it was his earnest
desire to keep as far away from royalty as possible on
the voyage over. (A remark that Mr. Blithers
couldn't quite fathom, then or afterward.)

Mrs. Blithers' retort to her husband's shocked comment on the un-princely appearance of the young man

and the wofully ordinary suit of clothes worn by the
Count, was sufficiently caustic, and he was silenced —
and convinced. Neither of the distinguished foreigners looked the part of a nobleman.

"I wouldn't talk about clothes if I were you," Mrs.
Blithers had said on the station platform. "Who
would suspect you of being one of the richest men in
America?" She sent a disdainful glance at his baggy
knees and bulging coat pockets, and for the moment
he shrank into the state of being one of the poorest
men in America.

They were surprised and not a little perplexed by
the fact that the Prince and his companion arrived at
the station quite alone. Neither of the Kings accompanied them. There was, Mrs. Blithers admitted, food
for thought in this peculiar omission on the part of
the Prince's late host and hostess, and she would have
given a great deal to know what was back of it. The
"luggage" was attended to by the admirable Hobbs,
there being no sign of a Red Roof servant about the
place. Moreover, there seemed to be considerable uneasiness noticeable in the manner of the two foreigners.
They appeared to be unnecessarily impatient for the
train to arrive, looking at their watches now and again,
and frequently sending sharp glances down the village
street in the direction of Red Roof. Blithers afterwards remarked that they made him think of a couple
of absconding cashiers. The mystery, however, was
never explained.

Arriving at the Grand Central Terminal, Prince

Robin and the Count made off in a taxi-cab, smilingly declining to reveal their hotel destination.

"But where am I to send my attorney with the agreement you are to sign, Prince?" asked Mr. Blithers, plainly irritated by the young man's obstinacy in declining to be "dropped" at his hotel by the Blithers motor.

"I shall come to your office at eleven to-morrow morning, Mr. Blithers," said Robin, his hat in his hand. He had bowed very deeply to Mrs. Blithers.

"But that's not right," blustered the financier. "A prince of royal blood hadn't ought to visit a money-grubber's office. It's not —"

"*Noblesse oblige,*" said Robin, with his hand on his heart. "It has been a pleasure to know you, Mrs. Blithers. I trust we may meet again. If you should ever come to Graustark, please consider that the castle is yours — as you hospitable Americans would say."

"We surely will," said Mrs. Blithers. Both the Prince and Count Quinnox bowed very profoundly, and did not smile.

"And it will be ours," added Mr. Blithers, more to himself than to his wife as the two tall figures moved off with the throng. Then to his wife: "Now to find out what ship they're sailing on. I'll fix it so they'll *have* to take the *Jupiter,* whether they want to or not."

"Wouldn't it be wisdom to find out what ship Maud is sailing on, Will? It seems to me that she is the real problem."

"Right you are!" said he instantly. "I must be getting dotty in my old age, Lou."

They were nearing the Ritz when she broke a prolonged period of abstraction by suddenly inquiring: "What did you mean when you said to him on the train: 'Better think it over, Prince,' and what did he mean by the insolent grin he gave you in reply?"

Mr. Blithers looked straight ahead.

"Business," said he, answering the first question but not the last.

CHAPTER VIII

ON BOARD THE " JUPITER "

A easy day at sea. The *Jupiter* seemed to be slinking through the mist and drizzle, so still was the world of waters. The ocean was as smooth as a mill pond; the reflected sky came down bleak and drab and no wind was stirring. The rush of the ship through the glassy, sullen sea produced a fictitious gale across the decks; aside from that there was dead calm ahead and behind.

A threat seemed to lurk in the smooth, oily face of the Atlantic. Far ahead stretched the grey barricade that seemed to mark the spot where the voyage was to end. There was no going beyond that clear-cut line. When the ship came up to it, there would be no more water beyond; naught but a vast space into which the vessel must topple and go on falling to the end of time. The great sirens were silent, for the fog of the night before had lifted, laying bare a desolate plain. The ship was sliding into oblivion, magnificently indifferent to the catastrophe that awaited its arrival at the edge of the universe. And she was sailing the sea alone. All other ships had passed over that sinister line and were plunging toward a bottom that would never be reached, so long is eternity.

The decks of the *Jupiter* were wet with the almost invisible drizzle that filled the air, yet they were

111

swarming with the busy pedestrians who never lose
an opportunity to let every one know that they are on
board.   No ship's company is complete without its leg-
stretchers.   They who never walk a block on dry land
without complaining, right manfully lop off miles when
walking on the water, and get to be known — at least
visually — to the entire first cabin before they have
paraded half way across the Atlantic.   (There was
once a man who had the strutting disease so badly
that he literally walked from Sandy Hook to Gaunt's
Rock, but, who, on getting to London, refused to walk
from the Savoy to the Cecil because of a weak heart.)
The worst feature about these inveterate water-walk-
ers is that they tread quite as proudly upon other
people's feet as they do upon their own, and as often
as not they appear to do it from choice.   Still, that
is another story.   It has nothing to do with the one
we are trying to tell.

To resume, the decks of the *Jupiter* were wet
and the sky was drab.   New York was twenty-four
hours astern and the brief Sunday service had come to
a peaceful end.   It died just in time to escape the
horrors of a popular programme by the band amid-
ships.   The echo of the last amen was a resounding
thump on the big bass drum.

Three tall, interesting looking men stood leaning
against the starboard rail of the promenade deck, unmindful of the mist, watching the scurrying throng of
exercise fiends.   Two were young, the third was old,
and of the three there was one who merited the second

glance that invariably was bestowed upon him by the
circling passers-by. Each succeeding revolution increased the interest and admiration and people soon
began to favour him with frankly unabashed stares
and smiles that could not have been mistaken for anything but tribute to his extreme good looks.

He stood between the gaunt, soldierly old man with
the fierce moustache, and the trim, military young man
with one that was close cropped and smart. Each
wore a blue serge suit and affected a short visored cap
of the same material, and each lazily puffed at a very
commonplace briar pipe. They in turn were watching
the sprightly parade with an interest that was calmly
impersonal. They saw no one person who deserved
more than a casual glance, and yet the motley crowd
passed before them, apparently without end, as if expecting a responsive smile of recognition from the tall
young fellow to whom it paid the honest tribute of
curiosity.

The customary he-gossip and perennial snooper who
is always making the voyage no matter what ship one
takes or the direction one goes, nosed out the purser
and discovered that the young man was R. Schmidt of
Vienna. He was busy thereafter mixing with the
throng, volunteering information that had not been
solicited but which appeared to be welcome. Especially were the young women on board grateful to the
he-gossip, when he accosted them as a perfect stranger
to tell them the name of another and even more perfect
stranger.

"Evidently an Austrian army officer," he always proclaimed, and that seemed to settle it.

Luckily he did not overhear R. Schmidt's impassive estimate of the first cabin parade, or he might have had something to repeat that would not have pleased those who took part in it.

"Queer looking lot of people," said R. Schmidt, and his two companions moodily nodded their heads.

"I am sorry we lost those rooms on the *Salammbo*," said the younger of his two companions. "I had them positively engaged, money paid down."

"Some one else came along with more money, Dank," observed R. Schmidt. "We ought to be thankful that we received anything at all. Has it occurred to you that this boat isn't crowded?"

"Not more than half full," said the older man. "All of the others appeared to be packed from hold to funnel. This must be an unpopular boat."

"I don't know where we'd be, however, if Mr. Blithers hadn't thought of the *Jupiter* almost at the last minute," said R. Schmidt.

"Nine day boat, though," growled the old man.

"I don't mind that in the least. She's a steady old tub and that's something."

"Hobbs tells me that it is most extraordinary to find the east bound steamers crowded at this season of the year," said Dank. "He can't understand it at all. The crowds go over in June and July and by this time they should be starting for home. I thought we'd have no difficulty in getting on any one of the big boats, but, by jove, everywhere I went they said they were full up."

"It was uncommonly decent of Blithers not coming down to see us off," said the elderly man, who was down on the passenger list as Totten. "I was apprehensive, 'pon my soul. He stuck like a leech up to the last minute."

R. Schmidt was reflecting. "It struck me as queer that he had not heard of the transfer of our securities in London."

"I cannot understand Bernstein & Sons selling out at a time when the price of our bonds is considerably below their actual value," said Totten, frowning. "A million pounds sterling is what their holdings really represented; according to the despatches they must have sold at a loss of nearly fifty thousand pounds. It is unbelievable that the house can be hard-pressed for money. There isn't a sounder concern in Europe than Bernstein's."

"We should have a Marconi-gram to-night or to-morrow in regard to the bid made in Paris for the bonds held by the French syndicate," said Dank, pulling at his short moustache. "Mr. Blithers is investigating."

"There is something sinister in all this," said R. Schmidt. "Who is buying up all of the out-standing bonds and what is behind the movement? London has sold all that were held there and Paris is approached on the same day. If Paris and Berlin should sell, nearly four million pounds in Graustark bonds will be in the hands of people whose identity and motives appear to be shrouded in the deepest mystery."

"And four million pounds represents the entire amount of our bonds held by outside parties," said Totten, with a significant shake of his grizzled head. "The remainder are in the possession of our own institutions and the people themselves. We should hear from Edelweiss, too, in response to my cablegram. Perhaps Romano may be able to throw light on the situation. I confess that I am troubled."

"Russia would have no object in buying up our general bonds, would she?" inquired R. Schmidt.

"None whatever. She would have nothing to gain. Mr. Blithers assured me that he was not in the least apprehensive. In fact, he declared that Russia would not be buying bonds that do not mature for twelve years to come. There must be some private — eh?"

A steward was politely accosting the trio.

"I beg pardon, is this Mr. Totten?"

"Yes."

"Message for you, sir, at the purser's."

"Bring it to my stateroom, Totten," said R. Schmidt briefly; and the old man hurried away on the heels of the messenger.

The two young men sauntered carelessly in an opposite direction and soon disappeared from the deck. A few minutes later, Totten entered the luxurious parlour of R. Schmidt and laid an unopened wireless message on the table at the young man's elbow.

" Open it, Totten."

The old man slit the envelope and glanced at the contents. He nodded his head in answer to an unspoken question.

" Sold?" asked R. Schmidt.

" Paris and Berlin, both of them, Prince. Every bond has been gobbled up."

" Does he mention the name of the buyer?"

" Only by the use of the personal pronoun. He says —' I have taken over the Paris and Berlin holdings. All is well.' It is signed ' B.' So! Now we know."

" By jove!" fell from the lips of both men, and then the three Graustarkians stared in speechless amazement at each other for the space of a minute before another word was spoken.

" Blithers !" exclaimed Dank, sinking back into his chair.

" Blithers," repeated Totten, but with an entirely different inflection. The word was conviction itself as he pronounced it.

R. Schmidt indulged in a wry little smile. " It amounts to nearly twenty million dollars, Count. That's a great deal of money to spend in the pursuit of an idle whim."

" Humph!" grunted the old Count, and then favoured the sunny-faced Prince with a singularly sharp glance. " Of course, you understand his game?"

" Perfectly. It's as clear as day. He intends to

be the crown father-in-law. I suppose he will expect Graustark to establish an Order of Royal Grandfathers."

"It may prove to be no jest, Robin," said the Count seriously.

"My dear Quinnox, don't look so sad," cried the Prince. "He may have money enough to buy Graustark but he hasn't enough to buy grandchildren that won't grow, you know. He is counting chickens before they're hatched, which isn't a good business principle, I'd have you to know."

"What was it he said to you at Red Roof?"

"That was nothing. Pure bluster."

"He said he had never set his heart on anything that he didn't get in the end, wasn't that it?"

"I think so. Something of the sort. I took it as a joke."

"Well, I took it as a threat."

"A threat?"

"A pleasant, agreeable threat, of course. He has set his heart on having the crown of Graustark worn by a Blithers. That is the long and short of it."

"I believe he did say to me in the woods that day that he could put his daughter on any throne in Europe if he set his mind to the job," said the Prince carelessly. "But you see, the old gentleman is not counting on two very serious sources of opposition when it comes to this particular case. There is Maud, you see,— and me."

"I am not so sure of the young lady," said the

Count sententiously. "The opposition may falter a bit there, and half of his battle is won."

"You seem to forget, Quinnox, that such a marriage is utterly impossible," said the Prince coldly. "Do you imagine that I would marry —"

"Pardon me, highness, I said *half* the battle would be won. I do contemplate a surrender on your part. You are a very pig-headed young man. The most pig-headed I've ever known, if you will forgive me for expressing myself so —"

"You've said it a hundred times," laughed the Prince, good-naturedly. "Don't apologise. Not only you but the entire House of Nobles have characterised me as pig-headed and I have never even thought of resenting it, so it must be that I believe it to be true."

"We have never voiced the opinion, highness, except in reference to our own great desire to bring about the union between our beloved ruler and the Crown Princess of —"

"So," interrupted R. Schmidt, "it ought to be very clear to you that if I will not marry to please my loyal, devoted cabinet I certainly shall not marry to please William W. Blithers. No doubt the excellent Maud is a most desirable person. In any event, she has a mind of her own. I confess that I am sorry to have missed seeing her. We might have got on famously together, seeing that our point of view is apparently unique in this day and age of the world. No, my good friends, Mr. Blithers is making a poor

investment. He will not get the return for his money
that he is expecting. If it pleases him to buy our
securities, all well and good. He shall lose nothing in
the end. · But he will find that Graustark is not a toy,
nor the people puppets. More than all that, I am
not a bargain sale prince with Christmas tree aspira-
tions, but a very unamiable devil who cultivates an
ambition to throw stones at the conventions. Not
only do I intend to choose my wife but also the court
grandfather. And now let us forget the folly of Mr.
Blithers and discuss his methods of business. What
does he expect to gain by this extraordinary investment? "

Count Quinnox looked at him rather pityingly. " It
appears to be his way of pulling the strings, my boy.
He has loaned us something like sixteen millions of
dollars. We have agreed to deposit our public service bonds as security against the loan, so that practically equalises the situation. It becomes a purely
business transaction. But he sees far ahead. This
loan of his matures at practically the same time that
our first series of government bonds are due for payment. It will be extremely difficult for a small country, such as Graustark, to raise nearly forty millions
of dollars in, say ten years. The European syndicates
undoubtedly would be willing to renew the loan under
a new issue — I think it is called refunding, or something of the sort. But Mr. Blithers will be in a position to say no to any such arrangement. He holds the
whip hand and —"

"But, my dear Count," interrupted the Prince, "what if he does hold it? Does he expect to wait ten years before exercising his power? You forget that marriage is his ambition. Isn't be taking a desperate risk in assuming that I will not marry before the ten years are up? And, for that matter, his daughter may decide to wed some other chap who —"

"That's just the point," said Quinnox. "He is arranging it so that you *can't* marry without his consent."

"The deuce you say!"

"I am not saying that he can carry out his design, my dear boy, but it is his secret hope, just the same. So far as Graustark is concerned, she will stand by you no matter what betides. As you know, there is nothing so dear to our hearts as the proposed union of Dawsbergen's Crown Princess and —"

"That's utterly out of the question, Count," said the Prince, setting his jaws.

The count sighed patiently. "So you say, my boy, so you say. But you are not reasonable. How can you know that the Crown Princess of Dawsbergen is not the very mate your soul has been craving —"

"That's not the point. I am opposed to this miserable custom of giving in marriage without the consent of the people most vitally concerned, and I shall never recede from my position."

"You are very young, my dear Prince."

"And I intend to remain young, my dear Count. Loveless marriages make old men and women of youths

and maidens. I remember thinking that remark out
for myself after a great deal of effort, and you may
remember that I sprung it with considerable effect on
the cabinet when the matter was formally discussed a
year or two ago. You heard about it, didn't you,
Dank?"

"I did, highness."

"And every newspaper in the world printed it as
coming from me, didn't they? Well, there you are.
I can't go behind my publicly avowed principles."

The young fellow stretched his long body in a sort
of luxurious defiance, and eyed his companions somewhat combatively.

"Sounds very well," growled the Count, with scant
reverence for royalty, being a privileged person.

"Now, Dank here can marry any one he likes — if
she'll have him — and he is only a lieutenant of the
guard. Why should I,— prince royal and master of
all he surveys, so to speak,— why should I be denied
a privilege enjoyed by every good-looking soldier who
carries a sword in my army — *my* army, do you understand? I leave it to you, Dank, is it fair? Who are
you that you should presume to think of a happy
marriage while I, your Prince, am obliged to twiddle
my thumbs and say 'all right, bring any old thing
along and I'll marry her'? Who are you, Dank, that's
what I'd like to know."

His humour was so high-handed that the two soldiers
laughed and Dank ruefully admitted that he was a
lucky dog.

"You shall not marry into the Blithers family, my lad, if we can help it," said the Count, pulling at his moustaches.

"I should say not!" said Dank, feeling for his.

"I should as soon marry a daughter of Hobbs," said R. Schmidt, getting up from his chair with restored sprightliness. "If he had one, I mean."

"The bonds of matrimony and the bonds of government are by no means synonymous," said Dank, and felt rather proud of himself when his companions favoured him with a stare of amazement. The excellent lieutenant was not given to persiflage. He felt that for a moment he had scintillated.

"Shall we send a wireless to Blithers congratulating him on his coup?" enquired the Prince gaily.

"No," said the Count. "Congratulating ourselves on his coup is better."

"Good! And you might add that we also are trusting to luck. It may give him something to think about. And now where is Hobbs?" said royalty.

"Here, sir," said Hobbs, appearing in the bed-room door, but not unexpectedly. "I heard wot you said about my daughter, sir. It may set your mind at rest, sir, to hear that I am childless."

"Thank you, Hobbs. You are always thinking of my comfort. You may order luncheon for us in the Ritz restaurant. The head steward has been instructed to reserve the corner table for the whole voyage."

"The 'ead waiter, sir," corrected Hobbs politely, and was gone.

In three minutes he was back with the information that two ladies had taken the table and refused to be dislodged, although the head waiter had vainly tried to convince them that it was reserved for the passage by R. Schmidt and party.

"I am quite sure, sir, he put it to them very hagreeably and politely, but the young lady gave 'im the 'aughtiest look I've ever seen on mortal fice, sir, and he came back to me so 'umble that I could 'ardly believe he was an 'ead waiter."

"I hope he was not unnecessarily persistent," said the Prince, annoyed. "It really is of no consequence where we sit."

"Ladies first, world without end," said Dank. "Especially at sea."

"He was not persistent, sir. In fact he was hextraordinary subdued all the time he was hexplaining the situation to them. I could tell by the way his back looked, sir."

"Never mind, Hobbs. You ordered luncheon?"

"Yes, your 'ighness. Chops and sweet potatoes and—"

"But that's what we had yesterday, Hobbs."

A vivid red overspread the suddenly dismayed face of Hobbs. "'Pon my soul, sir, I — I clean forgot that it was yesterday I was thinking of. The young lady gave me such a sharp look, sir, when the 'ead

waiter pointed at me that I clean forgot wot I was
there for. I will 'urry back and—"

"Do, Hobbs, that's a good fellow. I'm as hungry
as a bear. But no chops!"

"Thank you, sir. No chops. Absolutely, sir."
He stopped in the doorway. "I daresay it was 'er
beauty, sir, that did it. No chops. Quite so, sir."

"If Blithers were only here," sighed Dank. "He
would make short work of the female invasion. He
would have them chucked overboard."

"I beg pardon, sir," further adventured Hobbs,
"but I fancy not even Mr. Blithers could move that
young woman, sir, if she didn't 'appen to want to be
moved. Never in my life, sir, have I seen—"

"Run along, Hobbs," said the Prince. "Boiled
guinea hen."

"And cantaloupe, sir. Yes, sir, I quite remember
everything now, sir."

Twenty minutes later, R. Schmidt, seated in the
Ritz restaurant, happened to look fairly into the eyes
of the loveliest girl he had ever seen, and on the instant
forgave the extraordinary delinquency of the hitherto
infallible Hobbs.

CHAPTER IX

LATER on R. Schmidt sat alone in a sheltered corner
of the promenade deck, where chairs had been secured
by the forehanded Hobbs. The thin drizzle now as-
pired to something more definite in the shape of a
steady downpour, and the decks were almost deserted,
save for the few who huddled in the unexposed nooks
where the sweep and swish of the rain failed to penetrate. There was a faraway look in the young man's
eyes, as of one who dreams pleasantly, with little effort
but excellent effect. His pipe had gone out, so his
dream must have been long and uninterrupted. Eight
bells sounded, but what is time to a dreamer? Then
came one bell and two, and now his eyes were
closed.

Two women came and stood over him, but little did
they suspect that his dream was of one of them: the
one with the lovely eyes and the soft brown hair.
They surveyed him, whispering, the one with a little
perplexed frown on her brow, the other with distinct
signs of annoyance in her face. The girl was not more
than twenty, her companion quite old enough to be her
mother: a considerate if not complimentary estimate,
for a girl's mother may be either forty, fifty or even
fifty-five, when you come to think of it.

They were looking for something. That was quite clear. And it was deplorably clear that whatever it was, R. Schmidt was sitting upon it. They saw that he was asleep, which made the search if not the actual recovery quite out of the question. The older woman was on the point of poking the sleeper with the toe of her shoe, being a matter-of-fact sort of person, when the girl imperatively shook her head and frowned upon the lady in a way to prove that even though she was old enough to be the mother of a girl of twenty she was by no means the mother of this one.

At that very instant, R. Schmidt opened his eyes. It must have been a kindly poke by the god of sleep that aroused him so opportunely, but even so, the toe of a shoe could not have created a graver catastrophe than that which immediately befell him. He completely lost his head. If one had suddenly asked what had become of it, he couldn't have told, not for the life of him. For that matter, he couldn't have put his finger, so to speak, on any part of his person and proclaimed with confidence that it belonged to R. Schmidt of Vienna. He was looking directly up into a pair of dark, startled eyes, in which there was a very pretty confusion and a far from impervious blink.

"I beg your pardon," said the older woman, without the faintest trace of embarrassment,— indeed, with some asperity,—"I think you are occupying one of our chairs."

He scrambled out of the steamer rug and came to his feet, blushing to the roots of his hair.

"I beg your pardon," he stammered, and found his awkwardness rewarded by an extremely sweet smile — in the eyes of the one he addressed.

"We were looking for a letter that I am quite sure was left in my chair," said she.

"A letter?" he murmured vaguely, and at once began to search with his eyes.

"From her father," volunteered the elderly one, as if it were a necessary bit of information. Then she jerked the rug away and three pairs of eyes examined the place where R. Schmidt had been reclining. "That's odd. Did you happen to see it when you sat down, sir?"

"I am confident that there was no letter —" began he, and then allowed his gaze to rest on the name-card at the top of the chair. "This happens to be *my* chair, madam," he went on, pointing to the card. "'R. Schmidt.' I am very sorry."

"The steward must have put that card there while you were at luncheon, dear. What right has he to sell our chairs over again? I shall report this to the Captain —"

"I am quite positive that this is my chair, sir," said the girl, a spot of red in each cheek. "It was engaged two days ago. I have been occupying it since — but it really doesn't matter. It has your name on it now, so I suppose I shall have to —"

"Not at all," he made haste to say. "It is yours. There has been some miserable mistake. These deck stewards are always messing things up. Still, it is rather a mystery about the letter. I assure you I saw no —"

"No doubt the steward who changed the cards had sufficient intelligence to remove all incriminating evidence," said she coolly. "We shall find it among the lost, strayed and stolen articles, no doubt. Pray retain the chair, Mr.—" She peered at the namecard —"Mr. Schmidt."

Her cool insolence succeeded in nettling a nature that was usually most gentle. He spoke with characteristic directness.

"Thank you, I shall do so. We thereby manage to strike a fair average. I seize your deck chair, you seize my table. We are quits."

She smiled faintly. "R. Schmidt did not sound young and gentle, but old and hateful. That is why I seized the table. I expected to find R. Schmidt a fat, old German with very bad manners. Instead, you are neither fat, old, nor disagreeable. You took it very nicely, Mr. Schmidt, and I am undone. Won't you permit me to restore your table to you?"

The elderly lady was tapping the deck with a most impatient foot. "Really my dear, we were quite within our rights in approaching the head waiter. He —"

"He said it was engaged," interrupted the young lady. "R. Schmidt was the name he gave and I informed him it meant nothing to me. I am very sorry, Mr. Schmidt. I suppose it was all because I am so accustomed to having my own way."

"In that case, it is all very easy to understand," said he, "for I have always longed to be in a position where I could have my own way. I am sure that if I could have it, I would be a most overbearing, selfish person."

"We must enquire at the office for the letter, my dear, before —"

"It may have dropped behind the chair," said the girl.

"Right!" cried R. Schmidt, dragging the chair away and pointing in triumph at the missing letter. He stooped to recover the missive, but she was quick to forestall him. With a little gasp she pounced upon it and, like a child proceeded to hold it behind her back. He stiffened. "I remember that you said it was from your father."

She hesitated an instant and then held it forth for his inspection, rather adroitly concealing the post-mark with her thumb. It was addressed to "Miss B. Guile, S. S. *Jupiter*, New York City, N. Y.," and type-written.

"It is only fair that we should be quits in every particular," she said, with a frank smile.

He bowed. "A letter of introduction," he said, "in the strictest sense of the word. You have already had my card thrust upon you, so everything is quite regular. And now it is only right and proper that I should see what has become of your chairs. Permit me —"

"Really, Miss Guile," interposed her companion,

"this is quite irregular. I may say it is unusual. Pray allow me to suggest —"

"I think it is only right that Mr. Schmidt should return good for evil," interrupted the girl gaily. "Please enquire, Mr. Schmidt. No doubt the deck steward will know."

Again the Prince bowed, but this time there was amusement instead of uncertainty in his eyes. It was the first time that any one had ever urged him, even by inference, to "fetch and carry." Moreover, she was extremely cool about it, as one who exacts much of young men in serge suits and outing-caps. He found himself wondering what she would say if he were to suddenly announce that he was the Prince of Graustark. The thought tickled his fancy, accounting, no doubt, for the even deeper bow that he gave her.

"They can't be very far away," he observed quite meekly. "Oh, I say, steward! One moment here." A deck steward approached with alacrity. "What has become of Miss Guile's chair?"

The man touched his cap and beamed joyously upon the fair young lady.

"Ach! See how I have forgot! It is here! The best place on the deck — on any deck. See! Two — side by side,— above the door, away from the draft — see, in the corner, ha, ha! Yes! Two by side. The very best. Miss Guile complains of the draft from the door. I exchanged the chairs. See! But I forgot to speak. Yes! See!"

And, sure enough, there were the chairs of Miss

Guile and her companion snugly stowed away in the corner, standing at right angles to the long row that lined the deck, the foot rests pointed directly at the chair R. Schmidt had just vacated, not more than a yard and a half away.

"How stupid!" exclaimed Miss Guile. "Thank you, steward. This is much better. So sorry, Mr. Schmidt, to have disturbed you. I abhor drafts, don't you?"

"Not to the extent tha. I shall move out of this one," he replied gallantly, "now that I've got an undisputed claim to it. I intend to stano up for my rights, Miss Guile, even though you find me at your feet."

"How perfectly love —" began Miss Guile, a gleam of real enthusiasm in her eyes. A sharp, horrified look from her companion served as a check, and she became at once the coolly indifferent creature who exacts everything. "Thank you, Mr. Schmidt, for being so nice when we were trying so hard to be horrid."

"But you don't know how nice you are when you are trying to be horrid," he remarked. "Are you not going to sit down, now that we've captured the disappearing chair?"

"No," she said, and he fancied he saw regret in her eyes. "I am going to my room,— if I can find it. No doubt it also is lost. This seems to be a day for misplacing things."

"At any rate, permit me to thank you for discovering me, Miss Guile."

"Oh, I daresay I shall misplace you, too, Mr. Schmidt." She said it so insolently that he flushed as he drew himself up and stepped aside to allow her to pass. For an instant their eyes met, and the sign of the humble was not to be found in the expression of either.

"Even *that* will be something for me to look forward to, Miss Guile," said he. Far from being vexed, she favoured him with a faint smile of — was it wonder or admiration?

Then she moved away, followed by the uneasy lady — who was old enough to be her mother and wasn't.

Robin remained standing for a moment, looking after her, and somehow he felt that his dream was not yet ended. She turned the corner of the deck building and was lost to sight. He sat down, only to arise almost instantly, moved by a livelier curiosity than he ever had felt before. Conscious of a certain feeling of stealth, he scrutinised the cards in the backs of the two chairs. The steward was collecting the discarded steamer-rugs farther down the deck, and the few passengers who occupied chairs, appeared to be snoozing,— all of which he took in with his first appraising glance. "Miss Guile" and "Mrs. Gaston" were the names he read.

"Americans," he mused. "Young lady and chaperone, that's it. A real American beauty! And Blithers loudly boasts that his daughter is the prettiest girl in America! Shades of Venus! Can there be such a thing on earth as a prettier girl than this one?

Can nature have performed the impossible? Is
America so full of lovely girls that this one must take
second place to a daughter of Blithers? I wonder if
she knows the imperial Maud. I'll make it a point
to inquire."

Moved by a sudden restlessness, he decided that he
was in need of exercise. A walk would do him good.
The same spirit of restlessness, no doubt, urged him
to walk rather rapidly in the direction opposite to
that taken by the lovely Miss Guile. After completely circling the deck once he decided that he did
not need the exercise after all. His walk had not
benefitted him in the least. She *had* gone to her room.
He returned to his chair, conscious of having been
defeated but without really knowing why or how.
As he turned into the dry, snug corner, he came to
an abrupt stop and stared. Miss Guile was sitting in
her chair, neatly encased in a mummy-like sheath of
grey that covered her slim body to the waist.

She was quite alone in her nook, and reading. Evidently the book interested her, for she failed to look up
when he clumsily slid into his chair and threw the
rug over his legs — dreadfully long, uninteresting
legs, he thought, as he stretched them out and found
that his feet protruded like a pair of white obelisks.

Naturally he looked seaward, but in his mind's eye
he saw her as he had seen her not more than ten minutes
before: a slim, tall girl in a smart buff coat, with a
limp white hat drawn down over her hair by means of a
bright green veil; he had had a glimpse of staunch tan

walking-shoes. He found himself wondering how he had missed her in the turn about the deck, and how she could have ensconced herself so snugly during his brief evacuation of the spot. Suddenly it occurred to him that she had returned to the chair only after discovering that his was vacant. It wasn't a very gratifying conclusion.

An astonishing intrepidity induced him to speak to her after a lapse of five or six minutes, and so surprising was the impulse that he blurted out his question without preamble.

"How did you manage to get back so quickly?" he inquired.

She looked up, and for an instant there was something like alarm in her lovely eyes, as of one caught in the perpetration of a guilty act.

"I beg your pardon," she said, rather indistinctly.

"I was away less than eight minutes," he declared, and she was confronted by the wonderfully frank smile that never failed to work its charm. To his surprise, a shy smile grew in her eyes, and her warm red lips twitched uncertainly. He had expected a cold rebuff. "You must have dropped through the awning."

"Your imagination is superior to that employed by the author of this book," she said, "and that is saying a good deal, Mr.— Mr.—"

"Schmidt," he supplied cheerfully. "May I inquire what book you are reading?"

"You would not be interested. It is by an American."

"I have read a great many American novels," said he stiffly. "My father was an American. Awfully jolly books, most of them."

"I looked you up in the passenger list a moment ago," she said coolly. "Your home is in Vienna. I like Vienna."

He was looking rather intently at the book, now partly lowered. "Isn't that the passenger list you have concealed in that book?" he demanded.

"It is," she replied promptly. "You will pardon a natural curiosity? I wanted to see whether you were from New York."

"May I look at it, please?"

She closed the book. "It isn't necessary. I am from New York."

"By the way, do you happen to know a Miss Blithers,— Maud Blithers?"

Miss Guile frowned reflectively. "Blithers? The name is a familiar one. Maud Blithers? What is she like?"

"She's supposed to be very good-looking. I've never seen her."

"How queer to be asking me if I know her, then. Why *do* you ask?"

"I've heard so much about her lately. She is the daughter of William Blithers, the great capitalist."

"Oh, I know who he is," she exclaimed. "Perfect roodles of money, hasn't he?"

"Roodles?"

"Loads, if it means more to you. I forgot that you are a foreigner. He gave that wonderful ball last week for the Prince of — of — Oh, some insignificant little place over in Europe. There are such a lot of queer little duchies and principalities, don't you know; it is quite impossible to tell one from the other. They don't even appear on the maps."

He took it with a perfectly straight face, though secretly annoyed. "It was the talk of the town, that ball. It must have cost roodles of money. Is that right?"

"Yes, but it doesn't sound right when you say it. Naturally one doesn't say roodles in Vienna."

"We say noodles," said he. "I am very fond of them. But to resume; I supposed every one in New York knew Miss Blithers. She's quite the rage, I'm told."

"Indeed? I should think she might be, Mr. Schmidt, with all those lovely millions behind her."

He smiled introspectively. "Yes; and I am told that, in spite of them, she is the prettiest girl in New York."

She appeared to lose interest in the topic. "Oh, indeed?"

"But," he supplemented gracefully, "it isn't true."

"What isn't true?"

"The statement that she is the prettiest girl in New York."

"How can you say that, when you admit you've never seen her?"

"I can say it with a perfectly clear conscience, Miss Guile," said he, and was filled with delight when she bit her lip as a sign of acknowledgment.

"Oh, here comes the tea," she cried, with a strange eagerness in her voice. "I am so glad." She scrambled gracefully out of her rug and arose to her feet.

"Aren't you going to have some?" he cried.

"Yes," she said, quite pointedly. "In my room, Mr. Schmidt," and before he could get to his feet she was moving away without so much as a nod or smile for him. Indeed, she appeared to have dismissed him from her thoughts quite as completely as from her vision. He experienced a queer sensation of shrivelling.

At dinner that night, she failed to look in his direction, a circumstance that may not appear extraordinary when it is stated that she purposely or inadvertently exchanged seats with Mrs. Gaston and sat with her back to the table occupied by R. Schmidt and his friends. He had to be content with a view of the most exquisite back and shoulders that good fortune had ever allowed him to gaze upon. And then there was the way that her soft brown hair grew above the slender neck, to say nothing of — but Mrs. Gaston was watching him with most unfriendly eyes, so the feast was spoiled.

The following day was as unlike its predecessor as black is like white. During the night the smooth grey pond had been transformed into a turbulent, storm-threshed ocean; the once gentle wind was now a howling gale that swept the decks with a merciless lash in its grip and whipped into submission all who vaingloriously sought to defy its chill dominion. Not rain, but spray from huge, swashing billows, clouded the decks, biting and cutting like countless needles, each drop with the sting of a hornet behind it. Now the end of the world seemed far away, and the jumping off place was a rickety wall of white and black, leaning against a cold, drear sky.

Only the hardiest of the passengers ventured on deck; the exhilaration they professed was but another name for bravado. They shivered and gasped for breath as they forged their bitter way into the gale, and few were they who took more than a single turn of the deck. Like beaten cowards they soon slunk into the sheltered spots, or sought even less heroic means of surrender by tumbling into bed with the considerate help of unsmiling stewards. The great ship went up and the great ship came down: when up so high that the sky seemed to be startlingly near and down so horribly low that the bottom of the ocean was even nearer. And it creaked and groaned and sighed even above the wild monody of the wind, like a thing in misery, yet all the while holding its sides to keep from bursting with laughter over the plight of the little creature whom God made after His own image but not until after all of the big things of the universe had been designed.

R. Schmidt, being a good sailor and a hardy young
chap, albeit a prince of royal blood, was abroad early,
after a breakfast that staggered the few who remained
unstaggered up to that particular crisis.   A genial
sailor-man and an equally ungenial deck swabber advised him, in totally different styles of address, to
stay below if he knew what was good for him, only
to be thanked with all the blitheness of a man who
jolly well knows what is good for him, or who doesn't
care whether it is good for him or not so long as he is
doing the thing that he wants to do.

He took two turns about the deck, and each time as
he passed the spot he 'sent a covert glance into the
corner where Miss Guile's chair was standing. Of
course he did not expect to find her there in weather
like this, but — well, he looked and that is the end
to the argument.   The going was extremely treacherous and unpleasant he was free to confess to the
genial sailor-man after the second breathless turn, and
gave that worthy a bright silver dollar upon receiving a further bit of advice: to sit down somewhere out
of the wind, sir.

Quinnox and Dank were hopelessly bed-ridden, so
to speak. They were very disagreeable, cross and unpleasant, and somehow he felt that they hated their
cheerful, happy-faced Prince. Never before had
Count Quinnox scowled at him, no matter how mad
his pranks as a child or how silly his actions as a
youth. Never before had any one told him to go to
the devil. He rather liked it. And he rather ad-.

mired poor Dank for ordering him out of his cabin, with a perfectly astounding oath as a climax to the command. Moreover, he thought considerably better of the faithful Hobbs for an amazing exposition of human equality in the matter of a pair of boots that he desired to wear that morning but which happened to be stowed away in a cabin trunk. He told Hobbs to go to the devil and Hobbs repeated the injunction, with especial heat, to the boots, when he bumped his head in hauling them out of the trunk. Whereupon R. Schmidt said to Hobbs: "Good for you, Hobbs. Go on, please. Don'' mind me. It was quite a thump, wasn't it?" And Hobbs managed, between other words, to say that it was a whacking thump, and one he would not forget to his dying day — (if he lived through this one!).

"And you'd do well to sit in the smoke-room, sir," further advised the sailor-man, clinging to the rail with one hand and pocketing the coin with the other.

"No," said R. Schmidt resolutely. "I don't like the air in the smoke-room."

"There's quite a bit of air out 'ere, sir."

"I need quite a bit."

"I should think you might, sir, being a 'ealthy, strappin' sort of a chap, sir. 'Elp yourself. All the chairs is yours if you'll unpile 'em."

The young man battled his way down the deck and soon found himself in the well-protected corner. A half-dozen unoccupied chairs were cluttered about, having been abandoned by persons who over-estimated their hardiness. One of the stewards was engaged in stacking them up and making them fast.

Miss Guile's chair and that of Mrs. Gaston were staunchly fastened down and their rugs were in place. R. Schmidt experienced an exquisite sensation of pleasure. Here was a perfect exemplification of that much-abused thing known as circumstantial evidence. She contemplated coming on deck. So he had his chair put in place, called for his rug, shrugged his chin down into the collar of his thick ulster, and sat down to wait.

CHAPTER X

She literally was blown into his presence. He sprang to his feet to check her swift approach before she could be dashed against the wall or upon the heap of chairs in the corner. The deep roll of the vessel had ended so suddenly that she was thrown off her balance, at best precariously maintained in the hurricane that swept her along the deck. She was projected with considerable violence against the waiting figure of R. Schmidt, who had hastily braced himself for the impact of the slender body in the thick sea-ulster. She uttered an excited little shriek as she came bang up against him and found his ready arms closing about her shoulders.

"Oh, goodness!" she gasped, with what little breath she had left, and then began to laugh as she freed herself in confusion — a very pretty confusion he recalled later on, after he had recovered to some extent from the effects of an exceedingly severe bump on the back of his head. "How awkward!"

"Not at all," he proclaimed, retaining a grip on one of her arms until the ship showed some signs of resuming its way eastward instead of downward.

"I am sure it must have hurt dreadfully," she cried. "Nothing hurts worse than a bump. It seemed as though you must have splintered the wall."

"I have a singularly hard head," said he, and forth-with felt of the back of it.

"Will you please stand ready to receive boarders? My maid is following me, poor thing, and I can't afford to have her smashed to pieces.   Here she is!"

Quite a pretty maid, with wide, horrified eyes and a pale green complexion came hustling around the corner.   R. Schmidt, albeit a prince, received her with open arms.

"Merci, M'sieur!" she squealed and added something in muffled French that strangely reminded him of what Hobbs had said in English.   Then she deposited an armful of rugs and magazines at Robin's feet, and clutched wildly at a post actually some ten feet away but which appeared to be coming toward her with obliging swiftness, so nicely was the deck rotating for her.   "Mon dieu!   Mon dieu!"

"You may go back to bed, Marie," cried her mistress in some haste.

"But se rug, I feex it —" groaned the unhappy maid, and then once more: "Merci, M'sieur!"   She clung to the arm he extended, and tried bravely to smile her thanks.

"Here!   Go in through this door," he said, bracing the door open with his elbow.   "You'll be all right in a little while.   Keep your nerve."   He closed the door after her and turned to the amused Miss Guile. "Well, it's an ill wind that blows no good," he said enigmatically, and she flushed under the steady smile in his eyes. "Allow me to arrange your rug for you, Miss Guile."

"Thank you, no. I think I would better go inside. It is really too windy —"

"The wind can't get at you back here in this cubby-hole," he protested. "Do sit down. I'll have you as snug as a bug in a rug before you can say Jack Robin-son. See! Now stick 'em out and I'll wrap it around them. There! You're as neatly done up as a mummy and a good deal better off, because you are a long way short of being two thousand years old."

"How is your head, Mr. Schmidt?" she inquired with grave concern. "You seem to be quite crazy. I hope —"

"Every one is a little bit mad, don't you think? Especially in moments of great excitement. I dare-say my head *has* been turned quite appreciably, and I'm glad that you've been kind enough to notice it. Where is Mrs. Gaston?" He was vastly exhilarated.

She regarded him with eyes that sparkled and be-lied the unamiable nature of her reply.

"The poor lady is where she is not at all likely to be annoyed, Mr. Schmidt."

Then she took up a magazine and coolly began to run through the pages. He waited for a moment, con-siderably dashed, and then said "Oh," in a very un-friendly manner. She found her place in the maga-zine, assumed a more comfortable position, and, with noteworthy resolution, set about reading as if her life depended upon it.

He sat down, pulled the rug up to his chin, and stared out at the great, heaving bill ws. Suddenly remembering another injury, he felt once more of the back of his head.

"By jove!" he exclaimed. "There *is* a lump there."

"I can't hear you," she said, allowing the magazine to drop into her lap, but keeping her place carefully marked with one of her fingers.

"I can hear you perfectly," he said.

"It's the way the wind blows," she explained.

"Easily remedied," said he. "I'll move into Mrs. Gaston's chair if you think it will help any."

"Do!" she said promptly. "You will not disturb me in the least,—unless you talk." She resumed her reading, half a page above the finger tip.

He moved over and arranged himself comfortably, snugly in Mrs. Gaston's chair. Their elbows almost met. He was prepared to be very patient. For a long time she continued to read, her warm, rosy cheek half-averted, her eyes applied to their task with irritating constancy. He did not despair. Some wise person once had told him that it was only necessary to give a woman sufficient time and she would be the one to despair.

A few passengers possessed of proud sea-legs, staggered past the snug couple on their ridiculous rounds of the ship. If they thought of Miss Guile and R. Schmidt at all it was with the scorn that is usually devoted to youth at its very best. There could be no.

doubt in the passing mind that these two were sweethearts who managed to thrive on the smallest of comforts.

At last his patience was rewarded. She lowered the magazine and stifled a yawn — but not a real one.

"Have you read it?" she inquired composedly.

"A part of it," he said. "Over your shoulder."

"Is that considered polite in Vienna?"

"If you only knew what a bump I've got on the back of my head you wouldn't be so ungracious," he said.

"I couldn't possibly know, could I?"

He leaned forward and indicated the spot on the back of his head, first removing his cap. She laughed nervously, and then gently rubbed her fingers over the thick hair.

"There is a dreadful lump!" she exclaimed. "Oh, how sorry I am. Do — do you feel faint or — or — I mean, is it very painful?"

"Not now," he replied, replacing his cap and favouring her with his most engaging smile.

She smiled in response, betraying not the slightest sign of embarrassment. As a matter of fact, she was, if anything, somewhat too self-possessed.

"I remember falling down stairs once," she said, "and getting a stupendous bump on my forehead. But that was a great many years ago and I cried. How was I to know that it hurt you, Mr. Schmidt, when you neglected to cry?"

"Heroes never cry," said he. "It isn't considered first-class fiction, you know."

"Am I to regard you as a hero?"

"If you will be so kind, please."

She laughed outright at this. "I think I rather like you, Mr. Schmidt," she said, with unexpected candour.

"Oh, I fancy I'm not at all bad," said he, after a momentary stare of astonishment. "I am especially good in rough weather," he went on, trying to forget that he was a prince of the royal blood, a rather difficult matter when one stops to consider he was not in the habit of hearing people say that they rather liked him.

"Do your friends come from Vienna?" she inquired abruptly.

"Yes," he said, and then saved his face as usual by adding under his breath: "but they don't live there." It was not in him to lie outright, hence the handy way of appeasing his conscience.

"They are very interesting looking men, especially the younger. I cannot remember when I have seen a more attractive man."

"He is a splendid chap," exclaimed Robin, with genuine enthusiasm. "I am very fond of Dank."

She was silent for a moment. Something had failed, and she was rather glad of it.

"Do you like New York?" she asked.

"Immensely. I met a great many delightful people there, Miss Guile. You say you do not know the

Blithers family? Mr. Blithers is a rare old bird."

"Isn't there some talk of his daughter being engaged to the Prince of Graustark?"

He felt that his ears were red. "The newspapers hinted at something of the sort, I believe." He was suddenly possessed by the curious notion that he was being "pumped" by his fair companion. Indeed, a certain insistent note had crept into her voice and her eyes were searching his with an intentness that had not appeared in them until now.

"Have you seen him?"

"The Prince?"

"Yes.   What is he like?"

"I've seen pictures of him," he equivocated. "Rather nice looking, I should say."

"Of course he is like all foreign noblemen and will leap at the Blithers millions if he gets the chance. I sometimes feel sorry for the poor wretches." There was more scorn than pity in the way she said it, however, and her velvety eyes were suddenly hard and uncompromising.

He longed to defend himself, in the third person, but could not do so for very strong and obvious reasons. He allowed himself the privilege, however, of declaring that foreign noblemen are not always as black as they are painted. And then, for a very excellent reason, he contrived to change the subject by asking where she was going on the continent.

"I may go to Vienna," she said, with a smile that served to puzzle rather than to delight him. He was more than ever convinced that she was playing with him. "But pray do not look so gloomy, Mr. Schmidt; I shall not make any demands upon your time while I am there. You may —"

"I am quite sure of that," he interrupted, with his ready smile. "You see, I am a person of no consequence in Vienna, while you — Ah, well, as an American girl you will be hobnobbing with the nobility while the humble Schmidt sits afar off and marvels at the kindness of a fate that befell him in the middle of the Atlantic Ocean, and yet curses the fate that makes him unworthy of the slightest notice from the aforesaid American girl. For, I daresay, Miss Guile, you, like all American girls, are ready to leap at titles."

"That really isn't fair, Mr. Schmidt," she protested, flushing. "Why should you and I quarrel over a condition that cannot apply to either of us? You are not a nobleman, and I am not a title-seeking American girl. So, why all this beautiful irony?"

"It only remains for me to humbly beg your pardon and to add that if you come to Vienna my every waking hour shall be devoted to the pleasure of —"

"I am sorry I mentioned it, Mr. Schmidt," she interrupted coldly. "You may rest easy, for I shall not keep you awake for a single hour. Besides, I may not go to Vienna at all."

"I am sure you would like Vienna," he said, somewhat chilled by her manner.

"I have been there, with my parents, but it was

a long time ago. I once saw the Emperor and often have I seen the wonderful Prince Lichtenstein."

"Have you travelled extensively in Europe?"

She was smiling once more. "I don't know what you would consider extensively," she said. "I was educated in Paris, I have spent innumerable winters in Rome and quite as many summers in Scotland, England, Switzerland, Germ—"

"I know who you are!" he cried out enthusiastically. To his amazement, a startled expression leaped into her eyes. "You are travelling under an assumed name." She remained perfectly still, watching him with an anxious smile on her lips. "You are no other than Miss Baedeker, the well-known authoress."

It seemed to him that she breathed deeply. At any rate, her brow cleared and her smile was positively enchanting. Never, in all his life, had he gazed upon a lovelier face. His heart began to beat with a rapidity that startled him, and a queer little sensation, as of smothering, made it difficult for him to speak naturally in his next attempt.

"In that case, my pseudonym should be Guide, not Guile," she cried merrily. The dimples played in her cheeks and her eyes were dancing.

"B. stands for Baedeker, I'm sure. Baedeker Guide. If the B. isn't for Baedeker, what is it for?"

"Are you asking what the B. really stands for, Mr. Schmidt?"

"In a round-about way, Miss Guile," he admitted.

"My name is Bedelia," she said, with absolute sincerity. "Me mither is Irish, d'ye see?"

"By jove, it's worth a lot of trouble to get you to smile like that," he cried admiringly. "It is the first really honest smile you've displayed. If you knew how it improves you, you'd be doing it all of the time."

"Smiles are sometimes expensive."

"It depends on the market."

"I never take them to a cheap market. They are not classed as necessities."

"You couldn't offer them to any one who loves luxuries more than I do."

"You pay for them only with compliments, I see, and there is nothing so cheap."

"Am I to take that as a rebuke?"

"If possible," she said sweetly.

At this juncture, the miserable Hobbs hove into sight, not figuratively but literally. He came surging across the deck in a mad dash from one haven to another, or, more accurately, from post to post.

"I beg pardon, sir," he gasped, finally steadying himself on wide-spread legs within easy reach of Robin's sustaining person. "There is a wireless for Mr. Totten, sir, but when I took it to 'im he said to fetch it to you, being unable to hold up 'is head, wot with the wretched meal he had yesterday and the—"

"I see, Hobbs. Well, where is it?"

Hobbs looked embarrassed. "Well, you see, sir, I

'esitated about giving it to you when you appear to
be so —"

"Never mind. You may give it to me. Miss Guile
will surely pardon me if I devote a second or two to an
occupation she followed so earnestly up to a very short
time ago."

"Pray forget that I am present, Mr. Schmidt,'
she said, and smiled upon the bewildered Hobbs, who
after an instant delivered the message to his master.

Robin read it through and at the end whistled softly.

"Take it to Mr. Totten, Hobbs, and see if it will
not serve to make him hold up his head a little."

"Very good, sir. I hope it will. Wouldn't it be
wise for me to hannounce who it is from, sir, to sort
of prepare him for —"

"He knows who it is from, Hobbs, so you needn't
worry. It is from home, if it will interest you,
Hobbs."

"Thank you, sir, it does interest me. I thought it
might be from Mr. Blithers."

Robin's scowl sent him scuttling away a great deal
more rigidly than when he came.

"Idiot!" muttered the young man, still scowling.

There was silence between the two for a few seconds.
Then she spoke disinterestedly:

"Is it from the Mr. Blithers who has the millions
and the daughter who wants to marry a prince?"

"Merely a business transaction, Miss Guile," he said
absently. He was thinking of Romano's message.

"So it would appear."

"I beg pardon? I was — er — thinking —"

"It was of no consequence, Mr. Schmidt," she said airly.

He picked up the thread once more. "As a matter of fact, I've heard it said that Miss Blithers refused to marry the Prince."

"Is it possible?" with fine irony. "Is he such a dreadful person as all that?"

"I'm sure I don't know," murmured Robin uncomfortably. "He may be no more dreadful than she."

"I cannot hear you, Mr. Schmidt," she persisted, with unmistakeable malice in her lovely eyes.

"I'm rather glad that you didn't," he confessed. "Silly remark, you know."

"Well, I hope she doesn't marry him," said Miss Guile.

"So do I," said R. Schmidt, and their eyes met. After a moment, she looked away, her first surrender to the mysterious something that lay deep in his.

"It would prove that all American girls are not so black as they're painted, wouldn't it?" she said, striving to regain the ground she had lost by that momentary lapse.

"Pray do not overlook the fact that I am half American," he said. "You must not expect me to say that they paint at all."

"Schmidt is a fine old American name," she mused, the mischief back in her eyes.

"And so is Bedelia," said he.

"Will you pardon me, Mr. Schmidt, if I express

surprise that you speak English without the tiniest suggestion of an accent?"

"I will pardon you for everything and anything, Miss Guile," said he, quite too distinctly. She drew back in her chair and the light of raillery died in her eyes.

"What an imperial sound it has!"

"And why not? The R stands for Rex."

"Ah, that accounts for the King's English!"

"Certainly," he grinned. "The king can do no wrong, don't you see?"

"Your servant who was here speaks nothing but the King's English, I perceive. Perhaps that accounts for a great deal."

"Hobbs? I mean to say, 'Obbs? I confess that he has taught me many tricks of the tongue. He is one of the crown jewels."

Suddenly, and without reason, she appeared to be bored. As a matter of fact, she hid an incipient yawn behind her small gloved hand.

"I think I shall go to my room. Will you kindly unwrap me, Mr. Schmidt?"

He promptly obeyed, and then assisted her to her feet, steadying her against the roll of the vessel.

"I shall pray for continuous rough weather," he announced, with as gallant a bow as could be made under the circumstances.

"Thank you," she said, and he was pleased to take it that she was not thanking him for a physical service.

A few minutes later he was in his own room, and

she was in hers, and the promenade deck was as barren
as the desert of Sahara.

He found Count Quinnox stretched out upon his
bed, attended not only by Hobbs but also the re-
animated Dank. The crumpled message lay on the
floor.

"I'm glad you waited awhile," said the young
lieutenant, getting up from the trunk on which he had
been sitting. "If you had come any sooner you
would have heard words fit only for a soldier to hear.
It really was quite appalling."

"He's better now," said Hobbs, more respectfully
than was his wont. It was evident that he had sustained quite a shock.

"Well, what do you think of it?" demanded the
Prince, pointing to the message.

"Of all the confounded inpudence —" began the
Count healthily, and then uttered a mighty groan of
impotence. It was clear that he could not do justice
to the occasion a second time.

Robin picked up the Marconigram, and calmly
smoothed out the crinkles. Then he read it aloud,
very slowly and with extreme disgust in his fine young
face. It was a lengthy communication from Baron
Romano, the Prime Minister in Edelweiss.

"'Preliminary agreement signed before hearing
Blithers had bought London, Paris, Berlin. He cables
his immediate visit to G. Object now appears clear.
All newspapers in Europe print despatches from
America that marriage is practically arranged be-

"I shall **pray** for continuous rough weather"

tween R. and M. Interviews with Blithers corroborate reported engagement. Europe is amused. Editorials sarcastic. Price on our securities advance two points on confirmation of report. We are bewildered. Also vague rumour they have eloped, but denied by B. Dawsbergen silent. What does it all mean? Wire truth to me. People are uneasy. Gourou will meet you in Paris.'"

In the adjoining suite, Miss Guile was shaking Mrs. Gaston out of a long-courted and much needed sleep. The poor lady sat up and blinked feebly at the excited, starry-eyed girl.

"Wake up!" cried Bedelia impatiently. "What do you think? I have a perfectly wonderful suspicion — perfectly wonderful."

"How can you be so unfeeling?" moaned the limp lady.

"This R. Schmidt is Prince Robin of Graustark!" cried the girl excitedly. "I am sure of it — just as sure as can be."

Mrs. Gaston's eyes were popping, not with amazement but alarm.

"Do lie down, child," she whimpered. "Marie! The sleeping powders at once! Do —"

"Oh, I'm not mad," cried the girl. "Now listen to me and I'll tell you why I believe — yes, actually believe him to be the —"

"Marie, do you hear me?"

Miss Guile shook her vigorously. "Wake up! It isn't a nightmare. Now listen!"

CHAPTER XI

THE next day brought not only an agreeable change in
the weather but a most surprising alteration in the
manner of Mrs. Gaston, whose attitude toward R.
Schmidt and his friends had been anything but ami-
cable up to the hour of Miss Guile's discovery. The
excellent lady, recovering very quickly from her in-
disposition became positively polite to the hitherto
repugnant Mr. Schmidt. She melted so abruptly and
so completely that the young man was vaguely
troubled. He began to wonder if his incognito had
been pierced, so to speak.

It was not reasonable to suppose that Miss Guile
was personally responsible for this startling transi-
tion from the inimical to the gracious on the part of
her companion; the indifference of Miss Guile herself
was sufficient proof to the contrary. Therefore, when
Mrs. Gaston nosed him out shortly after breakfast
and began to talk about the beautiful day in a manner
so thoroughly respectful that it savoured of servility,
he was taken-aback, flabbergasted. She seemed to be
on the point of dropping her knee every time she
spoke to him, and there was an unmistakable tremor
of excitement in her voice even when she confided to
him that she adored the ocean when it was calm. He

forbore asking when Miss Guile might be expected to appear on deck for her constitutional but she volunteered the information, which was neither vague nor yet definite. In fact, she said that Miss Guile would be up soon, and soon is a word that has a double meaning when applied to the movements of capricious womanhood. It may mean ten minutes and it may mean an hour and a half.

Mrs. Gaston's severely critical eyes were no longer severe, albeit they were critical. She took him in from head to foot with the eye of an appraiser, and the more she took him in the more she melted, until at last in order to keep from completely dissolving, she said good-bye to him and hurried off to find Miss Guile.

Now it is necessary to relate that Miss Guile had been particularly firm in her commands to Mrs. Gaston. She literally had stood the excellent lady up in a corner and lectured her for an hour on the wisdom of silence. In the first place, Mrs. Gaston was given to understand that she was not to breathe it to a soul that R. Schmidt was not R. Schmidt, and she was not to betray to him by word or sign that he was suspected of being the Prince of Graustark. Moreover, the exacting Miss Guile laid great stress upon another command: R. Schmidt was never to know that she was *not* Miss Guile, but some one else altogether.

"You're right, my dear," exclaimed Mrs. Gaston in an excited whisper as she burst in upon her fair companion, who was having coffee and toast in her parlour. The more or less resuscitated Marie was waiting to do up her mistress's hair, and the young lady herself was alluringly charming in spite of the fact that it was not already " done up." " He is the — er — he is just what you think."

" Good heavens, you haven't gone and done it, have you," cried the girl, a slim hand halting with a piece of toast half way to her lips.

" Gone and done it? "

" You haven't been blabbing, have you? "

" How can you say that to me? Am I not to be trusted? Am I so weak and —"

" Don't cry, you old dear! Forgive me. But now tell me — absolutely — just what you've been up to. Don't mind Marie. She is French. She can always hold her tongue."

" Well, I've been talking with him, that's all. I'm sure he is the Prince. No ordinary male could be as sweet and agreeable and sunny as —"

" Stop! " cried Miss Guile, with a pretty moue, putting the tips of her fingers to her ears after putting the piece of toast into her mouth. " One would think you were a sentimental old maid instead of a cold-blooded, experienced, man-hating married woman."

" You forget that I am a widow, my dear. Besides, it is disgusting for one to speak with one's mouth full of buttered toast. It —"

" Oh, how I used to loathe you when you kept forever ding-donging at me about the way I ate when I was almost starving. Were you never a hungry little kid? Did you never lick jam and honey off your fingers and —"

" Many and many a time," confessed Mrs. Gaston, beaming once more and laying a gentle, loving hand on the girl's shoulder. Miss Guile dropped her head over until her cheek rested on the caressing hand, and munched toast with blissful abandon.

" Now tell me what you've been up to," she said, and Mrs. Gaston repeated every word of the conversation she had had with R. Schmidt, proving absolutely nothing but stoutly maintaining that her intuition was completely to be depended upon.

" And, oh," she whispered in conclusion, " wouldn't it be perfectly wonderful if you two should fall in love with each other —"

" Don't be silly!"

" But you have said that if he should fall in love with you for yourself and not because —"

" I have also said that I will not marry any man, prince, duke, king, count or anything else unless I am in love with him. Don't overlook that, please."

" But he is really very nice. I should think you could fall in love with him. Just think how it would please your father and mother. Just think —"

" I won't be bullied!"

" Am I bullying you?" in amazement.

" No; but father tries to bully me, and you know it."

"You must admit that the — this Mr. Schmidt is handsome, charming, bright —"

"I admit nothing," said Miss Guile resolutely, and ordered Marie to dress her hair as carefully as possible. "Take as long as you like, Marie. I shall not go on deck for hours."

"I — I told him you would be up soon," stammered the poor, man-hating ex-governess.

"You did?" said Miss Guile, with what was supposed to be a deadly look in her eyes.

"Well, he enquired," said the other.

"Anything else?" domineered the beauty.

"I forgot to mention one thing. He *did* ask me if your name was really Bedelia."

"And what did you tell him?" cried the girl, in sudden agitation.

"I managed to tell him that it was," said Mrs. Gaston stiffly.

"Good!" cried Miss Guile, vastly relieved, and not at all troubled over the blight that had been put upon a very worthy lady's conscience.

When she appeared on deck long afterward, she found every chair occupied. A warm sun, a far from turbulent sea, and a refreshing breeze had brought about a marvellous transformation. Every one was happy, every one had come back from the grave to gloat over the grim reaper's failure to do his worst, although in certain cases he had been importuned to do it without hesitation.

She made several brisk rounds of the deck; then,

feeling that people were following her with their eyes,
— admiringly, to be sure, but what of that? — she
abandoned the pleasant exercise and sought the seclusion of ·the sunless corner ' where her chair was
stationed.   The ship's daily newspaper was just off
the press and many of the loungers were reading the
brief telegraphic news from the capitals of the world.

During her stroll she passed several groups of
men and women who were lightly, even scornfully employed in discussing an article of news which had to
do with Mr. Blithers and the Prince of Graustark.
Filled with an acute curiosity, she procured a copy of
the paper from a steward, and was glancing at the
head lines as she made her way into her corner.
Double-leaded type appeared over the rumoured en-
gagment of Miss Maud Applegate Blithers, the beautiful and accomplished daughter of the great capitalist,
and Robin, Prince of Graustark.   A queer little smile
played about her lips as she folded the paper for
future perusal.   Turning the corner of the deck-
building she almost collided with R. Schmidt, who
stood leaning against the wall, scanning the little
newspaper with eyes that were blind to everything
else.

" Oh! " she gasped.

" I'm sorry," he exclaimed, crumpling the paper in
his hand as he backed away, flushing.   " Stupid of me.
Good morning."

" Good morning, Mr. Schmidt.   It wasn't your
fault.   I should have looked where I was going.

MICROCOPY RESOLUTION TEST CHART

(ANSI and ISO TEST CHART No. 2)

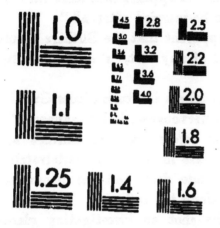

 APPLIED IMAGE Inc

1653 East Main Street
Rochester, New York   14609   USA
(716) 482 - 0300 - Phone
(716) 288 - 5989 - Fax

'Stop, look and listen,' as they say at the railway crossing."

"'Danger' is one of the commonest signs, Miss Guile. It lurks everywhere, especially around corners. I see you have a paper. It appears that Miss Blithers and the Prince are to be married after all."

"Yes; it is quite apparent that the Blithers family intends to have a title at any cost," she said, and her eyes flashed.

"Would you like to take a few turns, Miss Guile?" he inquired, a trace of nervousness in his manner. "I think I can take you safely over the hurdles and around the bunkers." He indicated the outstretched legs along the promenade deck and the immovable groups of chatterers along the rail.

Before deciding, she shot an investigating glance into the corner. Mrs. Gaston was not only there but was engaged in conversation with the grey-moustached gentleman in a near-by chair. It required but half a glance to show that Mr. Totten was unmistakably interested in something the voluble lady had just said to him.

"No, thank you, Mr. Schmidt," said Miss Guile hastily, and then hurried over to her chair, a distinct cloud on her smooth brow. Robin, considering himself dismissed, whirled and went his way, a dark flush spreading over his face. Never, in all his life, had he been quite so out of patience with the world as on this bright, sunny morning.

Miss Guile's frown deepened when her abrupt appearance at Mrs. Gaston's side caused that lady to look up with a guilty start and to break off in the middle of a sentence that had begun with: "International marriages, as a rule, are — Oh!"

Mr. Totten arose and bowed with courtly grace to the new arrival on the scene. He appeared to be immensely relieved.

"A lovely morning, Miss Guile," he said as he stooped to arrange her rug. "I hear that you were not at all disturbed by yesterday's blow."

"I was just telling Mr. Totten that you are a wonderful sailor," said Mrs. Gaston, a note of appeal in her voice. "He says his friend, Mr. Schmidt, is also a good sailor. Isn't it perfectly wonderful?"

"I can't see anything wonderful about it," said Miss Guile, fixing the ex-governess with a look that seared.

"We were speaking of this rumoured engagement of the Prince of Graustark and — er — what's the name?" He glanced at his newspaper. "Miss Blithers, of course. I enquired of Mrs.— er — Gaston if she happens to know the young lady. She remembers seeing her frequently as a very small child."

"In Paris," said Mrs. Gaston. "One couldn't very well help seeing her, you know. She was the only child of the great Mr. Blithers, whose name was on every one's lips at the —"

Miss Guile interrupted. "It would be like the

great Mr. Blithers to buy this toy prince for his daughter — as a family plaything or human lap-dog, or something of the sort, wouldn't it?"

Mr. Totten betrayed no emotion save amusement. Miss Guile was watching through half-closed eyes. There was a noticeable stiffening of the prim figure of Mrs. Gaston.

"I've no doubt Mr. Blithers can afford to buy the most expensive of toys for his only child. You Americans go in for the luxuries of life. What could be more extravagant than the purchase of a royal lap-dog? The only drawback I can suggest is that the Prince might turn out to be a cur, and then where would Mr. Blithers be?"

"It is more to the point to ask where Miss Blithers would be, Mr. Totten," said Miss Guile, with a smile that caused the fierce old warrior to afterwards declare to Dank that he never had seen a lovelier girl in all his life.

"Ah, but we spoke of the Prince as a lap-dog or a cur, Miss Guile, not as a watch-dog," said he.

"I see," said Miss Guile, after a moment. "He wouldn't sleep with one eye open. I see."

"The lap of luxury is an enviable resting-place. I know of no prince who would despise it."

"But a wife is sometimes a thing to be despised," said she.

"Quite true," said Mr. Totten. "I've no doubt that the Prince of Graustark will despise his wife, and for that reason will be quite content to close both eyes and let her go on searching for her heart's desire."

"She would be his Princess. Could he afford to allow his love of luxury to go as far as that?"

"Quite as justifiably, I should say, as Mr. Blithers when he delivers his only child into — into bondage."

"You were about to use another term."

"I was, but I thought in time, Miss Guile."

R. Schmidt sauntered briskly past at this juncture, looking neither to the right nor left. They watched him until he disappeared down the deck.

"I think Mr. Schmidt is a perfectly delightful young man," said Mrs. Gaston, simply because she couldn't help it.

"You really think he will marry Miss Blithers, Mr. Totten?" ventured Miss Guile.

"He? Oh, I see — the Prince?" Mr. Totten came near to being no diplomat. "How should I know, Miss Guile?"

"Of course! How *should* you know?" she cried.

Mr. Totten found something to interest him in the printed sheet and proceeded to read it with considerable avidity. Miss Guile smiled to herself and purposely avoided the shocked look in Mrs. Gaston's eyes.

"Bouillon at last," cried the agitated duenna, and peremptorily summoned one of the tray-bearing stewards. "I am famished."

Evidently Mr. Totten did not care for his mid-morning refreshment, for, with the most courtly of smiles, he arose and left them to their bouillon.

"Here comes Mr. Schmidt," whispered Mrs. Gaston

excitedly, a few moments later, and at once made a movement indicative of hasty departure.

"Sit still," said Miss Guile peremptorily.

R. Schmidt again passed them by without so much as a glance in their direction. There was a very sweet smile on Miss Guile's lips as she closed her eyes and lay back in her chair. Once, twice, thrice, even as many as six times R. Schmidt strode rapidly by their corner, his head high and his face aglow.

At last a queer little pucker appeared on the serene brow of the far from drowsy young lady whose eyes peeped through half closed lids. Suddenly she threw off her rug and with a brief remark to her companion arose and went to her cabin. Mrs. Gaston followed, not from choice but because the brief remark was in the form of a command.

Soon afterward, R. Schmidt who had been joined by Dank, threw himself into his chair with a great sigh of fatigue and said:

"'Gad, I've walked a hundred miles since breakfast. Have you a match?"

"Hobbs has made a very curious discovery," said the young lieutenant, producing his match-box. There was a perturbed look in his eyes.

"If Hobbs isn't careful he'll discover a new continent one of these days. He is always discovering something," said Robin, puffing away at his pipe.

"But this is really interesting. It seems that he was in the hold when Miss Guile's maid came down to get into one of her mistress's trunks. Now, the first

letter in Guile is G, isn't it?   Well, Hobbs says there
are at least half-a-dozen trunks there belonging to the
young lady and that all of them are marked with a
large red B.   What do you make of it? "

The Prince had stopped puffing at his pipe.
"Hobbs may be mistaken in the maid, Dank.   It
is likely that they are not Miss Guile's trunks, at all."

"He appears to be absolutely sure of his ground.
He heard the maid mention Miss Guile's name when
she directed the men to get one of the trunks out of the
pile.   That's what attracted his attention.   He confided to me that you are interested in the young lady,
and therefore it was quite natural for him to be simi-
larly affected.   'Like master, like man,' d'ye see? "

"Really, you know, Dank, I ought to dismiss
Hobbs," said Robin irritably.   "He is getting to be
a dreadful nuisance.   Always nosing around, trying
to —"

"But after all, sir, you'll have to admit that he has
made a puzzling discovery.   Why should her luggage
be marked with a B? "

"I should say because her name begins with a B,"
said Robin shortly.

"In that case, it isn't Guile."

"Obviously."   The young man was thinking very
hard.

"And if it isn't Guile, there must be an excellent
reason for her sailing under a false name.   She doesn't
look like an adventuress."

R. Schmidt rewarded this remark with a cold stare.

" Would you mind telling me what she does look like, Dank? " he enquired severely.

The lieutenant flushed. " I have not had the same opportunity for observation that you've enjoyed, sir, but I should say, off-hand, that she looks like a very dangerous young person."

" Do you mean to imply that she is — er — not altogether what one would call right? "

Dank grinned. " Don't you regard her as rather perilously beautiful? "

" Oh, I see. That's what you mean. I suppose you got *that* from Hobbs, too."

" Not at all. I have an excellent pair of eyes."

" What are you trying to get at, Dank? " demanded Robin abruptly.

" I'm trying to get to the bottom of Miss Guile's guile, if it please your royal highness," said the lieutenant coolly. " It is hard to connect the B and the G, you know."

" But why should we deny her a privilege that we are enjoying, all three of us? Are we not in the same boat? "

" Literally and figuratively. That explains nothing, however."

" Have you a theory? "

" There are many that we could advance, but, of course, only one of them could be the right one, even if we were acute enough to include it in our list of guesses. She may have an imperative reason for not disclosing her identity. For instance, she may be running away to get married."

"That's possible," agreed Robin.

"But not probable. She may be a popular music-hall favourite, or one of those peculiarly clever creatures known as the American newspaper woman, against whom we have been warned. Don't you regard it as rather significant that of all the people on this ship she should be one to attach herself to the unrecognised Prince of Graustark? Put two and two together, sir, and —"

"I find it singularly difficult to put one and one together, Dank," said the Prince ruefully. "No; you are wrong in both of your guesses. I've encountered music-hall favourites and I can assure you she isn't one of them. And as for your statement that she attached herself to me, you were never so mistaken in your life. I give you my word, she doesn't care a hang whether I'm on the ship or clinging to a life preserver out there in the middle of the Atlantic. I have reason to know, Dank."

"So be it," said Dank, but with doubt in his eyes. "You ought to know. I've never spoken to her, so —"

"She thinks you are a dreadfully attractive chap, Dank," said Robin mischievously. "She said so only yesterday."

Dank gave his prince a disgusted look, and smoked on in silence. His dignity was ruffled.

"Her Christian name is Bedelia," ventured Robin, after a pause.

"That doesn't get us anywhere," said Dank sourly.

"And her mother is Irish."

"Which accounts for those wonderful Irish blue eyes that —"

"So you've noticed them, eh?"

"Naturally."

"I consider them a very dark grey."

"I think we'd better get back to the luggage," said Dank hastily. "Hobbs thinks that she —"

"Oh, Lord, Dank, don't tell me what Hobbs thinks," growled Robin. "Let her make use of all the letters in the alphabet if it pleases her. What is it to us? Moreover, she may be utilising a lot of borrowed trunks, who knows? Or B may have been her initial before she was divorced and —"

"Divorced?"

"— her maiden name restored," concluded Robin airily. "Simple deduction, Dank. Dor't bother your head about her any longer. What w: know isn't going to hurt us, and what we don't know isn't —"

"Has it occurred to you that Russia may have set spies upon you —"

"Nonsense!"

"It isn't as preposterous as you —"

"Come, old fellow, let's forget Miss Guile," cried Robin, slapping the lieutenant on the shoulder. "Let's think of the real peril,— Maud Applegate

Blithers." He held up the ship's paper for Dank to see and then sat back to enjoy his companion's rage.

An hour later Dank and Count Quinnox might have been seen seated side by side on the edge of a skylight at the tip-top of the ship's structure, engaged in the closest conversation. There was a troubled look in the old man's eyes and the light of adventure in those of his junior. The sum and substance of their discussion may be given in a brief sentence: Something would have to be done to prevent Robin from falling in love with the fascinating Miss Guile.

"He is young enough and stubborn enough to make a fool of himself over her," the Count had said. "I wouldn't blame him, 'pon my soul I wouldn't. She is very attractive — ahem! You must be his safeguard, Dank. Go in and do as I suggest. You are a good looking chap and you've nothing to lose. So far as she is concerned, you are quite as well worth while as the fellow known as R. Schmidt. There's no reason why you shouldn't make the remainder of the passage pleasant for her, and at the same time enjoy yourself at nobody's expense."

"They know by instinct, confound 'em," lamented Dank; "they know the real article, and you can't fool 'em. She knows that he is the high muck-a-muck in this party and she won't even look at me, you take my word for it."

"At any rate, you can try, can't you?" said the Count impatiently.

"Is it a command, sir?"

"It is."

"Very well, sir. I shall do my best."

"We can't afford to have him losing his head over a pretty — er — a nobody, perhaps an adventuress, — at this stage of the game. I much prefer the impossible Miss Blithers, Dank, to this captivating unknown. At least we know who and what she is, and what she represents. But we owe it to our country and to Dawsbergen to see that he doesn't do anything — er — foolish. We have five days left of this voyage, Dank. They may be fatal days for him, if you do not come to the rescue."

"They may be fatal days for me," said Dank, looking out over the ocean.

CHAPTER XII

FIVE days later as the *Jupiter* was discharging passengers at Plymouth, Count Quinnox and Lieutenant Dank stood well forward on the promenade deck watching the operations. The younger man was moody and distrait, an unusual condition for him but one that had been noticeably recurrent during the past two or three days. He pulled at his smart little moustache and looked out upon the world through singularly lack-lustre eyes. Something had gone wrong with him, and it was something that he felt in duty bound to lay before his superior, the grim old Minister of War and hereditary chief of the Castle Guard. Occasionally his sombre gaze shifted to a spot farther down the deck, where a young man and woman leaned upon the rail and surveyed the scene of activity below.

"What is on your mind, Dank?" asked the Count abruptly. "Out with it."

Dank started. "It's true, then? I *do* look as much of a fool as I feel, eh?" There was bitterness in his usually cheery voice.

"Feel like a fool, eh?" growled the old soldier.

"Pretty mess I've made of the business," lamented Dank surlily. "Putting myself up as a contender against a fellow like Robin, and dreaming that I could win out, even for a minute! Good Lord, what an ass I am! Why we've only made it worse, Count. We've touched him with the spur of rivalry, and what could be more calamitous than that? From being a rather matter-of-fact, indifferent observer, he becomes a bewildering cavalier bent on conquest at any cost. I am swept aside as if I were a parcel of rags. For two days I stood between him and the incomparable Miss Guile. Then he suddenly arouses himself. My cake is dough. I am nobody. My feet get cold, as they say in America,— although I don't know why they say it. What has the temperature of one's feet to do with it? See! There they are. They are constantly together, walking, sitting, standing, eating, drinking, reading — *Eh bien!* You have seen with your own eyes. The beautiful Miss Guile has bewitched our Prince, and my labour is not only lost but I myself am lost. *Mon dieu!*"

The Count stared at him in perplexity for a moment. Then a look of surprise came into his eyes,— surprise not unmingled with scorn.

"You don't mean to say, Dank, that you've fallen in love with her? Oh, you absurd fledgelings. Will you —"

"Forgive my insolence, Count, but it is forty years since you were a fledgeling. You don't see things as you saw them forty years ago. Permit me to remind you that you are a grandfather."

"Your point is well taken, my lad," said the Count,

with a twinkle in his eye. "You can't help being young any more than I can help being old. Youth is perennial, old age a winding-sheet. I am to take it, then, that you've lost your heart to the fair —"

"Why not?" broke in Dank fiercely. "Why should it appear incredible to you? Is she not the most entrancing creature in all the world? Is she not the most appealing, the most adorable, the most feminine of all her sex? Is it possible that one can be so old that it is impossible for him to feel the charm, the loveliness, the —"

"For heaven's sake, Dank," said the old man in alarm, "don't gesticulate so wildly. People will think we are quarrelling. Calm yourself, my boy."

"You set a task for me and I obey. You urge me to do my duty by Graustark. You tell me I am a handsome dog and irresistible. She will be overwhelmed by my manly beauty, my valour, my soldierly bearing,— so say you! And what is the outcome? I — I, the vain-glorious,— I am wrapped around her little finger so tightly that all the king's horses and all the king's men —"

"Halt!" commanded his general softly. "You are turning tail like the veriest coward. Right about, face! Would you surrender to a slip of a girl whose only weapons are a pair of innocent blue eyes and a roguish smile? Be a man! Stand by your guns. Outwardly you are the equal of R. Schmidt, whose sole —"

"That sounds very well, sir, but how can I take up

arms against my Prince? He stands by *his* guns —
as you may see, sir,— and, dammit all, I'm no traitor.
I've just got to stand by 'em with him. That rot
about all being fair in love and war is the silliest —
Oh, well, there's no use whining about it. I'm mad
about her, and so is he. You can't —"

The Count stopped him with a sharp gesture. A
look of real concern appeared in his eyes.

" Do you believe that he is actually in love with this
girl? "

" Heels over head," barked the unhappy lieutenant.
" I've never seen a worse case."

" This is serious — more serious than I thought."

" It's horrible," declared Dank, but not thinking of
the situation from the Count's point of view.

" We do not know who or what she is. She may
be —"

" I beg your pardon, sir, but we do know what she
is," said the other firmly. " You will not pretend to
say that she is not a gentlewoman. She is cultured,
refined —"

" I grant all of that," said the Count. " I am not
blind, Dank. But it seems fairly certain that her
name is not Guile. We —"

" Nor is his name Schmidt. That's no argument,
sir."

" Still we cannot take the chance, my lad. We
must put an end to this fond adventure. Robin is
our most precious possession. We must not — Why
do you shake your head? "

"We are powerless, sir. If he makes up his mind to marry Miss Guile, he'll do it in spite of anything we can do. That is, provided she is of the same mind."

"God defend us, I fear you are right," groaned the old Count. "He has declared himself a hundred times, and he is a wilful lad. I recall the uselessness of the opposition that was set up against his lamented mother when she decided to marry Grenfell Lorry. 'Gad, sir, it was like butting into a stone wall. She said she *would* and she did. I fear me that Robin has much of his mother in him."

"Behold in me the first sacrifice," declaimed Dank, lifting his eyes heavenward.

"Oh, you will recover," was the unsympathetic rejoinder. "It is for him that I fear, not for you."

"Recover, sir?" in despair. "I fear you misjudge my humble heart —"

"Bosh! Your heart has been through a dozen accidents of this character, Dank, and it is good for a hundred more. I'll rejoice when this voyage is ended and we have him safe on his way to Edelweiss."

"That will not make the slightest difference, sir. If he sets his head to marry her he'll do it if we take him to the North Pole. All Graustark can't stop him, — nor old man Blithers either. Besides, he says he isn't going to Edelweiss immediately."

"That is news to me."

"I thought it would be. He came to the decision

not more than two hours ago. He is determined to spend a couple of weeks at Interlaken."

" Interlaken? "

" Yes. Miss Guile expects to stop there for a fort-night after leaving Paris."

" I must remonstrate with Robin — at once," declared the old man. " He is needed in Graustark. He must be made to realise the importance of —"

" And what are you going to do if he declines to realise anything but the importance of a fortnight in the shadow of the Jungfrau? "

" God help me, I don't know, Dank." The Count's brow was moist, and he looked anything but an uncon-querable soldier.

" I told him we were expected to reach home by the end of next week, and he said that a quiet fortnight in the Alps would make new men of all of us."

" Do you mean to say he expects me to daw-dle —"

" More than that, sir. He also expects me to daw-dle too. I shall probably shoot myself before the two weeks are over."

" I have it! I shall take Mrs. Gaston into my con-fidence. It is the only hope, I fear. I shall tell her that he is —"

" No hope there," said Dank mournfully. " Haven't you noticed how keen she is to have them together all the time? She's as wily as a fox. Never misses a chance. Hasn't it occurred to you to wonder why she drags you off on the slightest pretext when you happen to be in the way? She's done it a hundred times. Always leaving them alone together. My God, how I despise that woman! Not once but twenty times a day she finds an excuse to interfere when I am trying to get in a few words with Miss Guile. She's forever wanting me to show her the engine-room or the Captain's bridge or the wireless office or — why, by jove, sir, it was only yesterday that she asked me to come and look at the waves. Said she'd found a splendid place to see them from, just as if the whole damned Atlantic wasn't full of 'em. And isn't she always looking for porpoises on the opposite side of the ship? And how many whales and ice-bergs do you think she's been trying to find in the last five days? No, sir! There's no hope there!"

" 'Pon my soul!" was all that the poor Minister of War, an adept in strategy, was able to exclaim.

The *Jupiter* disgorged most of her passengers at Cherbourg and the descent upon Paris had scarcely begun when the good ship steamed away for Antwerp, Bremen and Hamburg. She was one of the older vessels in the vast fleet of ships controlled by the American All-Seas and All-Ports Company, and she called wherever there was a port open to trans-Atlantic navigation. She was a single factor in the great monopoly described as the " Billion Dollar Boast." The United States had been slow to recognise the profits of seas that were free, but when she did wake up she proceeded to act as if she owned them and all that therein lay. Her people spoke of the Gulf Stream as " ours ";

of the Banks of Newfoundland as "ours"?— or in some instances as "ourn"; of Liverpool, Hamburg, London, Bremen and other such places as "our European terminals"; and of the various oceans, seas and navigable waters as "a part of the system." Where once the Stars and Stripes were as rare as humming-birds in Baffin's Bay, the flags were now so thick that they resembled Fourth of July decorations on Fifth avenue, and it was almost impossible to cross the Atlantic without dodging a hundred vessels on which Dixie was being played, coming and going. A man from New Hampshire declared, after one of his trips over and back, that he cheered the good old tune so incessantly that his voice failed on the third day out, both ways, and he had to voice his patriotism with a tin horn.

Ships of the All-Seas and All-Ports Company fairly stuffed the harbours of the world. America was awake at last — wide awake! — and the necessity for prodding her was now limited to the task of putting her to sleep long enough to allow other nations a chance to scrape together enough able bodied seamen to man the ships.

William W. Blithers was one of the directors of the All-Seas and All-Ports Company. He was the first American to awake.

For some unaccountable reason Miss Guile and her companion preferred to travel alone to Paris. They had a private compartment, over which a respectful but adamantine conductor exercised an authority that

irritated R. Schmidt beyond expression.* The rest of
the t· ı was crowded to its capacity, and here was desirable space going to waste in the section occupied
by the selfish Miss Guile. He couldn't understand
it in her. Was it, after all, to be put down as a simple
steamer encounter? Was she deliberately snubbing
him, now that they were on land? Was he, a prince
of the royal blood, to be tossed aside by this purse-
proud American as if he were the simplest of simple-
tons? And what did she mean by stationing an offi-
cious hireling before her door to order him away when
he undertook to pay her a friendly visit?—to offer
his own and Hobbs' services in case they were needed
in Paris. Why should she lock her confounded door
anyway,—and draw the curtains? There were other
whys too numerous to mention, and there wasn't an
answer to a single one of them. The whole proceeding was incomprehensible.

To begin with, she certainly made no effort to con-
ceal the fact that she was trying to avoid him from
the instant the tender drew alongside to take off the
passengers. As a matter of fact, she seemed to be
making a point of it. And yet, the evening before,
she had appeared rather enchanted with the prospect
of seeing him at Interlaken.

It was not until the boat-train was nearing the en-
virons of Paris that Hobbs threw some light over the
situation, with the result that it instantly became
darker than ever before. It appears that Miss Guile
was met at the landing by a very good-looking young

man who not only escorted her to the train but actually entered it with her, and was even now enjoying the luxury of a private compartment as well as the contents of a large luncheon hamper, to say nothing of an uninterrupted view of something far more inspiring than the scenery.

"Frenchman?" inquired Dank listlessly.

"American, I should say, sir," said Hobbs, balancing himself in the corridor outside the door and sticking his head inside with more confidence than a traveller usually feels when travelling from Cherbourg to Paris. "But I wouldn't swear to it, sir. I didn't 'ear a word he said, being quite some distance away at the time. Happearances are deceptive, as I've said a great many times. A man may look like an American and still be almost anything else, see wot I mean? On the other hand, a man may look like almost nothing and still be American to his toes. I remember once saying to —"

"That's all right, Hobbs," broke in R. Schmidt sternly. "We also remember what you said, so don't repeat it. How soon do we get in?"

Hobbs cheerfully looked at his watch. "I couldn't say positive, sir, but I should think in about fourteen and a 'alf minutes, or maybe a shade under — between fourteen and fourteen and a 'alf, sir. As I was saying, he was a most intelligent looking chap, sir, and very 'andsome of face and figger. Between twenty-four and twenty-five, I dare say. Light haired, smooth-faced, quite tall and dressed in dark blue with a cravat, sir, that looked like cerise but may have been —"

"For heaven's sake, Hobbs, let up!" cried Robin, throwing up his hands.

"Yes, sir; certainly, sir. Did I mention that he wears a straw 'at with a crimson band on it? Well, if I didn't, he does. Hincidentally, they seemed greatly pleased to see each other. He kissed her hand, and looked as though he might have gone even farther than that if it 'adn't been for the crowd —"

"That will do!" said Robin sharply, a sudden flush mounting to his cheek.

"Very good, sir. Shall I get the bags down for the porters, sir? I beg pardon, sir,—" to one of the three surly gentlemen who sat facing the travellers from Graustark,—"my fault entirely. I don't believe it is damaged, sir. Allow me to —"

"Thank you," growled the stranger. "I can put it on myself," and he jerked his hat out of Hobbs' hand and set it at a rather forbidding angle above a lowering brow. "Look what you're doing after this, will you?"

"Certainly, sir," said Hobbs agreeably. "It's almost impossible to see without eyes in the back of one's head, don't you know. I 'ope —"

"All right, all right!" snapped the man, glaring balefully. "And let me tell you something else, my man. Don't go about knocking Americans without first taking a look. Just bear that in mind, will you?"

"The surest way is to listen," began Hobbs loftily,
but, catching a look from his royal master, desisted.
He proceeded to get down the hand luggage.

At the Gare St. Lazare, Robin had a brief glimpse
of Miss Guile as she hurried with the crowd down to
the cab enclosure, where her escort, the alert young
stranger, put her into a waiting limousine, bundled
Mrs. Gaston and Marie in after her, and then dashed
away, obviously to see their luggage through the
douane.

She espied the tall figure of her fellow voyager near
the steps and leaned forward to wave a perfunctory
farewell to him. The car was creeping out toward
the packed thoroughfare. It is possible that she expected him to dash among the chortling machines, at
risk of life or limb, for a word or two at parting. If
so, she was disappointed. He remained perfectly still,
with uplifted hat, a faint smile on his lips and not the
slightest sign of annoyance in his face. She smiled
securely to herself as she leaned back in the seat, and
was satisfied! Curiosity set its demand upon her an
instant later, however, and she peered slyly through
the little window in the back. He lifted his hat once
more and she flushed to her throat as she quickly drew
back into the corner. How in the world could he
have seen her through that abominable slit in the
limousine? And why was he now grinning so
broadly?

Count Quinnox found him standing there a few
minutes later, twirling his stick and smiling with his

eyes. Accompanying the old soldier was a slight, sharp-featured man with keen black eyes and a thin, pointed moustache of grey.

This man was Gou. ja, Chief of Police and Commander of the Tower in Edelweiss, successor to the celebrated Baron Dangloss. After he had greeted his prince, the quiet little man announced that he had reserved for him an apartment at the Bristol.

" I am instructed by the Prime Minister, your highness, to urge your immediate return to Edelweiss," he went on, lowering his voice. " The people are disturbed by the reports that have reached us during the past week or two, and Baron Romano is convinced that nothing will serve to subdue the feeling of uneasiness that prevails except your own declaration — in person — that these reports are untrue."

" I shall telegraph at once to Baron Romano that it is all poppy-cock," said Robin easily. " I refer, of course, to the reported engagement. I am not going to marry Miss Blithers and that's all there is to be said. You may see to it, baron, that a statement is issued to all of the Paris newspapers to-day, and to the correspondents for all the great papers in Europe and America. I have prepared this statement, under my own signature, and it is to be the last word in the matter. It is in my pocket at this instant. You shall have it when we reach the hotel — And that reminds me of another thing. I'm sorry that I shall have to ask you to countermand the reservation for rooms at the hotel you mention. I have already re-

served rooms at the Ritz,—by wireless. We shall
stop there.   Where is Dank?"

"The Ritz is hardly the place for —"

But Robin clapped him on the back and favoured
him with the good-natured, boyish smile that mastered
even the fiercest of his counsellors, and the Minister
of Police, being an astute man, heaved a deep sigh of
resignation.

"Dank is looking after the trunks, highness, and
Hobbs is coming along with the hand luggage," he
said. "The Ritz, you say? Then I shall have to
instruct Lieutenant Dank to send the luggage there
instead of to the Bristol. Pardon, your highness.'
He was off like a flash.

Count Quinnox was gnawing his moustache. "See
here, Robin," he said, laying his hand on the young
man's shoulder, "you are in Paris now and not on
board a ship at sea.   Miss Guile is a beautiful, charming, highly estimable young woman, and, I might as
well say it straight out to your face, you ought not to
subject her to the notoriety that is bound to follow if
the newspapers learn that she is playing around Paris,
no matter how innocently, with a prince whom —"

"Just a moment, Count," interrupted Robin, a old
light in his now unsmiling eyes. "You are getting
a little ahead of the game. Miss Guile is not going
to the Ritz, nor do I expect her to play around Paris
with me. As a matter of fact, she refused to tell me
where she is to stop while here, and I am uncomfortably certain that I shall not see her unless by

chance. On the other hand, I may as well be perfectly frank with you and say it straight out to your face that I am going to try to find her if possible, but I am not mean enough to employ the methods common to such enterprises. I could have followed her car in another when she left here a few minutes ago; I could manage in a dozen ways to run her to earth, as the detectives do in the books, but I'd be ashamed to look her in the face if I did any of these things. I shall take a gentleman's chance, my dear Count, and trust to luck and the generosity of fate. You may be sure that I shall not annoy Miss Guile, and you may be equally sure that she —"

"I beg your pardon, Robin, but I did not employ the word annoy," protested the Count.

"— that she takes me for a gentleman if not for a prince," went on Robin, deliberately completing the sentence before he smiled his forgiveness upon the old man. "I selected the Ritz because all rich Americans go there, I'm told. I'm taking a chance."

Quinnox had an obstinate strain in his make-up. He continued: "There is another side to the case, my boy. As a gentleman, you cannot allow this lovely girl to — er — well, to fall in love with you. That would be cruel, wantonly cruel. And it is just the thing that is bound to happen if you go on with —"

"My dear Count, you forget that I am only R. Schmidt to her and but one of perhaps a hundred young men who have placed her in the same perilous position. Moreover, it's the other way 'round, sir.

It is I who take the risk, not Miss Guile. I regret to say, sir, that if there is to be any falling in love, I am the one who is most likely to fall, and to fall hard. You assume that Miss Guile is heart-whole and fancy free. 'Gad, I wish that I could be sure of it!" He spoke with such fervour that the Count was indeed dismayed.

"Robin, my lad, I beg of you to consider the consequences that —"

"There's no use discussing it, old friend. Trust to luck. There is a bully good chance that she will send me about my business when the time comes and then 'the salvation of Graustark will be assured." He said it lightly but there was a dark look in his eyes that belied the jaunty words.

"Am I to understand that you intend to — to ask her to marry you?" manded the Count, profoundly troubled. "Remember, boy, that you are the Prince of Graustark, that you —"

"But I'm not going to ask her to marry the Prince of Graustark. I'm going to ask her to marry R. Schmidt," said Robin composedly.

"God defend us, Robin, I — I —"

"God has all he can do to defend us from William W. Blithers, Count. Don't ask too much of him. What kind of a nation are we if we can't get along without asking God to defend us every time we see trouble ahead? And do you suppose he is going to defend us against a slip of a girl —"

"Enough! Enough!" cried the Count, compressing his lips and glaring straight ahead.

"That's the way to talk," cried Robin enthusiastically. "By the way, I hope Dank is clever enough to find out who that young fellow is while they are clearing the luggage in there. I had a good look at him just now. He is all that Hobbs describes and a little more. He is a hustler."

CHAPTER XIII

In the Baron's room at the Ritz late that night there was held a secret conference. Two shadowy figures stole down the corridor at midnight and were admitted to the room, while Prince Robin slept soundly in his remote four-poster and dreamed of something that brought a gentle smile to his lips.

The three conspirators were of the same mind: it was clear that something must be done. But what? That was the question. Gourou declared that the people were very much disturbed over the trick the great capitalist had played upon the cabinet; there were sullen threats of a revolt if the government insisted on the deposit of bonds as required by the agreement. More than that, there were open declarations that the daughter of Mr. Blithers would never be permitted to occupy the throne of Graustark. Deeply as his subjects loved the young Prince, they would force him to abdicate rather than submit to the desecration of a throne that had never been dishonoured. They would accept William W. Blithers' money, but they would have none of William W. Blithers' daughter. That was more than could be expected of any self-respecting people! According to the Minister of Police, the name of Blithers was already a common synonym for affliction — and frequently employed in supposing a malediction. It signified all that was mean, treacherous, scurrilous. He was spoken of through clenched teeth as " the blood sucker." Children were ominously reproved by the threatening use of the word Blithers. " Blithers will get you if you don't wash your face," and all that sort of thing.

There was talk in some circles of demanding the resignation of the cabinet, but even the pessimistic Gourou admitted that it was idle talk and would come to nothing if the menacing shadow of Maud Applegate Blithers could be banished from the vicinity of the throne. Graustarkians would abide by the compact made by their leading men and would be content to regard Mr. Blithers as a bona fide creditor. They would pay him in full when the loan matured, even though they were compelled to sacrifice their houses in order to accomplish that end. But, like all the rest of the world, they saw through the rich American's scheme.

The world knew, and Graustark knew, just what Mr. Blithers was after, and the worst of it all was that Mr. Blithers also knew, which was more to the point. But, said Baron Gourou, Graustark knew something that neither the world nor Mr. Blithers knew, and that was its own mind. Never, said he, would Maud Applegate be recognised as the Princess of Graustark, not if she lived for a thousand years and married Robin as many times as she had hairs on her head. At least, he amended, that was the way every one felt about it at present.

The afternoon papers had published the brief statement prepared by Robin in the seclusion of his stateroom on board the *Jupiter* immediately after a most enjoyable hour with Miss Guile. It was a curt and extremely positive denial of the rumoured engagement, with the additional information that he never had seen Miss Blithers and was more or less certain that she never had set eyes on him.

A rather staggering co-incidence appeared with the published report that Miss Blithers herself was supposed to be somewhere in Europe, word having been received that day from sources in London that she had sailed from New York under an assumed name. The imaginative French journals put two and two together and dwelt upon the possibility that the two young people who had never seen each other might have crossed the Atlantic on the same steamer, seeing each other frequently and yet remaining entirely in the dark, so to speak. Inspired writers began to weave a romance out of the probabilities.

On one point Robin was adamantine. He refused positively to have his identity disclosed at this time, and Gourou had to say to the newspapers that the Prince was even then on his way to Vienna, hurrying homeward as fast as steel cars could carry him. He admitted that the young man had arrived on the *Jupiter* that morning, having remained in the closest seclusion all the way across the Atlantic.

This equivocation necessitated the most cautious rearrangement of plans on the part of the Baron. He was required to act as though he had no acquaintance with either of the three travellers stopping at the Ritz, although for obvious reasons he took up a temporary abode there himself. Moreover, he had to telegraph the Prime Minister in Edelweiss that the Prince was not to be budged, and would in all likelihood postpone his return to the capitol. All of which stamped the honest Baron as a most prodigious liar, if one stops to think of what he said to the reporters.

The newspapers also printed a definite bit of news in the shape of a despatch from New York to the effect that Mr. and Mrs. William W. Blithers were sailing for Europe on the ensuing day, bound for Graustark!

However, the chief and present concern of the three loyal gentlemen in midnight conclave was not centred in the trouble that Mr. Blithers had started, but in the more desperate situation created by Miss Guile. She was the peril that now confronted them, and she was indeed a peril. Quinnox and Dank explained the situation to the Minister of Police, and the Minister of Police admitted that the deuce was to pay.

"There is but one way out of it," said he, speaking officially, "and that is the simplest one I know of."

"Assassination, I suppose," said Dank scornfully.

"It rests with me, gentlemen," said the Baron, ignoring the lieutenant's remark, "to find Miss Guile and take her into my confidence in respect —"

"No use," said Dank, and, to his surprise, the Count repeated the words after him.

"Miss Guile is a lady, Baron," said the latter gloomily. "You cannot go to her with a command to clear out, keep her hands off, or any such thing. She would be justified in having you kicked out of the house. We must not annoy Miss Guile. That is quite out of the question."

"By jove!" exclaimed Dank, so loudly that his companions actually jumped in their seats. They looked at him in amazement,— the Count with something akin to apprehension in his eyes. Had the fellow lost his mind over the girl? Before they could ask what he meant by shouting at the top of his voice, he repeated the ejaculation, but less explosively. His eyes were bulging and his mouth remained agape.

"What ails you, Dank?" demanded the Baron, removing his eyes from the young man's face long enough to glance fearfully at the transom.

"I've — I've got it!" cried the soldier, and then sank back in his chair, quite out of breath. The Baron got up and took a peep into the hallway, and then carefully locked the door. "What are you locking the door for?" demanded Dank, sitting up suddenly. "It's only a theory that I've got — but it is wonderful. Absolutely staggering."

"Oh!" said Gourou, but he did not unlock the door. "A theory, eh?" He came back and stood facing the young man.

"Count," began Dank excitedly, "you remember the big red letter B on all of her trunks, don't you? Hobbs is positive he —"

Count Quinnox sprang to his feet and banged the table with his fist.

"By jove!" he shouted, suddenly comprehending.

"The letter B?" queried Gourou, perplexed.

"The newspapers say that she sailed from New York under an assumed name," went on Dank, thrilled by his own amazing cleverness. "There you are! Plain as day. The letter B explains everything. Now we know who Miss Guile really is. She's —"

"Maud!" exclaimed Quinnox, sinking back into his chair.

"Miss Blithers!" cried Gourou, divining at last. "By jove!" And thus was the jovian circle completed.

It was two o'clock before the three gentlemen separated and retired to rest, each fully convinced that the situation was even more complicated than before, for in view of this new and most convincing revelation there now could be no adequate defence against the alluring Miss Guile.

Robin was informed bright and early the next morning. In fact, he was still in his pajamas when the news was carried to him by the exhausted Dank, who had spent five hours in bed but none in slumber. Never in all his ardent career had the smart lieutenant been so bitterly afflicted with love-sickness as now.

"I don't believe a word of it," said the Prince promptly. "You've been dreaming, old chap."

"That letter B isn't a dream, is it?"

"No, it isn't," said Robin, and instantly sat up

in bed, his face very serious. "If she should turn out to be Miss Blithers, I've cooked my goose to a crisp. Good Lord, when I think of some of the things I said to her about the Blithers family! But wait! If she is Miss Blithers do you suppose she'd sit calmly by and hear the family ridiculed? No, sir! She would have taken my head off like a flash. She —"

"I've no doubt she regarded the situation as extremely humorous," said Dank, "and laughed herself almost sick over the way she was fooling you."

"That might sound reasonable enough, Dank, if she had known who I was. But where was the fun in fooling an utter outsider like R. Schmidt? It doesn't hold together."

"Americans have an amazing notion of humour, I am reliably informed. They appear to be able to see a joke under the most distressing circumstances. I'll stake my head that she is Miss Blithers."

"I can't imagine anything more terrible," groaned Robin, lying down flat again and staring at the ceiling.

"I shouldn't call her terrible," protested Dank, rather stiffly.

"I refer to the situation, Dank,— the mess, in other words. It *is* a mess, isn't it?"

"I suppose you'll see nothing more of her, your highness," remarked Dank, a sly hope struggling in his breast.

"You'd better put it the other way. She'll see nothing more of me," lugubriously.

"I mean to say, sir, you can't go on with it, can you?"

"Go on with what?"

"The — er — you know," floundered Dank.

"If there is really anything to go on with, Dank, I'll go on with it, believe me."

The lieutenant stared. "But if she *should* be Miss Blithers, what then?"

"It might simplify matters tremendously," said Robin, but not at all confidently. "I think I'll get up, Dank, if you don't mind. Call Hobbs, will you? And, I say, won't you have breakfast up here with me?"

"I had quite overlooked breakfast, 'pon my soul, I had," said Dank, a look of pain in his face. "No wonder I have a headache, going without my coffee so long."

Later on, while they were breakfasting in Robin's sitting room, Hobbs brought in the morning newspapers. He laid one of them before the Prince, and jabbed his forefinger upon a glaring headline.

"I beg pardon, sir; I didn't mean to get it into the butter. Very awkward, I'm sure. Hi, *garçon!* Fresh butter 'ere, and lively about it, too. *Buerre!* That's the word — buttah."

Robin and Dank were staring at the headline as if fascinated. Having successfully managed the butter, Hobbs at once restored his attention to t! ..adline, reading it aloud, albeit both of the young men were capable of reading French at sight. He translated with great profundity.

"'Miss Blithers Denies Report. Signed Statement Mysteriously Received. American Heiress not to wed Prince of Graustark.' Shall I read the harticle, sir?"

Robin snatched up the paper and read aloud for himself. Hobbs merely wiped a bit of butter from his finger and listened attentively.

The following card appeared at the head of the column, and was supplemented by a complete résumé of the Blithers-Graustark muddle:

"Miss Blithers desires to correct an erroneous report that has appeared in the newspapers. She is not engaged to be married to the Prince of Graustark, nor is there even the remotest probability that such will ever be the case. Miss Blithers regrets that she has not the honour of Prince Robin's acquaintance, and the Prince has specifically stated in the public prints that he does not know her by sight. The statements of the two persons most vitally affected by this disturbing rumour should be taken as final. Sufficient pain and annoyance already has been caused by the malicious and utterly groundless report." The name of Maud Applegate Blithers was appended to the statement, and it was dated Paris, August 29.

Thereafter followed a lengthy description of the futile search for the young lady in Paris, and an interview with the local representatives of Mr. Blithers, all of whom declared that the signature was genuine, but refused to commit themselves further without consulting their employer. They could throw no light upon the situation, even going so far as to declare that they were unaware of the presence of Miss Blithers in Paris.

It appears that the signed statement was left in the counting-rooms of the various newspapers by a heavily veiled lady at an hour agreed upon as "about ten o'clock." There was absolutely no clue to the identity of this woman.

Instead of following the suggestion of Miss Blithers that "sufficient pain and annoyance already had been caused," the journalists proceeded to increase the agony by venturing the hope that fresh developments would materialise before the day was done.

"Well, she appears to be here," said Robin, as he laid down the last of the three journals and stared at Dank as if expecting hope from that most unreliable source.

"I suppose you will now admit that I am right about the letter B," said Dank sullenly.

"When I see Miss Guile I shall ask point blank if she is Maud Applegate, Dank, and if she says she isn't, I'll take her word for it," said Robin.

"And if she says she is?"

"Well," said the Prince, ruefully, "I'll still take her word for it."

"And then?"

"Then I shall be equally frank and tell her that I

am Robin of Graustark. That will put us all square again, and we'll see what comes of it in the end."

"You don't mean to say you'll — you'll continue as you were!" gasped Dank.

"That depends entirely on Miss Guile, Boske."

"But you wouldn't dare to marry Maud Applegate Blithers, sir. You would be driven out of Graustark and —"

"I think that would depend a good deal on Miss Guile, too, old chap," said Robin coolly.

Dank swallowed very hard. "I want to be loyal to you, your highness," he said as if he did not think it would be possible to remain so.

"I shall count on you, Dank," said Robin earnestly.

"But —" began the lieutenant, and then stopped short.

"Let me finish it for you. You don't feel as though you could be loyal to Miss Blithers, is that it?"

"I think that would depend on Miss Blithers," said Dank, and then begged to be excused. He went out of the room rather hurriedly.

"Well, Hobbs," said Robin, after his astonishment had abated, "what do you think of it?"

"I think he's in love with her, sir," said Hobbs promptly.

"Good Lord! with — with Miss Guile?"

"Precisely so, sir."

"Well, I'll be darned!" said the American half of Prince Robin with great fervour,

"Tut, tut, sir," reproved Hobbs, who, as has been

said before, was a privileged character by virtue of long service and his previous calling as a Cook's interpreter. "Are you going out, sir?"

"Yes. I'm going out to search the highways and by-ways for Bedelia," said Robin, a gay light in his eyes. "By the way, did you, by any chance, learn the name of the 'andsome young gent as went away with 'er, 'Obbs?"

"I did not, sir. I stood at his helbow for quite some time at the Gare St. Lazare and the only words he spoke that I could hear distinctly was 'wot the devil do you mean, me man? Ain't there room enough for you here without standing on my toes like that? Move hover.' Only, of course, sir, he used the haspirates after a fashion of his own. The haitches are mine, sir."

"Is he an American?"

"It's difficult to say, sir. He may be from Boston, but you never can tell, sir."

"Do you know Boston, Hobbs?" inquired the Prince, adjusting his tie before the mirror.

"Not to speak it, sir," said Hobbs.

The day was warm and clear, and Paris was gleaming. Robin stretched his long legs in a brisk walk across the Place Vendome and up the Rue de la Paix to the Boulevard. Here he hesitated and then retraced his steps slowly down the street of diamonds, for he suspected Miss Guile of being interested in things that were costly. Suddenly inspired, he made his way to the ʼ ʼe de la Concorde and settled him-

self ou one of the seats near the entrance to the Champs
Elysees. It was his shrewd argument that if she
planned a ride on that exquisite morning it naturally
would be along the great avenue, and in that event he
might reasonably hope to catch her coming or going.
A man came up and took a seat beside him.

"Good morning, Mr. Schmidt," said the newcomer,
and Robin somewhat gruffly demanded what the deuce
he meant by following him. "I have some interesting
news," said Baron Gourou quietly, removing his hat
to wipe a damp brow. He also took the time to recover his breath after some rather sharp dodging of
automobiles in order to attain his present position of
security. Even a Minister of Police has to step lively
in Paris.

"From home?" asked Robin carelessly.

"Indirectly. It comes through Berlin. Our
special agent there wires me that the offices of Mr.
Blithers in that city have received instructions from
him to send engineers to Edelweiss for the purpose
of estimating the cost of remodelling and rebuilding
the castle,— in other words to restore it to its condition prior to the Marlanx rebellion fifteen years
ago."

There was a tantalising smile on the Baron's face
as he watched the changing expressions in that of his
Prince.

"Are you in earnest?" demanded Robin, a bright
red spot appearing in each cheek. The Baron nodded
his head. "Well, he's got a lot of nerve! '

"She was in the Rue de la Paix half an hour ago. I thought you might —"

"You saw her, Baron?"

"Yes, highness, and it may interest you to know that she saw you."

"The deuce you say! But how do you know that it was Miss Guile. You've no means of knowing."

"It is a part of my profession to recognise people from given descriptions. In this case, however, the identification was rendered quite simple by the actions of the young lady herself. She happened to emerge from a shop just as you were passing and I've never seen any one, criminal or otherwise, seek cover as quickly as she did. She darted back into the shop like one pursued by the devil. Naturally I hung around for a few minutes to see the rest of the play. Presently she peered forth, looked stealthily up and down the street, and then dashed across the pavement to a waiting taxi-metre. It affords me pleasure to inform your highness that I took the number of the machine." He glanced at his cuff-band.

"Where did she go from the Rue de la Paix?" asked Robin impatiently.

"To the Ritz. I was there almost as soon as she.

She handed an envelope — containing a letter, I fancy — to the carriage man and drove away in the direction of the Place de l'Opera. I have a sly notion, my Prince, that you will find a note awaiting you on your return to the hotel. Ah, you appear to be in haste, my young hunter."

"I am in haste. If you expect to keep alongside, Baron, you'll have to run I'm afraid," cried the Prince, and was instantly in his seven-league boots.

There was a note in Robin's rooms when he reached the hotel. It was not the delicately perfumed article that usually is despatched by fictional heroines but a rather business-like envelope bearing the well-known words "The New York Herald" in one corner and the name "R. Schmidt, Hotel Ritz," in firm but angular scrawl across its face. As Robin ripped it open with his finger, Baron Gourou entered the room, but not without giving vent to a slight cough in the way of an announcement.

"You forget, highness, that I am a short man and not possessed of legs that travel by yards instead of feet," he panted. "Forgive me for lagging behind. I did my best to keep up with you."

Robin stared at his visitor haughtily for a moment and then broke into a good-humoured laugh.

"Won't you sit down, Baron? I'll be at liberty in a minute or two," he said, and coolly proceeded to scan the brief message from Miss Guile.

"Well," said Gourou, as the young man replaced the letter in the envelope and stuck it into his pocket.

CHAPTER XIV

THE CAT IS AWAY

ROBIN's face was glowing with excitement. He put his hands in his trousers pockets and nervously jingled the coins therein, all the while regarding his Minister of Police with speculative eyes. Then he turned to the window and continued to stare down into the Place Vendome for several minutes, obviously turning something over in his mind before coming to a decision. The Baron waited. None knew better than he how to wait. He realised that a great deal hung upon the next few sentences to be uttered in that room, and yet he could be patient.

At last Robin faced him, but without speaking. An instant later he impulsively withdrew the letter from his pocket and held it out to the Baron, who strode across the room and took it from his hand. Without a word, he extracted the single sheet of paper and read what was written thereon.

"I gather from the nature of the invitation that you are expected to enjoy stolen fruit, if I may be so bold as to put it in just that way," said he grimly. "Apparently Miss Guile finds the presence of a duenna unnecessarily wise."

"There's no harm in a quiet little excursion such as she suggests, Baron," said Robin, defensively.

"You forget that I have seen the beautiful Miss Guile," said Gourou drily. "I take it, then, that you approve of the young lady's scheme."

"Scheme sounds rather sinister, doesn't it?"

"Trick, if it please you more than the other. Moreover, I cannot say that she *suggests* the quiet little excursion. It occurs to me that she commands, your highness." He held the missive to the light and read, a tender irony in his voice: "'My motor will call for you at three this afternoon, and we will run out to St. Cloud for tea; at the Pavillon Bleu. Mrs. Gaston is spending the day with relatives at Champigny, and we may as well be mice under the circumstances. If you have another engagement, pray do not let it interfere with the pleasure I am seeking.' Nothing could be more exacting, my dear Prince. She signs herself 'B. Guile,' and I am sure she is magnificently beguiling, if you will pardon the play on words."

"You wouldn't adopt that tone of suspicion if you knew Miss Guile," said Robin stiffly. "I am sure nothing could be more frank and above-board than her manner of treating the—"

"And nothing so cock-sure and confident," put in the Baron. "It would serve her right if you ignored the letter altogether."

"If I were as old as you, Baron, I haven't the least doubt that I should do so," said Robin coolly. "And by the same token, if you were as young as I, you'd do precisely the thing that I intend to do. I'm going to St. Cloud with her."

"Oh, I haven't been in doubt about that for an instant," said Gourou. "At your age I greatly favoured the clandestine. You will not pretend to assume that this is not a clandestine excursion."

"It's a jolly little adventure," was all that Robin could say, in his youthfulness.

The Baron was thoughtful. "There is something behind this extraordinary behaviour on the part of a lady generally accredited with sense and refinement," said he after a moment. "I think I have it, too. She is deliberately putting you to a rather severe test."

"Test? What do you mean?"

"She is trying you out, sir. Miss Guile,— or possibly Miss Blithers,— is taking a genuine risk in order to determine whether you are a real gentleman or only a make-believe. She is taking a chance with you. You may call it a jolly little adventure, but I call it the acid test. Young women of good breeding and refinement do not plan such adventures with casual, ship-board acquaintances. She intends to find out *what*, not *who*, you are. I must say she's exceedingly clever and courageous."

Robin laughed. "Thank you, Baron. Fore-warned is forearmed. I shall remain a gentleman at any cost."

"She is so shrewd and resourceful that I am almost

convinced she can be no other than the daughter of the amazing Mr. Blithers. I believe he achieved most of his success through sheer impudence, though it is commonly described as daring."

"In any case, Baron, I shall make it a point to find out whether she is the lady who defies the amazing Mr. Blithers, and goes into print about it."

"She has merely denied that she is engaged to the Prince of Graustark. Pray do not come back to us with the news that she is engaged to R. Schmidt," said Gourou significantly.

Robin smiled reflectively. "That *would* make a jolly adventure of it, wouldn't it?"

At three o'clock, a big limousine swung under the porte cochere at the Ritz and a nimble footman hopped down and entered the hotel. Robin was waiting just inside the doors. He recognised the car as the one that had taken Miss Guile away from the Gare St. Lazare, and stepped forward instantly to intercept the man.

"For Mr. Schmidt?" he inquired.

"Oui, M'sieur."

Thrilled by a pleasurable sense of excitement, the Prince of Graustark entered the car. He was quick to observe that the curtains in the side windows were partially drawn across the glass. The fact that she elected to journey to the country in a limousine on this hot day did not strike him as odd, for he knew that the comfort loving French people prefer the closed vehicle to the wind-inviting, dust-gathering touring body of the Americans and British. He observed the single letter L in gold in the panel of the door, and made mental note of the smart livery of the two men on the front seat.

A delicate perfume lingered in the car, convincing proof that Miss Guile had left it but a few minutes before its arrival at the Ritz. As a matter of fact, she was nearer than he thought, for the car whirled into the Rue de la Paix and stopped at the curb not more than a hundred yards from the Place Vendome.

Once more the nimble footman hopped down and threw open the door. A slender, swift-moving figure in a blue linen gown and a wide hat from which sprung two gorgeous blue plumes, emerged from the door of a diamond merchant's shop, and, before Robin could move from his corner, popped into the car and sat down beside him with a nervous little laugh on her lips — red lips that showed rose-like and tempting behind a thick chiffon veil, obviously donned for an excellent reason. The exquisite features of Miss Guile were barely distinguishable beneath the surface of this filmy barrier. The door closed sharply and, almost before the Prince had recovered from his surprise, the car glided off in the direction of the Place de l'Opera.

" Isn't it just like an elopement? " cried Miss Guile, and it was quite plain to him that she was vastly pleased with the sprightly introduction to the adventure. Her voice trembled slightly and she sat up very straight in the wide, comfortable seat.

"Is it really you?" cried Robin, and he was surprised to find that his own voice trembled.

"Oh," she said, with a sudden diffidence, "how do you do? What must you think of me, bouncing in like that and never once speaking to you?"

"If I were to tell you what I think of you, you'd bounce right out again without speaking to me," said he, smiling. "How do you do?" He extended his hand, but it was ignored. She sank back into the corner and looked at him for a moment as if uncertain what to say or do next. The shadowy red lips were smiling and the big dark eyes were eloquent, even through the screen.

"I may as well tell you at the outset, Mr. Schmidt, that I've never — *never* — done a thing like this before," she said, an uneasy note in her voice.

"I am quite sure of that," said he, "and therefore confess to a vast wealth of satisfaction."

"What *do* you think of me?"

"I think that you are frightened almost out of your boots," said he boldly.

"No, I'm not," said she resolutely. "I am only conscious of feeling extremely foolish."

"I shouldn't feel that way about stealing off for a cup of tea," said he. "It's all quite regular, you know, and is frequently done in the very best circles when the cat's away."

"You see, I couldn't quite scrape up the courage to go directly to the hotel for you," she said. "I know several people who are stopping there and I —

I —well you won't think I'm a dreadful person, will you?"

"Not at all," he declared promptly. Then he resolved to put one of the questions he had made up his mind to ask at the first opportunity. "Do you mind telling me why you abandoned me so completely, so heartlessly on the day we landed?"

"Because there was no reason why I should act otherwise, Mr. Schmidt," she said, the tremor gone from her voice.

"And yet you take me to St. Cloud for tea," he said pointedly.

"Ah, but no one is to know of this," she cried warmly. "This is a secret, a very secret adventure."

He could not help staring. "And that is just why I am mystified. Why is to-day so different from yesterday?"

"It isn't," she said. "Doesn't all this prove it?"

His face fell. "Don't you want to be seen with me, Miss Guile? Am I not —"

"Wait! Will you not be satisfied with things as they are and refrain from asking unnecessary questions?"

"I shall have to be satisfied," said he ruefully.

"I am sorry I said that, Mr. Schmidt," she cried, contrite at once. "There is absolutely no reason why I should not be seen with you. But won't you be appeased when I say that I wanted to be with you alone to-day?"

He suddenly remembered the Baron's shrewd con-

jecture and let the opportunity to say something banal
go by without a word. Perhaps it was a test, after
all. He merely replied that she was paying him a
greater compliment than he deserved.

"There are many things I want to speak about, Mr.
Schmidt, and — and you know how impossible it is to
— to get a moment to one's self when one is being
watched like a child, as I am being watched over by
dear Mrs. Gaston. She is my shield and armour, my
lovely one-headed dragon. I placed myself in her
care and — well, she is a very dependable person.
You *will* understand, won't you?"

"Pray do not distress yourself, Miss Guile," he
protested. "The last word is spoken. I am too
happy to spoil the day by doubting its integrity.
Besides, I believe I know you better than you think I
do."

He expected her to reveal some sign of dismay, but
she was suddenly on guard.

"Then you will not mind my eccentricities," she said
calmly, "and we shall have a very nice drive, some
tea and a — lark in place of the more delectable birds
prescribed by the chef at the Pavillon Bleu."

As the car turned into the Boulevard des Capucines
Robin suppressed an exclamation of annoyance on beholding Baron Gourou and Dank standing on the curb
almost within arm's length of the car as it passed.
The former was peering rather intently at the two
men on the front seat, and evinced little or no interest
in the occupants of the tonneau.

"Yes," said he, and then turned for another look at his compatriots. Gourou was jotting something down on his cuff-band. The Prince mentally promised him something for his pains. "But let us leave dull care behind," he went on gaily.

"He isn't at all dull," said she.

"But he *is* a care," said he. "He is always losing his heart, Miss Guile."

"And picking up some one else's, I fancy," said she.

"By the way, who was the good-looking chap that came to Cherbourg to meet you?"

"A very old friend, Mr. Schmidt. I've known him since I was that high." (That high was on a line with her knee.)

"Attractive fellow," was his comment.

"Do you think so?" she inquired innocently, and he thought she over-played it a little. He was conscious of an odd sense of disappointment in her. "Have you never been out to St. Cloud? No? I never go there without feeling a terrible pity for those poor prodigals who stood beside its funeral pyre and saw their folly stripped down to the starkest of skeletons while they waited. The day of glory is short, Mr. Schmidt, and the night that follows is bitterly long. They say possession is nine points of the law, but what do nine points mean to the lawless? The rich man

of to-day may be the beggar of to-morrow, and the
rich man's sons and daughters may be serving the
beggars of yesterday. I have been told that in the
lower east side of New York City there are men and
women who were once princes and princesses, counts
and countesses, dukes and duchesses. Why doesn't
some one write a novel about the royalty that hides
its beggary in the slums of that great city?"

"What's this? Epigrams and philosophy, Miss
Guile?" he exclaimed wonderingly. "You amaze me.
What are you trying to convey? That some day you
may be serving yesterday's beggar?"

"Who knows!" she said cryptically. "I am not a
philosopher, and I'm sorry about the epigrams. I
loathe people who make use of them. They are a
cheap substitution for wisdom. Do you take sugar
in your tea?" It was her way of abandoning the
topic, but he looked his perplexity. "I thought I'd
ask now, just for the sake of testing my memory later
on." She was laughing.

"Two lumps and cream," he said. "Won't you be
good enough to take off that veil? It seriously ob-
structs the view."

She complacently shook her head. "It doesn't ob-
struct mine," she said. "Have you been reading what
the papers are saying about your friend Mr. Blithers
and his obstreperous Maud?"

Robin caught his breath. In a flash he suspected
an excellent reason for keeping the veil in place. It
gave her a distinct advantage over him.

"Yes. I see that she positively denies the whole business."

"Likewise the prospective spouse," she added. "Isn't it sickening?"

"I wonder what Mr. Blithers is saying to-day," said he audaciously. "Poor old cock, he must be as sore as a crab. By the way, it is reported that she crossed on the steamer with us."

"I am quite certain that she did, Mr. Schmidt," said she.

"You really think so?" he cried, regarding her keenly.

"The man who came to meet me knows her quite well. He is confident that he saw her at Cherbourg."

"I see," said he, and was thoroughly convinced. "I may as well confess to you, Miss Guile, that I also know her when I see her."

"But you told me positively that you had never seen her, Mr. Schmidt," she said quickly.

"I had not seen her up to the second day out on the *Jupiter*," he explained, enjoying himself immensely.

"It was after that that you —"

"I know," he said, as she hesitated; "but you see I didn't know she was Miss Blithers until sometime after I had met you." There was a challenge in his manner amounting almost to a declaration.

She leaned forward to regard him more intently.

"Is it possible, Mr. Schmidt, that you suspect me of being that horrid, vulgar creature?"

Robin was not to be trapped.   There was something in the shadowy eyes that warned him.

"At least, I may say that I do not suspect you of being a horrid, vulgar creature," he said evasively.

"What else can this Miss Blithers be if not that?"

"Would you say that she is vulgar because she refuses to acknowledge a condition that doesn't exist? I think she did perfectly right in denying the engagement."

"You haven't answered my question, Mr. Schmidt."

"Well," he began slowly, "I don't suspect you of being Miss Blithers."

"But you did suspect it."

"I was pleasantly engaged in speculation, that's all.   It is generally believed that Miss Blithers sailed under an assumed name — literally, not figuratively."

"Is there any reason why you should imagine that my name is not Guile?"

"Yes.   Your luggage is resplendently marked with the second letter in the alphabet — a gory, crimson B."

"I see," she said reflectively.   "You examined my luggage, as they say in the customs office.   And you couldn't put B and G together, is that it?"

"Obviously."

"If you had taken the trouble to look, you would have found an equally resplendent G on the opposite end of each and every trunk, Mr. Schmidt," she said quietly.

"I did not examine your luggage, Miss Guile,"

said he stiffly. She hadn't left much for him to stand
upon. " Rather unique way to put one's initials on a
trunk, isn't it? "

" It possesses the virtue of originality," she admitted, "and it never fails to excite curiosity. I am
sorry you were misled. Nothing could be more distressing than to be mistaken for the heroine of a story
and then turn out to be a mere nobody in the end.
I've no doubt that if the amiable Miss Blithers were
to hear of it, she'd rush into print and belabour me
with the largest type that money could buy."

" Oh, come now, Miss Guile," he protested, " it really
isn't fair to Miss Blithers. She was justified in following an illustrious example. You forget that the
Prince of Graustark was the first to rush into print
with a flat denial. What else could the poor girl do? "

" Oh, I am not defending the Prince of Graustark.
He behaved abominably, rushing into print as you say.
Extremely bad taste, I should call it."

Robin's ears burned. He could not defend himself.
There was nothing left for him to do but to say that
it " served him jolly well right, the way Miss Blithers
came back at him."

" Still," she said, " I would be willing to make a
small wager that the well-advertised match comes off
in spite of all the denials. Given a determined father,
an ambitious mother, a purse-filled daughter and an
empty-pursed nobleman, and I don't see how the inevitable can be avoided."

His face was flaming. It was with difficulty that he

restrained the impulse to put her right in the matter without further ado.

"Are you sure that the Prince is so empty of purse as all that?" he managed to say, without betraying himself irretrievably.

"There doesn't seem to be any doubt that he borrowed extensively of Mr. Blithers," she said scornfully. "He is under some obligations to his would-be-father-in-law, I submit, now isn't he?"

"I suppose so, Miss Guile," he admitted uncomfortably.

"And therefore owes him something more than a card in the newspapers, don't you think?"

"Really, Miss Guile, I — I —"

"I beg your pardon. The Prince's affairs are of no importance to you, so why should I expect you to stand up for him?"

"I confess that I am a great deal more interested in Miss Blithers than I am in the Prince. By the way, what would you have done had you been placed in her position?"

"I think I should have acted quite as independently as she."

"If your father were to pick out a husband for you, whether or no, you would refuse to obey the paternal command?"

"Most assuredly. As a matter of fact, Mr. Schmidt, my father has expressed a wish that I should marry a man who doesn't appeal to me at all."

"And you refuse?"

"Absolutely."

"More or less as Miss Blithers has done," he said pointedly.

"Miss Blithers, I understand, has the advantage of me in one respect. I am told that she wants to marry another man and is very much in love with him."

"A chap named Scoville," said Robin, unguardedly.

"You know him, Mr. Schmidt?"

"No. I've merely heard of him. I take it from your remark that you don't want ɔ marry anybody — at present."

"Quite right. Not at present. Now let us talk of something else. *A bas* Blithers! Down with the plutocrats! Stamp out the vulgarians! Is there anything else you can suggest?" she cried gaily.

"Long live the Princess Maud!" said he, and doffed his hat. The satirical note in his voice was not lost on her. She started perceptibly, and caught her breath. Then she sank back into the corner with a nervous, strained little laugh.

"You think she will marry him?"

"I think as you do about it, Miss Guile," said he, and she was silenced.

CHAPTER XV

THE MICE IN A TRAP

THEY had a table in a cool, shady corner of the broad porch overlooking the Place d'Armes and the Seine and its vociferous ferries. To the right runs the gleaming roadway that leads to the hills and glades through which pomp and pride once strode with such fatal arrogance. Blue coated servitors attended them on their arrival, and watched over them during their stay. It was as if Miss Guile were the fairy princess who had but to wish and her slightest desire was gratified. Her guest, a real prince, marvelled not a little at the complete sway she exercised over this somewhat autocratic army of menials. They bowed and scraped, and fetched, and carried, and were not Swiss but slaves in Bagdad during the reign of its most illustrious Caliph, Al-haroun Raschid the great. The magic of Araby could have been no more potent than the spell this beautiful girl cast over the house of Mammon. She laid her finger upon a purse of gold and wished, and lo! the wonders of the magic carpet were repeated.

Robin remembered that Maud Applegate Blithers had spent the greater part of her life in Paris, and it was therefore not unreasonable to suppose that she had spent something else as well. At any rate, the

Pavillon Bleu was a place where it *had* to be spent if one wanted the attention accorded the few.

She had removed her veil, but he was not slow to perceive that she sat with her back to the long stretch of porch.

"Do you prefer this place to Armenonville or the Paillard at Pre Catelan, Miss Guile?" he inquired, quite casually, but with a secret purpose.

"No, it is stupid here, as a. rule, and common. Still every one goes to the other places in the after-noon and I particularly wanted to be as naughty as possible, so I came here to-day."

"It doesn't strike me as especially naughty," he re-marked.

"But it was very, very naughty before you and I were born, M. Schmidt. The atmosphere still re-mains, if one possesses a comprehensive imagination."

"I daresay," said he, "but the imagination doesn't thrive on tea. Those were the days of burgundy and a lot of other red things."

"One doesn't need to be in shackles to expatiate on the terrors of the Bridge of Sighs," she said.

"Are you going to take me up to the park?"

"Yes. Into the Shadows."

"Oh, that's good! I'm sure my imagination will work beautifully when it isn't subdued by all these blue devils. I — *Que voulez vous?*" The question was directed rather sharply to a particularly deferen-tial "blue devil" who stood at his elbow.

"Monsieur Schmidt?"

"Yes. What's this? A letter! 'Pon my soul, how the deuce could any one —" He got no farther, for Miss Guile's action in pulling down her veil and the subsequent spasmodic glance over her shoulder betrayed such an agitated state of mind on her part that his own sensations were checked at the outset.

"There must be some one here who knows you, Mr. Schmidt," she said nervously. "See what it says, please,— at once. I — perhaps we should be starting home immediately."

Robin tore open the envelope. A glance showed him that the brief note was from Gourou. A characteristic G served as a signature. As he read, a hard line appeared between his eyes and his expression grew serious.

"It is really nothing, Miss Guile," he said and prepared to tear the sheet into many pieces. "A stupid, alleged joke of a fellow who happens to know me, that's all."

"Don't tear it up!" she cried sharply. "What does it say? I have a right to know, Mr. Schmidt, even though it is only a joke. What has this friend of yours to say about me? What coarse, uncalled-for comment has he to make about —"

"Let me think for a moment, Miss Guile," he interrupted, suddenly realising that it was time for reflection. After a moment he said soberly: "I think it would be wise if we were to leave instantly. There is nothing to be alarmed about, I assure you, but — well, we'd better go."

"Will you allow me to see that letter?" she asked, extending her hand.

"I'd rather not, if you don't mind."

"But I insist, sir! I'll not go a step from this place until I know what all this is about."

"As it happens to concern you even more than it does me, I suppose you'd better see what it says." He passed the letter over to her and watched her narrowly as she read. Again the veil served as a competent mask.

"Who wrote this letter, Mr. Schmidt?" she demanded. Even through the veil he could see that her eyes were wide with — was it alarm or anger?

"A man named Gourou. He is a detective engaged on a piece of work for Mr. Totten."

"Is it a part of his duty to watch your movements?" she asked, leaning forward.

"No. He is my friend, however," said Robin steadily. "According to this epistle, it would appear that it is a part of his duty to keep track of you, not me. May I ask why you should be shadowed by two of his kind?"

She did not answer at once. When she spoke, it was with a determined effort to maintain her composure.

"I am sorry to have subjected you to all this, Mr. Schmidt. We will depart at once. I find that the cat is never away, so we can't be mice. What a fool I've been." There was something suspiciously suggestive of tears in her soft voice.

He laid a hand upon the small fingers that clutched the crumpled sheet of paper. To have saved his life, he could not keep the choked, husky tremor out of his voice.

"The day is spoiled for you. That is my only regret. As for me, Miss Guile, I am not without sin, so I may cast no stones. Pray regard me as a fellow culprit, and rest assured that I have no bone to pick with you. I too am watched and yet I am no more of a criminal than you. Will you allow me to say that I am a friend whose devotion cannot be shaken by all the tempests in the world?"

"Thank you," she said, and turned her hand under his to give it a quick, convulsive clasp. Her spirits seemed to revive under the responsive grip. "You might have said all the tempests in a tea pot, for that is really what it amounts to. My father is a very foolish man. Will you send for the car?"

He called an attendant and ordered him to find Miss Guile's footman at once. When he returned to the table, she was reading the note once more.

"It is really quite thrilling, isn't it?" she said, and there was still a quaver of indignation in her voice. "Are you not mystified?"

"Not in the least," said he promptly, and drew a chair up close beside hers. "It's as plain as day. Your father has found you out, that's all. Let's read it again," and they read it together.

"A word to the wise," it began. "Two men from

a private detective concern have been employed since yesterday in watching the movements of your companion, for the purpose of safe-guarding her against good-looking young men, I suspect. I have it from the most reliable of sources that her father engaged the services of these men almost simultaneously with the date of our sailing from New York. It may interest you to know that they followed you to St. Cloud in a high-power car and no doubt are watching you as you read this message from your faithful friend, who likewise is not far away."

"I should have anticipated this, Mr. Schmidt," she said ruefully. " It is just the sort of thing my father would do."

"You seem to take it calmly enough."

"I am quite used to it. I would be worth a great deal to any enterprising person who made it his business to steal me. There is no limit to the ransom he could demand."

"You alarm me," he declared. "No doubt these worthy guardians look upon me as a kidnapper. I am inclined to shiver."

" 'All's well that ends well,' " quoth she, pulling on her gloves. "I shall restore you safely to the bosom of the Ritz and that will be the end of it."

"I almost wish that some one would kidnap you, Miss Guile. It would afford me the greatest pleasure in the world to snatch you from their clutches. Your father would be saved paying the ransom but I should have to be adequately rewarded. I fancy, however, that he wouldn't mind paying the reward I should hold out for."

"I am quite sure he would give you anything you were to ask for, Mr. Schmidt," said she gaily. "You would be reasonable, of course."

"I might ask for the most precious of his possessions," said he, leaning forward to look directly into eyes that wavered and refused to meet his.

"Curiosity almost makes me wish that I might be kidnapped. I should then find out what you consider to be his most precious possession," she said, and her voice was perilously low.

"I think I could tell you in advance," said he, his eyes shining.

"I — I prefer to find out in my own way, Mr. Schmidt," she stammered hurriedly. Her confusion was immensely gratifying to him. There is no telling what might have happened to the Prince of Graustark at that moment if an obsequious attendant had not intervened with the earthly information that the car was waiting.

"Good Lord," Robin was saying to himself as he followed her to the steps, "was I about to go directly against the sage advice of old Gourou? Was I so near to it as that? In another minute — Gee, but it was a close shave. She is adorable, she is the most adorable creature in the world, even though she is the daughter of old man Blithers, and I —'gad I wonder what will come of it in the end? Keep a tight grip on yourself, Bobby, or you're a goner, sure as fate."

They were painfully aware of the fact that their progress down the long verandah was made under the surveillance of two, perhaps three pairs of unwavering eyes, and because of it they looked neither to right nor left but as those who walk tight-ropes over dangerous places. There was something positively uncanny in the feeling that their every movement was being watched by secret observers. Once inside the car, Miss Guile sank back with a long sigh of relief.

"Did you feel it, too?" she asked, with a nervous little catch in her voice.

"I did," said he, passing his hand over his brow. "It was like being alone in the dark with eyes staring at one from all sides of the room."

The car shot across the bridge and was speeding on its way toward the Bois when Robin ventured a glance behind. Through the little window in the back of the car he saw a big, swift-moving automobile not more than a quarter of a mile in their rear.

"Would you like to verify the report of my friend Gourou?" he asked, his voice quick with exhilaration. She knelt with one knee upon the seat and peered back along the road.

"There they are!" she cried. She threw the veil back over her hat as she resumed her seat in the corner. Her eyes were fairly dancing with excitement. The warm red lips were parted and she was breathing quickly. Suddenly she laid her hand over her heart as if to check its lively thumping. "Isn't it splendid? We are being pursued — actually chased by the man-hunters of Paris! Oh, I was never so happy in my life. Isn't it great?"

"It is glorious!" he cried exultantly. "Shall I tell the chauffeur to hit it up a bit? Let's make it a real chase."

"Yes, do! We'll see if we can foil them, as they say in the books. Oh, wouldn't it be wonderful if we were to — to — what do you call it? Give them the slip, isn't that it?"

"I'm game," said he, with enthusiasm. For a second or two they looked straight into each other's eyes and a message was exchanged that never could have been put into words. No doubt it was the flush of eager excitement that darkened their cheeks. In any case, it came swiftly and went as quickly, leaving them paler than before and vastly self-conscious. And after that brief, searching look they knew that they could never be as they were before the exchange. They were no longer strangers to each other, but shy comrades and filled with a delicious sense of wonder.

Robin gave hurried directions through the speaking tube to the attentive footman, and so explicit were these directions that the greatest excitement prevailed upon the decorous front seat of the car — first the footman looked back along the road, then the chauffeur, after which a thrill of excitement seemed to fairly race up and down their liveried backs. The car itself took a notion to quiver with the promise of joy unrestrained. In less than a minute they were going more than a mile a minute over a short stretch of the Avenue de Longchamp. At the Porte de Hippodrome they slowed down and ran into the Bois, taking the first road to the left. In a few minutes they were scudding past Longchamp at a "fair clip" to quote R. Schmidt. Instead of diverging into the Allee de Longchamp, the car took a sharp turn into the Avenue de l'Hippodrome and, at the intersection, doubled back over the Allee de la Reine Marguerite, going almost to the Boulogne gate, where again it was sent Parisward over the Avenue de St. Cloud.

Miss Guile was in command of the flight. She called out the instructions to the driver and her knowledge of the intricate routes through the park stood them well in hand. Purposely she evaded the Cascades, circling the little pools by narrow, unfrequented roads, coming out at last to the Porte de la Muette, where they left the park and took to the Avenue Henri Martin. It was her design to avoid the customary routes to the heart of the city, and all would have gone well with them had not fate in the shape of two burly *sergents de ville* intervened at a time when success seemed most certain. It was quite clear to the pursued that the car containing their followers had been successfully eluded and was no doubt in the Champs Elysees by this time. For some time there had been a worried look in the Prince's eyes. Once he undertook to remonstrate with his fair companion.

"My dear Miss Guile, we'll land in jail if we keep

up this hair-raising speed. There wouldn't be any fun in that, you know."

She gave him a scornful look. "Are you afraid, Mr. Schmidt?"

"Not on my own account," said he, "but yours. I've heard that the new regulations are extremely rigid."

"Pooh! I'm not afraid of the police. They — why, what's the matter? Oh, goodness!"

The car had come to a somewhat abrupt stop. Two policemen, dismounted from their bicycles, formed an insurmountable obstruction. They were almost in the shade of the Trocadero.

"Do not be alarmed," whispered Robin to the fast paling girl, into whose eyes the most abject misery had leaped at the sight of the two officers. "Leave it to me. I can fix them all right. There's nothing to be worried about — well, *sergent*, what is it?"

The polite officers came up to the window with their little note-books.

"I regret, m'sieur, that we shall be obliged to conduct yourself and mademoiselle to the office of a magistrate. Under the new regulations set forth in the order of last May, motorists may be given a hearing at once. I regret to add that m'sieur has been exceeding the speed limit. A complaint came in but a few minutes ago from the Porte de la Muette and we have been ordered to intercept the car. You may follow us to the office of the magistrate, m'sieur. It will soon be over, mademoiselle."

"But we can explain —" she began nervously.

The *sergent* held up his hand. "It is not necessary to explain, mademoiselle. Too many motorists have explained in the past but that does not restore to life the people they have killed in the pursuit of pleasure. Paris is enforcing her laws."

"But, *sergent*, I alone am to blame for any violation of the law," said Robin suavely. "Surely it is only necessary that I should accompany you to the magistrate. The young lady is in no way responsible —"

"Alas, m'sieur," said the man firmly but as if he were quite broken-hearted, "it is not for me to disobey the law, even though you may do so. It is necessary for the lady to appear before the Judge, and it is our duty to convey her there. The new law explicitly says that all occupants of said car shall be subject to penalty under the law without reprieve or pardon!"

"Where are your witnesses?" demanded Robin.

The two men produced their watches and their note-books, tapping them significantly.

"M'sieur will not think of denying that he has been running more rapidly than the law allows," said the second officer. "It will go harder with him if he should do so."

"I shall insist upon having an advocate to represent me before —"

"As you like, m'sieur," said the first officer curtly. "Proceed!" he uttered as a command to the chauffeur, and forthwith mounted his wheel. A score of people had gathered round them by this time, and Miss Guile was crouching back in her corner. Her veil was down. In single file, so to speak, they started off for the office of the nearest magistrate appointed under the new law governing automobiles. A policeman pedaled ahead of the car and another followed.

"Isn't it dreadful?" whispered Miss Guile. "What do you think they will do to us? Oh, I am so sorry, Mr. Schmidt, to have dragged you into this horrid —"

"I wouldn't have missed it for anything in the world," said he so earnestly that she sat up a little straighter and caught her breath. "After all, they will do no more than assess a fine against us. A hundred francs, perhaps. That is nothing."

"I am not so sure of that," said she gloomily. "My friends were saying only yesterday that the new law provides for imprisonment as well. Paris has constructed special prisons for motorists, and people are compelled to remain in them for days and weeks at a time. Oh, I hope —"

"I'll inquire of the footman," said Robin. "He will know." The footman, whose face was very long and serious, replied through the tube that very few violators escaped confinement in the "little prisons." He also said "Mon dieu" a half dozen times, and there was a movement of the driver's pallid lips that seemed to indicate a fervent echo.

"I shall telephone at once — to my friends," said

Miss Guile, a note of anger in her voice. "They are very powerful in Paris. We shall put those miserable wretches in their proper places. They—"

"We must not forget, Miss Guile, that we *were* breaking the law," said Robin, who was beginning to enjoy the discomfiture of this spoiled beauty, this girl whose word was a sort of law unto itself.

"It is perfect nonsense," she declared. "We did no harm. Goodness! What is this?"

Four or five policemen on wheels passed by the car, each with a forbidding glance through the windows.

"They are the boys we left behind us," paraphrased Robin soberly. "The park policemen. They've just caught us up, and, believe me, they look serious, too. I dare say we are in for it."

In a very few minutes the procession arrived at a low, formidable looking building on a narrow side street. The cavalcade of policemen dismounted and stood at attention while Mademoiselle and Monsieur got down from the car and followed a polite person in uniform through the doors. Whereupon the group of *sergents de ville* trooped in behind, bringing with them the neatly liveried servants with the golden letter L on their cuffs.

"I believe there is a jail back there," whispered the slim culprit, a quaver in her voice. She pointed down the long, narrow corridor at the end of which loomed a rather sinister looking door with thick bolt-heads studding its surface.

An instant later they were ushered into a fair-sized room on the left of the hall, where they were commanded to sit down. A lot of chairs stood about the room, filling it to the farthest corners, while at the extreme end was the Judge's bench.

"I insist on being permitted to telephone to friends — to my legal advisors,—" began Miss Guile, with praiseworthy firmness, only to be silenced by the attendant, who whispered shrilly that a trial was in progress, couldn't she see?

Two dejected young men were standing before the Judge, flanked by three *sergents de ville*. Robin and Miss Guile stared wide-eyed at their fellow criminals and tried to catch the low words spoken by the fat Magistrate. Once more they were ordered to sit down, this time not quite so politely, and they took seats in the darkest corner of the room, as far removed from justice as possible under the circumstances.

Presently a young man approached them. He was very nice looking and astonishingly cheerful. The hopes of the twain went up with a bound. His expression was so benign, so bland that they at once jumped to the conclusion that he was coming to tell them that they were free to go, that it had all been a stupid mistake. But they were wrong. He smilingly introduced himself as an advocate connected with the court by appointment and that he would be eternally grateful to them if they would tell him what he could do for them.

" I'd like to have a word in private with the Magistrate," said the Prince of Graustark eagerly.

" Impossible!" said the advocate, lifting his eyebrows and his smart little mustachios in an expression of extreme amazement. " It is imposs—" A sharp rapping on the Judge's desk reduced the remainder of the sentence to a delicate whisper—" ible, M'sieur."

" Will you conduct me to a telephone booth?" whispered Miss Guile, tearfully.

" Pray do not weep, Mademoiselle," implored thé advocate, profoundly moved, but at the same time casting a calculating eye over the luckless pair.

" Well, what's to be done?" demanded Robin. " We insist on having our own legal advisors here."

" The court will not delay the hearing, M'sieur," explained the young man. " Besides, the best legal advisor in Paris could do no more than to advise you to plead guilty. I at least can do that quite as ably as the best of them. No one ever pretends to defend a case in the automobile courts, M'sieur. It is a waste of time, and the court does not approve of wasting time. Perhaps you will feel more content if I introduce the assistant public prosecutor, who will explain the law. That is his only duty. He does not prosecute. There is no need. The *sergents* testify and that is all there is to the case."

" May I inquire what service you can be to us if the whole business is cut and dried like that?" asked Robin.

" Not so loud, M'si. .r. 'As I said before, I can advise you in respect to your plea, and I can tell you
how to present your statement to the court. I can
caution you in many ways. Sometimes a prisoner,
who is well-rehearsed, succeeds in affecting the honourable Magistrate nicely, and the punishment is not
so severe."

" So you advise us to plead guilty as delicately as
possible? "

" I shall not advise you, M'sieur, unless it pleases
you to retain me as your counsellor. The fee is
small. Ten francs. Inasmuch as the amount is
charged against you in the supplemental costs, it
seems foolish not to take advantage of what you are
obliged to pay for in any event. You will have to
pay my fee, so you may as well permit me to be of
service to you."

" My only concern is over Mademoiselle," said the
Prince. " You may send me to jail if you like, if
you'll only —"

" Mon dieu! I am not the one who enjoys the distinguished honour of being permitted to send people
to jail, but the Judge, M'sieur."

" It is ridiculous to submit this innocent young
lady to the humiliation of —"

" It is not only ridiculous but criminal," said the
advocate, with a magnificent bow. " But what is one
to do when it is the law? Of late, the law is peculiarly sexless. And now here is where I come in. It
is I who shall instruct you — both of you, Made-

moiselle — how to conduct yourselves before the Magistrate. Above all things, do not attempt to contradict a single statement of the police. Admit that all they say is true, even though they say that you have run over a child or an old woman with mortal results. It will go much easier with you. Exercise the gravest politeness and deference toward the honourable Magistrate and to every officer of the court. You are Americans, no doubt. The courts are prone to be severe with the Americans because they sometimes undertake to tell them how easy it is to get the right kind of justice in your wonderfully progressive United States. Be humble, contrite, submissive, for that is only justice to the court. If you have killed some one in your diversions, pray do not try to tell the magistrate that the idiot ought to have kept his eyes open. Another thing: do not inform the court that you require a lawyer. That is evidence of extreme culpability and he will consider you to be inexcusably guilty. Are you attending? Pray do not feel sorry for the two young men who are now being led away. See! They are weeping. It is as I thought. They are going to prison for — But that is their affair, not ours. I advised them as I am advising you, but they insisted on making a statement of their case. That was fatal, for it failed in many respects to corroborate the information supplied by the police. It —"

"What was the charge against them?" whispered Miss Guile, quaking. She had watched the exit of the tearful young men, one of whom was sobbing bitterly, and a great fear possessed her.

"Of that, Mademoiselle, I am entirely ignorant, but they were unmistakably guilty of denying it, whatever it was."

"Are they going to prison?" she gasped.

"It is not that which causes them to weep so bitterly, but the knowledge that their names are to be posted on the bulletin boards in the Place de l'Opera, the Place de l'Concorde, the —"

"Good Lord!" gasped Robin. "Is *that* being done?"

"It is M'sieur, and the effect is marvellous. Three months ago the boards were filled with illustrious names; to-day there are but few to be found upon them. The people have discovered that the courts are in earnest. The law is obeyed as it never was before. The prisons were crowded to suffocation at one time; now they are almost empty. It is a good law. To-day a mother can wheel her baby carriage in the thickest of the traffic and run no risk of — Ah, but here is the assistant prosecutor coming. Permit me to further warn you that you will be placed under oath to tell the absolute truth. The prosecutor will ask but three questions of you: your age, your name and your place of residence. All of them you must answer truthfully, especially as to your names. If it is discovered that you have falsely given a name not your own, the lowest penalty is sixty days in prison, imposed afterwards in addition to the sentence you will receive for violating the traffic laws. I have performed my duty as required by the commissioner. My fee is a fixed one, so you need not put your hand into your pocket, M'sieur. Good day, Mademoiselle — good day, M'sieur." He bowed profoundly and gave way to the impatient prosecutor, who had considerately held himself aloof while the final words were being uttered, albeit he glanced at his watch a couple of times.

"Come," he said, and he did not whisper; "let us be as expeditious as possible. Approach the court. It is —"

"See here," said Robin savagely, "this is too damned high-handed. Are we to have no chance to defend ourselves? We —"

"Just as you please, M'sieur," interrupted the prosecutor patiently. "It is nothing to me. I receive my fee in any event. If you care to defy the law in addition to what you have already done, it is not for me to object."

"Well, I insist on having —"

A thunderous pounding on the bench interrupted his hot-headed speech.

"Attend!" came in a sharp, uncompromising voice from the bench. "What is the delay? This is no time to think. All that should have been done before. Step forward! *Sergent*, see that the prisoners step forward."

Robin slipped his arm through Miss Guile's, expecting her to droop heavily upon it for support. To his

surprise she drew herself up, dis-engaged herself, and
walked straight up to the bench, without fear or hesitation.   It was Robin who needed an example of courage and fortitude, not she.   The chauffeur and footman, shivering in their elegance, already stood before
the bench.

"Will you be so kind as to raise your veil, Madam?"
spake the court.

She promptly obeyed.   He leaned forward with
sudden interest.   The prosecutor blinked and abruptly
overcame the habitual inclination to appear bored.
Such ravishing beauty had never before found its way
into that little court-room.   Adjacent moustaches
were fingered somewhat convulsively by several *sergents de ville*.

"Ahem!" said the court, managing with some difficulty to regain his judicial form.   "I am compelled
by law, Mademoiselle, to warn you before you are
placed under oath that the lowest penalty for giving
a false name in answer to the charge to be brought
against you is imprisonment for not less than sixty
days.   I repeat this warning to you, young man.   Be
sworn, if you please."

Robin experienced a queer sense of exultation, not
at all lessened by the knowledge that he would be forced
to reveal his own identity.   Would she call herself
Bedelia Guile or would she —"

"State your name, Mademoiselle," said the prosecutor.

CHAPTER XVI

Miss Guile lowered her head for an instant. Robin could see that her lip was quivering. A vast pity for her took possession of him and he was ashamed of what he now regarded as unexampled meanness of spirit on his own part. She lifted her shamed, pleading eyes to search his, as if expecting to find succour in their fearless depths. She found them gleaming with indignation, suddenly aroused, and was instantly apprehensive. There was a look in those eyes of his that seemed prophetic of dire results unless she checked the words that were rising to his lips. She shook her head quickly and, laying a hand upon his arm, turned to the waiting magistrate.

"My name is — Oh, is there no way to avoid the publicity —" she sighed miserably —" the publicity that —"

"I regret, Mademoiselle, that there is no alternative —" began the Judge, to be interrupted by the banging of the court-room door. He looked up, glaring at the offender with ominous eyes. The polite attendant from the outer corridor was advancing in great haste. He was not only in haste but vastly perturbed.

Despite the profound whack of the magistrate's

paper weight on the hollow top of the desk and the withering scowl that went with it, the attendant rushed forward, forgetting his manners, his habits and his power of speech in one complete surrender to nature. He thrust into the hand of the Judge a slip of paper, at the same time gasping something that might have been mistaken for an appeal for pardon but which more than likely was nothing of the sort.

"What is this?" demanded the Judge ferociously.

"Mon dieu!" replied the attendant, rolling his eyes heavenward.

The magistrate was impressed. He took up the slip of paper and read what was written thereon. Then he was guilty of a start. The next instant he had the prosecutor up beside him and then the advocate. Together they read the message from the outside and together they lifted three pairs of incredulous eyes to stare at the culprits below. There was a hurried consultation in excited whisperings, intermittent stares and far from magisterial blinkings.

Robin bent close to Bedelia's ear and whispered: "We must have killed some one, the way they are acting."

Her face was glowing with triumph. "No. Luck is with us, Mr. Schmidt. You'll see!"

The magistrate cleared his throat and beamed upon them in a most friendly fashion.

Robin grasped the situation in a flash. His own identity had been revealed to the Judge. It was not likely that the daughter of William Blithers could create such lively interest in a French court of justice, so it must be that Gourou or Quinnox had come to the rescue. The court would not think of fining a prince of the royal blood, law or no law!

"M'sieur, Mademoiselle, will you be so good as to resume your seats? An extraordinary condition has arisen. I shall be obliged to investigate. The trial must be interrupted for a few minutes. Pardon the delay. I shall return as quickly as possible. *Sergent!* See that Mademoiselle and M'sieur are made comfortable."

He descended from the bench and hurried into the corridor, followed closely by the prosecutor and the advocate, both of whom almost trod on his heels. This may have been due to the fact that they were slighter men and more sprightly, but more than likely it was because they were unable to see where they were going for the excellent reason that they were not looking in that direction at all.

Policemen and attendants, mystified but impressed, set about to make the culprits comfortable. They hustled at least a half dozen roomy chairs out of an adjoining chamber; they procured palm-leaf fans and even proffered the improbable — ice-water! — after which they betook themselves to a remote corner and whispered excitedly at each other, all the while regarding the two prisoners with intense interest. Even the despairing footman and chauffeur exhibited unmistakable signs of life.

"I fancy my friends have heard of our plight, Mr.

Schmidt," she said, quite composedly. "We will be released in a very few minutes."

He smiled complacently. He could afford to let her believe that her friends and not his were performing a miracle.

"Your friends must be very powerful," he said.

"They are," said she, with considerable directness.

"Still, we are not out of the scrape yet, Miss Guile," he remarked, shaking his head. "It may be a flash in the pan."

"Oh, please don't say that," she cried in quick alarm. "I — I should die if — if we were to be sent to —"

"Listen to me," he broke in eagerly, for an inspiration had come to him. "There's no reason why you should suffer, in any event. Apparently I am a suspected person. I may just as well be a kidnapper as not. You must allow me to inform the Judge that I was abducting you, so that he —"

"How absurd!"

"I don't in the least mind. Besides, I too have powerful friends who will see that I am released in a day or two. You —"

"You cannot hope to convince the Judge that you were abducting me in my own automobile — or at least in one belonging to my friends, who are irreproachable. I am very much obliged to you for thinking of it, Mr. Schmidt, but it is out of the question. I couldn't allow you to do it in the first place, and in the second I'm sure the court wouldn't believe you."

"It was I who suggested running away from those detectives," he protested.

"But I jumped at the chance, didn't I?" she whispered triumphantly. "I am even guiltier than thou. Can you ever forgive me for—"

"Hush!" he said, in a very low voice. His hand fell upon hers as it rested on the arm of the chair. They were in the shadows. She looked up quickly and their eyes met. After a moment hers fell, and she gently withdrew her hand from its place of bondage. "We are pals, Bedelia," he went on softly. "Pals never go back on each other. They sink or swim together, and they never stop to inquire the reason why. When it comes to a pinch, one or the other will sacrifice himself that his pal may be saved. I—"

"Please do not say anything more," she said, her eyes strangely serious and her voice vibrant with emotion. "Please!"

"I have a confession to make to you," he began, leaning still closer. "You have taken me on faith. You do not know who or what I am. I—"

She held up her hand, an engaging frown in her eyes. "Stop! This is no place for confessions. I will not listen to you. Save your confessions for the magistrate. Tell him the truth, Mr. Schmidt. I am content to wait."

He stared for an instant, perplexed. "See here,

Miss Guile,— Bedelia,— I've just got to tell you something that —"

"You may tell me at Interlaken," she interrupted,
and she was now quite visibly agitated.

"At Interlaken? Then you mean to carry out your
plan to spend—"

"Sh! Here they come. Now we shall see." ·

The magistrate and his companions re-entered the
room at that instant, more noticeably excited than
when they left it. The former, rubbing his hands
together and smiling as he had never smiled before,
approached the pair. It did not occur to him to resent the fact that they remained seated in his august
presence.

"A lamentable mistake has been made," he said.
"I regret that M'sieur and Mademoiselle have been
subjected to so grave an indignity. Permit me to
apologise for the misguided energy of our excellent
sergents. They —"

"But we were exceeding the speed limit," said
Robin comfortably, now that the danger was past.
"The officers were acting within their rights."

"I know, I know," exclaimed the magistrate.
"They are splendid fellows, all of them, and I beg
of you to overlook their unfortunate — er — zealous-
ness. Permit me to add that you are not guilty —
I should say, that you are honourably discharged by
this humble court. But wait! The *sergents* shall
also apologise. Here! Attend. It devolves upon
you —"

"Oh, I beg of you —" began Robin, but already the policemen, who had been listening open-mouthed to the agitated prosecutor, were bowing and scraping and muttering their apologies for enforcing a cruel and unjust law.

"And we are not obliged to give our names, *M'sieur le judge?*" cried Miss Guile gladly.

"Mademoiselle," said he, with a profound bow, "it is not necessary to acquaint me with something I already know. Permit me to again express the most unbounded regret that —"

"Oh, thank you," she cried. "We have had a really delightful experience. You owe us no apology, M'sieur. And now, may we depart?"

"Instantly! LaChance, conduct M'sieur and Mademoiselle into the fresh, sweet, open air and discover their car for them without delay. *Sergents*, remain behind. Let there be nothing to indicate that there has been detention. Mademoiselle, you have been merely making a philanthropic visit to our prison. There has been no arrest."

Robin and Miss Guile emerged from the low, forbidding door and stood side by side on the pavement looking up and down the street in search of the car. It was nowhere in sight. The chauffeur gasped with amazement — and alarm. He had left it standing directly in front of the door, and now it was gone.

"It is suggested, M'sieur," said the polite LaChance, "that you walk to the corner beyond, turn to the left and there you will find the car in plain

view. It was removed by two gentlemen soon after
you condescended to honour us with a visit of inspection, and thereby you have escaped much unnecessary
attention from the curious who always infest the vicinity of police offices." He saluted them gravely
and returned at once to the corridor.

Following leisurely in the wake of the hurrying
servants, Robin and Bedelia proceeded down the narrow street to the corner indicated. They were silent
and preoccupied. After all, *who* was to be thanked
for the timely escape, his god or hers?

And here it may be said that neither of them was
ever to know who sent that brief effective message to
the magistrate, nor were they ever to know the nature
of its contents.

The men were examining the car when they came up.
No one was near. There was no one to tell how it
came to be there nor whither its unknown driver had
gone. It stood close to the curb and the engine was
throbbing, proof in itself that some one had but re-
cently deserted his post as guardian.

"The obliging man-hunters," suggested Robin in
reply to a low-voiced question.

"Or your guardian angel, the great Gourou!" she
said, frowning slightly. "By the way, Mr. Schmidt,
do you expect to be under surveillance during your
stay at Interlaken?"

There was irony in her voice. "Not if I can help
it," he said. "And you, Miss Guile? Is it possible
that two of the best detectives in Paris are to continue

treading on your heels all the time you are in Europe?
Must we go about with the uncomfortable feeling that
some one is staring at us from behind, no matter
where we are? Are we to be perpetually attended
by the invisible? If so, I am afraid we will find it
very embarrassing."

They were in the car now and proceeding at a snail's
pace toward the Arc de Triomphe. Her eyes nar-
rowed. He was sure that she clutched her slim
fingers tightly although, for an excellent reason, he
was not by way of knowing. He was rapturously
watching those expressive eyes.

"I shall put a stop to this ridiculous espionage at
once, Mr. Schmidt. These men shall be sent kiting
— I mean, about their business before this day is
over. I do not intend to be spied upon an instant
longer."

"Still they may have been instruments of providence to-day," he reminded her. "Without them, we
might now be languishing in jail and our spotless
names posted in the Place de l'Opera. Bedelia Guile
and Rex Schmidt, malefactors. What would your
father say to that?'"

She smiled — a ravishing smile, it was. His heart
gave a stupendous jump. "He would say that it
served me right," said she, and then: "But what
difference can it possibly make to you, Mr. Schmidt,
if the detectives continue to watch over me?"

"None," said he promptly. "I suppose they are
used to almost anything in the way of human nature,

so if they don't mind, I'm sure I sha'n't. I haven't
the slightest objection to being watched by detectives,
if we can only keep other people from seeing us."

"Don't be silly," she cried. "And let me remind
you while I think of it: You are not to call me Bedelia."

"Bedelia," he said deliberately.

She sighed. "I am afraid I have been mistaken in
you," she said. He recalled Gourou's advice. Had
he failed in the test? "But don't do it again."

"Now that I think of it," he said soberly, "you are
not to call me Mr. Schmidt. Please bear that in
mind, Bedelia."

"Thank you. I don't like the name. I'll call
you —"

Just then the footman turned on the seat and excitedly pointed to a car that had swung into the boulevard from a side street.

"The man-hunters!" exclaimed Robin. "By
jove, we didn't lose them after all."

"To the Ritz, Pierre," she cried out sharply.
Once more she seemed perturbed and anxious.

"What are you going to call me?" he demanded,
insistently.

"I haven't quite decided," she replied, and lapsed
into moody silence.

Her nervousness increased as they sped down the
Champs Elysees and across the Place de la Concorde.
He thought that he understood the cause and pres-
ently sought to relieve her anxiety by suggesting that

she set him down somewhere along the Rue de Rivoli. She flushed painfully.

"Thank you, Mr. Schmidt, I — are you sure you will not mind?"

"May I ask what it is that you are afraid of, Miss Guile?" he inquired seriously.

She was lowering her veil. "I am not afraid, Mr. Schmidt," she said. "I am a very, very guilty person, that's all. I've done something I ought not to have done, and I'm — I'm ashamed. You don't consider me a bold, silly —"

"Good Lord, no!" he cried fervently.

"Then why do you call me Bedelia?" she asked, shaking her head.

"If you feel that way about it, I — I humbly implore you to overlook my freshness," he cried in despair.

"Will you get out here, Mr. Schmidt?" She pressed a button and the car swung alongside the curb.

"When am I to see you again?" he asked, holding out his hand. She gave it a firm, friendly grip and said:

"I am going to Switzerland the day after tomorrow. Good-bye."

In a sort of daze, he walked up the Rue Castiliogne to the Place Vendome. His heart was light and his eyes were shining with a flame that could have but one origin. He was no longer in doubt. He was in love. He had found the Golden Girl almost at the end of his journey, and what cared he if she did turn out to be the daughter of old man Blithers? What cared he for *anything* but Bedelia? There would be a pretty howdy-do when he announced to his people that their Princess had been selected for them, whether or no, and there might be such a thing as banishment for Himself. Even at that, he would be content, for Bedelia was proof against titles. If she loved him, it would be for himself. She would scorn the crown and mock the throne, and they would go away together and live happily ever afterward, as provided by the most exacting form of romance. And Blithers? What a joke it would be on Blithers if he gave up the throne!

As he approached the Ritz, a tall young man emerged from the entrance, stared at him for an instant, and then swung off at a rapid pace in the direction of the Rue de la Paix. The look he gave Robin was one of combined amazement and concern, and the tail end of it betrayed unmistakable annoyance, — or it might have been hatred. He looked over his shoulder once and found Robin staring after him. This time there could be no mistake. He was furious, but whether with Robin or himself there was no means of deciding from the standpoint of an observer. At any rate, he quickened his pace and soon disappeared.

He was the good-looking young fellow who had met her at the steamship landing, and it was quite obvious that he had been making investigations on his own account.

Robin permitted himself a sly grin as he sauntered into the hotel. He had given *that* fellow something to worry about, if he had accomplished nothing else. Then he found himself wondering if, by any chance, it could be the Scoville fellow. That would be a facer!

He found Quinnox and Dank awaiting him in the lobby. They were visibly excited.

"Did you observe the fellow who just went out?" inquired Robin, assuming a most casual manner.

"Yes," said both men in unison.

"I think we've got some interesting news concerning that very chap," added the Count, glancing around uneasily.

"Perhaps I may be able to anticipate it, Count," ventured Robin. "I've an idea he is young Scoville, the chap who is supposed to be in love with Miss Blithers — and *vice versa*," he concluded, with a chuckle.

"What have you heard?" demanded the Count in astonishment.

"Let's sit down," said Robin, at once convinced that he had stumbled upon an unwelcome truth.

They repaired to the garden and were lucky enough to find a table somewhat removed from the crowd of tea-drinkers. Robin began fanning himself with his broad straw-hat. He felt uncomfortably warm. Quinnox gravely extracted two or three bits of paper from his pocket, and spread them out in order before his sovereign.

"Read this one first," said he grimly.

It was a cablegram from their financial agents in New York City, and it said: "Mr. B. making a hurried trip to Paris. Just learned Scoville preceded Miss B. to Europe by fast steamer and has been seen with her in Paris. B. fears an elopement. Make sure papers are signed at once as such contingency might cause B. to change mind and withdraw if possible."

Robin looked up. "I think this may account for the two man-hunters," said he. His companions stared. "You will hear all about them from Gourou. We were followed this afternoon."

"Followed?" gasped Quinnox.

"Beautifully," said the Prince, with his brightest smile. "Detectives, you know. It was ripping."

"My God!" groaned the Count.

"I fancy you'll now agree with me that she is Miss Blithers," said Dank forlornly.

"Cheer up, Boske," cried Robin, slapping him on the shoulder. "You'll meet another fate before you're a month older. The world is absolutely crowded with girls."

"You can't crowd the world with one girl," said Dank, and it was quite evident from his expression that he believed the world contained no more than one.

"I had the feeling that evil would be the result of this foolish trip to-day," groaned Quinnox. "I should not have permitted you to —"

"The result is still in doubt," said Robin enigmatically. "And now, what comes next?"

"Read this one. It is from Mr. Blithers. I'll guarantee that you do not take this one so complacently."

He was right in his surmise. Robin ran his eye swiftly over the cablegram and then started up from his chair with a muttered imprecation.

"Sh!" cautioned the Count,—and just in time, for the young man was on the point of enlarging upon his original effort. "Calm yourself, Bobby, my lad. Try taking six or seven full, deep inhalations, and you'll find that it helps wonderfully as a preventive. It saves many a harsh word. I've—"

"You needn't caution me," murmured the Prince. "If I had the tongue of a pirate I couldn't begin to do justice to *this*," and he slapped his hand resoundingly upon the crumpled message from William W. Blithers.

The message had been sent by Mr. Blithers that morning, evidently just before the sailing of the fast French steamer on which he and his wife were crossing to Havre. It was directed to August Totten and read as follows:

"Tell our young friend to qualify statement to press at once. Announce reconsideration of hasty denial and admit engagement. This is imperative. I am not in mood for trifling. Have wired Paris papers that engagement is settled. Have also wired daughter. The sooner we get together on this the

MICROCOPY RESOLUTION TEST CHART

(ANSI and ISO TEST CHART No. 2)

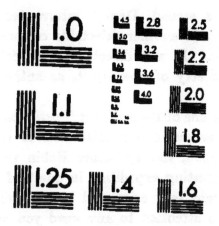

APPLIED IMAGE Inc

1653 East Main Street
Rochester, New York 14609 USA
(716) 482 - 0300 - Phone
(716) 288 - 5989 - Fax

better. Wait for my arrival in Paris." It was signed "W. B."

"There's Blitherskite methods for you," said Dank. "Speaking of pirates, he's the king of them all. Did you ever hear of such confounded insolence? The damned —"

"Wait a second, Dank," interrupted the Count. "There is still another delectable communication for you, Robin. It was directed to R. Schmidt and I took the liberty of opening it, as authorised. Read it."

This was one of the ordinary "*petits bleu*," dropped into the pneumatic tube letter-box at half-past two that afternoon, shortly before Robin ventured forth on his interesting expedition in quest of tea, and its contents were very crisp and to the point:

"Pay no attention to any word you may have received from my father. He cables a ridiculous command to me which I shall ignore. If you have received a similar message I implore you to disregard it altogether. Let's give each other a fighting chance."

It was signed "Maud Blithers."

CHAPTER XVII

Mr. Blithers received a marconigram from the *Jupiter* when the ship was three days out from New York. It was terse but sufficient.

"Have just had a glimpse of Prince Charming. He is very good-looking. Love to mother. Maud."

He had barely settled into a state of complete satisfaction with himself over the successful inauguration of a shrewd campaign to get the better of the recalcitrant Maud and the incomprehensible Robin, when he was thrown into a panic by the discovery that young Chandler Scoville had sailed for Europe two days ahead of Maud and her elderly companion. The gratification of knowing that the two young people had sailed away on the same vessel was not in the least minimised by Maud's declaration that she intended to remain in her cabin all the way across in order to avoid recognition, for he knew her too well to believe it possible that she could stay out of sight for any length of time, fair weather or foul. He even made a definite wager with his wife that the two would become acquainted before they were half-way across the Atlantic, and he made a bet with himself that nature would do the rest. And now here came the stagger-

ing suspicion that Scoville's hasty departure was the
result of a pre-arranged plan between him and Maud,
and that, after all, the silly girl might spoil everything
by marrying the confounded rascal before he could
do anything to prevent the catastrophe.

He even tried to engineer a scheme whereby young
Scoville might be arrested on landing and detained on
one pretext or another until he could reach Europe
and put an end to the fellow's vain-glorious conniving.

But after consulting with his lawyers he abandoned
the plan because they succeeded in proving to him that
Maud certainly would marry the fellow if she had
the least ground for believing that he was being op-
pressed on her account. The cables were kept very
busy, however, for the next twenty-four hours, and
it is certain that Scoville was a marked man from the
moment he landed.

Newspaper reporters camped on the trail of Mr.
Blithers. He very obligingly admitted that there was
something in the report that his daughter was to marry
the Prince of Graustark, although he couldn't say anything definite at the time. It wouldn't be fair to the
parties concerned, he explained. He gave away a
great many boxes of cigars, and not a few of the
more sagacious reporters succeeded in getting at least
three boxes by interviewing him on as many separate
occasions without being detected in the act of repeating. Then came the disgusting denials in Paris by
his daughter and the ungrateful Prince. This was

too much. He couldn't understand such unfilial behaviour on the part of one, and he certainly couldn't forgive the ingratitude of the other.

Instead of waiting until Saturday to sail, he changed ships and left New York on Friday, thereby gaining nothing by the move except relief from the newspapers, for it appears that he gave up a five day boat for one that could not do it under six. Still he was in active pursuit, which was a great deal better than sitting in New York twiddling his thumbs or looking at his watch and berating the pernicious hours that stood between him and Saturday noon.

" There will be something doing in Europe the day I land there, Lou," he said to his wife as they stood on deck and watched the Statue of Liberty glide swiftly back toward Manhattan Island. " I've got all the strings working smoothly. We've got Groostock where it can't peep any louder than a freshly hatched chicken, and we'll soon bring Maud to her senses. I tell you, Lou, there is nothing that makes a girl forget her lofty ideals so quickly as the chance to go shopping for princess gowns. She's seen the prince and I'll bet she won't be so stubborn as she was before. And if he has had a good, square look at her, — if he's had a chance to gaze into those eyes of hers,— why, I — well, I leave it to you. He can't help getting off his high horse, can he? "

Mrs. Blithers favoured him with a smile. It was acknowledged that Maud was the living image of what her mother had been at the age of twenty.

"I hope the child hasn't made any silly promise to Chaunie Scoville," she sighed.

"I've been thinking of that, Lou," said he, wiping his brow, "and I've come to one conclusion: Scoville can be bought off. He's as poor as Job and half a million will look like the Bank of England to him. I'll —"

"You are not to attempt anything of the kind, Will," she cried emphatically. "He would laugh in your face, poor as he is. He comes from one of the best families in New York and —"

"And I don't know where the best families need money any more than they do in New York," he interrupted irritably. " 'Gad, if the worst families need it as badly as they do, what must be the needs of the best? You leave it to me. It may be possible to insult him with a half million, so if he feels that way about it I'll apologise to him again with another half million. You'll see that he won't be capable of resenting two insults in succession. He'll —"

"He isn't a fool," said she significantly.

"He'd be a fool if he refused to take —"

"Are you losing your senses, Will?" she cried impatiently. "Why should he accept a million to give up Maud, when he can be sure of fifty times that much if he marries her?"

"But I'll cut Maud off with a dollar if she marries him, so help me Moses!" exclaimed Mr. Blithers, but he went a little pale just the same. "That will fix him!"

"You are talking nonsense," said she sharply. He put his fingers to his ears somewhat earlier than usual, and she turned away with a tantalising laugh. "I'm going inside," and inside she went. When he followed a few minutes later he was uncommonly meek.

"At any rate," he said, seating himself on the edge of a chair in her parlour, "I guess those cablegrams this morning will make 'em think twice before they go on denying things in the newspapers."

"Maud will pay no attention to your cablegram, and, if I am any judge of human nature, the Prince will laugh himself sick over the one you sent to Count Quinnox. I told you not to send them. You are not dealing with Wall Street. You are dealing with a girl and a boy who appear to have minds of their own."

He ventured a superior sniff. "I guess you don't know as much about Wall Street as you think you do."

"I only know that it puts its tail between its legs and howls every time some one points a finger at it," she observed scornfully.

"Now let's be sensible, Lou," he said, sitting back a little further in the chair, relieved to find that she was at least willing to tolerate his presence,— a matter on which he was in some doubt when he entered the room. There were times when he was not quite certain whether he or she was the brains of the family. "We'll probably have a wireless from Maud before long. Then we'll have something tangible to discuss.

By the way, did I tell you that I've ordered some Dutch architects from Berlin to go —"

"The Dutch are from Holland," she said wearily.

"— to go over to Growstock and give me a complete estimate on repairing and remodelling the royal castle? I dare say we'll have to do a good deal to the place. It's several hundred years old and must require a lot of conveniences. Such as bath-rooms, electric lights, steam heating appar —"

"Better make haste slowly, Will," she said, and he ought to have been warned by the light in her eye. "You are taking a great deal for granted, aren't you?"

"It's got to be fixed up some time, so we might just as well do it in the beginning," said he, failing utterly to grasp her meaning. "Probably needs refurnishing from top to bottom, too, and a new roof. I never saw a ruin yet that didn't leak. Remember those castles on the Rhine? Will you ever forget how wet we got the day we went through the one at —"

"They were abandoned, tumble-down castles," she reminded him.

"There isn't a castle in Europe that's any good in a rain-storm," he proclaimed. "A mortgage can't keep out the rain and that's what every one of 'em is covered with. Why old man Quiddox himself told me that their castle had been shot to pieces in one of the revolutions and —"

"It is time you informed yourself about the country you are trying to annex to the Blithers estate," she said sarcastically. "I can assist you to some extent if you will be good enough to listen. In the first place, the royal castle at Edelweiss is one of the most substantial in the world. It has not been allowed to fall into decay. In fact, it is inhabited from top to bottom by members of the royal household and the court, and I fancy they are not the sort of people who take kindly to a wetting. It is not a ruin, Will, such as you have been permitted to visit, but a magnificent building with all of the modern improvements. The only wettings that the inmates sustain are of a daily character and due entirely to voluntary association with porcelain bath-tubs and nickleplated showers, and they never get anything wet but their skins. As for the furnishings, I can assure you that the entire Blithers fortune could not replace them if they were to be destroyed by fire or pillage. They are priceless and they are unique. I have read that the hangings in the bed-chamber of the late Princess Yetive are the most wonderful in the whole world. The throne chair in the great audience chamber is of solid gold and weighs nearly three thousand pounds. It is studded with diamonds, rubies —"

"Great Scott, Lou, where did you learn all this?" he gasped, his eyes bulging.

"—emeralds and other precious stones. There is one huge carpet in the royal drawing-room that the Czar of Russia is said to have offered one hundred thousand pounds for and the offer was scorned. The park surrounding the castle is said to be beautiful beyond the power of description. The —"

"I asked you where you got all this information. Can't you answer me?"

"I obtained all this and a great deal more from a lady who spent a year or two inside the castle walls. I refer to Mrs. Truxton King, who might have told you as much if you had possessed the intelligence to inquire."

"Gee whiz!" exclaimed Mr. Blithers, going back to his buoyant boyhood days for an adequate expression. "What a wonder you are, Lou. But that's the woman of it, always getting at the inside of a thing while a man is standing around looking at the outside. Say, but won't it make a wonderful home for you and me to spend a peaceful old age in when we get ready to lay aside the —"

He stopped short, for she had arisen and was standing over him with a quivering forefinger levelled at his nose,— and not more than six inches away from it, — her handsome eyes flashing with fury.

"You may walk in where angels fear to tread, but you will walk alone, Will Blithers. I shall not be with you, and you may as well understand it now. I've told you a hundred times that money isn't everything, and it is as cheap as dirt when you put it alongside of tradition, honour, pride and loyalty. Those Graustarkians would take you by the nape of the neck and march you out of their castle so quick that your head would swim. You may be able `· ·uy their prince for Maudie to exhibit around the co'·.try, but you can't buy the intelligence of the people. They won't have you at any price and they won't have me, so there is the situation in a nutshell. They will hate Maudie, of course, but they will endure her for obvious reasons. They may even come to love and respect her in the end, for she is worthy. But as for you and me, William,— with all our money,— we will find every hand against us — even the hand of our daughter, I prophesy. I am not saying that I would regret seeing Maud the Princess of Graustark — far from it. But I do say that you and I will be expected to know our places. If you attempt to spend your declining years in the castle at Edelweiss you will find them reduced to days, and short ones at that. The people of Graustark will see to it that you die before your time."

"Bosh!" said Mr. Blithers. "Mind if I smoke?" He took out a cigar and began searching for matches.

"No," she said, "I don't mind. It is a sign that you need something to steady your nerves. I know you, Will Blithers. You don't want to smoke. You want to gain a few minutes of time, that's all."

He lit a cigar. "Right you are," was his unexpected admission. "I wonder if you really have the right idea about this business. What objection could any one have to a poor, tired old man sitting in front of his daughter's fireside and — and playing with her kiddies? It seems to me that —"

" You will never be a tired old man, that's the trouble," she said, instantly touched.

" Oh, yes, I will," said he slowly. " I'm rather looking forward to it, too."

" It will be much nicer to have the kiddies come to your own fireside, Will. I used to enjoy nothing better than going to spend a few days with my grandfather."

" But what's the use of going to all this trouble and expense if we are not to enjoy some of the fruits? " he protested, making a determined stand. " If these people can't be grateful to the man who helps 'em out in their time of trouble,— and who goes out of his way to present 'em with a bright, capable posterity, — I'd like to know what in thunder gratitude really means."

" Oh, there isn't such a thing as gratitude," she said. " Obligation, yes,— and ingratitude most certainly, but gratitude,— no. You are in a position to know that gratitude doesn't exist. Are you forgetting the private advices we already have had from Graustark? Does it indicate that the people are grateful? There are moments when I fear that we are actually placing Maud's life in peril, and I have had some wretched dreams. They do not want her. They speak of exile for the Prince if he marries her. And now I repeat what I have said before:— the people of Graustark must have an opportunity to see and become acquainted with Maud before the marriage is definitely arranged. I will not have my

daughter cast into a den of lions, Will,— for that
is what it may amount to. The people will adore her,
they will welcome her with open arms if they are given
the chance. But they will have none of her if she
is forced upon them in the way you propose."

"I'll — I'll think it over," said Mr. Blithers, and
then discovered that his cigar had gone out. "I
think I'll go on deck and smoke, Lou. Makes it stuffy
in here. We'll lunch in the restaurant at half-past
one, eh?"

"Think hard, Will," she recommended, with a
smile.

"I'll do that," he said, "but there's nothing on
earth that can alter my determination to make Maud
the Princess of Groostork. *That's* settled."

"Graustark, Will."

"Well, whatever it is," said he, and departed.

He did think hard, but not so much about a regal
home for aged people as about Channie Scoville who
had now become a positive menace to all of his well-
ordered and costly plans. The principal subject for
thought just now was not Graustark but this conniving young gentleman who stood ready to make a terrible mess of posterity. Mr. Blithers was sufficiently
fair-minded to concede that the fellow was good-looking, well-bred and clever, just the sort of chap that
any girl might fall in love with like a shot. As a
matter of fact, he once had admired Scoville, but that
was before he came to look upon him as a menace.
He would make a capital husband for any girl in the

world, except Maud. He could say that much for him, without reserve.

He thought hard until half-past one and then went to the wireless office, where he wrote out a message in cipher and directed the operator to waste no time in relaying it to his offices in Paris. His wife was right. It would be the height of folly to offer Scoville money and it would be even worse to inspire the temporary imprisonment of the young man.

But there was a splendid alternative. He could manage to have his own daughter abducted,— chaperon included,— and held for ransom!

The more he thought of it the better it seemed to him, and so he sent a cipher message that was destined to throw his Paris managers into a state of agitation that cannot possibly be measured by words. In brief, he instructed them to engage a few peaceable, trustworthy and positively respectable gentlemen,— he was particularly exacting on the score of gentility,— with orders to abduct the young lady and hold her in restraint until he arrived and arranged for her liberation! They were to do the deed without making any fuss about it, but at the same time they were to do it effectually.

He had the foresight to suggest that the job should be undertaken by the very detective agency he had employed to shadow young Scoville and also to keep an eye on Maud. Naturally, she was never to know the truth about the matter. She was to believe that her father came up with a huge sum in the shape of ran-

som, no questions asked. He also remembered in
time and added the imperative command that she was
to be confined in clean, comfortable quarters and given
the best of nourishment. But, above all else, it was
to be managed in a decidedly realistic way, for Maud
was a keen-witted creature who would see through the
smallest crack in the conspiracy if there was a single
false movement on the part of the plotters. It is also
worthy of mention that Mrs. Blithers was never —
decidedly never — to know the truth about the matter.

He went in to luncheon in a very amiable, even do-
cile frame of mind.

"I've thought the matter over, Lou," he said, "and
I guess you are right, after all. We will make all the
repairs necessary, but we won't consider living in it
ourselves. We'll return good for evil and live in a
hotel when we go to visit the royal family. As
for —"

"I meant that you were to think hard before attempting to force Maud upon Prince Robin's subjects without preparing them for the —"

"I thought of that, too," he interrupted cheerfully. "I'm not going to cast my only child into the
den of lions, so that's the end of it. Have you given
the order, my dear?"

"No," she said; "for I knew you would change
it when you came in."

Late that evening he had a reply from his Paris
managers. They inquired if he was responsible for
the message they had received. It was a ticklish job

and they wanted to be sure that the message was genuine. He wired back that he was the sender and to go ahead. The next morning they notified him that his instructions would be carried out as expeditiously as possible.

He displayed such a beaming countenance all that day that his wife finally demanded an explanation. It wasn't like him to beam when he was worried about anything, and she wanted to know what had come over him.

"It's the sea-air, Lou," he exclaimed glibly. "It always makes me feel like a fighting-cock. I —"

"Rubbish! You detest the sea-air. It makes you feel like fighting, I grant, but not like a fighting-cock."

"There you go, trying to tell me how I feel. I've never known any one like you, Lou. I can't say a word that —"

"Have you had any news from Maud?" she broke in suspiciously.

"Not a word," said he.

"What have you done to Chaunie Scoville?" she questioned, fixing him with an accusing eye.

"Not a thing," said he.

"Then, what is it?"

"You won't believe me if I tell you," said he warily.

"Yes, I will."

"No, you won't."

" Tell me this instant why you've been grinning like
a Cheshire cat all day."

" It's the sea-air," said he, and then: " I said you
wouldn't believe me, didn't I?"

" Do you think I'm a fool, Will Blithers?" she
flashed, and did not wait for an answer. He chuckled
to himself as she swept imperiously out of sight around
a corner of the deck-building.

He was up bright and early the next morning, tingling with anticipation. There ought to be word from
Paris before noon, and it might come earlier. He
kept pretty close to the wireless operator's office, and
was particularly attentive to the spitting crackle of
the instrument.

About eleven o'clock an incomprehensibly long message began to rattle out of the air. He contained
himself in patience for the matter of half an hour or
longer, and then, as the clatter continued without
cessation, he got up and made his way to the door of
the operator's office.

" What is it? The history of England?" he demanded sarcastically.

" Message for you, Mr. Blithers. It's a long one
and I'm having a hard time picking it up. Everybody seems to be talking at once. Do you want the
baseball scores, Mr. Blithers?"

" Not unless they come in cipher," said Mr. Blithers
acidly.

" Some of 'em do. Six to nothing in favor of the

Giants, two to nothing — Here we are at last. I've picked up the *Mauretania* again. She's relaying."

Mr. Blithers sat down on the steps and looked at his watch. It would be five o'clock in Paris. He wondered if they were giving Maud her afternoon tea, and then choked up with a sudden pity for the terrified captive. It was all he could do to keep from jumping up and ordering the operator to drop everything and take a message countermanding his inhuman instructions to those asses in Paris. Tears gushed from his eyes. He brushed them away angrily and tried to convince himself that it served Maud right for being so obstinate. Still the tears came. The corners of his mouth drooped and his chin began to quiver. It was too much! The poor child was —

But just then the operator sat back with a sigh of relief, mopped his brow, and said:

" Good thing you're a rich man, Mr. Blithers. It came collect and —"

" Never mind," blurted Mr. Blithers. " Hand it over."

There were four sheets of writing at some outlandish price per word, but what cared he? He wanted to get back to his stateroom and his cipher code as quickly — but his eyes almost started from his head as he took in the name at the bottom of the message. It was " Maud."

He did not require the cipher book. A fourth reader child could have read the message without a halt. Maud had taken his request literally. He had asked her to send him a nice long message, but he did not expect her to make a four-page letter of it. She was paying him out with a vengeance!

He took the precaution to read it before handing it over to his wife, to whom it was addressed in conjunction with himself:

"Dear father and mother," it began —(and he looked at the date line again to make sure it was from Paris)—"in reply to your esteemed favour of the nineteenth, or possibly the twentieth, I beg to inform you that I arrived safely in Paris as per schedule. Regarding the voyage, it was delightful. We had one or two rough days. The rest of the time it was perfectly heavenly. I met two or three interesting and amusing people on board and they made the time pass most agreeably. I think I wired you that I had a glimpse of a certain person. On my arrival in Paris I was met at the station by friends and taken at once to the small, exclusive hotel where they are stopping for the summer. It is so small and exclusive that I'm sure you have never heard of it. I may as well tell you that I have seen Chaunie,— you know who I mean, — Chandler Scoville, and he has been very nice to me. Concerning your suggestion that I reconsider the statement issued to the press, I beg to state that I don't see any sense in taking the world into my confidence any farther than it has been taken already, if that is grammatically correct. I have also sent word to a certain person that he is not to pay any attention to the report that we are likely to change our minds in order to help out the greedy newspapers who don't appear to know when they have had enough. I hope that the voyage will benefit both of you as much as it did me. If I felt any better than I do now I'd call for the police as a precaution. Let me suggest that you try the chicken a la Bombardier in the Ritz restaurant. I found it delicious. I daresay they serve it as nicely on your ship as they do on the *Jupiter*. as the management is the same. Of course one never can tell about chefs. My plans are a trifle indefinite. I may leave here at any moment. It is very hot and muggy and nearly ever· one is skipping off to the mountains or seashore. If I should happen to be away from Paris when you arrive don't worry about me. I shall be all right and in safe hands. I will let you know where I am just as soon as I get settled somewhere. I must go where it is quiet and peaceful. I am so distressed over what has occurred that I dou't feel as though I could ever be seen in public again without a thick veil and a pair of goggles. I have plenty of money for immediate use, but you might deposit something to my credit at the Credit Lyonnais as I haven't the least idea how long I shall stay over here. Miranda is well and is taking good care of me. She seldom lets me out of her sight if that is any comfort to you. I hope you will forgive the brevity of this communication and believe me when I say that it is not lack of love for you bo'h that curtails its length but the abominably hot weather. With endless love from your devoted daughter — Maud."

The tears had dried in ..r. Blithers' eyes but he wiped them time and again as he read this amazing letter, — this staggering exhibition of prodigality. He swore a little at first, but toward the end even that prerogative failed him. He set out in quest of his wife. Not that he expected her to say any more than he had said, but that he wanted her to see at a glance what kind of a child she had brought into the world and to forever hold her peace in future when he undertook to speak his mind.

He could not understand why his wife laughed softly to herself as she read, and he looked on in simple amazement when she deliberately undertook to count the words. She counted them in a whisper and he couldn't stand it. He went down where the children were shrieking over a game of quoits and felt singularly peaceful and undisturbed.

It was nearly bed-time before word came from his managers in Paris. Bed-time had no meaning for him after he had worked out the message by the code. It is true that he observed a life-long custom and went to bed, but he did not do it for the purpose of going to sleep.

"Your daughter has disappeared from Paris. All efforts to locate her have failed. Friends say she left ostensibly for the Pyrenees but inquiries at stations and along line fail to reveal trace of her. Scoville still here and apparently in the dark. He is being watched. Her companion and maid left with her last

night. Prince of Graustark and party left for Edelweiss to-day."

So read the message from Paris.

CHAPTER XVIII

One usually has breakfast on the porch of the Hotel Schweizerhof at Interlaken. It is not the most fashionable hostelry in the quaint little town at the head of the Lake of Thun, but it is of an excellent character, and the rolls and honey to be had with one's breakfast can not be surpassed in the Bernese Oberland. Straight ahead lies one of the most magnificent prospects in all the world: an unobstructed view of the snow-thatched Jungfrau, miles away, gleaming white and jagged against an azure sky, suggesting warmth instead of chill, grandeur instead of terror. Looking up the valley one might be led to say that an hour's ramble would take him to the crest of that shining peak, and yet some men have made a life's journey of it. Others have turned back in time.

One has a whiff of fragrant woodlands and serene hay-cocks, a breath of cool air from the Jungfrau's snows, a sniff of delectable bacon and toast — and a zest for breakfast. And one sets about it with interest, with the breakfast of the next day as a thing to look forward to.

R. Schmidt sat facing the dejected Boske Dank. His eyes were dancing with the joy of living, and nothing better can be said of a man's character than that

279

he is gay and happy at breakfast-time. He who wakes up, refreshed and buoyant, and eager for the day's adventure, is indeed a child of nature. He will never grow old and crabbed; he will grip the hand of death when the time comes with the unconquered zeal that makes the grim reaper despise himself for the advantage he takes of youth.

"Well, here we are and in spite of that, where are we?" said Dank, who saw nothing beautiful in the smile of any early morn. "I mean to say, what have we to show for our pains? We sneak into this God-forsaken hamlet, surrounded on all sides by abominations in the shape of tourists, and at the end of twenty-four hours we discover that the fair Miss Guile has played us a shabby trick. I daresay she is laughing herself sick over the whole business."

"Which is more than you can say for yourself, Boske," said Robin blithely. "Brace up! All is not lost. We'll wait here a day or two longer and then — well, I don't know what we'll do then."

"She never intended to come here at all," said Dank, filled with resentment. "It was a trick to get rid of us. She —"

"Be honest, old chap and say that it was a trick to get rid of *me*. Us is entirely too plural. But I haven't lost heart. She'll turn up yet."

"Count Quinnox is in despair over this extraordinary whim of yours, highness. He is really ill in bed this morning. I —"

"I'll run up and see him after breakfast," cried the

Prince, genuinely concerned. "I'm sorry he is taking it so seriously."

"He feels that we should be at home instead of dawdling about the —"

"That reminds me, Dank," broke in the Prince, fresh happiness in his smile; "I've decided th . home is the place for you and the Count — and Gourou too. I'm perfectly able to take care of myself,— with some assistance from Hobbs,— and I don't see any necessity for you three to remain with me any longer. I'll tell the Count that you all may start for Vienna to-night. You connect with the Orient express at —"

"Are you mad, highness?" cried Dank, startled out of his dejection. "What you speak of is impossible — utterly impossible. We cannot leave you. We were delegated to escort you —"

"I understand all of that perfectly, Dank," interrupted Robin, suddenly embarrassed, "but don't you see how infernally awkward it will be for me if Miss Guile does appear, according to plan? She will find me body-guarded, so to speak, by three surly, scowling individuals whose presence I cannot explain to save my soul, unless I tell the truth, and I'm not yet ready to do that. Can't you see what I mean? How am I to explain the three of you? A hawk-eyed triumvirate that camps on my trail from morn till night and refuses to budge! She'll suspect something, old fellow, and — well, I certainly will feel more comfortable if I'm not watched for the next few days."

"That's the point, highness. You've just got to

..e watched for the next few days. We would never dare to show our faces in Graustark again if we allowed anything to happen to you while you are under our care. You are a sacred charge. We must return you to Graustark as — er — inviolate as when you departed. We — we couldn't think of subjecting you to the peril of a — that is to say, it might prove fatal. Graustark, in that event, would be justified in hanging two of her foremost citizens and yours truly from gibbets designed especially for the blackest of traitors."

"I see, Dank. If I find happiness, you are almost sure to find disgrace and death, eh? It doesn't seem a fair division, does it? I suppose you all feel that the worst thing that can possibly happen is for me to find happiness."

"If I were the Prince of Graustark I should first think of the happiness of my subjects. I would not offend."

"Well put, Boske, but fortunately you are not the Prince. I sometimes wish that you were. It would relieve me of a tremendous responsibility. I am not mean enough, however, to wish a crown upon you, old fellow. You are lucky to be who and what you are. No one cares what you do, so long as you are honourable about it. With me it is different. I have to be watched day and night in order to be kept from doing what all the rest of the world looks upon as honourable."

"I implore you, highness, to give up this mad enterprise and return to your people as —"

"There is only one person in the world who can stop me now, Dank."

"And she isn't likely to do so, worse luck," was the other's complaint.

"When she tells me to go about my business, I'll go, but not until then. Don't you like honey, Dank?"

"No," said Dank savagely. "I hate it." He leaned back in his chair and glowered upon the innocent, placid Jungfrau. The Prince ate in silence. "May I be permitted a question, highness?"

"All you like, Boske. You are my best friend. Go ahead."

"Did you see Miss Guile after that visit to St. Cloud — and to the police station?"

"No. Evidently she was frightened out of her boots by the Hawkshaws. I don't blame her, do you?"

"And you've had no word from her?"

"None. Now you are going to ask what reason I have for believing that she will come to Interlaken. Well, I can't answer that question. I think she'll come, that's all."

"Do you think she is in love with you?"

"Ah, my dear fellow, you are asking me to answer my own prayer," said Robin, without a sign of resentment in his manner. "I'm praying that she isn't altogether indifferent. By the way, it is my turn to ask questions. Are you still in love with her?"

"I am proud to say that you are more in my prayers
that she," said Dank, with a profound sigh. "Nothing could please me more than to be the one to save
my prince from disaster, even if it meant the sacrifice of self. My only prayer is that you may be
spared, sir, and I taken in your place."

"That was a neat answer, 'pon my soul," cried
the Prince admiringly. "You — Hello, who is this
approaching? It is no other than the great Gourou
himself, the king of sleuths, as they say in the books
I used to read. Good morning, Baron."

The sharp-visaged little Minister of Police came up
to the table and fixed an accusing eye upon his
sovereign,— the literal truth, for he had the other
eye closed in a protracted wink.

"I regret to inform your majesty that the enemy
is upon us," he said. "I fear that our retreat is cut
off. Nothing remains save —"

"She has arrived?" cried the Prince eagerly.

"She has," said the Baron. "Bag and baggage,
and armed to the eyes. Each eye is a gatling-gun,
each lip a lunette behind which lies an unconquerable
legion of smiles and rows of ivory bayonets, each ear
a hardy spy, and every nut-brown strand a covetous
dastard on the warpath not for a scalp but for a
crown. Napoleon was never so well prepared for battle as she, nor Troy so firmly fortified. Yes, highness,
the foe is at our gates. We must to arms!"

"Where is she?" demanded Robin, unimpressed by
this glowing panegyric.

" At this instant, sir, I fancy she is rallying her forces in the very face of a helpless mirror. In other words, she is preparing for the fray. She is dressing."

" The devil! How dare you pry into the secret —"

" Abhorrent thought! I deduce, nothing more. Her maid loses herself in the halls while attempting to respond to the call for re-inforcements. She accosts a gentleman of whom she inquires the way. The gentleman informs her she is on the third, not the second *etage*, and she scurries away simpering, but not before confiding to me — the aforesaid gentleman — that her mistress will give her fits for being late with her hair, whatever that may signify. So, you see, I do not stoop to keyholes but put my wits to work instead."

" When did she arrive? "

" She came last night via Milan."

" From Milan? " cried Robin, astonished.

" A roundabout way, I'll admit," said the Baron, drily, " and tortuous in these hot days, but admirably suited to a purpose. I should say that she was bent on throwing some one off the track."

" And yet she came! " cried the Prince, in exultation. " She wanted to come, after all, now didn't she, Dank? " He gave the lieutenant a look of triumph.

" She is more dangerous than I thought," said the guardsman mournfully.

" Sit down, Baron," commanded the Prince. " I want to lay down the law to all of you. You three

will have to move on to Graustark and leave me to
look out for myself. I will not have Miss Guile —"

"No!" exclaimed the Baron, with unusual vehe-
mence. "I expected you to propose something of the
kind, and I am obliged to confess to you that we have
discussed the contingency in advance. We will not
leave you. That is final. You may depose us, exile
us, curse us or anything you like, but still we shall
remain true to the duty we owe to our country. We
stay here, Prince Robin, just so long as you are content to remain."

Robin's face was very red. "You shame me,
Baron," he said simply. "I am sorry that I spoke
as I did. You are my friends, my loyal friends, and I
would have humbled you in the eyes of my people.
I beg your pardon, and yours, Boske. After all, I
am only a prince and a prince is dependent on the
loyalty of such as you. I take back all that I said."

The Baron laid a kindly hand on the young man's
shoulder. "I was rough, highness, in my speech just
now, but you will understand that I was moved to —"

"I know, Baron. It was the only way to fetch me
up sharp. No apology is required. God bless you."

"Now I have a suggestion of my own to offer," said
the Baron, taking a seat at the end of the table. "I
confess that Miss Guile may not be favourably impressed by the constant attendance of three able-
bodied nurses, and, as she happens to be no fool, it
is reasonably certain that she will grasp the significance of our assiduity. Now I propose that the

Count, Dank and myself efface ourselves as completely as possible during the rest of our enforced stay in Interlaken. I propose that we take quarters in another hotel and leave you and Hobbs to the tender mercies of the enemy. It seems to me that —"

"Good!" cried Robin. "That's the ticket! I quite agree to that, Baron."

Dank wa prepared to object but a dark look from Gourou silenced him. "I've talked it over with the Count and he acquiesces," went on the Baron. "We recognise the futility of trying to induce you to leave at once for Graustark, and we are now content to trust Providence to watch over and protect you against a foe whose motives may in time become transparent, even to the blind."

The irony in the remark was not lost on Robin. He flushed angrily but held his tongue.

Ten o'clock found the three gentlemen,— so classified by Hobbs,— out of the Schweizerhof and arranging for accommodations at the Regina Hotel Jungfraublick, perched on an eminence overlooking the valley and some distance removed from the temporary abode of the Prince. Their departure from the hotel in the Hoheweg was accomplished without detection by Miss Guile or her friends, and, to all intents and purposes, Robin was alone and unattended when he sat down on the porch near the telescope to await the first appearance of the enchanting foe. He was somewhat puzzled by the strange submissiveness of his companions. Deep down in his mind lurked the disquieting suspicion that they were conniving to get the better of the lovely temptress by some sly and secret bit of strategy. What was back of the wily Baron's motive? Why were they now content to let him take the bit in his teeth and run wherever he would? What had become of their anxiety, their eagerness to drag him off to Graustark by the first train? There was food for reflection in the tranquil capitulation of the defenders. Were they acting under fresh instructions from Edelweiss? Had the Prime Minister directed them to put no further obstacle in front of the great Blithers invasion? Or — and he scowled darkly at the thought — was there a plan afoot to overcome the dangerous Miss Guile by means more sinister than subtle?

Enlightenment came unexpectedly and with a shock to his composure. He had observed the three spirited saddlehorses near the entrance of the hotel, in charge of two stable-boys, but had regarded them only as splendid specimens of equine aristocracy. It had not entered his mind to look upon them as agents of despair.

Two people emerged from the door and, passing by without so much as a glance in his direction, made their way to the mounting block. Robin's heart went down to his boots. Bedelia, a graceful figure in a smart riding habit, was laughing blithely over a soft-spoken remark that her companion had made as they were crossing the porch. And that companion was no other than the tall, good-looking fellow who had

met her at Cherbourg! The Prince, stunned and incredulous, watched them mount their horses and canter
away, followed by a groom who seemed to have sprung
up from nowhere.

"Good morning, Mr. Schmidt," spoke a voice, and,
still bewildered, he whirled, hat in hand, to confront
Mrs. Gaston. "Did I startle you?"

He bowed stiffly over the hand she held out for him
to clasp, and murmured something about being proof
against any surprise. The colour was slowly returning to his face, and his smile was as engaging as ever
despite the bitterness that filled his soul. Here was
a pretty trick to play on a fellow! Here was a slap
in the face!

"Isn't it a glorious morning? And how wonderful she is in this gorgeous sunlight," went on Mrs.
Gaston, in what may be described as a hurried, nervous manner.

"I had the briefest glimpse of her," mumbled
Robin. "When did she come?"

"Centuries and centuries ago, Mr. Schmidt," said
she, with a smile. "I was speaking of the Jungfrau."

"Oh!" he exclaimed, flushing. "I thought you —
er — yes, of course! Really quite wonderful. I have
heard it said that she never removes her night-cap,
but always greets the dawn in spotless — ahem! Of
course you understand that I am speaking of the Jungfrau," he floundered.

"Naturally, Mr. Schmidt. And so you came, after

all. We were afraid you might have concluded to alter your plans. Miss Guile will be delighted."

He appeared grateful for the promise. "I have been here for three days, Mrs. Gaston. You were delayed in leaving Paris?"

"Yes," she said, and changed the subject. "The riding is quite good, I understand. They are off for Lauterbrunnen."

"I see," said he. "There is a splendid inn there, I am told."

"They will return here for luncheon, of course," she said, raising her eyebrows slightly. His heart became a trifle lighter at this. "Mr. White is a life-long friend and acquaintance of the family," she volunteered, apropos of nothing.

"Oh, his name is White?" with a quiet laugh.

"If you have nothing better to do, Mr. Schmidt, why not come with me to the Kursaal? The morning concert will begin shortly, and I —"

"I think you will find that the band plays in the square across the way, Mrs. Gaston, and not in the Casino. At least, that has been the programme for the last two mornings."

"Nevertheless, there is a concert at the Casino to-day," she informed him. "Will you come?"

"Gladly," he replied, and they set off for the Kursaal. He found seats in the half-empty pavillion and prepared to listen to the music, although his real interest was following the narrow highway to Lanterbrunnen — and the Staubbach.

· "This is to be a special concert given at the request of the Grand Duke who, I hear, is leaving this afternoon for Berne."

" The Grand Duke? I was not aware of the presence of royalty," said he in surprise.

" No? He has been here for three days, but at another hotel. The Grand Duke Paulus and his family, you know."

Robin shot a swift, apprehensive glance about the big enclosure, sweeping the raised circle from end to end. On the opposite side of the pavillion he discovered the space reserved for the distinguished party. Although he was far removed from that section he sank deeper into his chair and found one pretext after another to screen his face from view. He did know the Grand Duke Paulus and the Grand Duke knew him, which was even more to the point.

The Prince of Graustark had been a prime favourite of the great man since his knickerbocker days. Twice as a boy he had visited in the ducal palace, far distant from Graustark, and at the time of his own coronation the Grand Duke and his sons had come to the castle in Edelweiss for a full month's stay. They knew him well and they would recognise him at a glance. At this particular time the last thing on earth that he desired was to be hailed as · a royal prince.

Never, in all his life, had he known the sun to penetrate so brightly into shadows as it did to-day. He felt that he was sitting in a perfect glare of light

and that every feature of his face was clear to the
most distant observer.

He was on the point of making an excuse to leave
the place when the ducal party came sauntering down
the aisle on their way to the reserved section. Every
one stood up, the band played, the Grand Duke bowed
to the right and to the left, and escape was cut off.
Robin could only stand with averted face and direct
mild execrations at the sunlight that had seemed so
glorious at breakfast-time.

"He is a splendid-looking man, isn't he?" Mrs.
Gaston was saying. She was gazing in rapt admiration upon the royal group.

"He is, indeed," said Robin, resolutely scanning a
programme, which he continued to hold before his face.
When he sat down again, it was with his back to the
band. "I don't like to watch the conductors," he explained. "They do such foolish things, you know."

Mrs. Gaston was eyeing him curiously. He was bitterly conscious of a crimson cheek. In silence they
listened to the first number. While the applause was
at its height, Mrs. Gaston leaned forward and said
to him:

"I am afraid you are not enjoying the music, Mr.
Schmidt. What is on your mind?"

He started. "I — I — really, Mrs. Gaston, I am
enjoying it. I —"

"Your mind has gone horse-back riding, I fear.
At present it is between here and Lauterbrunnen, jog-
ging beside that roaring little torrent that —"

" I don't mind confessing that you are quite right,"
said he frankly. " And I may add that the music
makes me so blue that I'd like to jump into that roaring torrent and — and swim out again, I suppose," he
concluded, with a sheepish grin.

" You are in love."

" I am," he confessed.

She laid her hand upon his. Her eyes were wide
with eagerness. " Would it drive away the blues if I
were to tell you that you have a chance to win her? "

He felt his head spinning. " If — if I could believe
that — that —" he began, and choked up with the
rush of emotion that swept through him.

" She is a strange girl. She will marry for love
alone. Her father is determined that she shall marry
a royal prince. That much I may confess to you.
She has defied her father, Mr. Schmidt. She will
marry for love, and I believe it is in your power to
awaken love in that adorable heart of hers. You —"

" For God's sake, Mrs. Gaston, tell me — tell me,
has she breathed a word to you that —"

" Not a single word. But I know her well. I have
known her since she was a baby, and I can read the
soul that looks out through those lovely eyes. Knowing her so well, I may say to you — oh, it must be in
the strictest confidence! — that you have a chance.
And if you win her love, you will *have* the greatest
treasure in all the world. She — but, look! The
Grand Duke is leaving. He —"

" I don't care what becomes of the Grand Duke,"

he burst out. "Tell me more. Tell me how you look into her soul, and tell me what you see —".

"Not now, sir. I have said enough. I have given you the sign of hope. It remains with you to make the most of it."

"But you — you don't know anything about me. I may be the veriest adventurer, the most unworthy of all —"

"I think, Mr. Schmidt, that I know you pretty well. I do not require the aid of Diogenes' lantern to see an honest man. I am responsible for her welfare. She has been placed under my protection. For twenty years I have adored her. I am not likely to encourage an adventurer."

"I must be honest with you, Mrs. Gaston," he said suddenly. "I am not —"

She held up her hand. "Mr. Totten has informed me that you are a life-long friend of Mrs. Truxton King. I cabled to her from Paris. There is no more to be said."

His face fell. "Did she tell you — everything?"

"She said no more than that R. Schmidt is the finest boy in all the world." Suddenly her face paled. "You are never — never to breathe a word of this to — to Bedelia," she whispered.

"But her father? What will he say to —"

"Her father has said all that can be said," she broke in quietly. "He cannot force her to marry the man he has selected. She will marry the man she

CHAPTER XIX

"WHAT WILL MY PEOPLE DO!"

THE Grand Duke and his party left Interlaken by special train early in the afternoon, and great was Robin's relief when Hobbs returned with the word that they were safely on their way to the capital of Switzerland. He emerged from the seclusion of his room, where he had been in hiding since noon, and set out for a walk through the town. His head was high and his stride jaunty, for his heart was like a cork. People stared after him with smiles of admiration, and never a *cocher'* passed him by without a genial, inviting tilt of the eyebrow and a tentative pull at the reins, only to meet with a pleasant shake of the head or the negative flourish of a bamboo cane.

Night came and with it the silvery glow of moonlight across the hoary headed queen of the Oberland. When Robin came out from dinner he seated himself on the porch, expectant, eager — and vastly lonesome. An unaccountable shyness afflicted him, rendering him quite incapable of sending his card up to the one who could have dispelled the gathering gloom with a single glance of the eye. Would she come stealing out ostensibly to look at the night-capped peak, but with furtive glances into the shadows of the porch in quest of — But no! She would not do that! She would come attended by the exasperating Mr. White and the friendly duenna. Her starry eyes, directed elsewhere, would only serve to increase the depth of the shadows in which he lurked impatient.

She came at last — and alone. Stopping at the rail not more than an arm's length from where he sat, she gazed pensively up at the solemn mistress of the valley, one slim hand at her bosom, the other hanging limp at her side. He could have touched that slender hand by merely stretching forth his own. Breathless, enthralled, he sat as one deprived of the power or even the wish to move. The spell was upon him; he was in thralldom.

She wore a rose-coloured gown, soft, slinky, seductive. A light Egyptian scarf lay across her bare shoulders. The slim, white neck and the soft dark hair — but she sighed! He heard that faint, quick-drawn sigh and started to his feet.

"Bedelia!" he whispered softly.

She turned quickly, to find him standing beside her, his face aglow with rapture. A quick catch of the breath, a sudden movement of the hand that lay upon her breast, and then she smiled, — a wavering, uncertain smile that went straight to his heart and shamed him for startling her. "I beg your pardon," he began lamely. "I — I startled you."

She held out her hand to him, still smiling. "I fear I shall never become accustomed to being pursued," she said, striving for comrl of her voice. "It is dreadful to feel that some one is forever watching you from behind. I am glad it is you, however. You at least are not 'the secret eye that never sleeps'!" She gently withdrew her hand from his ardent clasp. "Mrs. Gaston told me that she had seen you. I feared that you might have gone on your way rejoicing."

"Rejoicing?" he cried. "Why do you say that?"

"After our experience in Paris, I should think that you had had enough of me and my faithful watch-dogs."

"Rubbish!" he exclaimed. "I shall never have enough of you," he went on, with sudden boldness. "As for the watch-dogs, they are not likely to bite us, so what is there to be afraid of?"

"Have you succeeded in evading the watchful eye of Mr. Totten's friend?" she enquired, sending an apprehensive glance along the porch.

"Completely," he declared. "I am quite alone in this hotel and, I believe, unsuspected. And you? Are you still being—"

"Sh! Who knows? I think we have thrown them off the track, but one cannot be sure. I raised a dreadful rumpus about it in Paris, and—well, they said they were sorry and advised me not to be worried, for the surveillance would cease at once. Still, I am quite sure that they lied to me."

"Then you *are* being followed."

She smiled again, and there was mischief in her eyes. "If so, I have led them a merry chase. We have been travelling for two days and nights, Mr.

Schmidt, by train and motor, getting off at stations unexpectedly, hopping into trains going in any direction but the right one, sleeping in strange beds and doing all manner of queer things. And here we are at last. I am sure you must look upon me as a very silly, flibberty-gibbet creature."

"I see that your retinue has been substantially augmented," he remarked, a trace of jealousy in his voice. "The good-looking Mr. White has not been eluded."

"Mr. White? Oh, yes, I see. But he is to be trusted, Mr. Schmidt," she said mysteriously — and tantalisingly. "He will not betray me to my cruel monster of a father. I have his solemn promise not to reveal my whereabouts to any one. My father is the last person in the world to whom he would go with reports of my misdoings."

"I saw you this morning, riding with him," said he glumly.

"Through the telescope?" she inquired softly, laying a hand upon the stationary instrument.

He flushed hotly. "It was when you were starting out, Miss Guile. I am not one of the spies, you should remember."

"You are my partner in guilt," she said lightly. "By the way, have you forgiven me for leading you into temptation?"

"Certainly. I am still in the Garden of Eden, you see, and as I don't take any stock in the book of Genesis, I hope to prove to myself at least, that the conduct of an illustrious forebear of mine was not due to the frailties of Eve but to his own tremendous anxiety to get out of a place that was filled with snakes. I hope and pray that you will continue to put temptation in my path so that I may have the frequent pleasure of falling."

She turned her face away and for a moment was silent. "Shall we take those chairs over there, Mr. Schmidt? They appear to be as abandoned as we." She indicated two chairs near the broad portals.

He shook his head. "If we are looking for the most utterly abandoned, allow me to call your attention to the two in yonder corner."

"It is quite dark over there," she said with a frown.

"Quite," he agreed. "Which accounts, no doubt, for your failure to see them."

"Mrs. Gaston will be looking for me before —" she began hesitatingly.

"Or Mr. White, perhaps. Let me remind you that they have exceedingly sharp eyes."

"Mr. White is no longer here," she announced.

His heart leaped. "Then I, at least, have nothing to fear," he said quickly.

She ignored the banality. "He left this afternoon. Very well, let us take the seats over there. I rather like the — shall I say shadows?"

"I too object to the limelight,— Bedelia," he said, offering her his arm.

"You are not to call me Bedelia," she said, holding back.

"Then 'forgive us our transgressions' is to be applied in the usual order, I presume."

"Are you sorry you called me Bedelia?" she insisted, frowning ominously.

"No. I'm sorry you object, that's all."

They made their way through a maze of chairs and seated themselves in the dim corner. Their view of the Jungfrau from this vine-screened corner was not as perfect as it might have been, but the Jungfrau had no present power of allurement for them.

"I cannot stay very long," she said as she sank back in the comfortable chair.

He turned his back not only upon the occupants of the porch but the lustrous Jungfrau, drawing his chair up quite close to hers. As he leaned forward, with his elbows on the arms of the chair, she seemed to slink farther back in the depths of hers, as if suddenly afraid of him.

"Now, tell me everything," he said. "From beginning to eud. What became of you after that day at St. Cloud, whither have you journeyed, and wherefore were you so bent on coming to this now blessed Interlaken?"

"Easily answered. Nothing at all became of me. I journeyed thither, and I came because I had set my heart on seeing the Jungfrau."

"But you had seen it many times."

"And I hoped that I might find peace and quiet here," she added quite distinctly.

"You expected to find me here, didn't you?"

"Yes, but I did not regard you as a disturber of the peace."

"You knew I would come, but you didn't know why, did you, Bedelia?" He leaned a little closer.

"Yes, I knew why," she said calmly, emotionlessly. He drew back instantly, chilled by her directness. "You came because there was promise of an interesting adventure, which you now are on the point of making impossible by a rather rash exhibition of haste."

He stared at her shadowy face in utter confusion. For a moment he was speechless. Then a rush of protesting sincerity surged up within him and he cried out in low, intense tones: "I cannot allow you to think that of me, Miss Guile. If I have done or said anything to lead you to believe that I am —"

"Oh, I beg of you, Mr. Schmidt, do not enlarge upon the matter by trying to apologise," she cried.

"I am not trying to apologise," he protested. "I am trying to justify what you are pleased to call an exhibition of haste. You see, it's just this way: I am obliged to make hay while the sun shines, for soon I may be cast into utter darkness. My days are numbered. In a fortnight I shall be where I cannot call my soul my own. I —"

"You alarm me. Are you to be sent to prison?"

"You wouldn't look upon it as a prison, but it seems like one to me. Do not laugh. I cannot explain to you now. Another day I shall tell you everything, so pray take me for what I am to-day, and ask no questions.   I have asked no more of you, so do you be equally generous with me."

" True," she said, " you have asked no questions of me.   You take me for what I am to-day, and yet you know nothing of my yesterdays or my to-morrows.   It is only fair that I should be equally confiding.   Let there be no more questions.   Are we, however, to take each other seriously? "

" By all means," he cried.   " There will come a day when you may appreciate the full extent of my seriousness."

" You speak in riddles."

" Is the time ripe for me to speak in sober earnest? " he questioned softly.   She drew back again in swift alarm.

" No, no!   Not now — not yet.   Do not say anything now, Mr. Schmidt, that may put an end to our — to our adventure."

She was so serious, so plaintive, and yet so shyly prophetic of comfort yet to be attained, that his heart warmed with a mighty glow of exaltation.   A sweet feeling of tenderness swept over him.

" If God is good, there can be but one end to our adventure," he said, and then, for some mysterious reason, silence fell between them.   Long afterward — it seemed hours to him! — she spoke, and her voice was low and troubled.

" Can you guess why I am being watched so carefully, why I am being followed so doggedly by men who serve not me but another? "

"Yes. It is because you are the greatest jewel in the possession of a great man, and he would preserve you against all varlets,— such as I."

She did not reveal surprise at his shrewd conjecture. She nodded her head and sighed.

"You are right. I am his greatest jewel, and yet he would give me into the keeping of an utter stranger. I am being protected against that conscienceless varlet — Love! If love lays hands upon me — ah, my friend, you cannot possibly guess what a calamity that would be!"

"And love *will* lay hands upon you, Bedelia,—"

"I am sure of that," she said, once more serene mistress of herself after a peculiarly dangerous lapse. "That is why I shudder. What could be more dreadful than to fall into the clutches of that merciless foe to peace? He rends one's heart into shreds; he stabs in the dark; he thrusts, cuts and slashes and the wounds never heal; he blinds without pity; he is overbearing, domineering, ruthless and his victims are powerless to retaliate. Love is the greatest tyrant in all the world, Mr. Schmidt, and we poor wretches can never hope to conquer him. We are his prey, and he is rapacious. Do you not shudder also?"

"Bless you, no! I'd rather enjoy meeting him in mortal combat. My notion of bliss would be a fight to the death with love, for then the conflict would not be one-sided. What could be more glorious than to stand face to face with love, hand to hand, breast to breast, lip to lip until the end of time? Let him cut and slash and stab if you will, there would still be recompense for the vanquished. Even those who have suffered most in the conflict with love must admit that they have had a share in the spoils. One can't ignore the sweet hours when counting up the bitter ones, after love has withdrawn from the tender encounter. The cuts and slashes are cherished and memory is a store-house for the spoils that must be shared with vanity."

"It sounds like a book. Who is your favourite author?" she inquired lightly.

"Baedeker," he replied, with promptness. "Without my Baedeker, I should never have chanced upon the route travelled by love, nor the hotel where I now lodge in close proximity to —"

"Will you please be sensible?"

"You invite something to the contrary, Bedelia," he ventured.

"Haven't I requested you to —"

"I think of you only as Bedelia," he made haste to explain. "Bedelia will stick to you forever, you see, while Miss Guile is almost ephemeral. It cannot live long, you know, with so many other names eager to take its place. But Bedelia — ah, Bedelia is everlasting."

She laughed joyously, naturally. "You really are quite wonderful, Mr. Schmidt. Still I must change the subject. I trust the change will not affect your glibness, for it is quite exhilarating. How long do you purpose remaining in Interlaken?"

"That isn't changing the subject," said he. "I shall be here for a week or ten days — or perhaps longer." He put it in the form of a question, after all.

"Indeed? How I envy you. I am sorry to say I shall have to leave in a day or two."

His face fell. "Why?" he demanded, almost indignantly.

"Because I am enjoying myself," she replied.

"I don't quite get your meaning."

"I am having such a good time disobeying my father, Mr. Schmidt, and eluding pursuers. It is only a matter of a day or two before I am discovered here, so I mean to keep on dodging. It is splendid fun."

"Do you think it is quite fair to me?"

"Did I induce you to come here, good sir?"

"You did," said he, with conviction. "Heaven is my witness. I would not have come but for you. I am due at home by this time."

"Are you under any obligations to remain in Interlaken for a week or ten days?"

"Not now," he replied. "Do you mind telling me where you are going to, Miss Guile?"

"First to Vienna, then — well, you cannot guess where. I have decided to go to Edelweiss."

"Edelweiss!" he exclaimed in astonishment. He could hardly believe his ears.

"It is the very last place in the world that my father would think of looking for me. Besides I am curious to see the place. I understand that the great Mr. Blithers is to be there soon, and the stupid Prince who will not be tempted by millions, and it is even possible that the extraordinary Miss Blithers may take it into her head to look the place over before definitely refusing to be its Princess. I may find some amusement — or entertainment as an on-looker when the riots begin."

He was staring at her wide-eyed and incredulous. "Do you really mean to say you are going to Graustark?"

"I have thought of doing so. Don't you think it will be amusing to be on the scene when the grand climax occurs? Of course, the Prince will come off his high horse, and the girl will see the folly of her ways, and old Mr. Blithers will run rough shod over everybody, and — but, goodness, I can't even speculate on the possibilities."

He was silent. So this was the way the wind blew, eh? There was but one construction to be put upon her decision to visit the Capital of Graustark. She *had* taken it into her head "to look the place over before definitely refusing to be its Princess!" His first thrill of exultation gave way to a sickening sense of disappointment.

All this time she was regarding him through amused, half-closed eyes. She had a distinct advantage over him. She knew that he was the Prince of Graustark; she had known it for many days. Perhaps if she had known all the things that were in his cunning brain, she would not have ventured so far into the comedy she was constructing. She would have hesitated — aye, she might have changed her methods completely. But she was in the mood to do and say daring things. She considered her position absolutely secure, and so she could afford to enjoy herself for the time being. There would be an hour of reckon: 3, no doubt, but she was not troubled by its promise of castigation.

"Poor Prince!" she sighed pityingly. He started. The remark was so unexpected that he almost betrayed himself. It seemed profoundly personal. "He will be in very hot water, I fear."

He regarded her coldly. "And you want to be on hand to see him squirm, I suppose."

She took instant alarm. Was she going too far? His query was somewhat disconcerting.

"To be perfectly frank with you, Mr. Schmidt, I am going to Graustark because no one will ever think of looking for me in such an out-of-the-way place. I am serious now, so you must not laugh at me. Circumstances are such that I prefer to seek happiness after a fashion of my own. My parents love me, but they will not understand me. They wish me to marry a man they have picked out for me. I intend to pick out my own man, Mr. Schmidt. You may suspect, from all that you have seen, that I am running away from home, from those who are dearest in all the world to me. You knew that I was carefully watched in Paris. You know that my father fears that I may marry a man distasteful to him, and I suppose to my mother, although she is not so—"

"Are his fears well-founded?" he asked, rudely interrupting her. "Is there a man that he has cause to fear? Are—are you in love with some one, Bedelia?"

"Do not interrupt me. I want you to know that I am not running away from home, that I shall return to it when I see fit, and that I am not in love with the man they suspect. I want you to be just with me. You are not to blame my father for anything, no matter how absurd his actions may appear to you in the light of the past few days. It is right that he should try to safeguard me. I am wayward but I am not foolish. I shall commit no silly blunder, you may be sure of that. Now do you understand me better?"

She was very serious, very intense. He laid his hand on hers, and she did not withdraw it. Emboldened, his hand closed upon the dainty fingers and an instant later they were borne to his hot lips.

"You have said that I came here in search of a light adventure," he whispered, holding her hand close to his cheek as he bent nearer to her. "You imply that I am a trifler, a light-o'-love. I want you to understand me better. I came here because I—"

"Stop!" she pleaded. "You must not say it. I am serious—yes, I know that you are serious too. But you must wait. If you were to say it to me now

I should have to send you away and — oh, believe me, I do not want to do that. I — I —"

" You love no one else? " he cried, rapturously.

She swayed slightly, as if incapable of resisting the appeal that called her to his heart. Her lips were parted, her eyes glowed luminously even in the shad--ows, and she scarcely breathed the words:

" I love no one else."

A less noble nature than his would have seized upon the advantage offered by her sudden weakness. Instead, he drew a long, deep breath, straightened his figure and as he gently released the imprisoned hand, the prince in him spoke.

" You have asked me to wait. I am sure that you know what is in my heart. It will always be there. It will not cut and slash and stab, for it is the most tender thing that has ever come into my life — or yours. It must never be accused of giving pain to you, so I shall obey you — and wait. You are right to avoid the risk of entrusting a single word of hope to me. I am a passer-by. My sincerity, my honesty of purpose remain to be proved. Time will serve my cause. I can only ask you to believe in me — to trust me a little more each day — and to let your heart be my judge."

She spoke softly. " I believe in you, I trust you even now, or I would not be here. You are kind to me. Few would have been so generous. We both are passers-by. It is too soon for us to judge each other in the full. I must be sure — oh, I must be sure of myself. Can you understand? I must be sure of myself, and I am not sure now. You do not know how much there is at stake, you can not possibly know what it would mean to me if I were to discover that our adventure had no real significance in the end. I know it sounds strange and mysterious, or you would not look so puzzled. But unless I can be sure of one thing—one vital thing—our adventure has failed in every respect. Now, I must go in. No; do not ask me to stay—and let me go alone. I prefer it so. Good night, my comrade."

He stood up and let her pass. "Good night, my princess," he said, clearly and distinctly. She shot a swift glance into his eyes, smiled faintly, and moved away. His rapt gaze followed her. She entered the door without so much as a glance over her shoulder.

"My princess," he repeated wonderingly, to himself. "Have I kissed the hand of my princess? God in heaven, is there on earth a princess more perfect than she? Can there be in all this world another so deserving of worship as she?"

Late at night she sat in her window looking up at the peaceful Jungfrau. A dreamy, ineffably sweet smile lay in her dark eyes. The hand he kissed had lain long against her lips. To herself she had repeated, over and over again, the inward whisper:

"What will my dear, simple old dad say if I marry this man after all?"

In a window not ten feet away, he was staring out

into the night, with lowering eyes and troubled heart, and in his mind he was saying:

"What will my people do if I marry this woman after all?"

CHAPTER XX

Two days went by. They were fraught with an ever-increasing joy for the two who were learning to understand each other through the mute, though irresistible teachings of a common tutor. Each succeeding hour had its exquisite compensation; each presented the cup of knowledge to lips that were parched with the fever of impotence, and each time it was returned empty by the seekers after wisdom. There were days in which Love went harvesting and prospered amazingly in the fields, for each moment that he stored away against the future was ripe with promise. He was laying by the store on which he was to subsist to the end of his days; he allowed no moment to go to waste, for he is a miser and full of greed.

Not one word of love passed between these two who waited for the fruit to ripen. They were never alone together. Always they were attended by the calm, keen-eyed Mrs. Gaston, who, though she may have been in sympathy with their secret enterprise, was nevertheless a dependable barrier to its hasty consummation.

She had received her instructions from the one now most likely to be in need of a deterring influence; the girl herself. After that evening on the porch, Bedelia

313

had gone straight to her duenna with the truth. Then she made it clear to the good lady that she was not to be left alone for an instant to confront the welcome besieger. And so it was that when Robin and Bedelia walked or rode together, they were attended by prevention. In the Casino, at the gaming tables, at the concert, or even in the street he was never free to express a thought or emotion that, under less guarded conditions, might have exposed her to the risk she was so carefully avoiding.

He understood the situation perfectly and was not resentful. He appreciated the caution with which she was carrying on her own campaign, and he was not unmindful of the benefits that might also accrue to him through this proscribed period of reflection. While he was sure of himself by this time, and fully determined to risk even his crown for the girl who so calmly held him at bay, he was also sensible of the wisdom of her course. She was not willing to subject herself or him to the dangers of temptation. As she had said, there was a great deal at stake; the rest of their lives, in truth.

There was one little excursion to Grindelwald and its glacier, and later an ascent of the Schynige Platte. Even a desperate horror of the rack and pinion railway up and down the steep mountain did not daunt the incomparable chaperone. (True, she closed her eyes and shrank as far away from the edge of eternity as possible, but she stuck manfully to her post.) He dined with them on the two evenings, and with them heard the concerts.

There were times when he was perplexed, and uncertain of her. At no time did she relax into what might have been considered a receptive or even an encouraging mood. He watched eagerly for the love-light that he hoped to surprise in her eyes, but it never appeared. She was serene, self-contained, natural. That momentary dissolving on her part when she sat with him in the shadows was the only circumstance he had to base his hopes upon. She had betrayed herself then by word and manner, but now she had her emotions well in hand.

Her lovely eyes met his frankly and without the faintest sign of diffidence or self-consciousness. Her soft laugh was free and unconstrained, her smile gay and remotely suggestive of mischief. At times he thought she was playing the game too well for one who professed to be concerned about the future.

On the third day he was convicted of duplicity. She went off for a walk alone, leaving him safely anchored in what he afterwards came to look upon as a pre-arranged game of auction-bridge. When she came in after an absence of at least two hours, the game was just breaking up. He noted the questioning look that Mrs. Gaston bestowed upon her fair charge, and also remarked that it contained no sign of reproof. The girl went up to her room without so much as a word with him. Her face was flushed

and she carried her head disdainfully. He was greatly
puzzled.

The puzzle was soon explained. He waited for her
on the stairway as she came down alone to dinner.

"You told me that your friends were not in Interlaken, Mr. Schmidt," she said coldly. "Why did you
feel called upon to deceive me?"

He bit his lip. For an instant he reflected, and
then gave an evasive answer. "I think I told you that
I was alone in this hotel, Miss Guile. My friends are
at another hotel. I am not aware that—"

"I have seen and talked with that charming old
man, Mr. Totten," she interrupted. "He has been
here for days, and Mr. Dank as well. Do you think
that you have been quite fair with me?"

He lowered his eyes. "I think I have been most
fair to both of us," he replied. "Will you believe me
when I say that in a way I personally requested them
to leave this hotel and seek another? And will it de-
crease your respect for me if I add that I wanted to
have you all to myself, so to speak, and not to feel
that these good friends of mine were—"

"Why don't you look me in the face, Mr. Schmidt?"
she broke in. He looked up at once prepared to meet
a look of disdain. To his surprise, she was smiling.
"I have talked it all over with Mrs. Gaston, and she
advised me to forgive you if you were in the least peni-
tent and—honest. Well, you have made an honest
confession, I am satisfied. Now, I have a confession
to make. I have suspected all along that Mr. Totten

and Mr. Dank and the shadowy Mr. Gourou were in the town."

"You suspected?" he cried in amazement and chagrin.

"I was morally certain that they were here. To-day my suspicions were justified. I encountered Mr. Totten in the park beyond the Jungfraublick. He was very much upset, I can assure you, but he recovered with amazing swiftness. We sat on one of the benches in a nice little nook and had a long, long talk. He is a charming man. I have asked him to come to luncheon with us to-morrow, and to bring Mr. Dank."

"Good Lord, will wonders never —"

"But I did not include the still invisible Mr. Gourou. I was afraid that you would be too uncomfortable under the hawk-like eye of the gentleman who so kindly warned us at the Pavillon Bleu." There was gentle raillery in her manner. "I shall expect you to join us, Mr. Schmidt. You have no other engagement?"

"I — I shall be delighted," he stammered.

She laid her hand gently upon his arm and a serious sweetness came into her eyes.

"Come," she said; "let us go in ahead of Mrs. Gaston. Let us have just one little minute to ourselves, Mr. Schmidt."

It was true that she came upon the Count in one of the paths of the Kleine Rugen. He was walking slowly toward her, his eyes fixed thoughtfully upon the ground. When she accosted him, he was plainly confused, as she had said. After the first few passages in polite though stilted conversation, his keen, grey eyes resumed their thoughtful — it was even a calculating look.

"Will you sit here with me for a while, Miss Guile?" he asked gently. "I have something of the gravest importance to say to you."

She sat beside him on the sequestered bench, and when she arose to leave him an hour later, her cheek was warm with colour and her eyes were filled with tenderness toward this grim, staunch old man who was the friend of *her* friend. She laid her hand in his and suffered him to raise it to his lips.

"I hope, my dear young lady," said he with simple directness, "that you will not regard me as a stupid, interfering old meddler. God is my witness, I have your best interests at heart. You are too good and beautiful to —"

"I shall always look upon you as the kindest of men!" she cried impulsively, and left him.

He stood watching her slender, graceful figure as she moved down the sloping path and turned into the broad avenue. A smallish man with a lean face came up from the opposite direction and stopped beside him.

"Could you resist her, Quinnox, if you were twenty-two?" asked this man in his quiet voice.

Quinnox did not look around, but shook his head slowly. "I cannot resist her at sixty-two, my friend. She is adorable."

"I do not blame him. It is fate. *She* is fate.

Our work is done, my friend. We have served our country well, but fate has taken the matter out of our hands. There is nothing left for us to do but to fold our arms and wait." Gourou revealed his inscrutable smile as he pulled at his thin, scraggly moustache. He was shaking his head, as one who resigns himself to the inevitable.

After a long silence Quinnox spoke.

"Our people will come to love their princess, Gourou."

"Even as you and I, my friend," said the Baron.

And then they held their heads erect and walked confidently down the road their future sovereign had traversed before them.

When Mrs. Gaston joined Robin and Bedelia at the table which had been set for them in the *salle a manger*, she laid several letters before the girl who picked them up instantly and glanced at the superscription on each.

"I think that all of them are important," said Mrs. Gaston significantly. The smile on the girl's face had given way to a clouded brow. She was visibly perturbed.

"You will forgive me, Mr. Schmidt," she said nervously. "I must look at them at once."

He tried not to watch her face as she read what appeared to be a brief and yet evidently important letter, but his rapt gaze was not to be so easily managed. An exclamation of annoyance fell from her lips.

"This is from a friend in Paris, Mr. Schmidt," she

said, hesitatingly. Then, as if coming to a quick decision: "My father has heard that I am carrying on atrociously with a strange young man. It seems that it is a new young man. He is beside himself with rage. My friends have already come in for severe criticism. He blames them for permitting his daughter to run at large and to pick up with every Tom, Dick and Harry. Dear me, I shudder when I think of what he will do to you, Mrs. Gaston. He will take off your head completely. But never fear, you old dear, I will see that it is put on again as neatly as ever. So, you see, Mr. Schmidt, you now belong to that frightful order of nobodies, the Toms and the Dicks and the Harrys."

"I see that there is a newspaper clipping attached," he remarked. "Perhaps your father has been saying something to the newspapers." It was a mean speech and he regretted it instantly.

She was not offended, however. Indeed, she may not have heard what he said, for she was reading the little slip of printed matter. Suddenly she tore it into tiny bits and scattered them under the table. Her cheeks were red and her eyes glistened unmistakably with mortification. He was never to know what was in that newspaper cutting, but he was conscious of a sharp sensation of anger and pity combined. Whatever it was, it was offensive to her, and his blood boiled. He noted the expression of alarm and apprehension deepen in Mrs. Gaston's face.

Bedelia slashed open another envelope and glanced

at its contents. Her eyes flew open with surprise. For an instant she stared, a frown of perplexity on her brow.

"We are discovered!" she cried a moment later, clapping her hands together in an ecstasy of delight. "The pursuers are upon our heels. Even now they may be watching me from behind some convenient post or through some handy window pane. Isn't it fine? Don't look so horrified, you old dear. They can't eat us, you know, even though we are in a dining-room. I love it all! Followed by man-hunters! What could be more thrilling? The chase is on again. Quick! We must prepare for flight!"

"Flight?" gasped Robin. Her eyes were dancing. His were filled with dismay.

"It is as I feared," she cried. "They have found me out. Hurry! Let us finish this wretched dinner. I must leave here to-night."

"Impossible!" cried Mrs. Gaston. "Don't be silly. To-morrow will be time enough. Calm yourself, my dear."

"To-morrow at sunrise," cried Bedelia enthusiastically. "It is already planned, Mr. Schmidt. I have engaged an automobile in anticipation of this very emergency. The trains are not safe. To-morrow I fly again. This letter is from the little stenographer in Paris. I bribed her — yes, I bribed her with many francs. She is in the offices of the great detective agency—'the Eye that never Sleeps!' I

shall give her a great many more of those excellent
francs, my friends. She is an honest girl. She did
not fail me."

" I don't see how you can say she is honest if she accepted a bribe," said Mrs. Gaston severely.

" Pooh! " was Miss Guile's sufficient answer to this.
" We cross the Brunig Pass by motor. That really is
like flying, isn't it? "

" To Lucerne? " demanded Robin, still hazily.

" No, no! That would be madness. We shall
avoid Lucerne. Miles and miles to the north we will
find a safe retreat for a day or two. Then there will
be a journey by rail to — to your own city of Vienna,
Mr. Schmidt. You —"

" See here," said Robin flatly, " I don't understand
the necessity for all this rushing about by motor
and —"

" Of course you don't," she cried. " You are not
being sought by a cruel, inhuman monster of a father
who would consign you to a most shudderable fate!
You don't have to marry a man whose very name you
have hated. You can pick and choose for yourself.
And so shall I, for that matter. You —"

" You *adore* your father," cut in Mrs. Gaston
sharply. " I don't think you should speak of him in
that —"

" Of course I adore him! He is a dear old bear.
But he is a monster, an ogre, a tyrant, a — oh, well,
he is everything that's dreadful! You look dreadfully
serious, Mr. Schmidt. Do you think that I should

submit to my father's demands and marry the man he
has chosen for me?"

"I do," said Robin, abruptly and so emphatically
that both of his hearers jumped in their seats. He
made haste to dissemble. "Of course, I'd much
rather have you do that than to break your neck rolling over a precipice or something of the sort in a
crazy automobile dash."

Miss Guile recovered her poise with admirable
promptness. Her smile was a trifle uncertain, but
she had a dependable wit. "If that is all that you are
afraid of, I'll promise to save my neck at all costs,"
she said. "I could have many husbands but only one
poor little neck."

"You can have only one husband," said he, almost
savagely. "By the way, why don't you read the other
letter?" He was regarding it with jealous eyes, for
she had slipped it, face downward, under the edge of
her plate.

"It isn't important," she said, with a quick look
into his eyes. She convicted herself in that glance,
and knew it on the instant.

Angry with herself, she snatched up the letter and
tore it open. Her cheeks were flushed. She read
however without betraying any additional evidence of
uneasiness or embarrassment. When she had finished,
she deliberately folded the sheets and stuck them back
into the envelope without comment. One looking over
her shoulder as she read, however, might have caught
snatches of sentences here and there on the heavily

scrawled page. They were such as these: "You had led me to hope," . . . "for years I have been your faithful admirer," . . . "Nor have I wavered for an instant despite your whimsical attitude," . . . " therefore I felt justified in believing that you were sincere in your determination to defy your father." And others of an even more caustic nature: "You are going to marry this prince after all," . . . "not that you have ever by word or deed bound yourself to me, yet I had every reason to hope," . . . "Your father will be pleased to find that you are obedient," . . . "I am not mean enough to wish you anything but happiness, although I know you will never achieve it through this sickening surrender to vanity," . . . "if I were a prince with a crown and a debt that I couldn't pay," . . . "admit that I have had no real chance to win out against such odds," etc.

She faced Robin coolly. "It will be necessary to abandon our little luncheon for to-morrow. I am sorry. Still Mr. Totten informs me that he will be in Vienna shortly. The pleasure is merely postponed."

"Are you in earnest about this trip by motor to-morrow morning?" demanded Robin darkly. "You surely cannot be —"

"I am very much in earnest," she said decisively. He looked to Mrs. Gaston for help. That lady placidly shook her head. In fact, she appeared to be rather in favour of the preposterous plan, if one were to judge by the rapt expression on her countenance.

"I had the supposedly honest word of these crafty gentlemen that I was not to be interfered with again. They gave me their promise. I shall now give them all the trouble possible."

"But it will be a simple matter for them to find out how and when you left this hotel and to trace you perfectly."

"Don't be too sure of that," she said, exultantly. "I have a trick or two up my sleeve that will baffle them properly, Mr. Schmidt."

"My dear," interposed Mrs. Gaston severely, "do not forget yourself. It isn't necessary to resort to slang in order—"

"Slang is always necessary," avowed Bedelia, undisturbed. "Goodness, I know I shall not sleep a wink to-night."

"Nor I," said Robin gloomily. Suddenly his face lightened. A wild, reckless gleam shot into his eyes and, to their amazement, he banged the table with his fist. "By Jove, I know what I shall do. I'll go with you!"

"No!" cried Bedelia, aghast. "I—I cannot permit it, Mr. Schmidt. Can't you understand? You—you are the man with whom I am supposed to be carrying on atrociously. What could be more convicting than to be discovered racing over a mountain-pass—Oh, it is not to be considered—not for an instant."

"Well, I can tell you flatly just what I intend to do," said he, setting his jaws. "I shall hire another

car and keep you in sight every foot of the way.
You may be able to elude the greatest detective agency
in Europe, but you can't get away from me. I intend to keep you now that I've got you, Bedelia.
You can't shake me off. Where you go, I go."

"Do you mean it?" she cried, a new thrill in her
voice. He looked deep into her eyes and read there
a message that invited him to perform vast though
fool-hardy deeds. Her eyes were suddenly sweet with
the love she had never expected to know; her lips
trembled with the longing for kisses. "I shall travel
far," she murmured. "You may find the task an
arduous one — keeping up with me, I mean."

"I am young and strong," he said, "and, if God
is good to me, I shall live for fifty years to come, or
even longer. I tingle with joy, Bedelia, when I think
of being near you for fifty years or more. Have —
have you thought of it in that light? Have you looked
ahead and said to yourself: fifty years have I to live
and all of them with —"

"Hush! I was speaking of a week's journey, not
of a life's voyage, Mr. Schmidt," she said, her face
suffused.

"I was speaking of a honeymoon," said he, and
then remembered Mrs. Gaston. She was leaning back
in her chair, smiling benignly. He had an uncomfortable thought: was he walking into a trap set for
him by this clever woman? Had she an ulterior motive in advancing his cause?

"But it would be perfectly silly of you to foll'w me in a car," said Bedelia, trying to regain her lost composure. "Perfectly silly, wouldn't it, Mrs. Gaston?"

"Perfectly," said Mrs. Gaston.

"I will promise to see you in Vienna —"

"I intend to see you every day," he declared, "from now till the end of time."

"Really, Mr. Schmidt, you —"

"If there is one thing I despise beyond all reason, Bedelia, it is the name of 'Schmidt'! I wish you wouldn't call me by that name."

"I can't just call you 'Mister,'" she demurred.

"Call me Rex for the present," said he. "I will supply you with a better one later on."

"May I call him Rex?" she inquired of her companion.

"In moderation," said Mrs. Gaston.

"Very well, then, Rex, I have changed my mind. I shall not cross the Brunig by motor since you insist upon risking your neck in pursuit of me. I shall go by train in the morning,— calmly, complacently, stupidly by train. Instead of a thrilling dash for liberty over rocky heights and through perilous gorges, I shall travel like any bourgeoise in a second — or third class carriage, and the only thrill I shall have will be when we stop for Baker's chocolate at the top of the Pass. By that time I expect to be sufficiently hungry to be thrilled even by the sight of a cake of chocolate. Will you travel in the carriage behind me? I fancy it will be safe and convenient and you can't possibly be far from my heels."

"That's a sensible idea," he cried. "And we may be able to accommodate your other pursuers on the same train. What's the sense of leaving them behind? They'd only catch us up in the end, so we might just as well take them along with us."

"No. We will keep well ahead of them. I insist on that. They can't get here before to-morrow afternoon, so we will be far in the lead. We will be in Vienna in two days. There I shall say good-bye to you, for I am going on beyond. I am going to Graustark, the new Blithers estate. Surely you will not follow me there."

"You are very much mistaken. I shall be there as soon as you and I shall stay just as long, provided Mr. Blithers has no objections," said Robin, with more calmness than he had hoped to display in the face of her sudden thrust.

"We are forgetting our dinner," said Mrs. Gaston quietly. "I think the waiter is annoyed."

CHAPTER XXI

MR. BLITHERS ARRIVES IN GRAUSTARK

MR. WILLIAM W. BLITHERS arrived in Edelweiss, the Capital of Graustark, on the same day that the Prince returned from his tour of the world. As a matter of fact, he travelled by special train and beat the Prince home by the matter of three hours. The procession of troops, headed by the Royal Castle Guard, it was announced would pass the historic Hotel Regengetz at five in the afternoon, so Mr. Blithers had front seats on the extension porch facing the Platz.

He did not know it, but if he had waited for the regular train in Vienna, he would have had the honour of travelling in the same railway carriage with the royal young man. ("Would" is used advisedly in the place of "might," for he *would* have travelled in it, you may be sure.)

Moreover, he erred in another particular, for arriving at the same instant and virtually arm-in-arm with the country's sovereign, he could hardly have been kept out of the procession itself. When you stop to think that next to the Prince he was the most important personage in the realm on this day of celebration, it ought not to be considered at all unreasonable for him to have expected some notable attention, such as being placed in the first carriage immediately behind the country's sovereign, or possibly on the seat facing him. Missing an opportunity like this, wasn't at all Mr. Blithers' idea of success. He was very sorry about the special train. If it hadn't been for that train he might now be preparing to ride castlewards behind a royal band instead of sitting with his wife in the front row of seats on a hotel porch, just like a regular guest, waiting for the parade to come along. It certainly was a wasted opportunity.

He had lost no time in his dash across the continent. In the first place, his agents in Paris made it quite clear to him that there was likely to be " ructions " in Graustark over the loan and the prospect of a plebeian princess being seated on the throne whether the people liked it or not; and in the second place, Maud Applegate had left a note on his desk in the Paris offices, coolly informing him that she was likely to turn up in Edelweiss almost as soon as he. She added an annoying postscript. She said she was curious to see what sort of a place it was that he had been wasting his money on!

To say that he was put out by Maud's aggravating behaviour would be stating the case with excessive gentleness. He was furious. He sent for the head of the detective agency and gave him a blowing up that he was never to forget. It appears that the detectives had followed a false lead and had been fooled by the wary Maud in a most humiliating manner. They hadn't the remotest notion where she was, and evinced great surprise when informed in a voice loud enough to be heard a half-block away that she was on her way to Graustark. They said it couldn't be possible, and he said they didn't know what they were talking about. He was done with them. They could step out and ask the cashier to give them a check for their services, and so on and so forth. He did not forget to notify them that they were a gang of loafers.

Then he dragged Mrs. Blithers off to the Gare de l'Este and took the Express to Vienna. He would see to the loan first and to Maud afterward.

He had no means of knowing that a certain Miss Guile was doing more to shape the destiny of the principality of Graustark than all the millions he had poured into its treasury. Nor had he the faintest suspicion that she was even then on Graustark soil and waiting as eagerly as he for the procession to pass a given point.

Going back a day or two, it becomes necessary to report that while in Vienna the perverse Bedelia played a shabby trick on the infatuated Robin. She stole away from the Bristol in the middle of the night and was half-way to the Graustark frontier before he was aware of her flight. She left a note for him, the contents of which sufficed to ease his mind in the presence of what otherwise might have been looked upon as a calamity. Instead of relapsing into despondency over her defection, he became astonishingly exuberant. It was relief and not despair that followed the receipt of the brief letter. She had played directly into his hand, after all. In other words, she had removed a difficulty that had been troubling him for days: the impossibility of entering his own domain without betraying his identity to her. Naturally his entrance to the Capital would be attended by the most incriminating manifestation on the part of the populace. The character of R. Schmidt would be effaced in an instant, and, according to his own notion, quite a bit too soon to suit his plans. He preferred to remain Schmidt until she placed her hand in his and signified a readiness to become plain Mrs. R. Schmidt of Vienna. That would be his hour of triumph.

In her note she said: "Forgive me for running away like this. It is for the best. I must have a few days to myself, dear friend,—— days for sober reflection uninfluenced by the presence of a natural enemy to composure. And so I am leaving you in this cowardly, graceless fashion. Do not think ill of me. I give you my solemn promise that in a few days I shall let you know where I may be found if you choose to come to me. Even then I may not be fully convinced in my own mind that our adventure has reached its climax. You have said that you would accompany me to Graustark. I am leaving to-night for that country, where I shall remain in seclusion for a few days before acquainting you with my future plans. It is not my intention to stop in Edelweiss at present. The newspapers proclaim a state of unrest there

over the coming visit of Mr. Blithers and the return
of the Prince, both of whom are very much in the
public eye just now. I prefer the quiet of the country to the excitement of the city, so I shall seek some
remote village and give myself up to — shall I say
prayerful meditation? Believe me, dear Rex, to be
your most devoted, though whimsical, Bedelia."

He was content with this. Deep down in his heart
he thanked her for running away at such an opportune time! The situation was immeasurably sim-
plified. He had laid awake nights wondering how he
could steal into his own domain with her as a companion and still put off the revelation that he was
not yet ready to make. Now the way was comparatively easy. Once the demonstration was safely over,
he could carry on his adventure with something of the
same security that made the prowlings of the Bagdad Caliphs such happy enterprises, for he could
with impunity traverse the night in the mantle of R.
Schmidt.

Immediately upon receiving her letter, he sent for
Quinnox and Gourou, who were stopping at a hotel
nearby.

"I am ready to proceed to Edelweiss, my friends,"
said he. "Miss Guile has departed. Will you book
accommodations on the earliest train leaving for
home?"

"I have already seen to that, highness," said Gourou
calmly. "We leave at six this evening. Count Quinnox has wired the Prime Minister that you will arrive

in Edelweiss at three to-morrow afternoon, God willing."

"You knew that she had gone?"

"I happened to be in the Nordbahnhof when she
boarded the train at midnight," replied the Baron,
unmoved.

"Do you never sleep?" demanded Robin hotly.

"Not while I am on duty," said Gourou.

The Prince was thoughtful, his brow clouding with
a troubled frown. "I suppose I shall now have to
face my people with the confession that will confirm
their worst fears. I may as well say to you, my
friends, that I mean to make her my wife even though
it costs me my kingdom. Am I asking too much of
you, gentlemen, when I solicit your support in my
fight against the prejudice that is certain to —"

Quinnox stopped him with a profound gesture of
resignation and a single word: "Kismet!" and
Gourou, with his most ironic smile, added: "You
may count on us to support the crown, highness, even
though we lose our heads."

"Thank you," said Robin, flushing. "Just because I appear to have lost my head is no reason for
your doing the same, Baron Gourou."

The Baron's smile was unfaltering. "True," he
said. "But we may be able to avoid all that by in-
ducing the people of Graustark to lose their hearts."

"Do you think they will accept her as — as their
princess?" cried Robin, hopefully.

"I submit that it will first be necessary for you

to induce Miss Guile to accept you as her prince,"
said Gourou mildly. " That doesn't appear to be
settled at present."

He took alarm. " What do you mean? Your remark has a sinister sound. Has anything transpired
to —"

" She has disappeared, highness, quite effectually.
That is all that I can say," said Gourou, and Robin
was conscious of a sudden chill and the rush of cold
moisture to his brow. " But let us prepare to confront an even more substantial condition. A prospective father-in-law is descending upon our land.
He is groping in the dark and he is angry. He has
lost a daughter somewhere in the wilds of Europe,
and he realises that he cannot hope to become the
grandfather of princes unless he can produce a
mother for them. At present he seems to be desperate. He doesn't know where to find her, as Little
Bo-peep might have said. We may expect to catch
him in a very ugly and obstreperous mood. Have I
told you that he was in this city last night? He arrived at the Bristol a few hours prior to the significant departure of Miss Guile. Moreover, he has
chartered a special train and is leaving to-day for
Edelweiss. Count Quinnox has taken the precaution
to advise the Prime Minister of his approach and
has impressed upon him the importance of decrying
any sort of popular demonstration against him on his
arrival. Romano reports that the people are in an
angry mood. I would suggest that you prepare, in

a way, to placate them, now that Miss Guile has more
or less dropped out of sight. It behooves you to —"

"See here," broke in Robin harshly, "have you
had the effrontery to make a personal appeal to
Miss Guile in your confounded efforts to prevent
the —"

"Just a moment, Robin," exclaimed Count Quinnox, his face hardening. "I am sorry to hear words
of anger on your lips, and directed toward your most
loyal friends. You ask us to support you and in the
next breath imply that we are unworthy. It is beneath the dignity of either Baron Gourou or myself
to reply to your ungenerous charge."

"I beg your pardon," said Robin, but without lowering his head. He was not convinced. The barb
of suspicion had entered his brain. Were they, after
all, responsible for Bedelia's flight? Had they revealed his identity to the girl and afterward created
such alarm in her breast that she preferred to slink
away in the night rather than to court the humiliation that might follow if she presumed to wed Graustark's prince in opposition to his country's wish?
"You must admit that the circumstance of her secret flight last night is calculated to — But, no matter. We will drop the subject. I warn you, however, that my mind is fixed. I shall not rest until I
have found her."

"I fancy that the state of unrest will be general,"
said Gourou, with perfect good-nature. "It will go
very hard with Graustark if we fail to find her. And

now, to return to our original sin: What are we to
do about the ambitious Mr. Blithers? He is on my
conscience and I tremble."

It must not be supposed for an instant that the City
of Edelweiss and the court of Graustark was unimpressed by the swift approach and abrupt arrival
of Mr. Blithers. His coming had been heralded for
days in advance. The city was rudely expectant, the
court uneasy. The man who had announced his determination to manage the public and private affairs
of the principality was coming to town. He was
coming in state, there could be no doubt about that.
More than that, he was coming to propitiate the people
whether they chose to be mollified or not. He was
bringing with him a vast store of business acumen, an
unexampled confidence and the self-assurance of one
who has never encountered failure. Shylock's mantle
rested on his hated shoulders, and Judas Iscariot was
spoken of with less abhorrence than William W.
Blithers by the Christian country of Graustark. He
was coming to get better acquainted with his daughter's future subjects.

Earlier in the week certain polite and competent
gentlemen from Berlin had appeared at the Castle
gates, carrying authority from the dauntless millionaire. They calmly announced that they had come
to see what repairs were needed in and about the
Castle and to put the place in shape. A most regrettable incident followed. They were chased out
of town by an angry mob and serious complications

with the German Empire were likely to be the result
of the outrage.

Moreover, the citizens of Graustark were openly
reluctant to deposit their state bonds as security for
the unpopular loan, and there was a lively sentiment
in favour of renouncing the agreement entered into
by the cabinet.

The Prime Minister, in the absence of the Prince,
called mass meetings in all the towns and villages and
emissaries of the crown addressed the sullen crowds.
They sought to clarify the atmosphere. So eloquent
were their pleadings and so sincere their promises
that no evil would befall the state, that the more en-
lightened of the people began to deposit their bonds
in the crown treasury. Others, impressed by the confidence of their more prosperous neighbours, showed
signs of weakening. The situation was made clear
to them. There could be no possible chance of loss
from a financial point of view. Their bonds were safe,
for the loan itself was a perfectly legitimate transaction, a conclusion which could not be gainsaid by the
most pessimistic of the objectors. Mr. Blithers would
be paid in full when the time came for settlement, the
bonds would be restored to their owners, and all would
be well with Graustark.

As for the huge transactions Mr. Blithers had made
in London, Paris and Berlin, there could be but one
conclusion: he had the right to invest his money as
he pleased. That was his look-out. The bonds of
Graustark were open to purchase in any market.

Any investor in the world was entitled to buy all that
he could obtain if he felt inclined to put his money
to that use. The earnest agents of the government
succeeded in convincing the people that Mr. Blithers
had made a good investment because he was a good
business man. What did it matter to Graustark who
owned the outstanding bonds? It might as well be
Blithers as Bernstein or any one else.

As for Miss Blithers becoming the Princess of
Graustark, that was simple poppy-cock, declared the
speakers. The crown could take oath that Prince
Robin would not allow *that* to happen. Had he not
declared in so many words that he would never wed
the daughter of William Blithers, and, for that matter, hadn't the young woman also announced that she
would have none of him? There was one thing that
Mr. Blithers couldn't do, and that was to marry his
daughter to the Prince of Graustark.

And so, by the time that Mr. Blithers arrived in
Edelweiss, the people were in a less antagonistic frame
of mind,—though sullenly suspicious,—and were
even prepared to grin in their sleeves, for, after all,
it was quite clear that the joke was not on them but
on Mr. Blithers.

When the special train pulled into the station Mr.
Blithers turned to his wife and said:

"Cheer up, Lou. This isn't a funeral."

"But there is quite a mob out there," she said,
peering through the car window. "How can we be
sure that they are friendly?"

"Don't you worry," said Mr. Blithers confidently. "They are not likely to throw rocks at the goose that lays the golden egg." If he had paused to think, he would not have uttered such a careless indictment. The time would come when she was to remind him of his thoughtless admission, omitting, however, any reference to the golden egg.

The crowd was big, immobile, surly. It lined the sidewalks in the vicinity of the station and stared with curious, half-closed eyes at the portly capitalist and his party, which, by the way, was rendered somewhat imposing in size by augmentation in the shape of lawyers from Paris and London, clerks and stenographers from the Paris office, and four plain clothes men who were to see to it that Midas wasn't blown to smithereens by envious anarchists; to say nothing of a lady's maid, a valet, a private secretary and a doctor. (Mr. Blithers always went prepared for the worst.)

He was somewhat amazed and disgruntled by the absence of silk-hat ambassadors from the Castle, with words of welcome for him on his arrival. There was a plentiful supply of policemen but no cabinet mininsters. He was on the point of censuring his secretary for not making it clear to the government that he was due to arrive at such and such an hour and minute, when a dapper young man in uniform — he couldn't tell whether he was a patrolman or a captain — came up and saluted.

"I am William W. Blithers," said he sharply.

"I am an official guide and interpreter, sir," announced the young man suavely. "May I have the honour—"

"Not necessary — not necessary at all," exploded Mr. Blithers. "I can get about without a guide."

"You will require an interpreter, sir," began the other, only to be waved aside.

"Any one desiring to speak to me will have to do it in English," said Mr. Blithers, and marched out to the carriages.

He was in some doubt at first, but as his carriage passed swiftly between the staring ranks on the sidewalks, he began to doff his hat and bow to the right and the left. His smiles were returned by the multitude, and so his progress was more or less of a triumph after all.

At the Regengetz he found additional cause for irritation. The lords and nobles who should have met him at the railway station were as conspicuously absent in the rotunda of the hotel. No one was there to receive him except the ingratiating manager of the establishment, who hoped that he had had a pleasant trip and who assured him that it would not be more than a couple of hours before his rooms would be vacated by the people who now had them but were going away as soon as the procession had passed.

"Get 'em out at once," stormed Mr. Blithers. "Do you think I want to hang around this infernal lobby until—"

"Pardon me," said the manager blandly, "but your

rooms will not be ready for you before four or five
o'clock. They are occupied. We can put you tem-
porarily in rooms at the rear if your lady desires to
rest and refresh herself after the journey."

"Well, I'll be ——" began Mr. Blithers, purple in
the face, and then leaned suddenly against the counter,
incapable of finishing the sentence.

The manager rubbed his hands and smiled. "This
is one of our gala days, Mr. Blithers. You could not
have arrived at a time more opportune. I have taken
the precaution to reserve chairs for you on the verandah. The procession will pass directly in front of
the hotel on its way to Castle avenue."

"What procession?" demanded Mr. Blithers. He
was beginning to recall the presence of uniformed
bands and mounted troops in the side streets near the
station.

"The Prince is returning to-day from his trip
around the world," said the manager.

"He ought to have been back long ago," said Mr.
Blithers wrathfully, and mopped his brow with a hand
rendered unsteady by a mental convulsion. He was
thinking of his hat-lifting experience.

True to schedule, the procession passed the hotel
at five. Bands were playing, people were shouting,
banners were waving, and legions of mounted and foot
soldiers in brilliant array clogged the thoroughfare.
The royal equipage rolled slowly by, followed by less
gorgeous carriages in which were seated the men who

failed to make the advent of Mr. Blithers a conspicuous success.

Prince Robin sat in the royal coach, faced by two
unbending officers of the Royal Guard. He was alone
on the rear seat, and his brown, handsome face was
aglow with smiles. Instead of a hat of silk, he lifted
a gay and far from immaculate conception in straw;
instead of a glittering uniform, he wore a suit of blue
serge and a peculiarly American tie of crimson hue.
He looked more like a popular athlete returning from
conquests abroad than a prince of ancient lineage.
But the crowd cheered itself hoarse over this bright-
faced youngster who rode by in a coach of gold and
brandished a singularly unregal chapeau.

His alert eyes were searching the crowd along the
street, in the balconies and windows with an eager
intensity. He was looking for the sweet familiar face
of the loveliest girl on earth, and knew that he looked
in vain, for even though she were one among the many
her features would be obscured by an impenetrable
veil. If she were there, he wondered what her
thoughts might be on beholding the humble R. Schmidt
in the rôle of a royal prince receiving the laudations
of the loving multitude!

Passing the Regengetz, his eyes swept the rows of
cheering people banked upon its wide terrace and
verandahs. He saw Mr. and Mrs. Blithers well down
in front, and for a second his heart seemed to stand
still. Would she be with them? It was with a dis-

tinct sensation of relief that he realised that she was not with the smiling Americans.

Mr. Blithers waved his hat and, instead of shouting the incomprehensible greeting of the native spectators, called out in vociferous tones:

"Welcome home! Welcome! Hurrah!"

As the coach swerved into the circle and entered the great, tree-lined avenue, followed by the clattering chorus of four thousand horse-shoes, Mrs. Blithers after a final glimpse of the disappearing coach, sighed profoundly, shook out her handkerchief from the crumpled ball she had made of it with her nervously clenched fingers, touched her lips with it and said:

"Oh, what a remarkably handsome, manly boy he is, Will."

Mr. Blithers nodded his head proudly. "He certainly is. I'll bet my head that Maud is crazy about him already. She can't help it, Lou. That trip on the *Jupiter* was a God-send."

"I wish we could hear something from her," said Mrs. Blithers, anxiously.

"Don't you worry," said he. "She'll turn up safe and sound and enthusiastic before she's a week older. We'll have plain sailing from now on, Lou."

CHAPTER XXII

MR. BLITHERS indeed experienced plain sailing for the ensuing twenty hours. It was not until just before he set forth at two the next afternoon to attend, by special appointment, a meeting of the cabinet in the council chamber at the Castle that he encountered the first symptom of squalls ahead.

He had sent his secretary to the Castle with a brief note suggesting an early conference. It naturally would be of an informal character, as there was no present business before them. The contracts had already been signed by the government and by his authorised agents. So far as the loan was concerned there was nothing more to be said. Everything was settled. True, it was still necessary to conform to a certain custom by having the Prince affix his signature to the contract over the Great Seal of State, but as he previously had signed an agreement in New York this brief act was of a more or less perfunctory nature.

The deposit of bonds by the state and its people would follow in course of time, as prescribed by contract, and Mr. Blithers was required to place in the Bank of Graustark, on such and such a date, the sum of three million pounds sterling. Everybody was satisfied with the terms of the contract. Mr. Blithers was to get what really amounted to nearly nine per-cent on a gilt-edged investment, and Graustark was to preserve its integrity and retain its possessions.

There was a distant cloud on the financial horizon, however, a vague shadow at present,—but prophetic of storm. It was perfectly clear to the nobles that when these bonds matured, Mr. Blithers would be in a position to exact payment, and as they matured in twelve years from date he was likely to be pretty much alive and kicking when the hour of reckoning arrived.

Mr. Blithers was in the mood to be amiable. He anticipated considerable pleasure in visiting the an-cient halls of his prospective grandchildren. During the forenoon he had taken a motor ride about the city with Mrs. Blithers, accompanied by a guide who created history for them with commendable glibness and some veracity, and pointed out the homes of great personages as well as the churches, monuments and museums. He also told them in a confidential under-tone that the Prince was expected to marry a beauti-ful American girl and that the people were enchanted with the prospect! That sly bit of information realised ten dollars for him at the end of the trip, aside from his customary fee.

The first shock to the placidity of Mr. Blithers came with the brief note in reply to his request for an informal conference. The Lord Chamberlain curtly informed him that the Cabinet would be in session at two and would be pleased to grant him an audience of half an hour, depending on his promptness in appearing.

Mr. Blithers was not accustomed to being granted audiences. He had got into the habit of having them thrust upon him. It irritated him tremendously to have any one measure time for him. Why, even the President of the United States, the Senate, or the District Attorney in New York couldn't do *that* for him. And here was a whipper-snapper Lord Chamberlain telling him that the Cabinet would grant him half-an-hour! He managed to console himself, however, with the thought that matters would not always be as they were at present. There would be a decided change of tune later on.

It would be folly to undertake the depiction of Mr. Blithers' first impressions of the Castle and its glories, both inside out. To begin with, he lost no small amount of his assurance when he discovered that the great gates in the wall surrounding the park were guarded by resplendent dragoons who politely demanded his " pass." After the officer in charge had inspected the Lord Chamberlain's card as if he had never seen one before, he ceremoniously indicated to a warden that the gates were to be opened. There was a great clanking of chains, the drawing of iron bolts, the whirl of a windlass, and the ponderous gates swung slowly ajar.

Mr. Blithers caught his breath — and from that instant until he found himself crossing the great hall

in the wake of an attendant delegated to conduct him
to the council chamber his sensations are not to be
described. It is only necessary to say that he was
in a reverential condition, and that is saying a great
deal for Mr. Blithers. A certain bombastic confidence in himself gave way to mellow timidity. He
was in a new world. He was cognisant of a distinct
sensation of awe. His ruthless Wall Street tread became a mincing, uncertain shuffle; he could not conquer the absurd notion that he ought to tip-toe his
way about these ancient halls with their thick, velvety
rugs and whispering shadows.

Everywhere about him was pomp, visible and invisible. It was in the great stairway, the vaulted
ceilings, the haughty pillars, over all of which was the
sheen of an age that surpassed his comprehension.
Rigid servitors watched his progress through the vast
spaces — men with grim, unsmiling faces. He knew,
without seeing, that this huge pile was alive with noble
lords and ladies: The court! Gallantry and beauty
to mock him with their serene indifference!

Somewhere in this great house beautiful women
were idling, or feasting, or dreaming. He was conscious of their presence all about him, and shrank
slightly as he wondered if they were scrutinising his
ungainly person. He was suddenly ashamed of his
tight-fitting cut-a-way coat and striped trousers.
Really he ought to get a new suit! These garments
were much too small for him.

Were ironic eyes taking in the fresh creases in those New York trousers? Were they regarding his shimmering patent leather shoes with an intelligence that told them that he was in pain? Were they wondering how much he weighed and why he didn't unbutton his coat when he must have known that it would look better if it didn't pinch him so tightly across the chest? Above all things, were they smiling at the corpulent part of him that preceded the rest of his body, clad in an immaculate waistcoat? He never had felt so conspicuous in his life, nor so certain that he was out of place.

Coming in due time — and with a grateful heart — to a small ante-chamber, he was told to sit down and wait. He sat down very promptly. In any other house he would have sauntered around, looking at the emblems, crests and shields that hung upon the walls. But now he sat and wondered. He wondered whether this could be William W. Blithers. Was this one of the richest men in the world — this fellow sitting here with his hands folded tightly across his waistcoat? He was forced to admit that it was and at the same time it wasn't.

The attendant returned and he was ushered into a second chamber, at the opposite end of which was a large, imposing door — closed. Beside this door stood a slim, erect figure in the red, blue and gold uniform of an officer of the Castle guard. As Mr. Blithers approached this rigid figure, he recognised

a friend and a warm glow pervaded his heart. There
could be no mistaking the smart moustache and super-
cilious eye-brows. It was Lieutenant Dank.

"How do you do?" said Mr. Blithers. "Glad to
see you again." His voice sounded unnatural. He
extended his hand.

Dank gave him a ceremonious salute, bowed slightly
but without a smile, and then threw open the door.

"Mr. Blithers, my lords," he announced, and stood
aside to let the stranger in a strange land pass within.

A number of men were seated about a long table
in the centre of this imposing chamber. No one
arose as Mr. Blithers entered the room and stopped
just inside the door. He heard it close gently behind him. He was at a loss for the first time in his
life. He didn't know whether he was to stop just
inside the door fingering his hat like a messenger boy,
or go forward and join the group. His gaze fell upon
a huge oaken chair at the far end of the table. It
was the only unoccupied seat that came within the
scope of his rather limited vision. He could not see
anything beyond the table and the impassive group
that surrounded it. Was it possible that the big
chair was intended for him? If so, how small and insignificant he would look upon it. He had a ghastly
notion that his feet would not touch the floor, and
he went so far as to venture the hope that there would
be a substantial round somewhere about midway from
the bottom.

He had appeared before the inquisitorial commit-

tees in the United States Senate, and had not been op-
pressed by the ponderous gravity of the investigation.
He had faced the Senators without a tremor of awe.
He had even regarded them with a confidence, equal
if not superior to their own. But now he faced a
calm, impassive group of men who seemed to strip
him down to the flesh with a cool, piercing interest,
and who were in no sense impressed by what they saw.

Despite his nervousness he responded to the life
long habit of calculation. He counted the units in
the group in a single, rapid glance, and found that
there were eleven. Eleven lords of the realm!
Eleven stern, dignified, unsmiling strangers to the arrogance of William W. Blithers! Something told him
at once that he could not spend an informal half-hour
with them. Grim, striking, serious visages, all of
them! The last hope for his well-fed American
humour flickered and died. He knew that it would
never do to regale them in an informal off-hand way
— as he had planned — with examples of native wit.

Reverting to the precise moment of his entrance to
the Castle, we find Mr. Blithers saying to himself that
there wasn't the slightest use in even hoping that he
might be invited to transfer his lodgings from the
Regengetz to the Royal bed-chambers. The chance
of being invited to dine there seemed to dwindle as
well. While he sat and waited in the first ante-
chamber he even experienced strange misgivings in
respect to parental privileges later on.

After what appeared to him to be an interminable

MICROCOPY RESOLUTION TEST CHART

(ANSI and ISO TEST CHART No. 2)

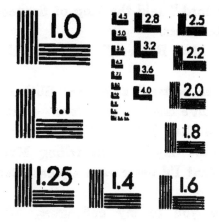

APPLIED IMAGE Inc

1653 East Main Street
Rochester, New York 14609 USA
(716) 482 - 0300 - Phone
(716) 288 - 5989 - Fax

length of time, but in reality no more than a few seconds, a tall man arose from his seat and advanced with outstretched hand. Mr. Blithers recognised Count Quinnox, the Minister of War. He shook that friendly hand with a fervour that must have surprised the Count. Never in all his life had he been so glad to see any one.

"How are you, my lord," said the king of finance, fairly meek with gratefulness.

"Excellently well, Mr. Blithers," returned the Count. "And you?"

"Never better, never better," said Mr. Blithers, again pumping the Count's hand up and down — with even greater heartiness than before. "Glad to see you. Isn't it a pleasant day? I was telling Mrs. Blithers this morning that I'd never seen a pleasanter day. We —"

"Let me introduce you to my colleagues, Mr. Blithers," interrupted the Count.

"Happy, I'm sure," mumbled Mr. Blithers. To save his life, he couldn't tell what had got into him. He had never acted like this before.

The Count was mentioning the names of dukes, counts and barons, and Mr. Blithers was bowing profoundly to each in turn. No one offered to shake hands with him, although each rose politely, even graciously. They even smiled. He remembered that very well afterwards. They smiled kindly, almost benignly. He suddenly realised what had got into him. It was respect.

"A chair, Franz," said the white haired, gaunt man who was called Baron Romano. "Will you sit here, Mr. Blithers? Pray forgive our delay in admitting you. We were engaged in a rather serious discussion over —"

"Oh, that's all right," said Mr. Blithers, magnanimously. "Am I interfering with any important business, gent— my lords? If so, just —"

"Not at all, Mr. Blithers. Pray be seated."

"Sure I'm not taking any one's seat?"

"A secretary's, sir. He can readily find another."

Mr. Blithers sat down. He was rather pleased to find that the big chair was not meant for him. A swift intuition told him that it was reserved for the country's ruler.

"The Prince signed the contracts just before you arrived, Mr. Blithers," said Baron Romano. "The seal has been affixed to each of the documents, and your copy is ready for delivery at any time."

Mr. Blithers recovered himself slightly. "You may send it to the hotel, Baron, at any time to-morrow. My lawyers will have a look at it." Then he made haste to explain: "Not that it is really necessary, but just as a matter of form. Besides, it gives the lawyers something to do." He sent an investigating glance around the room.

"The Prince has retired," said the Baron, divining the thought. "He does not remain for the discussions." Glancing at the huge old clock above the door, the Prime Minister assumed a most business-like

air. "It will doubtless gratify you to know that
three-fourths of the bonds have been deposited, Mr.
Blithers, and the remainder will be gathered in during the week. Holders living in remote corners of our
country have not as yet been able to reach us with
their securities. A week will give them sufficient time,
will it not, Count Lazzar?"

"I may safely say that all the bonds will be in our
hands by next Tuesday at the latest," said the Minister of the Treasury. He was a thin, ascetic man;
his keen eyes were fixed rather steadily upon Mr.
Blithers. After a moment's pause, he went on: "We
are naturally interested in your extensive purchases
of our outstanding bonds, Mr. Blithers. I refer to
the big blocks you have acquired in London, Paris and
Berlin."

"Want to know what I bought them for?" inquired Mr. Blithers amiably.

"We have wondered not a little at your readiness
to invest such a fortune in our securities."

"Well, there you have it. Investment, that's all.
Your credit is sound, and your resources unques-
tioned, your bonds gilt-edge. I am glad of the opportunity to take a few dollars out of Wall Street
uncertainties and put 'em into something absolutely
certain. Groo — Gras — er — Groostock bonds are
pretty safe things to have lying in a safety vault in
these times of financial unrest. They create a pretty
solid fortune for my family,— that is to say, for my
daughter and her children. A sensible business man,

— and I claim to be one,— looks ahead, my lords. Railroads are all right as long as you are alive and can run them yourself. It's after you are dead that they fail to do what is expected of them. New fingers get into the pie, and you never can tell what they'll pull out in their greediness. I cannot imagine anything safer in the shape of an investment than the bonds of a nation that has a debt of less than fifty million dollars. As a citizen of a republic whose national debt is nearly a billion, I confess that I can't see how you've managed so well."

"We are so infinitesimal, Mr. Blithers, that I daresay we could be lost in the smallest of your states," said Baron Romano, with a smile.

"Rhode Island is pretty small," Mr. Blithers informed him, without a smile.

"It is most gratifying to Graustark to know that you value our securities so highly as a legacy," said Count Lazzar, suavely. "May I venture the hope, however, that your life may be prolonged beyond the term of their existence? They expire in a very few years — a dozen, in fact."

"Oh, I think I can hang on that long," said Mr. Blithers, a little more at ease. He was saying to himself that these fellows were not so bad, after all. "Still one never knows. I may be dead in a year. My daughter — but, of course, you will pardon me if I don't go into my private affairs. I fear I have already said too much."

"On the contrary, sir, we are all only too willing

to be edified. The workings of an intelligence such
as yours cannot fail to be of interest to us who are
so lacking in the power to cope with great undertak-
ings. I confess to a selfish motive in asking you about
your methods of — er — investment," said the Minister of Finance. Mr. Blithers failed to see that he
was shrewdly being led up to a matter that was of
more importance to Graustark just then than anything along financial lines.

"I am only too willing, my lords, to give you the
benefit of my experience. Any questions that you
may care to ask, I'll be glad to answer to the best of
my ability. It is only natural that I should take a
great personal interest in Graustock from now on.
I want to see the country on the boom. I want to
see it taking advantage of all the opportunities that
— er — come its way. There may be a few pointers
that William W. Blithers can give you in respect to
your railways and mines — and your general policy,
perhaps. I hope you won't hesitate about asking."

The Prime Minister tapped reflectively upon the
table-top with his fingers for a moment or two.

"Thank you," he said. "We are at this very
moment in something of a quandary in respect to the
renewal of a treaty with one of our neighbours. For
the past twenty years we have been in alliance with
our next door neighbours, Axphain on the north and
Dawsbergen on the south and east. The triple alliance will end this year unless renewed. Up to the
present our relations have been most amiable. Ax-

phain stands ready to extend our mutual protective agreement for another term of years, but Dawsbergen is lukewarm and inclined to withdraw. When you become better acquainted with the politics of our country you will understand how regrettable such an action on the part of a hitherto friendly government will be."

"What's the grievance?" inquired Mr. Blithers, bluntly. He was edging into familiar waters now. "What's the matter with Dawsbergen? Money controversy?"

"Not at all," said Lazzar hastily.

"Why not let 'em withdraw?" said Mr. Blithers. "We can get along without them."

There was a general uplifting of heads at the use of the pronoun, and a more fixed concentration of gaze.

"I daresay you are already acquainted with the desire on the part of Dawsbergen to form an alliance in which Axphain can have no part," said Baron Romano. "In other words, it has been the desire of both Dawsbergen and Graustark to perfect a matrimonial alliance that may cement the fortunes of the two countries —"

"Count Quinnox mentioned something of the sort," interrupted Mr. Blithers. "But suppose this matrimonial alliance doesn't come off, who would be the sufferer, you or Dawsbergen? Who will it benefit the most?"

There was a moment's silence. Doubtless it had

never occurred to the Ministry to speculate on the point.

"Dawsbergen is a rich, powerful country," said Romano. "We will be the gainers by such an alliance, Mr. Blithers."

"I don't go much on alliances," said the capitalist. "I believe in keeping out of them if possible."

"I see," said the Baron reflectively. There was another silence. Then: "It has come to our notice in a most direct manner that the Prince of Dawsbergen feels that his friendly consideration of a proposal made by our government some years ago is being disregarded in a manner that can hardly be anything but humiliating to him, not only as a sovereign but as a father."

"He's the one who has the marriageable daughter, eh? I had really forgotten the name."

The Baron leaned forward, still tapping the table-top with his long, slim fingers.

"The report that Prince Robin is to marry your daughter, Mr. Blithers, has reached his ears. It is only natural that he should feel resentful. For fifteen years there has been an understanding that the Crown Princess of Dawsbergen and the Prince of Graustark were one day to be wedded to each other. You will admit that the present reports are somewhat distressing to him and unquestionably so to the Crown Princess."

Mr. Blithers settled back in his chair. "It seems

to me that he is making a mountain out of a mole-hill."

Baron Romano shrank perceptibly. "It devolves upon me, sir, as spokesman for the Ministry, the court and the people of Graustark, to inform you that marriage between our Prince and any other than the Crown Princess of Dawsbergen is not to be considered as possible."

Mr. Blithers stared. "Hasn't the Prince any voice in the matter?" he demanded.

"Yes. He has already denied, somewhat publicly, that he is not contemplating marriage with your daughter. He has had a voice in that matter at least."

A fine moisture started out on the purplish brow of Mr. Blithers. Twenty-two eyes were upon him. He realised that he was not attending an informal conference. He had been brought here for a deliberate purpose.

"I may be permitted the privilege of reminding you, my lords, that his denial was no more emphatic than that expressed by my daughter," he said, with real dignity.

"We have accepted her statement as final, but it is our earnest desire that the minds of the people be set at rest," said the Baron gravely. "I sincerely trust that you will appreciate our position, Mr. Blithers. It is not our desire or intention to offend in this matter, but we believe it to be only fair and

just that we, should understand each other at the outset. The impression is afoot that —"

"My lords," said Mr. Blithers, rising, his face suddenly pale, " I beg leave to assure you that my daughter's happiness is of far more importance to me than
all the damned principalities in the world. Just a
moment, please. I apologise for the oath — but I
mean it, just the same. I do not resent your attitude, nor do I resent your haste in conveying to me
your views on the subject. It may be diplomacy to
go straight to a question and get it over with, but it
isn't always diplomatic to go off half-cocked. I will
say, with perfect candour, that I should like to see my
daughter the Princess of Graustark, but — by God!
I want you to understand that her own wishes in the
matter are to govern mine in the end. I have had
this marriage in mind, there's no use denying it. I
have schemed to bring these two young people together with a single object in view. I knew that if
they saw enough of each other they would fall in love,
and they would want the happiness that love brings to
all people. Just a moment, Barc l I want to say
to you now, all of you, that if my g: .l should love your
prince and he should love her in return, there isn't
a power below heaven that can keep them apart. If
she doesn't love him, and he should be unlucky enough
to love her, I'd see him hanged before he could have
her. I'll admit that I have counted on seeing all of
this come to pass, and that I have bungled the thing
pretty badly because I'm a loving, selfish father,—

but, my lords, since you have brought me here to tell me that it is impossible for my girl to marry your prince, I will say to you, here and now, that if they ever love each oth r and want to get married, I'll see to it that it isn't impossible. You issue an ultimatum to me, in plain words, so I'll submit one to you, in equally plain words. I intend to leave this matter entirely to my daughter and Prince Robin. They are to do the deciding, so far as I am concerned. And if they decide that they love each other and want to get married, *they will get married*. Do I make myself perfectly plain, my lords?"

The dignified Ministry of Graustark sat agape. With his concluding words, Mr. Blithers deposited his clenched fist upon the table with a heavy thud, and, as if fascinated, every eye shifted from his face to the white knuckles of that resolute hand.

Baron Romano also arose. "You place us in the extremely distressing position of being obliged to oppose the hand of a benefactor, Mr. Blithers. You have come to our assistance in a time of need. You have —"

"If it is the loan you are talking about, Baron, that is quite beside the question," interrupted Mr. Blithers. "I do not speculate. I may have had a personal motive in lending you this money, but I don't believe you will find that it enters into the contract we have signed. I don't lend money for charity's sake. I sometimes give it to charity, but when it comes to business, I am not charitable. I have made

a satisfactory loan and I am not complaining. You
may leave out the word benefactor, Baron. It doesn't
belong in the game."

"As you please, sir," said Romano coldly. "We
were only intent upon conveying to you our desire
to maintain friendly relations with you, Mr. Blithers,
despite the unpleasant conditions that have arisen.
I may at least question your right to assume that
we are powerless to prevent a marriage that is
manifestly unpopular with the subjects of Prince
Robin."

"I had it on excellent authority to-day that the
people are not opposed to the union of my daughter
and the prince," said Mr. Blithers.

"I am compelled to say that you have been misinformed," said the Baron, flatly.

"I think I have not been misinformed, however,
concerning the personal views of Prince Robin. If
I am not mistaken, he openly declares that he will
marry to suit himself and not the people of Graustark. Isn't it barely possible, my lords, that he may
have something to say about who he is to marry?"

"I confess that his attitude is all that you describe," said the Baron. "He has announced his
views quite plainly. We admit that he may have
something to say about it."

"Then I submit that it isn't altogether an improb-
ability that he may decide to marry according to the
dictates of his heart and not for the sake of appear-
ances," said Mr. Blithers scathingly. "I have an

The dignified Ministry of Graustark sat agape

idea that he will marry the girl he loves, no matter who she may be."

Count Quinnox and Baron Gourou exchanged glances. These two men were guilty of having kept from their colleagues all information concerning a certain Miss Guile. They, as well as Dank, were bound by a promise exacted by their sovereign prince. They alone knew that Mr. Blithers was supported by an incontrovertible truth. For the present, their lips were sealed, and yet they faced that anxious group with a complete understanding of the situation. They knew that Mr. Blithers was right. Prince Robin would marry the girl that he loved, and no other. They knew that their prince expected to marry the daughter of the man who now faced these proud noblemen and virtually defied them!

"Am I not right, Count Quinnox?" demanded Mr. Blithers, turning suddenly upon the Minister of War. "You are in a position to know something about him. Am I not right?"

Every eye was on the Count. "Prince Robin will marry for love, my lords," he said quietly. "I am forced to agree with Mr. Blithers."

Baron Romano sank into his chair. There was silence in the room for many seconds.

"May I enquire, Count Quinnox, if you know anything of the present state of Prince Robin's — er — heart?" inquired the Prime Minister finally.

A tinge of red appeared in each of Count Quinnox's swarthy cheeks.

"I can only surmise," said he briefly.

"Has — has he met some one in whom he feels a — er — an interest?"

"Yes."

"May we have the benefit of your conclusions?" said Baron Romano, icily.

"I am not at liberty to supply information at present," said the Count, visibly distressed.

Mr. Blithers leaned forward, his hands upon the table. "Some one he met after leaving New York?" he inquired eagerly.

"Time will reveal everything, Mr. Blithers," said the Count, and closed his jaws resolutely. His colleagues looked at him in consternation. The worst, then, had happened!

A gleam of triumph shot into the eyes of Mr. Blithers. His heart swelled. He felt himself stepping out upon safe, solid ground after a period of floundering. The very best, then, had happened!

"My lords, I find that my half-hour is almost up," he said, pulling out his gold watch and comparing its time with that of the clock on the wall. "Permit me to take my departure: I am content to let matters shape themselves as they may. Shakespeare says 'there is a destiny that shapes our ends, rough hew them' — er — and so forth. Allow me, however, before leaving, to assure you of my most kindly interest in the welfare of your State. You may be pleased to know that it is not from me that Graustark — did I get it right that time? — will redeem her bonds when they mature, but from my only daughter. She is nearly twenty-one years of age. On her twenty-fifth birthday I shall present to her — as a gift — all of my holdings in Graustark. She may do as she sees fit with them. Permit me to wish you all good day, my lords. You may send the contract to my hotel, Baron. I expect to remain in the city for some time."

As he traversed the vast halls on his way to the outer world, he was again overcome by the uneasy conviction that ironic eyes were looking out upon him from luxurious retreats. Again he felt that his coat fitted him too tightly and that his waistcoat was painfully in evidence. He hurried a bit. If he could have had his way about it, he would have run. Once outside the castle doors, he lighted a big cigar, and threw the burnt-out match upon the polished flagstones of the terrace. He regretted the act on the instant. He wished he had not thrown it there. If the solemn grooms had not been watching, he would have picked it up and stuck it into his pocket for disposal on the less hallowed stones of a city thoroughfare.

Outside the gates he felt more at ease, more at home, in fact. He smoked in great contentment. In the broad, shady avenue he took out his watch and pried open the case. A great pride filled his eyes as he looked upon the dainty miniature portrait of his daughter Maud. She *was* lovely — she was even lovelier than he had ever thought before.

At the Regengetz a telegram awaited him.   It was from Maud.

" I shall be in Edelweiss this week without fail.   I have something very important to tell you."   So it read.

CHAPTER XXIII

NINE o'clock of a rainy night, on the steep, winding road that climbed the mountain-side from the walled-in city to the crest on which stood the famed monastery of St. Valentine,— nine o'clock of a night fraught with pleasurable anticipation on the part of one R. Schmidt, whose eager progress up the slope was all too slow notwithstanding the encouragement offered by the conscienceless Jehu who frequently beat his poor steeds into a gallop over level stretches and never allowed them to pause on the cruel grades.

Late in the afternoon there had come to the general post-office a letter for Mr. R. Schmidt. He had told her that any message intended for him would reach his hands if directed to the post-office. Since his arrival in the city, three days before, he had purposely avoided the main streets and avenues of Edelweiss, venturing forth but seldom from the Castle grounds, and all because he knew that he could not go abroad during the day-time without forfeiting the privileges to be enjoyed in emulation of the good Caliphs of Baghdad. His people would betray their prince because they loved him: his passage through the streets could only be attended by respectful homage on the part of every man, woman and child in the place. If Bedelia were there, she could not help knowing who and what he was, with every one stupidly lifting his hat and bowing to him as he passed, and he did not want Bedelia to know the truth about him until she had answered an all-important question, as has been mentioned before on more than one occasion in the course of this simple tale.

Her letter was brief. She merely acquainted him with the fact that she had arrived in Edelweiss that day from Ganlook, twenty miles away, and was stopping at the Inn of the Stars outside the city gates and half way up the mountain-side, preferring the quiet, ancient tavern to the stately Regengetz for reasons of her own.

In closing she said that she would be delighted to see him when it was convenient for him to come to her. On receipt of this singularly matter-of-fact letter, he promptly despatched a message to Miss Guile, Inn of the Stars, saying that she might expect him at nine that night.

Fortunately for him, the night was wet and blustering. He donned a rain-coat, whose cape and collar served to cover the lower part of his face fairly well, and completed his disguise by pulling far down over his eyes the villainous broad-brimmed hat affected by the shepherds in the hills. He had a pair of dark eye-glasses in reserve for the crucial test that would come with his entrance to the Inn.

Stealing away from the Castle at night, he entered the ram-shackle cab that Hobbs had engaged for the expedition, and which awaited him not far from the private entrance to the Park. Warders at the gate looked askance as he passed them by, but not one presumed to question him. They winked slyly at each other, however, after he had disappeared in the shadows beyond the rays of the feeble lanterns that they carried. It was good to be young!

The driver of that rattling old vehicle was no other than the versatile Hobbs, who, it appears, had rented the outfit for a fixed sum, guaranteeing the owner against loss by theft, fire or dissolution. It is not even remotely probable that the owner would have covered the ground so quickly as Hobbs, and it is certain that the horses never suspected that they had it in them.

The mud-covered vehicle was nearing the Inn of the Stars when Robin stuck his head out of the window and directed Hobbs to drive slower.

"Very good, sir," said Hobbs. "I thought as how we might be late after losing time at the city gates, sir, wot with that silly guard and the ——"

"We are in good time, Hobbs. Take it easy."

The lights of the Inn were gleaming through the drizzle not more than a block away. Robin's heart was thumping furiously. Little chills ran over him, delicious chills of excitement. His blood was hot and cold, his nerves were tingling. The adventure!

"Whoa!" said Hobbs suddenly. "'Ello, wot the 'ell is ——"

A dark figure had sprung into the road-way near the horses' heads, and was holding up a warning hand.

"Is this Mr. Schmidt's carriage?" demanded a hoarse, suppressed voice.

"It is," said Hobbs, "for the time being. Wot of it?"

Robin's head came through the window.

"What do you want?"

"Some one is coming out here to meet you, sir. Do not drive up to the doors. Those are the orders. You are to wait here, if you please."

Then the man shot away into the darkness, leaving the wayfarers mystified by his words and action.

"Wot am I to do, sir?" inquired Hobbs. "Most hextraordinary orders, and who the deuce is behind them, that's wot I'd like to know."

"We'll wait here, Hobbs," said Robin, and then put his hand suddenly to his heart. It was acting very queerly. For a moment he thought it was in danger of pounding its way out of his body!

Below him lay the lighted city, a great yellow cloud almost at his feet. Nearer, on the mountain-side were the misty lights in the windows of dwellers on the slope, and at points far apart the street lamps, dim splashes of light in the gloom. Far above were the almost obscured lights of St. Valentine, hanging in the sky. He thought of the monks up there. What a life! He would not be a monk, not he.

"My word!" exclaimed Hobbs, but instantly resumed his character as cabby.

A woman came swiftly out of the blackness and stopped beside the cab. She was swathed in a long gossamer, and hooded. The carriage lamps gleamed strong against the dripping coat.

"Is it you?" cried Robin, throwing open the door and leaping to the ground.

"It is I, M'sieur," said the voice of Marie, Miss Guile's French maid.

Bleak disappointment filled his soul. He had hoped for — but no! He might have known. She would not meet him in this manner.

"What has happened?" he cried, grasping the girl's arm. "Has she —"

"Sh! May we not speak in French?" said Marie, lowering her voice after a significant look at the motionless cabman. "He may understand English, M'sieur. My mistress has sent me to say to M'sieur that she has changed her mind."

"Changed her mind," gasped Robin.

"Yes, M'sieur. She will not receive you at the Inn of the Stars. She bids you drive to the end of this street, where there is a garden with a Magyar band, and the most delicious of refreshments to be had under vine-covered —"

"A public garden?" exclaimed Robin in utter dismay.

"Pingari's, sir," said Hobbs, without thinking. "I know the place well. It is a very quiet, orderly place — I beg pardon!"

"So he understands French, eh?" cried Marie sharply.

"It doesn't matter," cried Robin impatiently. "Why, in heaven's name, did she select a public eating-house in which to receive me?"

"If M'sieur chooses to disregard the wishes of —" began the maid, but he interrupted her.

"I am not accustomed to meeting people in public gardens. I —"

"Nor is my mistress, M'sieur. I assure you it is the first time she has committed an indiscretion of this kind. May I put a flea in M'sieur's ear? The place is quite empty to-night, and besides there is the drive back to the Inn with Mademoiselle. Is not that something, M'sieur?"

"By jove!" exclaimed Robin. "Drive on,— you! But wait! Let me take you to the Inn, Marie. It —"

"No! I may not accept M'sieur's thoughtful invitation. Bon soir, M'sieur."

She was off like a flash. Robin leaped nimbly into the cab.

"Pingari'a, driver!" he said, his heart thumping once more.

"Very good, sir," and they were off at a lively rate, rattling quite gaily over the cobble-stones.

Pingari's is the jumping-off place. It stands at the sharp corner of an elbow in the mountain, with an almost sheer drop of a thousand feet into the quarries below. A low-roofed, rambling building, once used as a troop-house for nomadic fighting-men who came from all parts of the principality on draft by feudal barons in the days before real law obtained, it was something of a historic place. Parts of the structure are said to be no less than five hundred years old, but time and avari : have relegated history to a rather uncertain background, and unless one is pretty well up in the traditions of the town, he may be taken in nicely by shameless attendants who make no distinction between the old and the new so long as it pays them to procrastinate.

As a matter of fact, the walls of the ancient troop-house surround what is now considered the kitchen, and one never steps inside of them unless he happens to be connected in a somewhat menial way with the green grocer, the fish-monger, the butcher or the poultry-man. The wonderful vine-covered porches, reeking with signs of decay and tottering with age, are in truth very substantial affairs constructed by an ancestor of the present Signor Pingari no longer ago than the Napoleonic era — which is quite recent as things go in Graustark.

Hobbs drove bravely into the court yard, shouted orders to a couple of hostlers and descended from the box. The Magyar band was playing blithely to the scattered occupants of the porches overlooking the precipice.

" 'Ere we are, sir," said he to the Prince, as he jerked open the door of the cab. " Shall I wait, sir? "

"Certainly," said Robin, climbing out. "I am a long way from home, my good man."

He hurried up the steps and cast an eye about the place. There were no ladies unattached. As he was about to start on a tour of investigation, a polite person in brass buttons came up to him.

"Alone, sir?" he inquired pityingly.

"Quite," said Robin, still peering into the recesses.

"Then come with me, if you please. I am directed to escort you to one who is also alone. This way, sir."

Robin followed him through a door, down a narrow hallway, up a flight of stairs and out another door upon a small portico, sheltered by a heavy canvas awning. Two men were standing at the railing, looking down upon the impressionistic lights of the sunken city. The Prince drew back, his face hardening.

"What does this mean, sirrah? You said —"

At the sound of his voice the two men turned, stared at him intently for an instant and then deliberately strode past him, entered the door and disappeared. The person in brass buttons followed them.

A soft, gurgling laugh fell upon his ears — a laugh of pure delight. He whirled about and faced — one who was no longer alone.

She was seated at the solitary little table in the corner; until now it had escaped his notice for the excellent reason that it was outside the path of light

from the open doorway, and the faint glow from the
adjacent porches did not penetrate the quiet retreat.

He sprang toward her with a glad cry, expecting
. ·r. to rise. She remained seated, her hand extended.
This indifference on her part may have been the result of cool premeditation. In any event, it served to
check the impulsive ardour of the Prince, who, it is
to be feared, had lost something in the way of self-
restraint. It is certain — absolutely certain — that
had she come forward to meet him, she would have
found herself imprisoned in a pair of strong, eager
arms,— and a crisis precipitated. He had to be content with a warm hand-clasp and a smile of welcome
that even the gloom could not hide from his devour-
ing eyes.

"My dear, dear Bedelia," he murmured. "I had
almost given you up. Three long days have I waited
for you. You —"

"I have never broken a promise, Rex," she said
coolly. "It is you who are to be commended, not I,
for you see I was coming to Graustark anyway. I
should not have been surprised if you had failed me,
sir. . It is a long way from Vienna to this out-of-the-
way—"

"The most distant spot in the world would not
have been too far away to cause an instant's hesitation
on my part," said he, dropping into the chair opposite her. "I would go to the end of the world,
Bedelia."

"But your personal affairs — your business," she protested. "Can you neglect it so —"

"My business is to find happiness," said he. "I should be neglecting it indeed if I failed to pursue the only means of attaining it. You are happiness, Bedelia."

"What would you sacrifice for happiness?" she asked softly.

"All else in the world," he replied steadily. "If I were a king, my realm should go if it stood between me and — you, Bedelia."

She drew back with a queer little gasp, as if suddenly breathless.

"Wait — wait just for a moment," she said, with difficulty steadying her voice. "This night may see the end of our adventure, Rex. Let us think well before we say that it is over. I know, if you do not, that a great deal depends upon what we are to say to each other to-night. You will ask me to be your wife. Are you sure that you appreciate all that it means to you and to your future if I should say yes to that dear question?"

He looked at her intently. "What do you know, Bedelia?"

"I know that you are the Prince of Graustark and that it is ordained that you shall wed one whose station is the equal of your own. You must think well, dear Rex, before you ask Bedelia Guile to be your wife."

"You know that I am —" he began, dully, and then

burst into a mirthless laugh. "And knowing who I am, why do you not leap at the chance to become the Princess of Graustark? Why not realise an ambition that —"

"Hush! You see how well I considered when I advised you to think before speaking? You are now saying things that are unworthy of you. You are forgetting that it is my privilege to say no to the am in search of happiness. I too —"

He stood up, leaning far over the table, a penetrating look in his eyes.

"How long have you known, Bedelia?"

"Since the second day out on the *Jupiter*," she replied serenely.

He slowly resumed his seat, overwhelmed by the sickening realisation that his bubble had burst. She had known from the beginning. She had played with him. She had defied him!

"I know what you are thinking, Rex," she said, almost pleadingly. "You are thinking ill of me, and you are unjust. It was as fair for me as it was for you. We played a cautious game. You set about to win my love as you saw fit, my friend, and am I to be condemned if I exercised the same privilege? I was no more deliberate, no more reprehensible than you. Am I more guilty of deceit than you?"

He gave a great sigh of relief. "You are right," he said. "It is my turn to confess. I have known

for many days that you are not Bedelia Guile. We
are quits."

She laughed softly. "I rather like Bedelia. I
think I shall keep it as a good-luck name. We have
now arrived at the time for a profound contemplation
of the results of our experiments. In the meantime, I
have had no dinner. I trust that the Prince of Graustark has dined so lightly that he will not decline to
share my repast with me. It has already been ordered — for two."

"By jove, you — you amaze me!" he exclaimed.

"Please remove that dreadful mackintosh and touch
the bell for me. You see, I am a very prosaic person,
after all. Even in the face of disaster I can have a
craving for food and drink. That's better."

In a sort of daze, he tapped the little table bell.
A waiter appeared on the instant.

"Give us more light, waiter," was her command,
"and serve dinner at once."

The lights went up, and Robin looked into her soft,
smiling eyes.

"It doesn't matter," he whispered hoarsely. "I
don't care what happens to me, Bedelia, I — I shall
never give you up. You are worth all the kingdoms
in the world. You are the loveliest, most adorable —"

"Hush! The eyes of your people are upon you.
See! Even the waiter recognises his prince. He is
overcome. Ah! He falters with the consommé. It
is a perilous moment. There! I knew something

would happen, poor fellow. He has spilled — but, all
is well; he has his wits again. See! He replenishes
from the steaming tureen. We are saved."

Her mood was so gaily satiric, so inconsequential,
that he allowed a wondering, uncertain smile to banish
the trouble from his eyes as he leaned back in the chair
and studied the vivid, excited face of the girl who had
created havoc with his senses. She was dressed as he
had seen her on board the *Jupiter* during those delightful days on deck: the same trim figure in a blue
serge suit and a limp white hat, drawn well down over
her .soft brown hair, with the smart red tie and the
never-to-be-forgotten scent of a perfume that would
linger in his nostrils forever and forever.

" Do you think it strange that I should have asked
you to meet me here in this unconventional way instead of at the Inn? " she inquired, suddenly serious.
Again the shy, pleading expression stole into her eyes.

" I did think so, but no longer. I am glad that we
are here."

" Mrs. Gaston is inside," she informed him quickly.
" I do not come alone. An hour ago the Inn became
quite impossible as a trysting place. A small party
from the Regengetz arrived for dinner. Can you
guess who is giving the dinner? The great and only
William W. Blithers, sir, who comes to put an obstinate daughter upon the throne of Graustark,
whether she will or no."

" Did he see you? " cried Robin.

" No," she answered, with a mischievous gleam in

her eyes. "I stole out through the back door, and sent Marie out with one of the porters to head you off. Then I came on here. I didn't even stop to change my gown."

"Hide and seek is a bully game," said he. "It can't last much longer, Bedelia. I think it is only right that we should go to your father and tell him that — everything is all right. It is his due. You've solved your own problem and are satisfied, so why not reveal yourself. There is nothing to be gained by further secrecy."

She was watching him closely. "Are you, after all is said and done, sure that you want to marry the daughter of William Blithers, in the face of all the bitter consequences that may follow such an act? Think hard, my dear. She is being forced upon you, in a way. Mr. Blithers' money is behind her. Your people are opposed to the bargain, for that is the way in which they will look upon it. They may act very harshly toward you. The name of Blithers is detested in your land. His daughter is reviled. Are you sure that you want to marry her, Re— Robin?"

"Are you through?" he asked, transfixing her with a determined look. "Well, then, I'll answer you. I do want to marry you, and, more than that, I mean to marry you. I love —"

"You may tell me, Robin, as we are driving back to the Inn together — not here, not now," she said softly, the lovelight in her eyes.

Happiness blurred his vision. He was thrilled by

an enchantment so stupefying that the power of speech, almost of thought, was denied him for the time being. He could only sit and stare at her with prophetic love in his eyes, love that bided its time and trembled with anticipation.

Long afterward, as they were preparing to leave Pingari's she said to him:

"My father is at the Inn, Robin. I ran away from him to-night because I wanted to be sure that our adventure was closed before I revealed myself to him. I wanted to be able to say to him that love will find its way, no matter how blind it is, nor how vast the world it has to traverse in search of its own. My father is at the Inn. Take me to him now, Robin, and make the miracle complete."

His fingers caressed her warm cheek as he adjusted the collar of the long seacoat about her throat and chin. Her eyes were starry bright, her red lips were parted.

"My Princess!" he whispered tenderly. "My Princess!"

"My Prince," she said so softly that the words barely reached his ears. "We have proved that Love is the king. He rules us all. He laughs at locksmiths — and fathers — but he does not laugh at sweethearts. Come, I am ready."

He handed her into the cab a moment later, and drew the long deep breath of one who goes down into deep water. Then he followed after her. The attendant closed the door.

"Where to, sir?" called Hobbs from the driver's seat.

He received no answer, yet cracked his whip gaily over the horses' backs and drove out into the slanting rain.

Hobbs was a dependable fellow. He drove the full length of the street twice, passing the Inn of the Stars both times at a lively clip, and might have gone on forever in his shuttlecock enterprise, had not the excited voice of a woman hailed him from the sidewalk.

"Stop! *Attendez!* You! Man!"

He pulled up with a jerk. The dripping figure of Marie ran up from behind.

"My mistress? Where is she?" panted the girl.

"In heaven," said Hobbs promptly, whereupon Marie pounded on the glass window of the cab.

Robin quickly opened the door.

"Wha — what is it?"

"Yes, Marie," came in muffled tones from the depths of the cab.

"Madame Gaston returns long ago. She is beside herself. She is like a maniac. She has lost you; she cannot explain to — to Mademoiselle's father. Mon dieu, when he met her unexpectedly in the hall, he shouts, 'where is my daughter?' And poor Madame she has but to shiver and stammer and — run away! *Oui!* She dash out into the rain! It is terrible. She —"

Bedelia broke in upon this jumbled recitation. "Where have we been, Robin? Where are we now?"

"Where are we, Hobbs?"

"We are just getting back to the Inn of the Stars, sir,—descending, you might say, sir," said Hobbs.

"Drive on, confound you."

"To the Inn, sir?"

"Certainly!"

The door slammed and the final block was covered in so short a time that Robin's final kiss was still warm on Bedelia's lips when the gallant cab rolled up to the portals of the Inn of the Stars.

"Did you ever know such a night, sir?" inquired Hobbs, as the Prince handed his lady out. He was referring to the weather.

CHAPTER XXIV

JUST WHAT MIGHT HAVE BEEN EXPECTED

EVEN the most flamboyant of natures may suffer depression at times, and by the same token arrogance may give way to humility,—or, at the very least, conviction.

Mr. Blithers had had a trying day of it. To begin with, his wife raked him over the coals for what she was pleased to call his senseless persistence in the face of what she regarded as unalterable opposition on the part of the Cabinet and House of Nobles. It appears that he had experienced a second encounter with the Ministry only the day before. After sleeping over the results of his first visit to the Council Chamber, he awoke to the fact that matters were in such a condition that it behooved him to strike while the iron was hot. So he obtained a second hearing, principally because he had not slept as well over it as he would have liked, and secondarily because he wanted to convince himself that he could parade their ancient halls without feeling as self-conscious as a whipped spaniel.

He came off even worse in his second assault upon the ministry, for this time the members openly sneered at his declarations. As for his progress through the enchanted halls he was no end worse off than before.

It so happened that he arrived at the castle at the very hour when the ladies and gentlemen of the royal household were preparing to fare forth to the tennis courts. He came upon them, first on the terrace, then in the entrance, and later on was stared at with evident curiosity by white flanneled and duck-skirted persons in the lofty halls. He wished that he was back at Blitherwood where simplicity was not so infernally common.

He made the mistake of his life when he gave to his wife the details of this second conference with the Cabinet. He did it in the hope that a sympathetic response would be forthcoming. To his surprise, she merely pitied him, but in such a disgustingly personal way that he wondered if he could ever forgive her.

" Can't you appreciate what I am doing for Maud? " he argued, almost tearfully.

" I can appreciate what you are doing *to* her," said she, and swept out of the room.

" It's bad enough to have one stubborn woman in the family," said he to himself, glaring at the closed door — which had been slammed, by the way,—" but two of 'em — Good Lord: "

And so it was that Mr. Blithers, feeling in need of cheer, arranged a little dinner for that evening, at the Inn of the Stars. He first invited his principal London lawyer and his wife — who happened to be *his* principal — and then sent a more or less peremptory invitation to the President of the Bank of Graustark, urging him to join the party at the Regengetz

and motor to the Inn. He was to bring his wife and
any friends that might be stopping with them` at the
time. The banker declined. His wife had been dead
for twenty years; the only friends he possessed were
directors in the bank, and they happened to be having
a meeting that night. So Mr. Blithers invited his
secondary London lawyer, his French lawyer and two
attractive young women who it appears were related
to the latter, although at quite a distance, and then
concluded that it was best to speak to his own wife
about the little affair. She said she couldn't even
think of going. Maud might arrive that very night
and she certainly was not going out of the hotel with
such an event as that in prospect.

"But Simpson's wife is coming," protested Mr.
Blithers, "and Pericault's cousins. Certainly you
must come. Jolly little affair to liven us up a bit.
Now Lou,—"

"I am quite positive that Lady Simpson will change
her mind when she hears that Pericault's cousins are
going," said Mrs. Blithers acidly.

"Anything the matter with Pericault's cousins?"
he demanded, inclined to the bellicose.

"Ask Pericault," she replied briefly.

He thought for a moment. "If that's the case,
Lou, you'll have to come, if only to save my reputa-
tion," he said. "I didn't think it of Pericault. He
seems less like a Frenchman than any man I've ever
known."

Mrs. Blithers relented. She went to the dinner and

so did Lady Simpson, despite Pericault's cousins, and
the only ones in the party who appeared to be uneasy
were the cousins themselves. It is safe to say that it
was not the rain that put a dampener on what otherwise might have been an excessively jovial party.

Stupendous was the commotion at the Inn of the
Stars when it became known that one of the richest men
in the world — and a possible father-in-law apparent
to the crown,— was to honour the place with his presence that night. Every one, from the manager down
to the boy who pared potatoes, laid himself out to make
the occasion a memorable one.

The millionaire's table was placed in the very centre
of the dining-room, and plates were laid for eight.
At the last minute, Mr. Blithers ordered the number
increased to nine.

"My daughter may put in an appearance," he explained to Lady Simpson. "I have left word at the
hotel for her to come up if by any chance she happens
to arrive on the evening train."

"Haven't you heard from her, Mr. Blithers?" inquired the austere lady, regarding the top of his head
with an illy-directed lorgnon.

They were entering the long, low dining-room. Mr.
Blithers resented the scrutiny: It was lofty. and yet
stooping. She seemed to be looking down upon him at
right angles, due no doubt to her superior height and
to the fact that she had taken his arm.

"We have," said he, "but not definitely. She is
likely to pop in on us at any moment, and then again

she's likely not to. My daughter is a very uncertain person, Lady Simpson. I never seem to be able to put my finger upon her."

"Have you ever tried putting the whole hand upon her?" inquired her ladyship, and Mr. Blithers stared straight ahead, incapable of replying.

He waited until they were seated at the table and then remarked: "I am sorry you got splashed, Lady Simpson. You'd think they might keep the approach to a place like this free of mud and water."

"Oh, I daresay the gown can be cleaned, Mr. Blithers," she said. "I am quite ready to discard it, in any event, so it really doesn't matter."

"My dear," said he to his wife, raising his voice so that diners at nearby tables could not help hearing what he said, "I forgot to tell you that we are expected to dine with the Prince at the Castle." Then he wondered if any one in the room understood English.

"When?" she inquired.

"Very shortly," said he, and she was puzzled for a moment by the stony glare he gave her.

Lord Simpson took this opportunity to mention that he had taken reservations for the return of himself and wife to Vienna on the next day but one.

"We shall catch the Orient Express on Friday and be in London by Monday," he said. "Our work here is completed. Everything is in ship-shape. Jenkins will remain, of course, to attend to the minor details, such as going over the securities and —"

" Don't you like that caviare? " asked Mr. Blithers with some asperity.

" It has a peculiar taste," said Lord Simpson.

" Best I've ever tasted," said Mr. Blithers, spreading a bun thickly. Pericault's cousins were fingering the champagne glasses. " We've got sherry coming first," said he.

" Everything satisfactory, M'sieur Blithers? " inquired the *maître d'hotel* softly, ingratiatingly, into his left ear.

" Absolutely," said Mr. Blithers with precision. " You needn't hurry things. We've got the whole evening ahead of us."

Lady Simpson shivered slightly. The Pericault cousins brightened up. There was still a chance that the " dowagers " would retire early from the scene of festivity.

" By the way," said Simpson, " how long do you purpose remaining in Edelweiss, Blithers? "

For the first time, the capitalist faltered. He was almost ready to admit that his enterprise had failed in one vital respect. The morning's experience in the Council Chamber had shaken his confidence considerably.

" I don't know, Simpson," said he. " It is possible that we may leave soon."

" Before the Prince's dinner? " inquired Lady Simpson, again regarding his bald spot through the lorgnon.

" Depends on what my daughter has to say when

she gets here," said he almost gruffly. "If she wants to stay for a while, we will remain. I don't mind saying that I have a curious longing for Wall Street. I am at home there and — well, by George, I'm like a fish out of water here."

His wife looked up quickly, but did not speak.

"I am a business man. Lady Simpson, not a philanderer. I'd like to take this town by the neck and shake some real enterprise into it, but what can you do when everybody is willing to sit down and let tradition look after 'em? I've put a lot of money into Grosstock and I'd like to see the country prosper. Still I'm not worried over my investment. It is as good as gold."

"Perfectly safe," said Lord Simpson.

"Absolutely," said the secondary London lawyer.

Pericault's comment was in French and not intended to be brief, but as Mr. Blithers was no longer interested, the privilege of completing his remarks was not accorded him. He did say *Mon dieu* under his breath, however, in the middle of his employer's next sentence.

"As I said before, everything depends on whether my daughter wants to remain. If she says she wants to stay, that settles the point so far as I am concerned. If she says she doesn't want to stay, we'll — well, that will settle it also. I say, waiter, can't you hurry the fish along?"

"Certainly, sir. I understood M'sieur to say that there was no hurry —"

"Well, pour the champagne anyway. I think we need it."

Two hours later, Mr. Blithers looked at his watch again. The party was quite gay: at least fifty percent disorderly.

"That train has been in for an hour," said the host. "I guess Maud didn't come. I left word for the hotel to call me up if she arrived — I say, waiter, has there been a telephone message for me?"

"No, M'sieur. We have kept a boy near the telephone all evening, M'sieur. No message."

"I also told 'em to send up any telegram that might come," he informed his wife, who merely lifted her eyebrows. They had been lowered perceptibly in consequence of the ebullience of Pericault's cousins.

The vivacious young women were attracting a great deal of attention to their table. Smart diners in the immediate neighbourhood appeared to be a trifle shocked. Three dignified looking gentlemen, seated near the door, got up and left the room.

"We really must be going," said Mrs. Blithers nervously, who had been watching the three men for some time with something akin to dismay in her soul. She had the sickening notion that they were members of the Cabinet — lords of the realm.

"All right," said Mr. Blithers. "Call the cars up, waiter. Still raining?"

"Yes, M'sieur. At this season of the year—"

"Call the cars. Let's have your bill."

Pericault's cousins were reluctant to go. In fact,

they protested shrilly that it was silly to break up such a successful party at such an unseemly hour.

"Never mind," whispered Pericault softly, and winked.

"I'll leave 'em in your care, Pericault," said Mr. Blithers grimly. "They are *your* cousins, you know."

"Trust me implicitly, Monsieur," said Pericault, bowing very deeply. Then he said good-night to Mrs. Blithers and Lady Simpson. The secondary London lawyer did the same.

Out in the wide, brilliantly lighted foyer, a few late-stayers were waiting for their conveyances to be announced. As the four departing members of the Blithers party grouped themselves near the big doors, impatient to be off, a brass-buttoned boy came up and delivered a telegram to the host.

He was on the point of tearing open the envelope when his eyes fell upon two people who had just entered the hall from without, a man and woman clad in raincoats. At the same instant the former saw Mr. Blithers. Clutching his companion's arm he directed her attention to the millionaire.

"Now for it, Bedelia," he whispered excitedly.

Bedelia gazed calmly at Mr. Blithers and Mr. Blithers gazed blankly at the Prince of Graustark. Then the great financier bowed very deeply and called out:

"Good evening, Prince!"

He received no response to his polite greeting, for the Prince was staring at Bedelia as if stupefied. The millionaire's face was very red with mortification as he turned it away.

" He — he doesn't recognise you," gasped Robin in amazement.

" Who? " she asked, her eyes searching the room with an eager, inquiring look.

" Your father," he said.

She gave him a ravishing, delighted smile.

" Oh, it is so wonderful, Robin.   I have fooled you completely.   That man isn't my father."

" That's Mr. Blithers or I am as blind as a bat," he exclaimed.

" Is it, indeed?   The one reading the telegram, with his eyes sticking out of his head? "

Robin's head was swimming.   " Good heaven, Bedelia, what are you —"

" Ah! " she cried, with a little shriek of joy.   " See! There he is! "

One of the three distinguished men who had been remarked by Mrs. Blithers now separated himself from his companions and approached the couple.   He was a tall, handsome man of fifty.   Although his approach was swift and eager, there was in his face the signs of wrath that still struggled against joy.

She turned quickly, laid her hand upon the Prince's rigid arm, and said softly:

" My father is the Prince of Dawsbergen, dear."

.   .   .   .

A crumpled telegram dropped from Mr. Blithers' palsied hand to the floor as he turned a white, despairing face upon his wife. The brass-buttoned boy picked it up and handed it to Mrs. Blithers.   It was from Maud.

"We were married in Vienna today. After all I think I shall not care to see Graustark. Channie is a dear. I have promised him that you will take him into the business as a partner. We are at the Bristol.

"MAUD."

THE END

Lightning Source UK Ltd.
Milton Keynes UK
UKHW02n0615140218
317658UK00008B/1020/P